THE ELSON READERS—BOOK SIX
A Teacher's Guide

Catherine Andrews

B.A. English Education, National Board Certified, Teacher of English, International Baccalaureate/Bartow High School

Mary Jane Newcomer

B.A. English Education, Teacher of English, Frostproof Middle-Senior High School, Frostproof, Florida

LOST CLASSICS BOOK COMPANY
Lake Wales, Florida

Publisher's Note

Recognizing the need to return to more traditional principles in education, Lost Classics Book Company is republishing forgotten late 19th and early 20th century literature and textbooks to aid parents in the education of their children.

This guide is designed to accompany *The Elson Readers—Book Six,* which was reprinted from the 1920 copyright edition. This guide contains all the original questions and exercises from the reader along with suggested answers. It also includes new "Extended Activities" that reinforce and enhance the original study sections.

We have included the same glossary and pronunciation guide of more than 1380 terms at the end of the book that is included in the reader, and which has been updated with pronunciation notation currently in use.

The Elson Readers—Book Six, which this volume is meant to accompany, has been assigned a reading level of 1060L. More information concerning this reading level assessment may be attained by visiting www.lexile.com.

ISBN 978-1-890623-30-2

Designed to Accompany
The Elson Readers—Book Six
ISBN 978-1-890623-20-3
Part of
The Elson Readers
Nine Volumes: *Primer* through *Book Eight*
ISBN 978-1-890623-23-4

On the Cover:
Circe Pouring Poison into a Vase and Awaiting the Arrival of Ulysses (w/c) by Sir Edward Burne-Jones (1833-98)
Private Collection/Bridgeman Art Library

Table of Contents

A Note about This Guide

Teachers and students alike may notice a difference in punctuation, capitalization, and spelling between the prose and poetry sections in the reader. Rules concerning these matters have changed since the original reader's publication, and we have decided that in the prose sections it would be in the best interest of the student to update these items so they will learn these rules as practiced today. However, the stories remain completely unabridged. We have exercised constraint, and typical changes consist of, for example: commas used in place of semicolons when appropriate, lowercase treatment of words not personified, or hyphenated spelling of words being contracted to modern spellings. We have, however, followed the traditional editorial practice of not changing these items in works of poetry, leaving these matters to the prerogative of the poet.

Language is always changing, and when the student notices these changes it is often a good place to start a discussion on topics such as: personification, comma usage, "up" or "down" style of capitalization, etc.

We have used *The Chicago Manual of Style,* 14th Edition, published by the University of Chicago, as our primary reference for these changes.

Student worksheets do not inlude those exercises designed as group activities, which may result in non-sequential numbering of questions on those pages.

The reader was originally published just after World War One and many discussion questions refer to this great event. These questions can often be used to start discussions on that war and conflicts that occured after it. See the "Appendix" for a brief description of World War One.

Finally, we have provided references to Internet sites that may be useful for some of the exercises. These sites are the property of their creators, not Lost Classics Book Company, and we take no responsibility for their content. Considering the very changeable nature of the Internet, these sites may or may not exist by the time of printing and should only be considered a starting point for research.

The Elson Readers—Book Six
A Teacher's Guide

How to Use This Book

This *Teacher's Guide* was developed to provide teachers with a guideline for appropriate, grade-level, student responses to the questions found in the "Notes and Questions" sections of the reader. Some extension activities have been added to those discussion questions in this manual and may be used at the teacher's discretion to reinforce comprehension and appreciation of the work in question. "Vocabulary Worksheets" have also been added at the end of each major section in the *Teacher's Guide* to encourage students to broaden their use of language.

Teachers may wish to have students begin with "Part One" and read the book in order, or they may pick and choose the works that fit their classroom goals. The parts are not sequential; however, skills introduced in one part may be reinforced in later parts allowing students to practice and master the various literary skills as outlined in the objectives found at the beginning of each part in the *Teacher's Guide.*

These questions and activities were designed to give the students a greater understanding of the world around them and a deeper appreciation of the contributions of those who have helped to build that world. In addition, students will receive instruction in the qualities so essential to their development as future productive citizens in the world they will inherit.

Prediction—It is important that students are able to make predictions about a text based on evidence from the story as well as from prior knowledge. Many of the selections in *Book Six* are lengthy and are divided into sections. Have students discuss at the end of each section, based on what they have read and what they already know, what they think is going to occur next. Also at the end of each section, have students discuss whether their predictions were correct. It may be helpful to have students write their predictions and explanations in a reading journal.

Words in Context—Most of the selections in *Book Six* have a list of glossary terms. Before students define the term from the glossary, have them identify the word in context and "guess" what they think the word means. Have students create their own definition of the word before they use the glossary. Students tend to be better able to apply and use the word if they can put the definition in their own words. It is also suggested that the students use the terms in their own sentences. Make sure when students do use the word that they are using it correctly. Have students look for context clues. These may be: 1. antonyms 2. synonyms 3. appositives.

Instructional Aids—Additional aids have been provided for instructing and evaluating students' progress in the "Appendix."

PART I: NATURE—HOME AND COUNTRY

In This Section—

Objectives—

THE WORLD OF NATURE

HOME AND COUNTRY

By completing "Part I," the following objectives will be met.

1. The student will use effective reading strategies to construct meaning and identify the purpose of a text including:
    a. using illustrations
    b. defining unfamiliar words
    c. retelling and summarizing
    d. predicting events and outcomes
2. The student will determine the main idea or essential message and identify relevant supporting details and facts of a text.
3. The student will read and organize facts from the text and other sources to make a report, outline, and perform an authentic task.
4. The student will prepare for writing by focusing on the topic and organizing supporting details in a logical sequence.
5. The student will draft and revise writing.
6. The student will produce final documents that have been edited for correct spelling, punctuation, and grammar.
7. The student will write for a variety of audiences and purposes.
8. The student will write in a variety of genres including narrative and expository writing.
9. The student will use reference materials (dictionaries, encyclopedias, maps, charts).
10. The student will use speaking strategies effectively such as eye contact, gestures, and visuals that engage the audience.
11. The student will identify the development of plot and how conflicts are resolved in a story.
12. The student will identify and understand similarities and differences among the characters, settings, and events presented in various texts.
13. The student will identify the author's purpose and point of view.
14. The student will identify and use literary terminology such as rhyme scheme, personification, alliteration, and meter.
15. The student will respond critically to fiction, nonfiction, and poetry.
16. The student will recognize cause-and-effect relationships in literary texts.
17. The student will respond to a text by explaining how the motives of the characters or events compare with those in his or her own life.
18. The student will use context clues to understand words and ideas.
19. The student will predict events that may occur in the text and explain the reasoning behind the prediction.
20. The student will understand the qualities necessary for people to become good citizens and apply those qualities to his/her personal life.
21. The student will understand the qualities necessary to develop good character and apply those qualities to his/her personal life.

THE WORLD OF NATURE

Animals

American Bighorn Sheep, p. 25

1. **This is a story of ranch life; what picture of the roundup does the author give?**

   "All the forenoon we spent riding the long circle with the cowpunchers of the roundup; in the afternoon we worked the herd, cutting the cattle, with much breakneck galloping and dexterous halting and wheeling. Then came the excitement and hard labor of roping, throwing, and branding the wild and vigorous range calves—in a corral, if one was handy; otherwise, in a ring of horsemen." The author paints a vivid picture of the hard work and skill needed for a successful roundup.

2. **Can you give a reason for branding the ranch cattle?**

   Ranchers allowed their cattle to roam the open range, mingling with cattle from other ranches. In order to recognize their own cattle, cowboys had to round them up, sort them out, and brand the new calves with the rancher's unique mark. Thus the rancher could easily spot his cattle in a large herd.

3. **Describe the ranch house.**

   "The roomy, homelike ranchhouse, with its log walls, shingled roof, and big chimneys and fireplaces, stands in a glade, in the midst of the thick forest, which covers half the bottom; behind rises, bare and steep, the wall of peaks, ridges, and tablelands."

4. **Why does the author call the democracy of the roundup "healthy"?**

   In order for the roundup to succeed, "every man had to do his full share." Both a healthy roundup and a healthy democracy require everyone's participation.

5. **Notice what he says about "laggards and idlers"; do you think Roosevelt did his share of the work?**

   The author says laggards and idlers "get no mercy" if they do not do their job well. Student responses may vary but will likely agree that Roosevelt did his share of the work.

If the hardest and most unpleasant task had fallen to him, how would he have performed it?

He would have faced the task with determination and worked to see it through to completion.

6. **What reason for hunting does the author give?**

"I hunted chiefly to keep the ranch in meat."

7. **How did Roosevelt's life on the ranch differ from the life of the ordinary cowboy?**

While the cowboys continued to work on the ranch, Roosevelt "would go back to the ranch to turn to my books with added zest." He also states that he did a good deal of writing.

What do you think of his way of dividing his time while on the ranch? Was it a wise plan? Was it easy to follow? What temptations to irregularity do you think he met? What qualities must Roosevelt have had to make him hold to such a course?

Student responses will vary. These questions could be assigned as a class discussion of Roosevelt's work ethic.

8. **Compare Roosevelt's way of breaking a colt with the cowboy's way. Compare the results obtained.**

Roosevelt says "I took my time, breaking them gradually and gently—not, after the usual cowboy fashion, in a hurry, by sheer main strength and rough riding, with the attendant danger to the limbs of the man and very probable ruin to the manners of the horse." Roosevelt felt that gentleness and time was more valuable than speed and strength. His method was safer for him and resulted in a well-trained horse.

9. **Why did the chase of the bighorn attract Roosevelt?**

The bighorn sheep lived further away, were marvelous climbers, heavier than deer, wary and noble. "The chase of no other kind of American big game ranks higher, or more thoroughly tests the manliest qualities of the hunter."

What do you think are the "manliest qualities of the hunter"?

Roosevelt refers to "a steady head, sound lungs, and trained muscles" in the actual hunt. However, additional needed qualities are patience, alertness, and tenacity.

How does the chase of the bighorn test these qualities?

The sheep live on the highest crests, are wonderful climbers, and live "by choice always among cliffs and jagged, broken ground." The qualities that Roosevelt mentioned are all required to reach the bighorn's habitat.

Are these qualities possessed by hunters only? What other circumstances in life test these qualities?

Student responses will reflect a variety of ideas. Encourage a class discussion of circumstances that would demand patience, alertness, and tenacity.

10. Where are the Bad Lands? Locate them on a map. Why were they given this name?

The Bad Lands are located in southwestern South Dakota and were named for their rugged terrain and lack of good, arable farming land.

Read aloud lines that give the most vivid description of the "heart of the Bad Lands."

"At last I got into the heart of the Bad Lands proper, where the hard, wrinkled earth was torn into shapes as sullen and grotesque as those of dreamland. Bands of black, red, and purple varied the gray and yellow-brown of their sides; the tufts of scanty vegetation were dull green. Sometimes I rode my horse at the bottom of narrow washouts, between straight walls of clay but a few feet apart; sometimes I had to lead him as he scrambled up, down, and across the sheer faces of the buttes. The glare from the bare clay walls dazzled the eye; the air was burning under the hot August sun. I saw nothing living except the rattlesnakes, of which there were many."

Read aloud the description of the valley in the midst of the wilderness.

"At last, in the midst of the wilderness, I came on a lovely valley. A spring trickled out of a cedar cañon, and below this spring the narrow, deep ravine was green with luscious grass, and was smooth for some hundreds of yards. Here I unsaddled and turned old Manitou loose to drink and feed at his leisure."

11. Tell the story of the hunt for mountain sheep, giving the main incidents under the following topics:

a. the preparation and first day:

Roosevelt left early in the morning with his favorite horse, a blanket, oilskin slicker, salt, hardtack, tea, sugar, a metal cup for boiling water, a rifle and cartridges. He rode for six hours through grassy plateaus and wooded coulees, through the Bad Lands until he came at last to a valley where he set up camp. He spent part of the afternoon climbing the ridges and peaks looking for signs of the bighorn then he went back to camp and settled down for the night.

b. the chase and the conclusion:

He awoke before dawn and began the hunt. From a high ridge he spotted movement and identified three sheep in the distance. Roosevelt left his spot and began to follow them to their drinking pool. Through gullies, narrow washouts, and over clay trails he moved soundlessly. He approached them at last, whistled, and as they looked, shot the biggest of the sheep. Initially, the sheep ran off with the others, but soon lagged behind and Roosevelt finished him. After dressing the sheep, Roosevelt returned to camp, ate breakfast, got his horse and returned to the sheep where he loaded him on his horse and returned to the ranch by midday.

12. **You will find Hagedorn's *The Boys' Life of Theodore Roosevelt* an interesting biography.**
13. **Find in the glossary the following: roundup, cowpuncher, corral, bottom, prongbuck, sheer, picketed, loom, quarry.**
14. **Pronounce: buttes, fortnight, haunting, route, plateau, cañon, leisure, gorge, supple, wary, clamber.**

Extended Activity:

1. This story is suggested as a silent reading activity. To further gauge silent reading comprehension, give the students this short true/false quiz.

F. a. The setting for this story begins in the mountains.

F. b. Manitou, Roosevelt's favorite horse, was young.

T. c. The bighorns of the Bad Lands do not move far from their home.

F. d. Bighorn sheep and deer tracks are indistinguishable from each other.

T. e. Roosevelt shot twice to kill his game.

2. Students may be assigned any of the additional activities.

a. Using a good encyclopedia or the Internet, research the Bad Lands. Discover how they were formed and what they look like today. Create a three-dimensional replica of the Bad Lands as Roosevelt described them. Draw a map of South Dakota on poster board and identify the location of the Bad Lands. Using Playdough or other moldable materials, along with paint, create a miniature version of the Bad Lands.

b. On Roosevelt's ride through the Bad Lands, he took only those items essential for survival for a day and a night. Your family is planning an overnight campout in the Bad Lands. No campers, no luxuries! Remember, Roosevelt slept under the stars with his saddle for a pillow. Like Roosevelt, you want to see a bighorn sheep. You will be climbing rugged terrain in heat and facing a cool night. What essential items will you need? After you have prepared your list, create a story about your adventure. What did you encounter? Were you well prepared? What items should you have taken or left behind? Were you successful in your quest to see a bighorn sheep? See "More Extended Activities" (page 24) at the end of this section on animals for other related activities.

NAME______________________________CLASS__________DATE______

AMERICAN BIGHORN SHEEP, P. 25

1. For a reading check, circle true or false to the following statements:

True False a. The setting for this story begins in the mountains.

True False b. Manitou, Roosevelt's favorite horse, was young.

True False c. The bighorns of the Bad Lands do not move far from their home.

True False d. Bighorn sheep and deer tracks are indistinguishable from each other.

True False e. Roosevelt shot twice to kill his game.

2. Complete the additional assigned activity.
   a. Using a good encyclopedia or the Internet, research the Bad Lands. Discover how they were formed and what they look like today. Create a three-dimensional replica of the Bad Lands as Roosevelt described them. Draw a map of South Dakota on poster board and identify the location of the Bad Lands. Using Playdough or other moldable materials, along with paint, create a miniature version of the Bad Lands.
   b. On Roosevelt's ride through the Bad Lands, he took only those items essential for survival for a day and a night. Your family is planning an overnight campout in the Bad Lands. No campers, no luxuries! Remember, Roosevelt slept under the stars with his saddle for a pillow. Like Roosevelt, you want to see a bighorn sheep. You will be climbing rugged terrain in heat and facing a cool night. What essential items will you need? After you have prepared your list, create a story about your adventure. What did you encounter? Were you well prepared? What items should you have taken or left behind? Were you successful in your quest to see a bighorn sheep?

A Furious Elephant Charge, p. 34

1. **Tell briefly the story of the charge.**
   On an elephant hunt, the hunters heard the roar of the huge animals. Making their way toward the sound, they discovered a herd of elephants in the tall grasses. The gun-bearers became excited and knocked their guns together, attracting the attention of the elephants. As the elephants watched, the hunters approached and fired. Some of the elephants scattered, but the hunter saw one "rogue" elephant coming his way in full charge. The hunter could not shoot because the elephant's trunk protected his forehead. Just as the elephant reached the hunter, the hunter fired, but it was too late. The elephant slashed the hunter with his tusk and sent him sprawling. As the hunter lay hidden in the grass, trembling for his life, the elephant beat the grass looking for him, but, blinded by gun powder and smoke, his sense of scent was destroyed. He failed to find the hunter and eventually walked away. The hunter was spared.
2. **To what does the author compare the growl of the elephant?**
   "The growl of an elephant is exactly like the rumbling of thunder."
3. **Why did the author feel more helpless in this adventure than in previous dangers?**
   "The tangled grass rendered retreat impossible. I had only one barrel loaded, and that was useless, as the upraised trunk protected his forehead. I felt myself doomed."
4. **How do you think he felt when the elephant had failed to find him and pushed on?**
   "To my joy I heard the rustling of the grass grow fainter."
5. **What qualities do you think a good hunter must have?**
   Allow students to brainstorm those qualities.
6. **Read aloud in class the story of the charge, from page 36, line 23, to the end of the selection.**
7. **You will enjoy reading "Toomai of the Elephants" in Rudyard Kipling's *Second Jungle Book* and reporting the story to your classmates, reading aloud parts that you think are most interesting.**

8. Find in the glossary the meaning of: arrested, jungle, reverberating, interspersed, margin, crevices, inspection, respective, compact, velocity, rendered, whip-thong, concealment, momentarily, acute.

9. Pronounce: often, ponderous.

Extended Activity:

1. This story is suggested as a silent reading activity. To further gauge silent reading comprehension, give the students this short true/false quiz.

T. a. The setting for this story takes place in the mountains.

F. b. The elephants moved stealthily, leaving no tracks.

T. c. The elephants growled like thunder and screamed like a train engine.

T. d. Elephants can run as fast as a horse at full speed.

F. e. The elephant used his trunk to throw the hunter into the air.

2. In the biographical section, students learn that the author of this story has traveled, explored, and hunted around the world. Have the students identify on a globe or world map all the places listed in the section: England, Ceylon, Nile River, Lake Albert Nyanza, Egypt, Cyprus, India, Japan, and the United States.

3. See "More Extended Activities" (page 24) at the end of this section on animals for other related activities.

NAME______________________________CLASS__________DATE______

A FURIOUS ELEPHANT CHARGE, P. 34

1. For a reading check, circle true or false to the following statements:

True False a. The setting for this story takes place in the mountains.

True False b. The elephants moved stealthily, leaving no tracks.

True False c. The elephants growled like thunder and screamed like a train engine.

True False d. Elephants can run as fast as a horse at full speed.

True False e. The elephant used his trunk to throw the hunter into the air.

2. In the biographical section, you learn that the author of this story has traveled, explored and hunted around the world. Identify on a globe or world map all the places listed in the section: England, Ceylon, Nile River, Lake Albert Nyanza, Egypt, Cyprus, India, Japan, and the United States.

How An Elk Swam to Safety, p. 39

Note: the first three questions are designed to elicit a variety of valid student responses. Use these questions as a classroom discussion.

1. **What part of the story is most interesting to you?**
2. **What description do you like best?**
3. **Read aloud descriptions that would make fine subjects for movies.**
4. **Make an outline of the more important incidents of the story.**

   Outlines may vary but should include these general headings:

   Setting: beside a river on an open plain; the boys had prepared a fire, eaten, and were exploring their surroundings when they noticed a herd of wapiti, or elk, milling about.

   The wolves: Upon investigation, the boys saw that a pack of wolves were chasing the wapiti. They singled out a large one and chased him near the boys' camp where he veered into the thicket, and the wolves sneaked away.

   A panther and death: thinking they could chase out the wapiti with their dog, the boys sent him into the thicket, only to see the wapiti run out with a panther clinging to his back. In a wild run for his life, the wapiti ran to the lake where he jumped in and swam, dumping the panther into the water. Unable to swim, the panther floundered in the water where the boys shot him. The wapiti swam to a shoal where he emerged from the water. The boys discovered an arrowhead in his thigh which finally led to his death.
5. **Tell the substance of the story, following your outline.**
6. **What incident gained for the elk the sympathy of the boys?**

   The elk had been attacked by wolves and a wolverine. "Persecution by so many enemies had won for him their sympathy."
7. **How is the attack on the elk by the wolves explained?**

   The boys discovered an arrowhead from an Indian sticking in his thigh. "The wound explained why the wolves had assailed an animal that otherwise, from his great size and strength, would have defied them."
8. **Find in the glossary the meaning of: indicated, towering, majestic, imposing, doubling, rejoined,**

antlers, swerved, wolverine, persecution, visible, mortal, assailed, defied, accounted.

9. Pronounce: François, wapiti, toward, wounded, reappearance, creature, farther, shoal, pursuit.

Extended Activity:

1. This story is suggested as a silent reading activity. To further gauge silent reading comprehension, give the students this short true/false quiz.

F. a. The setting for this story occurs in a forest beside a river.

T. b. Wapiti belong to the deer family.

F. c. Wolves often attack healthy, full-grown wapiti.

F. d. The boys' presence and the smoke from the fire stopped the wolves from going into the thicket after the elk.

T. e. Wolves, wolverines, and an arrowhead all contributed to the wapiti's death.

2. Have students complete any of the following activities.

a. The elk was very adept at losing his predators. He kept both the wolves and the wolverine from destroying him. Research animal behavior to find other examples of tactics animals use to fend off their attackers.

b. In the biographical sketch at the end of this story, the students learn more about the voyageurs in this story. Early French-Canadian voyageurs traveled throughout the north in their birch-bark canoes, exploring as they went. As a tribute to their explorations, Voyageurs National Park is locate in northern Minnesota. Research early voyageurs, discover more about their adventures, and map their river voyages through the vast wilderness. The Internet is an excellent research source.

See "More Extended Activities" (page 24) at the end of this section on animals for other related activities.

NAME______________________________CLASS__________DATE______

HOW AN ELK SWAM TO SAFETY, p. 39

1. For a reading check, circle true or false to the following statements:

True False a. The setting for this story occurs in a forest beside a river.

True False b. Wapiti belong to the deer family.

True False c. Wolves often attack healthy, full-grown wapiti.

True False d. The boys' presence and the smoke from the fire stopped the wolves from going into the thicket after the elk.

True False e. Wolves, wolverines, and an arrowhead all contributed to the wapiti's death.

2. Complete the additional assigned activity.
   a. The elk was very adept at losing his preditors. He kept both the wolves and the wolverine from destroying him. Research animal behavior to find other examples of tactics animals use to fend off their attackers.
   b. In the biographical sketch at the end of this story you learned more about the voyageurs in this story. Early French-Canadian voyageurs traveled throughout the north in their birch-bark canoes, exploring as they went. As a tribute to their explorations, Voyageurs National Park is located in northern Minnesota. Research early voyageurs, discover more about their adventures, and map their river voyages through the vast wilderness. The Internet is an excellent research source.

The World of Nature—*Animals,* pp. 25-44

More Extended Activities:

1. In these stories students have met a variety of animals. Roosevelt writes about horses, cattle, blacktails, prongbuck, elk, and, of course, the bighorn sheep. In Baker's story, he mentions elephants, and finally in Captain Reid's story he identifies elk, wolves, a dog, and a wolverine. In the first two stories, the hunters had to recognize footprints and be able to track their game. Have students research several animals mentioned in these stories and create a poster of their identifying paw/hoof prints. Have their classmates identify the animals by their prints.

2. Students should research the habitat, size, and habits of one or more of the main animals mentioned in these stories. On a large floor space, tape the outline of the actual size of their chosen animal, making sure to duplicate the identifying marks described by the authors: the bighorn's curled horns, the elephant's large ears, and the elk's towering horns.

3. Students could choose one animal mentioned in any of the stories. After researching its habitat and characteristics, complete the following web.

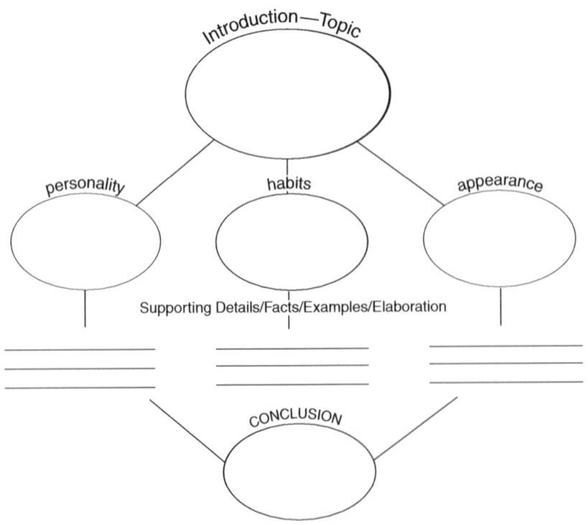

In the big circle name the animal. In the following three small circles identify personality, habits, and appearance. After completing the web, students should write an essay in first person (using I, me, we, us) as if they are the animal. Papers must be edited for correct grammar and punctuation. Students can then create a drawing of their animal and present their research to the rest of the class, using their artwork as a visual aid.

The research paper should be written in blue or black ink and in cursive. Be sure students plan their writing before they compose the final paper. The web may be helpful in planning their writing and verifying there is enough information.

The presentation should be a minimum of two minutes. It must include at least one visual. This may be props, posters, pictures, video, overhead slides, computer and/or television. Arrangements should be made ahead of time with the teacher for use of materials. Each student will be graded on proper treatment of the topic as well as proper elements of public speaking.

4. Students could create a poster describing any of the stories in the section. The poster should include the story title, a scene from the story, and a catchy slogan that captures the main idea of the story.

5. Roosevelt refers to the "manly qualities of hunters." After reading these three stories, students should identify in the chart below all the qualities they can think of that these hunters showed. When they have completed their list, draw a character that represents all of these qualities.

American Bighorn Sheep	A Furious Elephant Charge	How an Elk Swam to Safety

NAME______________________________CLASS__________DATE______

THE WORLD OF NATURE—*ANIMALS,* EXTENDED EXERCISES, PP. 25-44

1. In these stories you have met a variety of animals. Roosevelt writes about horses, cattle, blacktails, prongbuck, elk, and, of course, the bighorn sheep. In Baker's story, he mentions elephants, and finally in Captain Reid's story he identifies elk, wolves, a dog, and a wolverine. In the first two stories, the hunters had to recognize footprints and be able to track their game. Research several animals mentioned in these stories and create a poster of their identifying paw/hoof prints. Have your classmates identify the animals by their prints.

2. Research the habitat, size, and habits of one or more of the main animals mentioned in these stories. On a large floor space, tape the outline of the actual size of your chosen animal, making sure to duplicate the identifying marks described by the authors: the bighorn's curled horns, the elephant's large ears, and the elk's towering horns.

3. Choose one animal mentioned in any of the stories. After researching its habitat and characteristics, complete the following web on the following page.

   In the big circle name the animal. In the following three small circles identify personality, habits, and appearance. After completing the web, write an essay in first person (using I, me, we, us) as if you are the animal. Papers must be edited for correct grammar and punctuation. You can then create a drawing of your animal and present your research to the rest of the class, using your artwork as a visual aid.

   The research paper should be written in blue or black ink and in cursive. Be sure you plan your writing before you compose the final paper. The web may be helpful in planning your writing and verifying there is enough information.

   The presentation should be a minimum of two minutes. It must include at least one visual. This may be props, posters, pictures, video, overhead slides, computer and/or television. Arrangements should be made ahead of time with the teacher for use of materials. Each student will be graded on proper treatment of the topic as well as proper elements of public speaking.

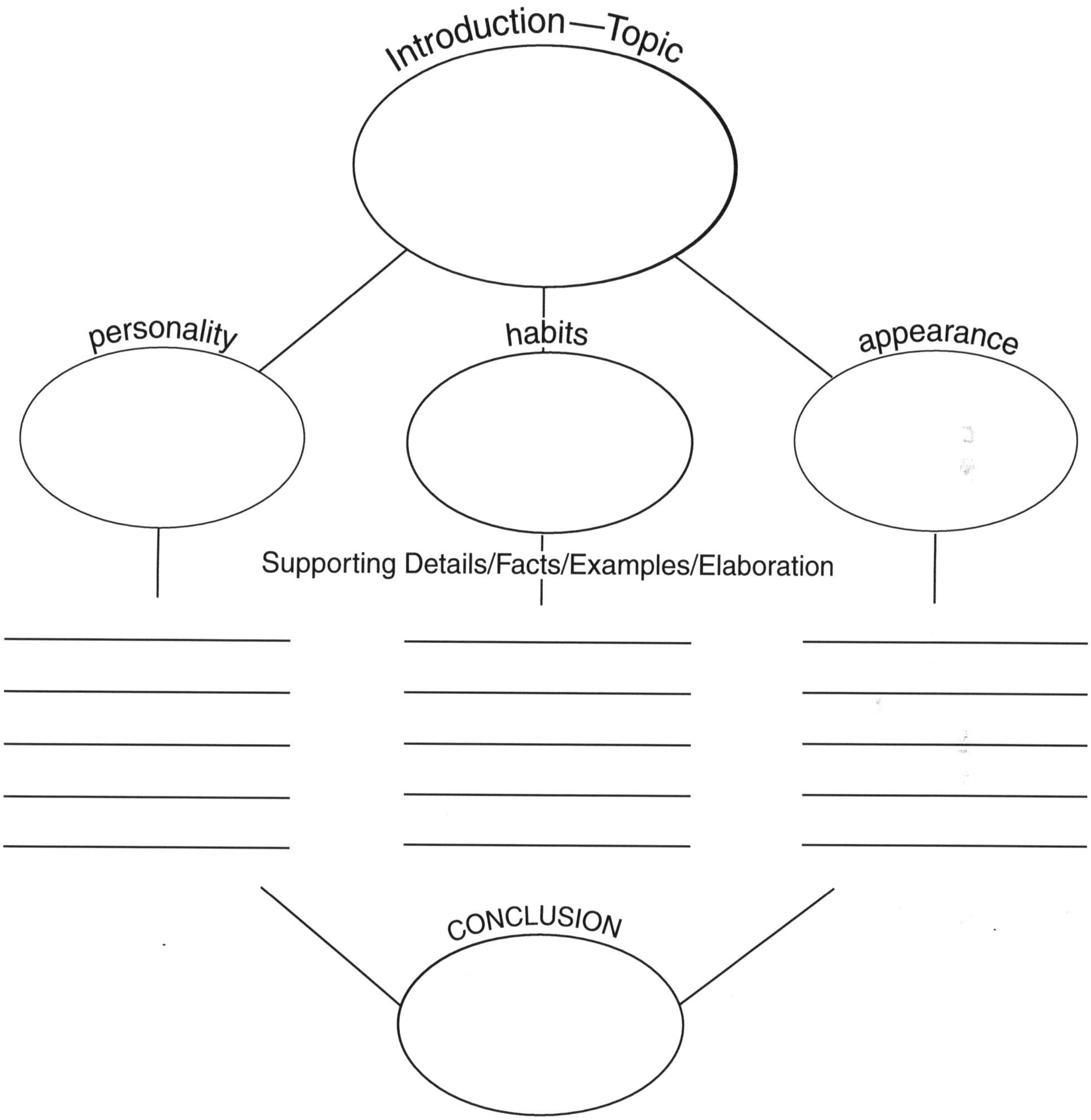
Introduction—Topic
personality
habits
appearance
Supporting Details/Facts/Examples/Elaboration
CONCLUSION

4. Create a poster describing any of the stories in the section. The poster should include the story title, a scene from the story, and a catchy slogan that captures the main idea of the story.

5. Roosevelt refers to the "manly qualities of hunters." After reading these three stories, identify in the chart below all the qualities you can think of that these hunters showed. When you have completed your list, draw a character that represents all of these qualities.

American Bighorn Sheep	A Furious Elephant Charge	How an Elk Swam to Safety

Birds and Their Songs

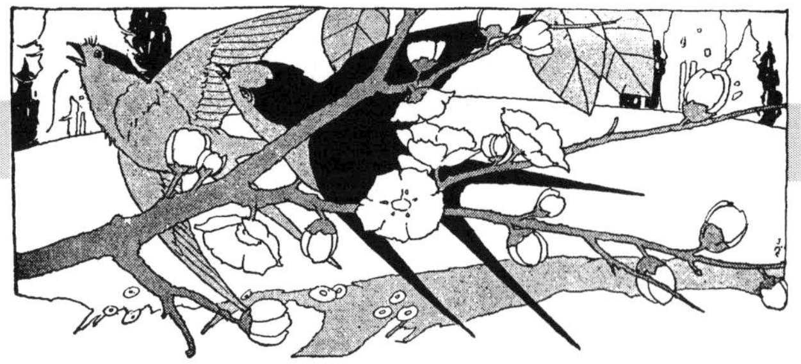

The Cardinal Bird, p. 45

1. **The cardinal bird is an American songster; have you ever seen this bird?**
   Answers will vary.
2. **What tells you in the poem that it stays all winter?**
   "Where snowdrifts are deepest he frolics along…"
3. **The poet says that this bird is a preacher; what is his church?**
   "A plump little prelate, the park is his church;"
   What pulpit does he like best?
   "The pulpit he loves is a cliff-sheltered birch;"
   To whom does he preach?
   "He preaches, with most unconventional glee, A sermon addressed to the squirrels and me.
   What belief does he preach?
   "Commending the wisdom of those that display The brightest of colors when heavens are gray."
4. **Do you agree that we should appear bright and cheerful on gray days? Why?**
   Encourage students to explain their responses.
5. **You will enjoy "Training Cardinals," Muller (in *St. Nicholas*, June, 1918), and also the Victor Records, "Songs of Our Native Birds," Kellogg, and "Songs and Calls of Our Native Birds," Gorst.**
6. **Find in the glossary the meaning of: lyrics, prelate, rubicund, livery, unconventional, commending.**

The Bluebird, p. 46

1. **Have you ever seen a bluebird?**
   Answers will vary.
2. **At what time of the year does this bird "seek our maple groves"?**
   "When ice is thawed, and snow is gone…Drifting down the first warm wind That thrills the earliest days of spring, The bluebird seeks our maple groves."
3. **What do you know of its song?**
   "He sings, and his is nature's voice—A gush of melody sincere From that great fount of harmony Which thaws and runs when spring is here."
4. **What faith do the spring winds and the bluebird's songs give the poet?**
   "They tell me after frost and death There comes a time of blossoming; And after snow and cutting sleet, The cold, stern mood of Nature yields To tender warmth, when bare pink feet Of children press her greening fields."
5. **What effect on the poet has the bluebird's song?**
   "While through my life spring's freshness runs Like music through a poet's dream."
6. **Explain the comparison found in the last stanza.**
   The poet says spring's freshness is like music running through a poet's dream. Encourage students to explore the meaning of the comparison.
7. **Which stanza do you like best? Why?**
   Answers will vary.
8. **Find in the glossary the meaning of: swarm, thrills, gush, greening, splendor, gladden, vales.**

To the Cuckoo, p. 48

1. **Make a list of all the names by which the poet speaks of the cuckoo in this poem.**
The poet says the cuckoo is a: beauteous stranger, messenger of Spring, delightful visitant, sweet bird.
2. **Mention the various things he says come at the same time that the cuckoo's song is heard.**
Spring, flowers, music of birds, and peas in bloom come when the cuckoo's song is heard.
3. **What tells you that this bird's song is one of cheer?**
"Thou hast no sorrow in thy song."
4. **Express the meaning of the fifth stanza in your own words.**
Student responses may vary but should reflect that though the cuckoo is gone to other places in the winter, he always returns in spring
5. **What does the poet mean by "No winter in thy year"?**
The cuckoo always migrates to warmer climates and therefore, knows nothing about winter.
6. **Memorize the last two stanzas. In memorizing a selection, become familiar with the thought as well as the words through both the eye and the ear. Writing and then saying aloud the lines will help to fix them in your memory.**
The last two stanzas are these:

    Sweet bird! thy bower is ever green;
    Thy sky is ever clear;
    Thou hast no sorrow in thy song,
    No Winter in thy year!

    O could I fly, I'd fly with thee!
    We'd make, with joyful wing,
    Our annual visit o'er the globe,
    Companions of the Spring.
7. **Contest: Who can memorize these two stanzas in the shortest time?**
8. **Find in the glossary the meaning of: cuckoo, decks, hail, bowers, starts, lay.**
9. **Pronounce: beauteous, visitant.**

The Humming Bird, p. 50

1. **Have you ever seen a humming bird?**
   Answers will vary.
2. **What service does the bird render to the flowers?**
   The humming bird visits every flower "like a curious florist, removing from each the injurious insects that otherwise would ere long cause its beauteous petals to drop and decay."
3. **How does the bird capture the insect?**
   "Its long delicate bill enters the cup of the flower, and the tongue touches each insect in succession and draws it from its lurking place, to be instantly swallowed."
4. **How does the author excuse the bird's theft of food from the flower?**
   The theft of food "is looked upon with a grateful feeling by a flower, which is thus kindly relieved from the attacks of her destroyers."
5. **Make a program for Bird Day; or for exercises, with a birdhouse exhibit.**
   Students may want to contact the National Audubon Society for ideas and suggestions.
6. **You will find valuable suggestions in the illustrated bulletins: *Bird Houses and How to Build Them* and *How To Attract Birds*, which are sent free by the Department of Agriculture, Washington, D. C.; also *Good Bungalows for Good Birds*, sent free by Southern Cypress Manufacturers' Association, New Orleans, Louisiana.**
   These resources are from the 1920 edition of the reader. Similar documents may be available now, however, from governmental departments and/or industry organizations. The Internet is a good place to start a search for current resources.
7. **Find in the glossary the meaning of: expand, pinions, baffles, competition, precaution.**
8. **Pronounce: genial, poised, recesses, resplendent.**

FORBEARANCE, P. 52

1. **Which one of these five examples of forbearance do you think most difficult to practice?**
   The five examples of forbearance are: not harming birds, not picking flowers, eating simply with the wealthy, facing danger with trust, and loving good behavior. Students' responses will vary.
2. **Why should we protect birds and flowers?**
   Birds and flowers are important to our environment. They help control insects and provide enjoyment to those who observe them.
   What society has for its purpose the protection of birds?
   The National Audubon Society exists to encourage the protection of birds, along with all wildlife.
3. **What feeling similar to that described in the fifth example have you experienced in greeting a war hero?**
   Answers will vary.
4. **Which do most people prefer in daily life—appreciation that is expressed, or silent appreciation?**
   Most people prefer appreciation that is expressed.
5. **What two words are sharply contrasted in the second line?**
   Loved and left are contrasted. The poet is asking if one can admire the wood-rose and still leave it on its stem without picking it.
6. **Read the poem aloud to bring out all the contrasts.**
7. **What word shows that Emerson feels that he does not possess all of these qualities?**
   He uses the word "teach" showing that he has not learned forbearance in all of these.
8. **How does he express his admiration for the person who does possess them?**
   "Oh, be my friend, and teach me to be thine!"
9. **Find in the glossary the meaning of: forbearance, wood-rose, pulse, high, behavior**
10. **Pronounce: stalk.**

THE WORLD OF NATURE—*BIRDS AND THEIR SONGS*, PP. 45-52

Extended Activities:

Note to the teacher: Students should be encouraged to research various birds and become familiar with their habitats. Research information related to the specific birds mentioned in these entries are available on a wide variety of Internet sites. Several of the sites have educational materials for students and teachers that will aid them in their exploration of the bird kingdom. A few are listed below.

National Audubon Society http://www.audubon.org/
Hummingbird Society http://www.hummingbird.org/
North American Bluebird Society http://nabluebirdsociety.org/
Northern Cardinal http://prince.thinkquest.org/5078/Wildbirds.dir
The Cuckoo Bird http://www.sintercom.org/sef/cuckoo.html
State Birds http://www.50states.com/bird

The following activities can be adapted to any of the entries in this section.

1. Have students choose one of the five entries in this section. Students should rewrite the piece on poster board then, drawing their own pictures or using magazine pictures, illustrate the poem based on the images they find in it.

2. Students should research two of the birds described in these pieces. Learn about their nesting habits, migration patterns, habitat, and appearance. Then complete the following diagram describing what they learned.

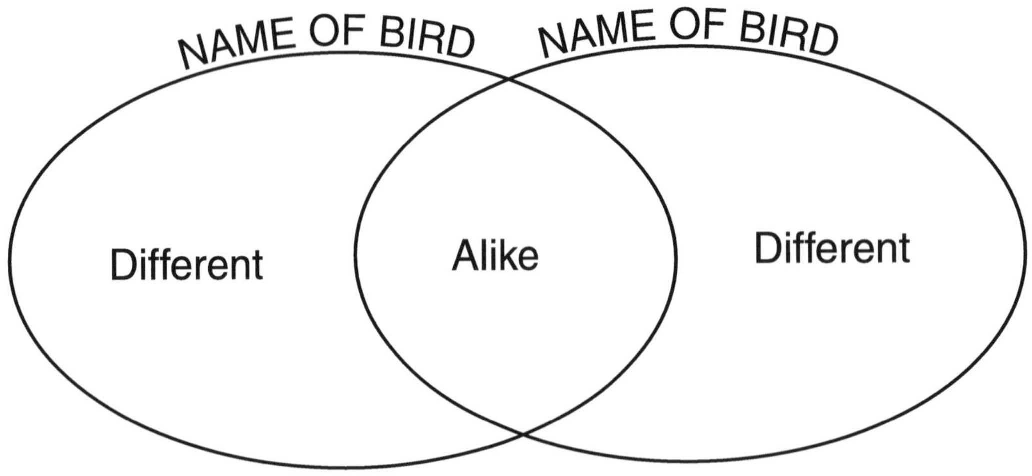

3. Have students identify which of the birds mentioned in these passages are state birds. Of which states? Answers—The cardinal is the state bird of the following states: Illinois, Indiana, Kentucky, North Carolina, Ohio, Virginia, and West Virginia. The bluebird is the state bird for Missouri and New York.

4. Poets frequently use a term called *alliteration* in their poetry. Alliteration repeats beginning consonant sounds as in "cool and crisp." Have students scan the poems and identify all the examples of alliteration they can find.

Obvious answers may include:

"The Cardinal Bird": plump little prelate; the park is his church; sermon addressed to the squirrels.

"To the Cuckoo": woods thy welcome ring; daisy decks; sound of music sweet; wandering through the wood; pull the primrose; pea puts on; vocal vale; an annual; We'd make with joyful wing.

"Forbearance": man or maid; nobility more nobly.

NAME______________________________ **CLASS**__________ **DATE**______

THE WORLD OF NATURE—*BIRDS AND THEIR SONGS*, EXTENDED EXERCISES, PP. 45-52

1. Choose one of the five entries in this section. Rewrite the piece on poster board then, drawing your own pictures or using magazine pictures, illustrate the poem based on the images you find in it.

2. Research two of the birds described in these pieces. Learn about their nesting habits, migration patterns, habitat, and appearance. Then complete the following diagram describing what you learned.

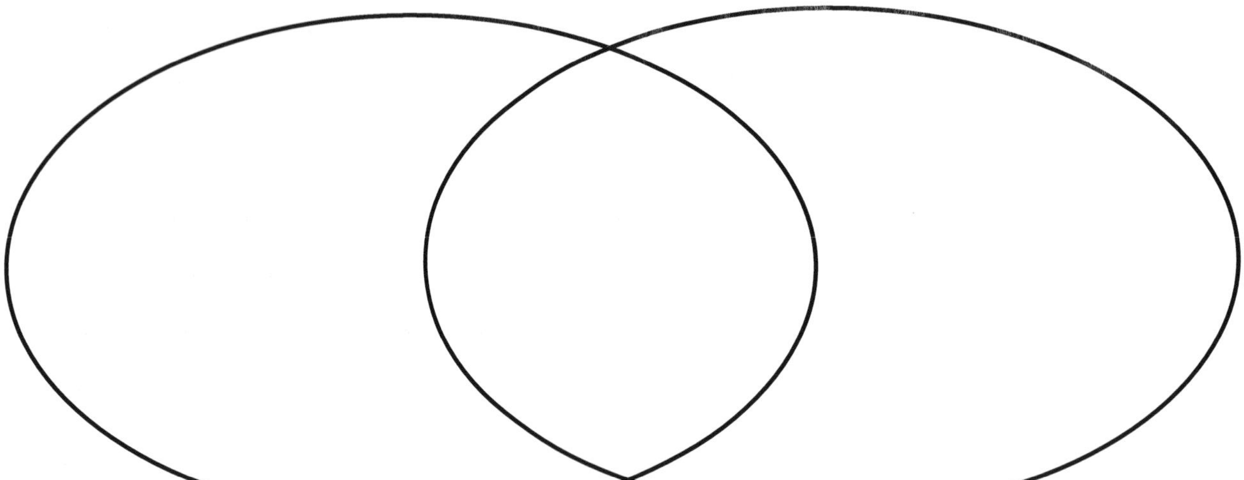

3. Identify which of the birds mentioned in these passages are state birds. Of which states?

Bird______________________

Bird______________________

4. Poets frequently use a term called *alliteration* in their poetry. Alliteration repeats beginning consonant sounds as in "cool and crisp." Scan the poems and identify all the examples of alliteration you can find.

Flowers

Roadside Flowers, p. 53

1. **Who is speaking in the poem?**
   The roadside flowers are speaking.
2. **What do we commonly call roadside flowers?**
   We call them wildflowers.
3. **What characteristics of roadside flowers that differ from those of cultivated flowers are noted in the first two stanzas?**
   "Straying from garden grounds, Lovers of idle hours, Breakers of ordered bounds. We blossom for those who need us, The strangers left behind." Roadside flowers are not planted nor cared for by humans. They grow where they please.
4. **What service do the flowers say they render? To whom?**
   They "blossom for those who need them, The strangers left behind."
5. **How does "the Lord of the Garden" help the roadside flowers in their task? What is their task?**
   "He makes the sun to rise, And His rain to fall like pardon On our dusty paradise." Their task is "to better the world with beauty, Wherever the way may lead."
6. **Do you think the last stanza means that the humble roadside flowers believe, with the poet Browning, that "all service ranks the same with God"?**
   Yes, the roadside flowers believe "all service ranks the same with God."
7. **What does the last stanza mean to you?**
   Encourage the students to justify their responses to the last stanza.

The Dandelions, p. 54

1. **To what is the coming of the dandelions likened in the first stanza?**
The coming of the dandelions is likened to a band of soldiers.
2. **Can you tell why the poet set the coming of the dandelions "upon a showery night"?**
The night rain brought out the dandelions in "a trooper band."
3. **What does the second stanza tell you?**
The second stanza points out that, unlike soldiers, the dandelions did not come with bugles and cheer; they just quietly appeared in the morning.
4. **To what does the poet liken the dandelions in the third stanza?**
The poet likens the dandelions to veterans—white with age.
5. **What becomes of the dandelions?**
They blow away in the spring winds.
6. **Find in the glossary the meaning of: slopes, paraded, selfsame.**

Apple Blossoms, p. 56

1. **The poem describes an English apple orchard; does it picture equally well an American apple orchard?**
   Yes, the apple orchard looks the same everywhere.
2. **What is the "promised glory" of the apple tree?**
   The "promised glory" refers to the apple crop that will be harvested in the fall.
3. **What picture does "baby-white" bring before you?**
   "Baby-white" refers to the soft fresh skin of a newborn baby.
4. **What other signs of spring does the poet mention?**
   He mentions the mavis, a song bird, and the pink buds that pop out in the spring.
5. **How could blossoms falling from a tree make the poet think of a "cascade"?**
   A cascade is a waterfall. The blossoms fall from the trees like a waterfall.
6. **What made the brooklets look like silver?**
   The spring sun sparkling on the water could make the brooklets look like silver.
7. **What effect does the repetition of "In the spring" give?**
   The poet is emphasizing the beauty and gentleness of spring.
8. **Find three lines in each stanza that rhyme.**
   Stanza 1: "When the spreading trees are hoary, With their wealth of promised glory, And the mavis pipes his story"
   Stanza 2: "Pink buds bursting at the light, Crumpled petals baby-white—Just to touch them a delight!"
   Stanza 3: "When the pink cascades are falling, And the silver brooklets brawling, And the cuckoo bird is calling"
   Stanza 4: "When the bride and maidens wear Apple blossoms in their hair; Apple blossoms everywhere,"
   Stanza 5: "No sight can I remember Half so precious, half so tender, As the apple blossoms render"
9. **What makes this poem so pleasing when read aloud?**
   The poet's meter and rhyme make the poem so pleasing.
10. **Find in the glossary the meaning of: mavis, crumpled, brawling, bridal, render.**
11. **Pronounce: hoary, subtle, beneath.**

THE WORLD OF NATURE—*FLOWERS*, PP. 53-57

Extended Activities:

The following activities can be adapted to any of the entries in this section.

1. Meter in poetry refers to the pattern of stressed and unstressed syllables that create the rhythm in the poem. Stressed or accented syllables are indicated with a '; unstressed or unaccented syllables are indicated with a ˘. Have students choose a poem from these selections, recopy the poem, then above each syllable mark a ' or a ˘ to indicate the meter of the poem.

2. Poems are often organized in patterns called rhyme schemes: lines that rhyme are assigned the same letters of the alphabet beginning with A. All of the poems in this section have clear rhyming patterns. Have students read the poems again and identify their rhyme schemes.

"Roadside Flowers"—ABAB CDCD EFEF GHGH IJIJ
"The Dandelions"—ABAB CDCD EFEF GHGH
"Apple Blossoms"—AAABBBA AAACCCA AAADDDA AAAEEEA AAAFFFA

3. Poets often use figurative language to help communicate the poem's message. At least three types of figurative language appear in these poems. A metaphor compares two unlike objects saying one is the other. "The dog, a speeding bullet, raced across the yard." A simile compares two unlike objects saying one is like or as the other. "The dog was like a flash of lightning speeding across the yard." Personification gives nonhuman objects human thoughts or actions. "The wind whispered in my ear." Have students read the poems and find examples of each of the figurative languages described above. Then explain how they help to communicate the poet's meaning. (Students' responses may vary.)

Metaphor:
"The Dandelions"—The dandelions are renamed as troops in an army;
"Apple Blossoms"—the blossoms are renamed as pink cascades.

Simile:
"Roadside Flowers"—"And His rain to fall like pardon."

Personification:

"Roadside Flowers"—flowers are talking;

"The Dandelions"—dandelions are behaving like soldiers;

"Apple Blossoms"—blossoms are falling and brooklets are brawling.

NAME______________________________CLASS__________DATE______

THE WORLD OF NATURE—*FLOWERS*, EXTENDED EXERCISES, PP. 53-57

1. **Meter in poetry refers to the pattern of stressed and unstressed syllables that create the rhythm in the poem. Stressed or accented syllables are indicated with a '; unstressed or unaccented syllables are indicated with a ˘. Choose a poem from these selections, recopy the poem, then above each syllable mark a ' or a ˘ to indicate the meter of the poem.**

2. Poems are often organized in patterns called rhyme schemes: lines that rhyme are assigned the same letters of the alphabet beginning with A. All of the poems in this section have clear rhyming patterns. Read the poems again and identify their rhyme schemes.

"Roadside Flowers"____________________________________

"The Dandelions"____________________________________

Apple Blossoms"____________________________________

3. Poets often use figurative language to help communicate the poem's message. At least three types of figurative language appear in these poems. A metaphor compares two unlike objects saying one is the other. "The dog, a speeding bullet, raced across the yard." A simile compares two unlike objects saying one is like or as the other. "The dog was like a flash of lightning speeding across the yard." Personification gives nonhuman objects human thoughts or actions. "The wind whispered in my ear." Read the poems and find examples of each of the figurative languages described above. Then explain how they help to communicate the poet's meaning.

Metaphor:

____

____

____

Simile:

____

____

____

Personification:

____

____

____

Spring and Summer

The Voice of Spring, p. 58

1. **Who is speaking in this poem?**
   Spring is speaking.
2. **How may the steps of Spring be traced?**
   Her steps may be traced "By the winds which tell of the violet's birth, By the primrose-stars in the shadowy grass, By the green leaves opening as I pass."
3. **How does the wind tell that the violets are in bloom?**
   The wind has seen their "birth."
4. **Read the lines from the second stanza which tell where Spring has been and the result of her visit there.**
   "I have breathed on the South, and the chestnut flowers By thousands have burst from the forest-bowers. And the ancient graves and the fallen fanes Are veiled with wreaths on Italian plains."
5. **Where does the third stanza tell us that Spring has been? What was the result of her visit there?**
   "I have looked on the hills of the stormy North, And the larch has hung all his tassels forth, The fisher is out on the sunny sea, And the reindeer bounds o'er the pastures free, And the pine has a fringe of softer green, And the moss looks bright where my foot hath been."
6. **Why could not the fisherman go out before Spring came?**
   The lakes and rivers would be covered with ice in the North.
7. **What places mentioned in the fourth stanza show how far Spring has traveled?**
   The poet says he has been from the "Hesperian clime," an Italian reference, to the "Iceland lakes." From south to north, Spring has traveled far.
8. **What is the name of the "night bird" which sings through the "starry time"?**
   The nightingale is the night bird, known for its sad song.
9. **What bird is mentioned in connection with the Iceland lakes? Why is not a singing bird mentioned instead of this bird?**
   The swan's wild note is connected to the Iceland lakes. Singing birds may not be as common in Iceland's climate.

10. **What was the chain which bound the streams before the coming of Spring?**

The chain refers to the frozen waters of winter that kept them from moving.

11. **Select the words from the fifth stanza which tell of the movement of the waters.**

"They are sweeping on to the silvery main, They are flashing down from the mountain brows, They are flinging spray o'er the forest boughs, They are bursting forth from their sparry caves, And the earth resounds with the joy of waves!"

12. **Which of the flowers and trees named in the poem do you know?**

Answers will vary.

13. **Find in the glossary the meaning of: ancient, fanes, clime, sparry, lyre.**

14. **Pronounce: violet, Italian, loosed, Hesperian, verdure.**

SPRING PROPHECIES, P. 60

1. **What "prophecy" of spring does the first stanza give?**
   The breezes bring "The delicate odor of buds to be."
   The second?
   The green of the elm is "A gracious token of leaves to be."
   The third?
   The orchard sends "The subtle fragrance of fruit to be."
   The fourth?
   A bird "Foretells the sweetness of songs to be."
2. **Which of these signs of spring have you noticed?**
   Answers will vary.
3. **Why would you call this poem a lyric?**
   A lyric expresses the poet's personal feelings about a topic using poetry that is musical. This poem describes the author's feelings about spring.
4. **Find lines that seem to you especially musical.**
   Answers will vary.
5. **Point out the lines that rhyme.**
   The rhyme scheme is as follows: AABBB CCBBB DDBBB EEBBB (Spring may be considered near rhyme.)
6. **How does the poet avoid repeating the word "wind" in the first stanza?**
   He refers to the wind as "the gossipy breezes."
7. **There is a national club called "The United States School Garden Army"; are you a member?**
   "The United States School Garden Army" could not be located. However, an Internet search for School Gardens produced many opportunities to explore educational resources for children and gardening. Students are encouraged to pursue those resources to expand their gardening skills.
8. **Write to the Bureau of Education, Washington, D.C., for *Home Gardening for City Children*, and for *A Manual of School-Supervised Gardening;* or to the Department of Agriculture for *Circular 48* of the "Boys' and Girls' Club Work."**
   See note on page 32, question 6.
9. **Find in the glossary the meaning of: range, gossipy, nook, gracious, token, rigor, foretells.**
10. **Pronounce: unsheathes, elm, melodious.**

Spring in Kentucky, p. 62

1. **In what poetic words does the author say that in March he begins to think of spring?**

   "March is a month when the needle of my nature dips toward the country."

2. **How do plants "stretch arms upward and legs downward"?**

   Their branches and leaves reach up to the sun, and their roots dig into the earth.

3. **How does "Nature do her spring house-cleaning"?**

   Nature uses the "rain clouds for her water buckets, and the wind for her brooms." She drenches the earth and sweeps in every dirty corner until the earth is clean. She scatters the leaves, and with her brooms, beats down the icicles.

4. **After house-cleaning, what does Nature do?**

   "This done, she begins to hang up soft new curtains at the forest windows and to spread over her floor a new carpet of an emerald loveliness such as no mortal looms could ever have woven."

5. **To whom does she send invitations to visit her?**

   She sends invitations throughout the South "for the birds to come and spend the summer in Kentucky."

6. **When are these invitations accepted?**

   They are accepted "in April and May, and by June her house is full of visitors."

7. **Compare the picture of spring in this selection with those in the two poems preceding; which picture do you like best?**

   Answers will vary.

8. **Find in the glossary the meaning of: cranny, emerald.**

MARCH, P. 63

1. **Which of the things mentioned in this poem have you noticed in the spring?**
   The poem mentions cocks, streams, birds, lakes, fields, old, young, strong, cattle, plowboy, mountains, fountains, clouds, and blue sky. Student responses will vary.
2. **How many of these may be seen in the city?**
   Responses will vary based on the student's concept of the city, but birds, old, young, strong, fountains, clouds, and blue sky may be seen in the city.
3. **How many can be seen only in the country?**
   Cocks, streams, lakes, fields, cattle, plowboy, and mountains can only be seen in the country.
4. **From what places has the snow "retreated"?**
   The snow has retreated from the streams, lakes, and green fields.
5. **In what battle has it been "defeated"?**
   It has been defeated in the battle with spring.
6. **Where does it still linger?**
   It still lingers "On the top of the bare hill."
7. **What are the "fountains" of which the poet speaks?**
   The fountains may be the waterfalls, the result of melting snows. Encourage students to think of other possibilities.
8. **What tells you that the plowboy feels happy?**
   He "is whooping-anon-anon," which means he is whooping continually.
9. **To what are the small clouds compared?**
   The clouds are compared to sailboats sailing on the water.
10. **Which words sound like the thought they express?**
    Words that sound like their meaning are referred to as onomatopoeia. Twitter and whooping sound like the thought they express.
11. **Which lines rhyme?**
    The rhyme scheme is as follows: AABBCDDEEC FFGGCHHIIC.
12. **Find in the glossary the meaning of: grazing, prevailing, laureate.**

JUNE, P. 65

1. **By what signs does the poet know that June has come?**
The poet hears a partridge, feels a softness in the air, sees the bursting buds, and hears the warblers in the woods.
2. **In the first stanza notice the repetition of "I heard a partridge drumming," with the addition, "a welcome with his wings"; what similar instance is there in the second stanza?**
"I saw it in the bursting buds of roses in the clearing; The roses in the clearing, June, were blushing pink and red."
3. **What is the effect of this repetition?**
It emphasizes the wonder of the month of June with the coming of the partridge and the roses.
4. **Why does the poet call June "the laughter of the year"?**
The poet uses imagery throughout the poem that gives the reader a sense of happiness. A partridge drumming, buds bursting, blushing pink and red, and warblers humming songs of joy all paint a picture of "The fairy month, the merry month, the laughter of the year."
5. **What rhymes do you like particularly well?**
Answers will vary.
6. **Divide your class into groups or teams, each having two or three members. Each group will prepare a program for Arbor and Bird Day, the programs to be reported in class. Select the three best programs.**
Information about Arbor Day can be requested from the American Forestry Association, 1516 P St. NW, Washington, D.C. 20002. Information on birds can be requested from the National Audubon Society. See the reference to that organization in the Extended Activities under Birds in "Part I" of this *Guide*.
7. **Find in the glossary the meaning of: nearing, clearing, warbler.**
8. **Pronounce: alders, partridge.**

THE WORLD OF NATURE—*SPRING AND SUMMER*, PP. 58-66

Extended Activities:

1. Have students choose one of the poems in this section. In a web consisting of a circle with spokes extending from it, have students identify the name of the poem in the center circle. Have them list all the vivid images that appear in the poem on the spokes extending from the circle. After they have shared the poetic phrases they have found, provide detailed pictures of various seasons for the students, or have them find pictures to share with the class. In the same type of web consisting of a circle with spokes coming from it, have students choose a specific season from the pictures and name the season in the center circle. Have them list all the images that appear in the picture on the spokes extending from the circle. Teachers may use this as a single activity or use it as a springboard for the following activity.

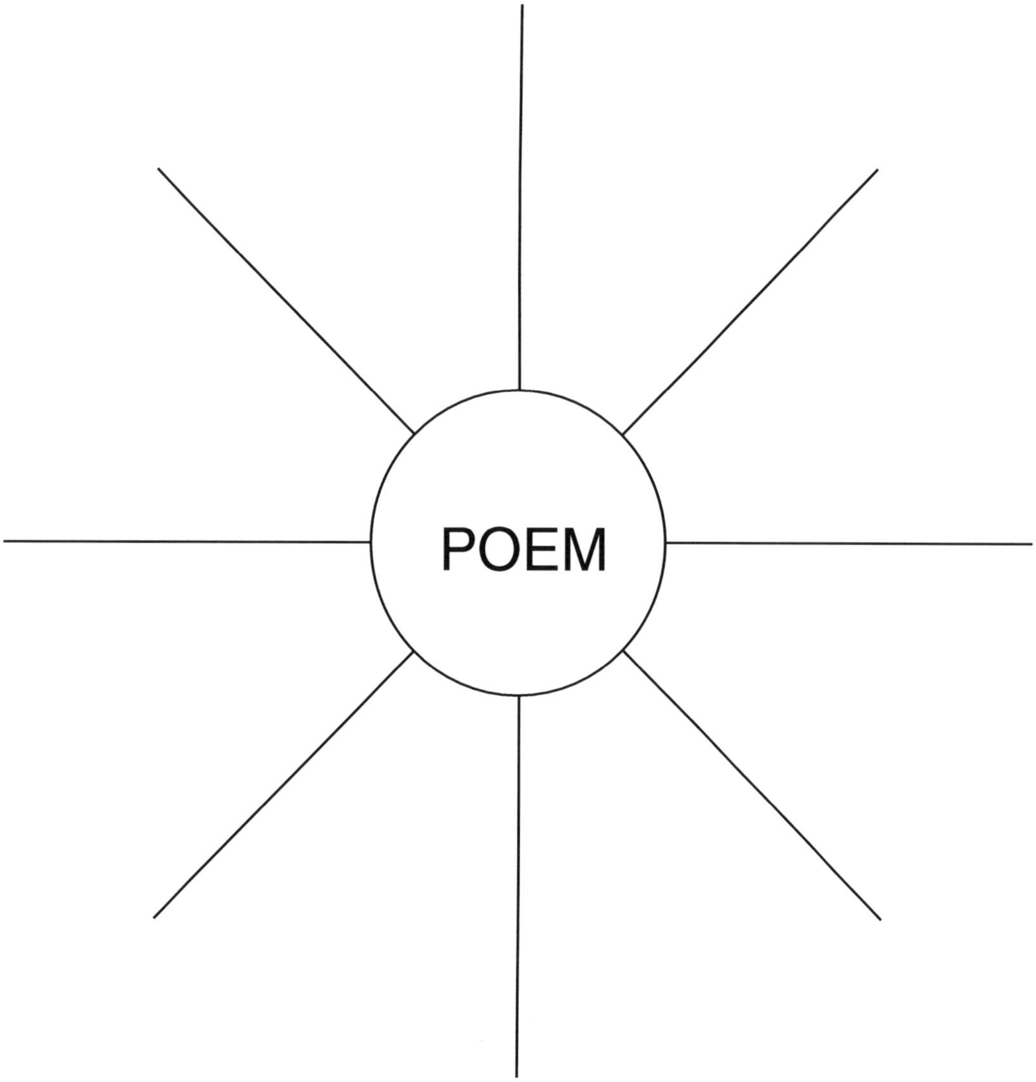

2. In these works, the poets describe their love for spring and summer seasons. Students should choose a season of the year that they particularly like. Then they are to create a lyric poem describing their personal feelings about that season. They should include vivid imagery so the readers can experience that season as they read. In the poem entitled "March" students became familiar with the term *onomatopoeia*. In the poems about flowers, they saw examples of metaphors, simile, and personification. (See Extended Activities under "Flowers.") Students should include at least two of any of those figures of speech in their lyric poem.

3. In the poem titled "Spring in Kentucky" the author uses prose instead of poetry to express his thoughts about spring. Have the students rewrite the piece as a poem, using his musical language and main ideas to create their piece.

NAME______________________________CLASS__________DATE______

THE WORLD OF NATURE—*SPRING AND SUMMER*, EXTENDED EXERCISES, PP. 58-66

1. Choose one of the poems in this section. In a web consisting of a circle with spokes extending from it, identify the name of the poem in the center circle. List all the vivid images that appear in the poem on the spokes extending from the circle. After you have shared the poetic phrases you have found, find detailed pictures of various seasons to share with the class.

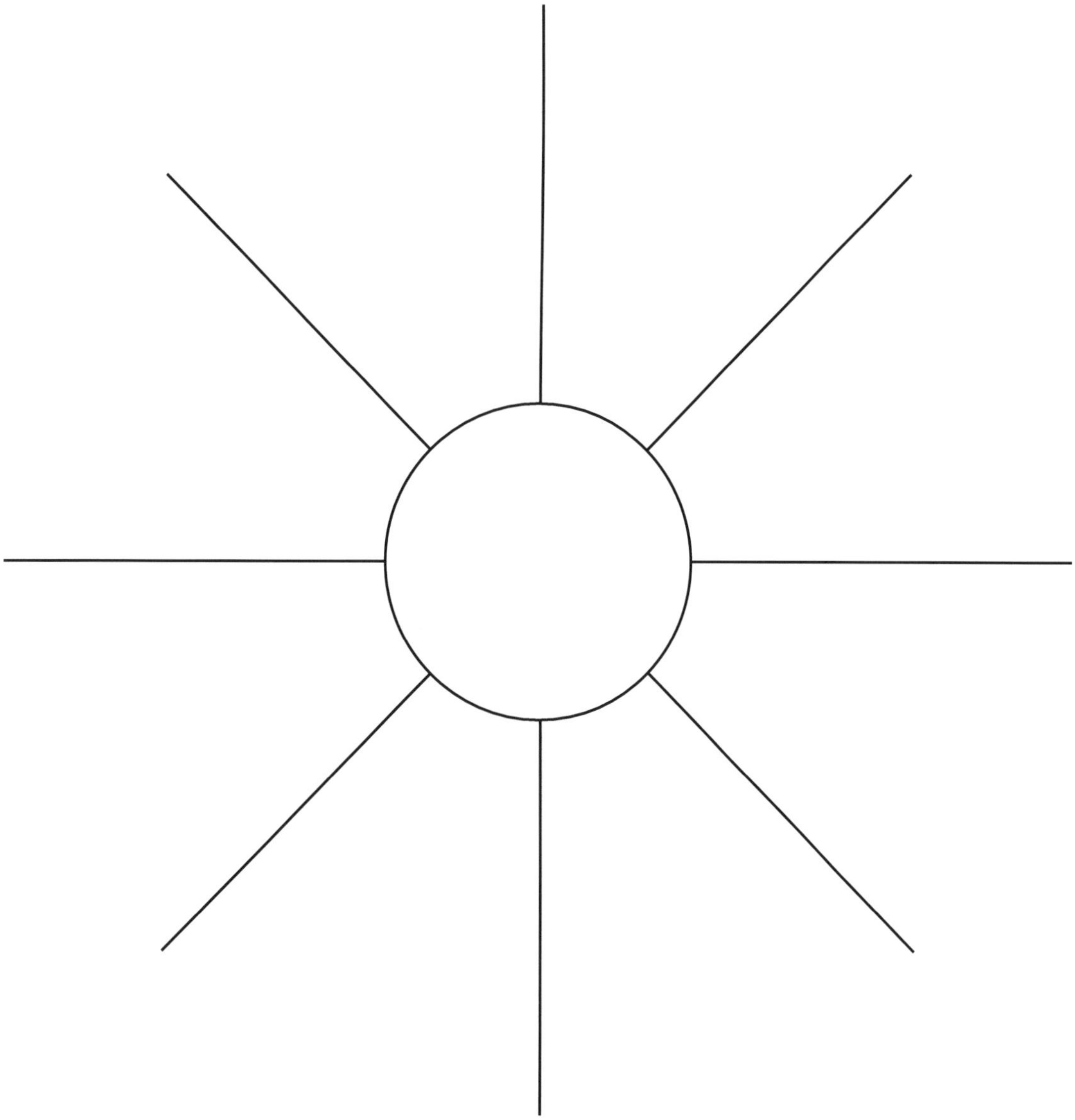

In the same type of web consisting of a circle with spokes coming from it, choose a specific season from the pictures and name the season in the center circle. List all the images that appear in the picture on the spokes extending from the circle.

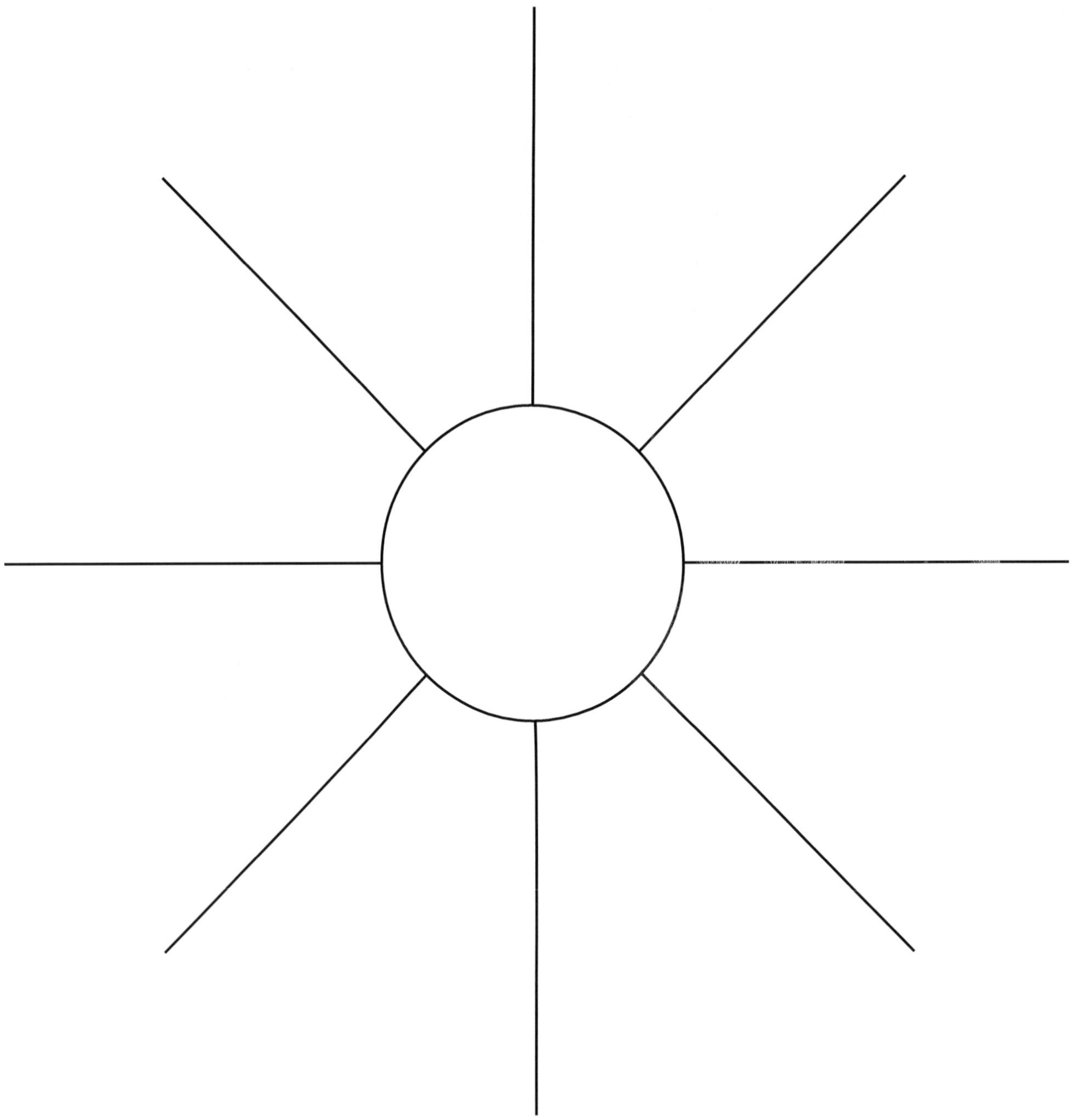

2. In these works, the poets describe their love for spring and summer seasons. Choose a season of the year that you particularly like. Then create a lyric poem describing your personal feelings about that season. Include vivid imagery so the readers can experience that season as they read. In the poem entitled "March," you became familiar with the term *onomatopoeia*. In the poems about flowers, you saw examples of metaphors, simile and personification. Include at least two of any of those figures of speech in your lyric poem.

3. **In the poem titled "Spring in Kentucky" the author uses prose instead of poetry to express his thoughts about spring. Rewrite the piece as a poem, using his musical language and main ideas to create your piece.**

Sky and Water

My Heart Leaps Up, p. 67

1. **What do you think Wordsworth means when he says his heart "leaps up"? Can you remember any occasion on which your heart leaped up?**

   Student responses will vary.

2. **How does the poet tell us that the sight of a rainbow gave him the same joy when he was a child that it gives him now?**

   "So it was when my life began; So is it now I am a man."

   How can the child be "father" of the man he will become?

   Possible responses may include the concept that just as a father teaches his child, the innocence and wonder of a child can teach us about life. Holding on to the sense of wonder one has as a child makes one a better adult.

3. **What things sometimes make boys and girls forget the wonderful world of nature?**

   Answers will vary but may reflect that busy schedules and modern technology all detract from time we spend in nature.

4. **What difference do you think the lack of this feeling would have made in Wordsworth's life?**

   We probably would not have his great poems on nature.

5. **How can we keep this feeling in our hearts?**

   In order to keep this feeling, it must be nurtured, not just by reading about nature, but by taking time to become a part of nature.

The Fountain, p. 68

1. **What picture does the first stanza give you?**
   The stanza gives a picture of sunshine and light.
   The second?
   It gives a picture of a bright moonlit night.
   The third?
   It gives a picture of a starry night.
2. **Which do you like best?**
   Answers will vary.
3. **How could the fountain change every moment and still be the same?**
   The fountain is always in motion, day and night, but it is always "climbing heavenward, Never aweary."
4. **In what qualities would Lowell have his heart like the fountain?**
   He would like to be "Ceaseless aspiring, Ceaseless content" and "Fresh, changeful, constant" like the fountain.
5. **What is addressed in the last stanza?**
   The poet addresses the fountain.
6. **Find in the glossary the meaning of: element, constant, upward.**
7. **Pronounce: blithesome, aspiring.**

THE SEA, P. 70

1. **Who is supposed to be speaking in the poem?**
   The sailor is speaking in the poem.
2. **When does the sea play "with the clouds"?**
   The sea plays with the clouds in storms and sunshine.
3. **When does it lie "Like a cradled creature"?**
   It is a "cradled creature" when it is at rest, with no winds to lash at it.
4. **What is meant by "the blue above"?**
   The "blue above" is the sky.
5. **What is "the blue below"?**
   The "blue below" refers to the ocean depths.
6. **Why does the shore seem "tame" to the sailor?**
   The shore does not hold the thrill of adventure that the "wild, unbounded" sea does.
7. **To what does the speaker compare himself when he returns from the shore?**
   He compares himself to a bird. "And backward flew to her billowy breast, Like a bird that seeketh its mother's nest."
8. **Find a line in the poem which speaks of the silence of the ocean.**
   "With the blue above, and the blue below, And silence whereso'er I go."
9. **Find lines which speak of the noise of the ocean.**
   "On the fierce, foaming, bursting tide, when every mad wave drowns the moon." "And Death, whenever he comes to me, Shall come on the wild, unbounded sea."
10. **What caused the noise described in these lines?**
    "The sou'west blasts" caused the noise.
11. **What famous American or English sailors might have loved the sea as this sailor did?**
    Answers will vary.
12. **Find in the glossary the meaning of: mark, bound, deep, bursting, aloft, tame, billowy, dolphins, outcry, range.**
13. **Pronounce: regions, porpoise, calm.**

THE WORLD OF NATURE—*SKY AND WATER*, PP. 67-71

Extended Activities:

1. In each of these poems, the poet describes a memorable encounter in nature. Have students think of one of their most memorable experiences in nature. What gave them the greatest pleasure, or, as Wordsworth put it, caused their hearts to leap up? Have them create a poem describing that adventure. Vivid imagery and rich vocabulary will make their poems more meaningful.

2. Before assigning the poems to the class, copy and cut the poems into one-line segments. Divide the class into small groups and assign each group a poem. Along with the separated lines, give the students the first line in the poem, the rhyme scheme, and the number of stanzas in the poem. Students will collaborate to reassemble the poem and in the process, become familiar with the poet's words and imagery.

Rhyme schemes are as follows:

"My Heart Leaps Up" ABCCABCDD. It has one stanza.

"The Fountain" ABCB DEFE GHIH JKLK MNON PQRQ STUT VWXW. It has eight stanzas.

"The Sea" AABBCC DDEEFF GGHHII JJKKLL MMNNOO PPQQRR. It has six stanzas.

3. Have students choose a picturesque, well-written line from any of the poems, such as Procter's line "The whale it whistled, the porpoise rolled." Have them illustrate the image through artwork in such a way that classmates can readily identify the line.

NAME______________________________CLASS__________DATE_______

THE WORLD OF NATURE—*SKY AND WATER,* EXTENDED EXERCISES, PP. 67-71

1. In each of these poems, the poet describes a memorable encounter in nature. Think of one of your most memorable experiences in nature. What gave you the greatest pleasure, or, as Wordsworth put it, caused your heart to leap up? Create a poem describing that adventure. Vivid imagery and rich vocabulary will make your poems more meaningful.

3. **Choose a picturesque, well-written line from any of the poems, such as Procter's line "The whale it whistled, the porpoise rolled." Illustrate the image through artwork in such a way that classmates can readily identify the line.**

Home and Its Festivals

Roofs, p. 79

1. **What preference for home does the poet express in the first stanza?**
   The poet describes the time of "wanderlust" when wide roads and starlit skies lure him. "But I'm glad to turn from the open road and the star light on my face, And to leave the splendor of out-of-doors for a human dwelling place."
2. **The poet thinks the gypsy is not a vagabond; what reason does he give for this belief?**
   A vagabond is defined in the glossary as "an idle wanderer; idle fellow," or one who wanders aimlessly without a care for a house of his own. The poet says a gypsy-man will sleep in his cart or his tent, or sit on the grass and rest all day. "But when it is dark, he wants a roof to keep away the sky." So he takes his home with him when he travels.
3. **What does the poet give as the only reason a road is good?**
   The only reason a road is good "is just because of the homes, the homes, the homes to which it goes."
4. **Explain the comparison found in the last stanza.**
   The poet compares life to a highway, milestones to years, and tollgates to times of tears. Encourage students to explain how those things are alike, using the "Phrases for Study" at the end of the selection to guide their discussion. The phrases are defined in the glossary as follows: "life is a highway—we go on living in the same way that we march along a main road"; "milestone—stone which marks distance; boundary marker"; "buy your way with tears—pay your dues by suffering."
5. **What is the "Golden Town where Golden Houses are"?**
   A "Golden Town where Golden Houses are" is heaven.
6. **What other titles might the author have given to this poem?**
   Encourage student responses.
7. **Listen while the entire poem is read aloud by a good reader.**

8. Find in the glossary the meaning of: wanderlust, vagabond, milestone, tollgate.

Extended Activity:

Gypsies were much more common at the time this poem was written than they are today. To help students understand the poem better, have them research gypsies. Students should identify when and where they were most popular, describe their lifestyle, and record some of their adventures. Have them prepare a classroom presentation to share their findings. Then read the poem and compare Kilmer's description of gypsies to their own findings.

Home Song, p. 81

1. **What reason does the poet give in the first stanza for believing that "To stay at home is best"?**

   To stay at home is best "For those that wander they know not where Are full of trouble and full of care."

   In the second?

   Those that wander "Are baffled and beaten and blown about By the winds of the wilderness of doubt."

   In the third?

   Danger lurks for those that leave their homes. "O'er all that flutter their wings and fly A hawk is hovering in the sky."

2. **Does it seem to you that "Home-keeping hearts are happiest"?**

   Answers will vary.

3. **Does this poem make you think of the song, "Keep the Home Fires Burning"? Can you sing this song?**

   "Keep the Home Fires Burning" was a popular song during World War One. The lyrics were written by Lena Guilbert Ford and the melody was written by Ivor Novello in 1915. Web sites containing information about the era and this song are available on the Internet. Encourage students to research this song and compare it to the poem. Suggested sites to begin the research are:

   http://www.emory.edu/ENGLISH/LostPoets/index.html
   http://www.ebs.hw.ac.uk/EDC/CAC/m100/5fires.html
   http://ingeb.org/songs/keeptheh.html

4. **In reading Longfellow's biography, note that he lived abroad for a number of years; what do you think this experience taught him?**

   Based on his reflections in this poem, the reader can assume that his travels made him more appreciative of his home.

5. **Compare this poem with "Roofs"; in what way are they alike? In what way are they unlike?**

   These poems are alike because they both describe the safety of home and the longing for a roof over one's head. The poems are different because while Kilmer acknowledges the urge to wander, Longfellow says "To stay at home is best."

6. **Find in the glossary the meaning of: distressed, baffled.**

Extended Activity:

Students should be familiar with the term *alliteration*—the same beginning consonant sounds within a group of words. Have them list as many examples as they can from Longfellow's poem "Home Song." Obvious answers should include: Stay, stay at home, my heart; home-keeping hearts are happiest; For those that wander they know not where; baffled and beaten and blown about; winds of the wilderness; flutter their wings and fly; hawk is hovering.

NAME______________________________ **CLASS**__________ **DATE**______

HOME SONG, P. 81

You should be familiar with the term *alliteration*—the same beginning consonant sounds within a group of words. List as many examples as you can from Longfellow's poem "Home Song."

THE OLD OAKEN BUCKET, P. 82

1. **Why do you think the "scenes" of the poet's childhood are so dear to him?**
   They bring back images of his childhood that are special to him—the orchard, the meadow, the wild-wood, the pond, the mill, the bridge, the waterfall, and his father's cot.
2. **What words does he use to describe the bucket?**
   The poet describes it as "The old oaken bucket, the iron-bound bucket, The moss-covered bucket that hung in the well."
3. **When did the boy find greatest pleasure in the old oaken bucket?**
   His greatest pleasure in the bucket came "at noon, when returned from the field, I found it the source of an exquisite pleasure." When the bucket came to the surface of the well, "dripping with coolness," the poet says it was better than wine. "Not a full, blushing goblet could tempt me to leave it."
4. **Listen while the poem is read aloud by three good readers, each reading a stanza.**
5. **What does the poet say is "the emblem of truth"?**
   "The emblem of truth" was the pure water from the well.
6. **How did the boy drink from the bucket?**
   "As, poised on the curb, it inclined to my lips" indicates that the boy drank from the edge of the bucket.
7. **Have you ever seen the kind of well and bucket described in this poem?**
   Answers will vary.
8. **Find in the glossary the meaning of: cataract, cot, rude, iron-bound, yield, glowing, inclined.**
9. **Pronounce: exquisite, ardent, situation.**

Extended Activities:

1. Wordsworth's poem is filled with vivid images describing the scenes from his childhood, particularly the old oaken bucket. Have students choose a particular line or scene that paints a picture with words and illustrate that scene with as many details from the poem as they can find.

2. The poets of these three poems based on home have several things in common. Have students read their biographies, listed

after each poem. Along with research information from other sources, have students identify their common characteristics: age, education, profession, adventures, etc. What contributions did they make to the world? What can we learn from them?

NAME______________________________ CLASS__________ DATE______

THE OLD OAKEN BUCKET, P. 82

1. Wordsworth's poem is filled with vivid images describing the scenes from his childhood, particularly the old oaken bucket. Choose a particular line or scene that paints a picture with words and illustrate that scene with as many details from the poem as you can find.

2. The poets of these three poems based on home have several things in common. Read their biographies, listed after each poem. Along with research information from other sources, identify their common characteristics: age, education, profession, adventures, etc. What contributions did they make to the world? What can we learn from them?

The Landing of Columbus, p. 84

1. **Describe the island as Columbus saw it from the ships.**
Columbus saw "a level and beautiful island, covered with trees, like a continual orchard. Though everything appeared in the wild luxuriance of untamed nature, yet the island was evidently populous." He also was "delighted by the beauty of the forests and the variety of unknown fruits on the trees which overhung the shores."
2. **What was the ceremony of taking possession of the island?**
"On landing, Columbus threw himself upon his knees, kissed the earth, and returned thanks to God with tears of joy," as did his men. "Columbus, then rising, drew his sword, displayed the royal standard, and took possession, in the names of the Castilian sovereigns."
3. **What name did Columbus give the island?**
He named the island San Salvador.
4. **How did the natives regard the ships and the white men?**
Initially the natives thought the ships were monsters from the ocean depths. "When they beheld the boats approach the shore, and a number of strange beings, clad in glittering steel, or raiment of various colors, landing upon the beach," the natives ran in fright to the woods. Seeing that they were not being chased, the natives gradually returned and watched the possession ceremony with awe. Finally, "they approached the Spaniards, touched their beards, and examined their hands and faces, admiring their whiteness."
5. **Describe the natives as the Spaniards saw them. Tell about their arms of defense.**
The natives appeared to be covered with colorful paint over copper complexions, with straight coarse hair, and beardless. They had high foreheads and fine eyes, they were of medium height, and they seemed to be young, friendly, and simple. "Their only arms were lances, hardened at the end by fire, or pointed with a flint or the bone of a fish."
6. **How did they receive the name Indian?**
Columbus thought that he had landed on the shores of India, so he called the natives Indians.

7. **How do you think Columbus and his men felt on finding land?**

   Answers will vary.

8. **Find in the glossary the meaning of: luxuriance, Castilian, veering, affright, properties, extremity.**
9. **Pronounce: populous, gestures, raiment, ceremony.**

Extended Activity:

Washington Irving wrote this story from a third-person point of view. He was describing the scenes as though he were on the outside looking in and describing what he saw using words like he, him, they, and them. The writer is not part of the story in a third-person account. A first-person point of view tells the story as if the writer was one of the characters in the scene using words like I, me, we, and us. Ask students to choose a character from this story, Columbus, one of his men, or one of the natives, and re-create this story from a first-person point of view, using first-person terms as though the student were really there and saw and felt it all. Students should use descriptive, sensory details to describe the sights and sounds of the event. Students should plan, write, and edit their work then write a final draft to share with the class.

NAME________________________________CLASS__________DATE______

THE LANDING OF COLUMBUS, p. 84

Washington Irving wrote this story from a third-person point of view. He was describing the scenes as though he were on the outside looking in and describing what he saw using words like he, him, they, and them. The writer is not part of the story in a third-person account. A first-person point of view tells the story as if the writer was one of the characters in the scene using words like I, me, we, and us. Choose a character from this story, Columbus, one of his men, or one of the natives. Re-create this story from a first-person point of view, using first-person terms as though you were really there and saw and felt it all. You should use descriptive, sensory details to describe the sights and sounds of the event. Plan, write, and edit your work, then write a final draft to share with the class.

Thanksgiving at Todd's Asylum, p. 87

1. **Read the story silently and time yourself by the clock.**
2. **Tell the story from the following outline: (a) the inmates of the asylum (Uncle Eph, Aunt Tildy, the inventor, Fisherman Jones, the clock, Miltiades); (b) how Fisherman Jones caught Miltiades; (c) Thanksgiving Day (the trip to the village, the dinner, the new inmates).**

   a. Uncle Eph, Eph Todd, was a poor farmer who lived on an annuity. His house was called Todd's asylum and was open to anyone down on their luck. Aunt Tildy, the first inmate in the asylum, was on her way to the poor farm when Eph rescued her from the overseer and took her to the asylum. The inventor had lost his possessions in the failed invention of an incubator and immediately showed up at the asylum where he used the annuity to try to invent another incubator. Fisherman Jones came to the asylum old and nearly blind and spent his days fishing in the dry pasture with his new rod and reel from the annuity. The clock had been rescued from the old schoolhouse by Eph and ticked away in his kitchen where Aunt Tildy cared for it. Finally, Miltiades had been the sole survivor of the inventor's attempts to hatch turkey eggs in his incubator.

   b. Thanksgiving was coming and the asylum had nothing with which to make a feast, so the inventor set out traps to catch Miltiades. Meanwhile, Fisherman Jones dug up a grub for bait and returned to his dry pasture for another day of fishing. Miltiades was watching from the bushes, ran for the bait, and was snagged. Fisherman Jones thought he had caught his fish at last and ran frantically through the pasture trying to hold onto the runaway reel being pulled by Miltiades in his escape. In his attempt to help the fisherman, Eph got caught in the line and Eph, the fisherman, and Miltiades all ended up in a big tangled heap, while the inventor, eager to help, got caught in his own trap set for Miltiades.

   c. In the morning, Eph started to town to get Aunt Tildy's supplies for the dinner. However, in his haste, he had hitched his horse to a wagon frozen in mud and the horse broke loose, leaving the wagon, and pulling Eph helplessly behind him. By the time Eph discovered his mistake, thawed the wagon, and returned to town, he had forgotten everything Aunt Tildy asked him to buy, so he came home empty-handed. In the meantime, the clock had stopped running which upset Aunt Tildy so that she was incapable of tending to her dinner, so the occupants of the asylum sat down to overcooked vegetables, burnt pie, and an overdone turkey. However, the neighbors in turn came by with turkey, plum pudding, and baskets laden with good things. Just as the occupants of the asylum were ready to eat, another knock came at the door. Thinking someone else was bringing more food, Eph went to the door to refuse their entrance when he met a poor couple, pale, tired, cold, and looking for work. Eph invited them in to join the feast, and they became permanent residents of the asylum.

3. **How does Eph spare Aunt Tildy's feelings?**

"He cheered Aunt Tildy, and he cracked jokes." In addition, he told her that ever since he was a boy he wanted bread and milk for Thanksgiving and, finally, he could have it.

4. **Compare Eph's feelings with that of the inventor about the neighbors' gifts.**

While Eph hesitated, speechless, before all the gifts, the inventor was overjoyed and wasted no time welcoming the neighbors and accepting their gifts.

5. **Give instances of Eph's unselfishness.**

Students should be encouraged to find all the examples they can locate. Included in their list should be Eph's asylum that housed his guests and his annuity that bought their supplies, his concern for Aunt Tildy's feelings and the rescue of the old clock.

6. **How do you explain the "steam" in Eph's eyes?**

The "steam" was his tears.

7. **How did Aunt Tildy show her appreciation of Eph?**

She stood before the group and questioned Eph, "Aren't you the kindest man yourself that ever lived? Aren't you always doing something for everybody, and helping every one of those neighbors in all sorts of ways? I'd like to know what the whole place would do without you?"

8. **Who furnishes the most fun?**

Answers will vary.

9. **Read aloud in class the most humorous passages.**
10. **Dramatize the dinner scene, using the information given in the first part of the story for the table conversation. Let the inventor, with interruptions by the others, tell about his incubator; Fisherman Jones about how he caught Miltiades; Eph about going to the village; while Aunt Tildy busies herself with the clock. The entrance of the children and of the old couple will furnish enough action. Try to make each person express by his manner and conversation the characteristics brought out in the story.**
11. **Find in the glossary the meaning of: annuity, asylum, infirmities, committeeman, inmate, legacy, overseer, mused, incubator, juniper, lurked, tense, commissions, wake, panorama, flusterated.**
12. **Pronounce: Miltiades, nary, Ishmael, whoppingest, writhed.**

Extended Activity:

1. Connecting with a character in the story helps students to understand and relate more effectively to the story. Ask students to choose one character from the story with whom they can relate or are most like. After reading all the events that refer specifically to that character, have them list all the ways that they and the character are alike.

2. Good writers use sensory details, details that affect the five senses, to stir the reader's imagination and create mental pictures of the events in the story. As students read the story, have them complete the following chart of all the references to the five senses they can locate.

TOUCH	TASTE	SMELL	SIGHT	SOUND

NAME____________________________**CLASS**__________**DATE**______

THANKSGIVING AT TODD'S ASYLUM, P. 87

1. **Choose one character from the story with whom you can relate or are most like. After reading all the events that refer specifically to that character, list all the ways that you and the character are alike.**

____

CHARACTER

ALIKE	DIFFERENT

2. **Good writers use sensory details, details that affect the five senses, to stir the reader's imagination and create mental pictures of the events in the story. As you read the story, complete the following chart of all the references to the five senses you can locate.**

TOUCH	TASTE	SMELL	SIGHT	SOUND

The Twenty-second of December, p. 98

1. **What event does this poem celebrate?**
   This poem celebrates the landing of the Pilgrims.
2. **Do you know where in this country the Pilgrims first "trod the desert land"?**
   They landed in what later became Plymouth, Massachusetts.
3. **What does the poet tell about "our fathers" in the first stanza?**
   They were "thoughtful and free."
4. **Could the pioneer Pilgrims have imagined the vast country into which the colonies developed?**
   No, the second stanza says that "They little thought how pure a light, With years should gather round that day," or "How wide a realm their sons should sway."
5. **Why did the first World War produce a fresh thrill of reverence for "the thoughtful and the free" Pilgrims?**
   Without "the thoughtful and the free" Pilgrims, we would not have had our liberties to defend. Their bravery and leadership made this the great nation it is today.
6. **Explain the last stanza.**
   From coast to coast, where the sun sets on the western shores of America, the descendants of the Pilgrims will honor their courage and sacrifice.
7. **Find in the glossary the meaning of: strand, realm, sway, bays, reverence, sires, hallowed.**

Extended Activity:

To appreciate this poem, students should be acquainted with the perils the Pilgrims faced when they first landed. Have students research one of the following topics: Pilgrims, Plymouth Colony, colonial life in America, or the Mayflower. Record the hardships as well as the successes they experienced. (*Mary of Plymouth,* Lost Classics Book Company, is an account of the daily life in Plymouth Colony during its first ten years which may be helpful.) Have them create a pictorial representation of their findings.

NAME______________________________CLASS__________DATE______

THE TWENTY-SECOND OF DECEMBER, P. 98

To appreciate this poem, you should be acquainted with the perils the Pilgrims faced when they first landed. Research one of the following topics: Pilgrims, Plymouth Colony, colonial life in America, or the Mayflower. Record the hardships as well as the successes they experienced. Create a pictorial representation of your findings.

A Christmas Tree, p. 99

1. **What did Dickens begin to think about when he returned home?**
   Dickens began to think, "What do we all remember best upon the branches of the Christmas tree of our own young Christmas days?"
2. **How did his "shadowy tree" appear to grow?**
   He observed that his tree "appears to grow downward toward the earth."
3. **On what part of the tree were the toys?**
   He found his toys at the top of the tree, "Up yonder, among the green holly and red berries."
4. **What would the phrase "lower and maturer branches," page 105, line 24, seem to indicate as the thing to which Dickens is comparing his imaginary tree and its branches?**
   The "lower and maturer branches" seem to hold for him the memories of earlier years—"Schoolbooks shut up; cricket-bats, stumps and balls, left higher up, with the smell of trodden grass and the softened noise of shouts in the evening air." Perhaps, he, like the "lower and maturer branches" has aged and matured and stored his childhood delight in the tree.
5. **What stories from *The Arabian Nights* have you read?**
   Answers will vary. *The Elson Readers, Book Five* includes stories from *The Arabian Nights* referred to by Dickens which students may want to read.
6. **Read aloud lines that refer to the stories you have read.**
   Answers will vary.
7. **Read lines that show the love Dickens felt for children.**
   Responses will vary. An example could include these lines: "If I no more come home at Christmastime, there will be boys and girls (thank Heaven!) while the world lasts; and they do! Yonder they dance and play upon the branches of my tree, God bless them, merrily, and my heart dances and plays too!"
8. **Read aloud lines containing humorous descriptions or comparisons.**
   Answers will vary.

9. In which lines do you think Dickens has best remembered the thoughts and feeling of his childhood?

Answers will vary.

10. Find in the glossary the meaning of: tapers, devices, fascination, counselor, mammoth, sinister, perpetually, free-irons, garnished, nectar, inadvertently, dissolved, versatility, indifferent, talismans, Ali Baba, cricket-bats, stumps.

11. Pronounce: bouquet, ghastly, panniers, Parliament, diminutive, profile, miniature, dissembling, scimitar, genie.

Extended Activity:

1. In this story, Dickens describes in great detail the toys on his childhood tree. Have students select one of the toys he describes and re-create it through art using Dickens' details to bring it to life. Some possible choices include: the tumbler, counselor, frog, cardboard lady and man, the great black horse or the four horses of no color, Jacob's Ladder, the doll's house.

2. Dickens had fond memories of his childhood Christmas tree. Everyone has unique memories of their favorite holiday event. Have students identify and describe their favorite holiday memory, using vivid details to describe it as Dickens did.

NAME____________________________________**CLASS**____________**DATE**________

A CHRISTMAS TREE, P. 99

1. In this story, Dickens describes in great detail the toys on his childhood tree. Select one of the toys he describes and re-create it through art using Dickens' details to bring it to life.

2. Dickens had fond memories of his childhood Christmas tree. Everyone has unique memories of their favorite holiday event. Identify and describe your favorite holiday memory, using vivid details to describe it as Dickens did.

Christmas Bells, p. 107

1. **Who is speaking in this poem?**
   The poet is speaking in this poem.
2. **What words describe the sound of the bells?**
   The sound of the bells is "wild and sweet."
3. **What words do these bells repeat?**
   They repeat the words, "Of peace on earth, good will to men!"
4. **Who "thought how, as the day had come," etc.?**
   The poet thought that as Christmas approached, "The belfries of all Christendom" rang out the song of peace and goodwill.
5. **What day is meant?**
   The poet was thinking of a future day when the "world revolved from night to day" singing "peace on earth, good will to men."
6. **In what sense is it an "unbroken song"?**
   It is a song that continues, always bringing the hope that peace will come to the world.
7. **Why does the poet say "rolled"?**
   Perhaps the poet was envisioning the day when peace and goodwill would "roll" like ocean waves across the world.
8. **What does the second stanza tell you?**
   The poet was perhaps reflecting on history and recalling that, though peace and goodwill had been promoted for centuries, the world was not yet at peace.
9. **What is meant by "revolved from night to day"?**
   The poet was suggesting that perhaps one day, the world will turn from the darkness and blackness of hatred and war to the sunshine "Of peace on earth, good will to men!"
10. **Find in the glossary the meaning of: carols, belfries, chime.**

Extended Activity:

Peace on earth and goodwill to all men is a common Christmas theme. This particular poem has been set to music and is sung as a Christmas carol. Have the students read other Christmas carols and identify those that speak of peace and goodwill. Have students identify examples throughout the world where peace and goodwill have occurred and where they are yet to be realized.

NAME______________________________**CLASS**__________**DATE**______

CHRISTMAS BELLS, P. 107

Peace on earth and goodwill to all men is a common Christmas theme. This particular poem has been set to music and is sung as a Christmas carol. Read other Christmas carols and identify those that speak of peace and goodwill. Identify examples throughout the world where peace and goodwill have occurred and where they are yet to be realized.

Christmas Carols:

Peace Realized:

Peace Not Realized:

Ring Out, Wild Bells, p. 108

1. **When were the bells described in this poem ringing?**
   The bells in this poem are ringing at the end of the year as it "is dying in the night."
2. **Explain the description of the bells in line one.**
   The poet describes the bells as wild, ringing out "to the wild sky, The flying cloud, the frosty light." A symbol is a real object that represents an idea, as the American eagle, a real object, represents freedom, an idea. Encourage students to explain the symbolisms of the wild bell, the wild sky, the flying cloud, the frosty light.
3. **What picture does the poet give in the first stanza to explain his use of the phrase "wild sky"?**
   He uses the picture of a "flying cloud, a frosty light," an image of scudding clouds on a cold winter day.
4. **Find in the second stanza what the poet hopes will go with the old year; what does he hope will come with the new year?**
   With the old year he hopes to "Ring out the false"; with the new year he hopes to "Ring in the true."
   How does the poet's beautiful hope explain his description of the bells in this stanza?
   He describes the bells as "happy bells," indicating the happiness that truth would bring to the world.
5. **What "false" things are mentioned in each stanza and what "true" things does the poet hope will replace them during the new year?**
   The poet defines the false things as grief for those we no longer see, the feud of rich and poor, the slowly dying cause, party strife, want, care, sin, faithless coldness, mournful rhymes, false pride, civic slander and spite, disease, lust for gold, wars, and the darkness of the land. The poet hopes to ring in: justice for all men, nobler modes of life, sweeter manners, purer laws, minstrels, love of truth and right, love of good, a thousand years of peace, valiant and free men, larger hearts, kinder hands, and, finally, "The Christ that is to be."
6. **What do you think the poet meant by "sweeter manners"?**

Student responses will vary but should include the importance of common courtesy, respect, and decency.

What does the mention of "sweeter manners" and "purer laws" in the same line tell you of the importance of manners? Read what Tennyson tells us about manners in another poem and see if this will help you to understand: For manners are not idle, but the fruit of loyal nature and of noble mind.

Tennyson suggests that manners are a reflection of loyalty and goodness; they require action as do purer laws. "Sweeter manners" and "purer laws" can only be seen through the actions and behaviors of those who practice them.

7. **What does the poet hope will prevent "the feud of rich and poor"?**

"Redress" or justice for all people will prevent "the feud of rich and poor."

Can you show that this feud is with us still?

Have students cite current examples of the feuds between the rich and the poor.

8. **How does Tennyson describe his own poetry in the fifth stanza?**

He refers to his poems as "mournful rhymes".

9. **What does he mean by a "fuller minstrel"?**

In medieval times, minstrels provided entertainment for their audiences through music and poetry. The poet is suggesting that "fuller minstrels," those better than he, bring the world new music and poems of hope.

10. **What things does the poet hope will remove men's false pride and their petty jealousies?**

He wants to replace them with "the love of truth and right."

11. **Why does the poet describe "lust of gold" as "narrowing"?**

By longing for wealth as our chief source of happiness, we narrow our horizons and limit our possibilities for happiness.

12. **What organizations in your city or county are helping to "Ring out old shapes of foul disease"?**

Answers will vary.

13. **What attempt is being made in the world today to secure "a thousand years of peace"?**

Have students identify attempts in their local area that promote peace.

14. What is meant by "the darkness of the land"?
The darkness may refer to the lack of education that prohibits people from achieving their dreams.

15. How does the public school help to "ring out" this darkness?
Education and knowledge empower students to pursue their goals.

16. Name some other false things not mentioned in this poem that are found in the world.
Encourage a class discussion of "false things" that the students experience in their daily routines.

17. What should take the place of these?
Answers will reflect their responses to the previous question.

18. Why is this poem appropriate for Armistice Day?
Known as Veterans Day in America, Armistice Day is celebrated in Great Britain to recognize the armistice that ended World War One. This poem is appropriate for those veterans who fought to ring out the false things mentioned in this poem.

19. Listen while the poem is read aloud by a good reader.

20. Find in the glossary the meaning of: saps, mankind, modes, spite, common.

21. Pronounce: redress, valiant.

Extended Activity:

Although Tennyson, the author of this poem, was an English poet, Longfellow, the author of "Christmas Bells," was an American poet, but they express similar longings in their poems. Have students compare these poems. What symbols or images do they have in common? What is their common wish? What common events in their lives may have contributed to this common wish?

NAME______________________________CLASS__________DATE______

RING OUT, WILD BELLS, P. 108

Although Tennyson, the author of this poem, was an English poet, Longfellow, the author of "Christmas Bells," was an American poet, but they express similar longings in their poems. Compare these poems. What symbols or images do they have in common? What is their common wish? What common events in their lives may have contributed to this common wish?

Common Symbols and Images:

____

____

____

____

____

____

____

Common Wish:

____

____

____

____

Common Events in Authors' Lives:

____

____

____

____

____

____

____

____

Our Country and Its Flag

One Country, p. 111

1. **To whom is this poem addressed?**
   It is addressed to the "Sons of the South and brothers of the North."
2. **What is "the Supreme Republic"?**
   The "Supreme Republic" is the United States of America.
3. **What kind of deeds makes the glory of a country?**
   Standing as one on the soil and sea makes the glory of a country.
4. **Of what does the poet say we must be the makers?**
   The poet says we must be the makers of "her immortality—her freedom, fame, Her glory, or her shame."
5. **Why should boys and girls think of such things?**
   Boys and girls should think of these things so that they learn to be good citizens.
6. **From whom do you think the command given in the second stanza comes?**
   Answers will vary. Teachers should direct students to think about Abraham Lincoln.
7. **Read aloud the lines that give "the command imperious".**
   The lines that give "the command imperious" read "Stand forth, Sons of the South and brothers of the North! Stand forth and be As one on soil and sea—Your country's honor more than empire's worth."
8. **How may many people "be as one" in the performance of an act?**
   Many people can "be as one" when they agree and work together.
9. **How were the North and South to be as one? Tell several ways in which this was true in the first World War.**
   The North and South can be as one by putting aside their differences and working towards the good of America. Americans from both the North and the South fought in World War One. People of different countries can work together for the good of the world.
10. **What is worth more than empire?**
    A country's honor is worth more than an empire.

11. **Read aloud the line that tells us the poet thinks Freedom's work has only begun.**

    The line that tells us the poet thinks Freedom's work has only begun is "We must be the makers of her immortality."

12. **Find the lines that tell how Freedom makes patriots rise to defend her.**

    Freedom makes patriots rise to defend her because she "wears the loveliest coronal" and "she breathes the breath of patriots."

13. **Listen while the entire poem is read aloud by a good reader.**

14. **Find in the glossary the meaning of: immortality, clarion, empire, coronal, clod.**

15. **Pronounce: imperious, patriots.**

AMERICA, P. 113

1. **How does the poet address his country?**
The poet addresses his country as "dear land of all my love."
2. **How long does he say her "name shall shine" and her "fame shall glow"?**
Her "name shall shine" and her "fame shall glow" as long as she loves true love, her science tells the truth, her eagle harms no dove, her law by law shall grow, and her God is God above.
3. **In the third line, the poet expresses the idea that large countries should protect small countries. What did the United States do in World War One to live up to this ideal?**
The United States helped protect democracy in countries who could not alone stand against the European aggressors. For example we helped Belgium, Serbia, and England.
4. **How are our laws made, and how may they be changed?**
A bill is proposed in either the House of Representatives or the Senate. Then, the two houses, one at a time, vote on the bill. Then the president of the United States either signs the bill, making it into law, or he vetoes it sending it back to Congress for reevaluation. To change a law the same process is followed.
5. **What is meant by "thy God is God above"?**
The author means by "God above," the divine God, as opposed to earthly gods such as money, power, or fame.
6. **What can Americans do to show that they regard every man as a brother?**
Answers will vary. Direct students to think about treating each other fairly and disregarding prejudices.
7. **What selections have you read in this book that show this spirit of brotherhood?**
All the reading selections in "Service and Thrift" show the spirit of brotherhood.

Our Country, p. 114

1. **To what does the author wish to call our attention when he speaks of the two oceans?**
   The author is calling attention to how vast America is when he speaks of the two oceans.
2. **In the second stanza what things are mentioned which make up "many a goodly prospect"?**
   "Rich prairies," "sunlit oceans," "broad lakes," "mighty rivers," and forests make up "many a goodly prospect."
3. **Why are the prairies compared to "sunlit oceans"?**
   The prairies are compared to the ocean because they are vast, undulate like ocean waves, and reflect the sun.
4. **What broad lakes lie on the breast of our country?**
   The Great Lakes lie on the breast of our country.
5. **What makes the stars "tremble"?**
   The sparkling of the stars make it look like they are trembling. The stars may also tremble at America's greatness.
6. **Name a river which is "mountain born."**
   Many rivers are mountain born. Have students research on the Internet or look in an encyclopedia for specific rivers near them, to find out if they are mountain born.
7. **Why do "wanderers from afar" come to America?**
   "Wanderers from afar" come to America to "breath the air of liberty."
8. **From what places do they come?**
   Foreigners come from many places all over the world. America is often compared to a melting pot because these people come to the United States and become Americans combining, or melting, their culture with that of America in general.
9. **What do they find here?**
   They find freedom and the riches of the land.
10. **How long a time is meant in line 23?**
    The word *time* in line 23 means eternity.
11. **Memorize the last stanza.**
12. **Find in the glossary the meaning of: chafes, nurtured, ample, azure, fawn.**
13. **Pronounce: prospect, grandeur, bounteous.**

Extended Activities:

1. Research Ellis Island and write a report. Ellis Island is located in New York and from 1892-1954 was the headquarters of an immigration and naturalization district. It is estimated that over 20 million immigrants entered the country through Ellis Island. It is now a museum. Students may look up Ellis Island or the Department of Immigration and Naturalization for information. Students may use the following map to help organize their information.

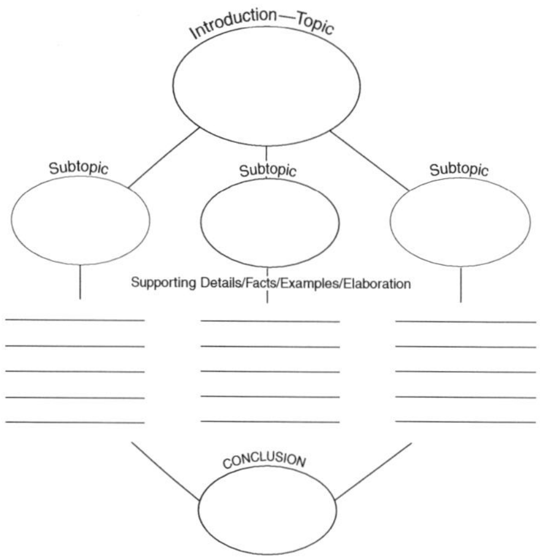

2. Research your family history and make a family tree. Use poster board for the display and include pictures if and where possible. Students may use the following diagram as a model.

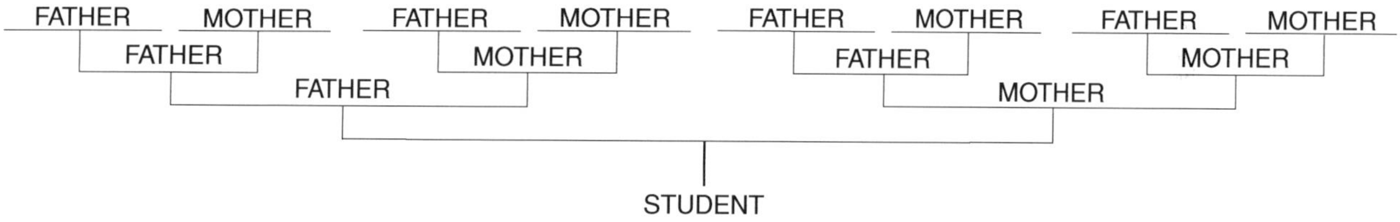

Name______________________________ Class__________ Date______

Our Country, p. 114

1. Research Ellis Island and write a report. Ellis Island is located in New York and from 1892-1954 was the headquarters of an immigration and naturalization district. It is estimated that over 20 million immigrants entered the country through Ellis Island. It is now a museum. You may look up Ellis Island or the Department of Immigration and Naturalization for information. You may use the following map to help organize your information.

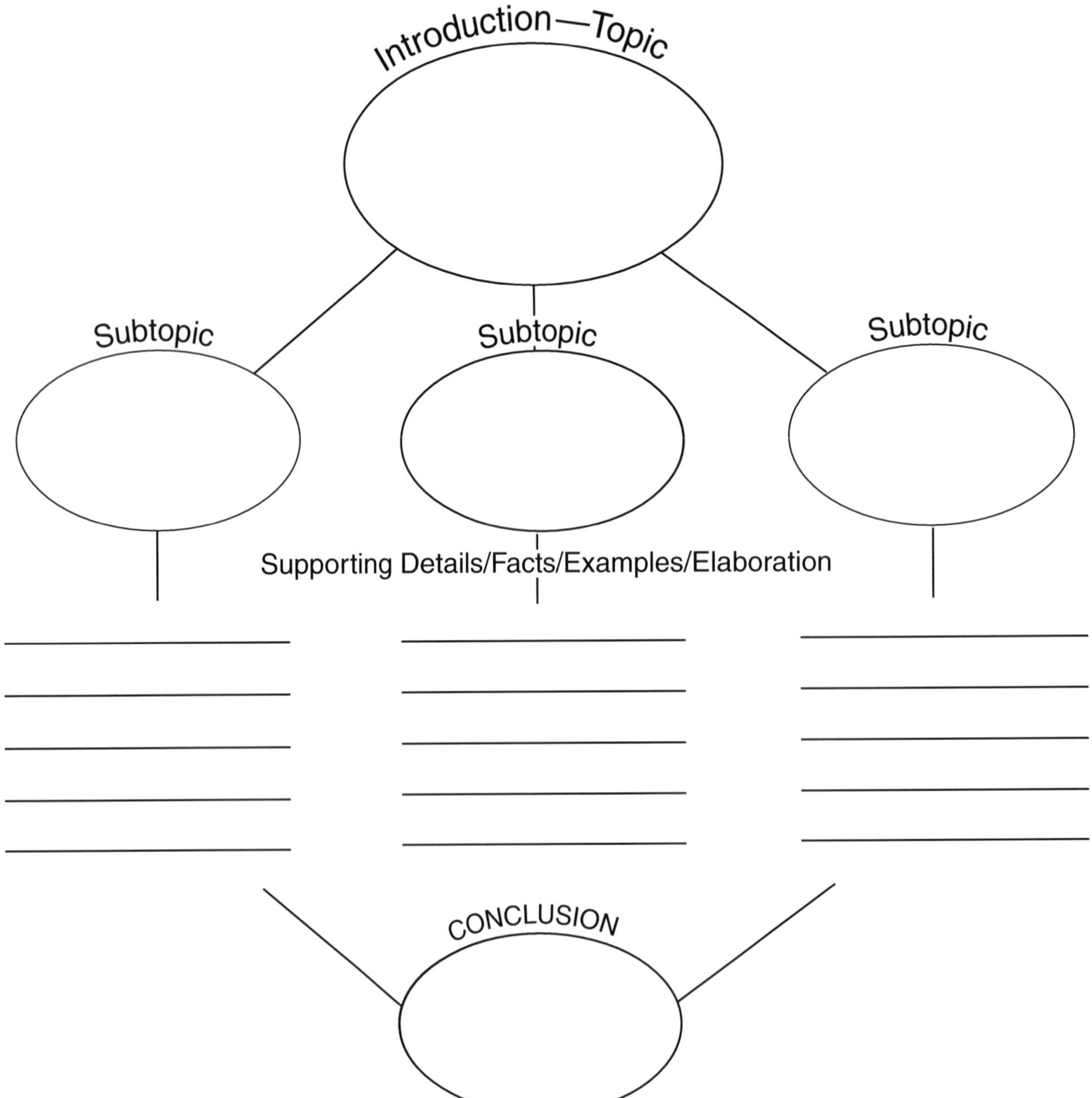

2. Research your family history and make a family tree. Use poster board for the display and include pictures if and where possible. You may use the following diagram as a model.

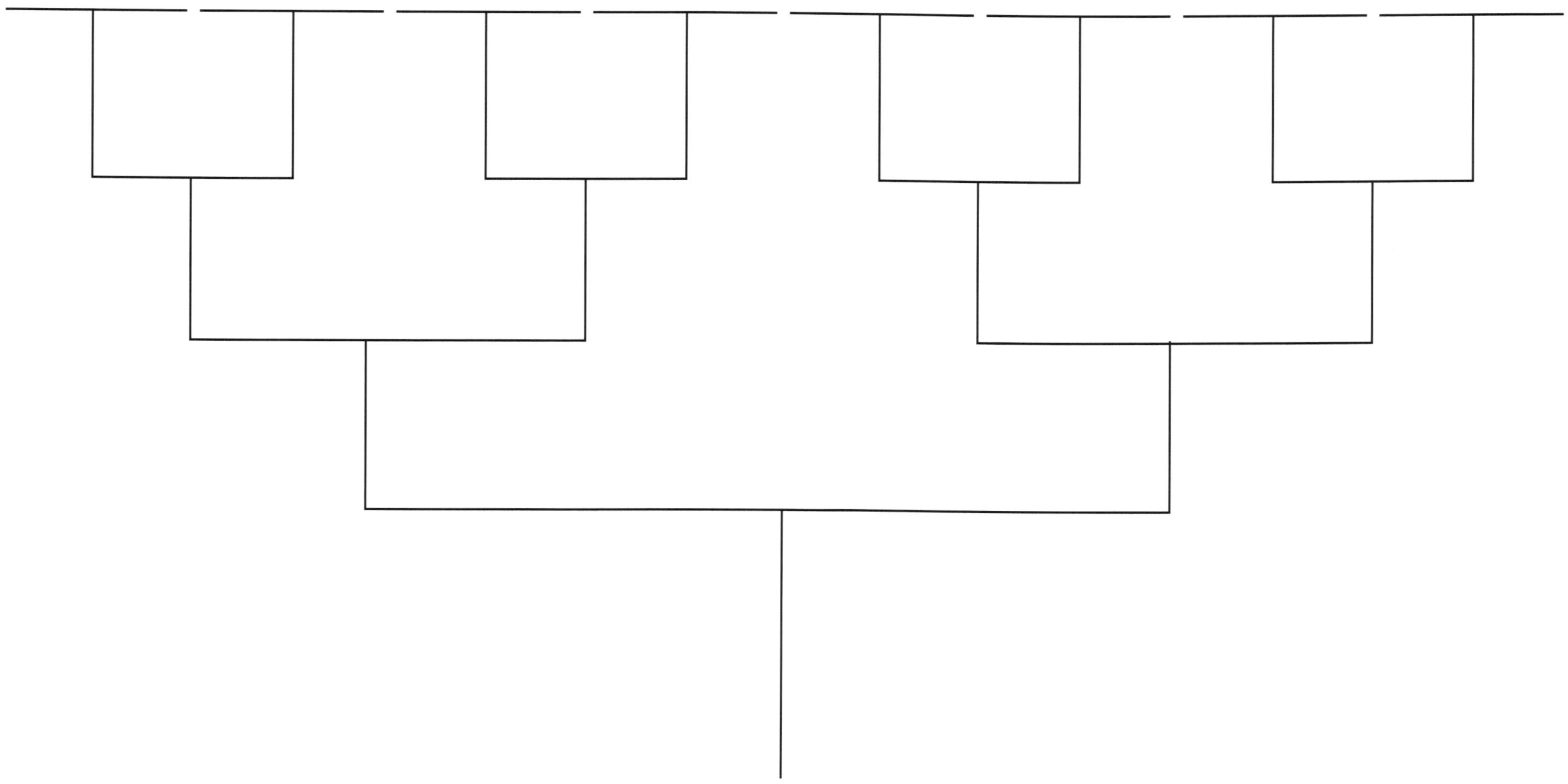

THE BOSTON TEA PARTY, P. 115

1. **Why did the American colonists refuse to import tea?**
   The American colonists refused to import tea because the English were taxing them without representation.
2. **What did they do when they heard that three ships loaded with tea were on their way to America?**
   When the colonists heard three ships loaded with tea were on their way to America, the colonists "held a great many meetings at Faneuil Hall" deciding what should be done.
3. **What request did they make of the British governor of the American colonies?**
   They requested the tea be sent back to England. The governor refused until they paid the taxes.
4. **Tell of the incident of the tea party in the Boston Harbor.**
   The Boston Tea party occurred when colonists, dressed like Indians, dumped the tea into the harbor.
5. **Tell of the new governor and of his acts.**
   The new governor made Salem the new metropolis of Massachusetts and made Boston a "garrisoned and fortified" town.
6. **What did Governor Gage do to fortify Boston?**
   To fortify Boston, General Gage "built a battery across the Neck, in the road to Roxbury, and placed guards for its defense."
7. **What did the Continental Congress do that showed that the colonists intended to fight?**
   The Continental Congress met and exhorted the colonists "to arm and discipline themselves."
8. **What is said about the minutemen?**
   The minutemen were said to be ready to fight within a minute's notice.
9. **Tell how the colonists resisted the British troops at Salem.**
   At Salem "Colonel Timothy Rickering, with thirty or forty militiamen, prevented the English colonel, Leslie, with four times as many regular soldiers from taking possession of some military stores."
10. **Read the poem "Lexington," by Holmes, page 417.**

11. **In what battle did General Warren fall?**
General Warren fell at the Battle of Bunker Hill in June, 1775.
12. **Tell what you know of the battle of Bunker Hill.**
The Battle of Bunker Hill was the first big battle of the American Revolution. It was fought on June 17, 1775, in Charlestown, Massachusetts. About 1,200 American troops were led by Colonel William Prescott. Prescott allegedly said the famous quote, "Don't fire until you see the whites of their eyes." The British won the battle allowing them to retain their occupation of Boston.
13. **What do you think became of the famous Grandfather's chair?**
Answers will vary.
14. **Find in the glossary the meaning of: Tories, customhouse, coffee house, incensed, ministry, Faneuil Hall, Liberty Tree, common, garrisoned, battery, provincial, exhorted, affirmed, provocation, ascertained, aspect, diorama.**
15. **Pronounce: wharf, warriors, hoisted, metropolis, desolate, conducive, strewn, yeomanry, precincts.**

HAIL, COLUMBIA, P. 122

1. **Who were the heroes to whom the second line is addressed?**
   The heroes addressed in the second line are those men who fought in the Revolutionary War.
2. **When had they "fought in Freedom's cause"?**
   They fought in Freedom's cause from 1775 (Battles of Lexington and Concord) until 1783 when the Peace Treaty was signed.
3. **How does the author say they had won peace?**
   They won peace with their valor.
4. **What has independence cost?**
   Independence cost people their lives, and some of the men who fought also lost their livelihoods.
5. **Read aloud the lines in the refrain, or chorus, which tell how liberty must be protected.**
   A refrain is the repetition of a line or groups of lines in a poem for the purpose of effect. The refrain that tells how liberty must be protected reads, "Firm, united, let us be, Rallying round our Liberty."
6. **Whom does the author address as "Immortal patriots"?**
   The "Immortal patriots" are those Americans willing to fight and die for their rights and to defend their shores.
7. **What "rude foe" might he have had in mind when writing the song?**
   The "rude foe" might have been France. Refer to the "Biographical and Historical Note" on page 123.
8. **What does he mean by the "well-earned prize" of "toil and blood"?**
   The "well-earned prize" of "toil and blood" is the independence and freedom America gained.
9. **Who had toiled and shed blood for this prize?**
   The colonists who rejected British rules toiled and shed blood for this prize.
10. **To whom was Columbia offering peace at this time?**
    Columbia was offering peace to its citizens.
11. **Read aloud lines that show the author believed the United States would conquer if forced into war.**
    The lines that show the author believed the United States would conquer if forced into war read, "In heaven we place

a manly trust That truth and justice shall prevail And every scheme of bondage fail."

12. In whose praise was the third stanza written?

The third stanza was praising George Washington, America's first president.

13. Find lines in this stanza which explain the words: "First in war, first in peace."

"And when the storm of war was gone, Enjoyed the peace your Valor won," explains the words, "First in war, first in peace."

14. Who was the chief described in the fourth stanza?

The chief described in the fourth stanza was President Adams who was president in 1798 when Hopkinson wrote this poem. Refer to "Biographical and Historical Note" on page 123.

15. What comparison indicates the author's faith in this chief's ability to save his country.

The author compares the president to a rock who can withstand the storms.

16. How had he served his country before?

He had served his country before by being part of the Revolution and organizing the new country.

17. When had Washington "resolved on death or liberty"?

Washington "resolved on death or liberty" when he agreed to fight for America's freedom and lead the colonists into war with England.

18. Read aloud the lines that express a thought that should guide our country for all time.

The lines that should guide our country read,

"Firm, united, let us be,
Rallying round our Liberty!
As a band of brothers joined,
Peace and safety we shall find."

19. How do lines 4 and 5, page 122, fit the present time? Why do you think those who fought overseas in the World Wars enjoy peace even more than those who remained at home?

Answers will vary.

20. Find in the glossary the meaning of: shrine, prevail, trump.

21. Pronounce: valor, impious.

The Flag, p. 124

1. **What feeling does this poem express?**
The feeling expressed by this poem is pride in our flag.
2. **Why should men and boys uncover their heads to the flag?**
It is respectful to take off one's hat when saluting the flag.
3. **What word is generally used for the "bars" in our flag?**
Stripes is the word used for the "bars" of our flag.
4. **Why is the white in America's flag "unsullied"?**
The white on America's flag is unsullied because it represents purity of purpose.
5. **What line in the poem by Lanier (page 113) expresses his hope that it never will be sullied?**
The line that expresses the author's hope that the flag will never be sullied is "All shall maintain it."
6. **Give another phrase for "tread to it."**
Another phrase for "tread to it" is "to march after it."
7. **Why do tyrants dread our flag?**
Tyrants dread our flag because they know it represents a strong country which stands for justice.
8. **Why were Americans willing to go to France to fight in World War One? For what were they fighting?**
Answers will vary. They were fighting to help France maintain its freedom and democracy.
9. **Listen while the entire poem is read aloud by a good reader.**
10. **What picture does the whole poem suggest?**
Answers will vary.
11. **What does the poem say "valley and crag" will hear?**
"Valley and crag" shall hear the cheers for the flag.
12. **How may all "maintain" the flag?**
We all may "maintain" the flag by being good citizens and by serving our country.
13. **When did men go "down to the grave" for the flag?**
Men went "down to the grave" for the flag when they died protecting America's freedom.
14. **How may we honor these men?**
Answers will vary. Students should realize that Veterans' Day (what we now call Memorial Day) was meant to remember the sacrifice made by soldiers defending our flag.

15. **Why is this poem easy to read?**
    Answers will vary.
16. **Find in the glossary the meaning of: trail, unsullied, crag.**

Washington and the American Army, p. 126

1. **What did you learn about the Continental Congress?**
The Continental Congress assembled at Philadelphia and was composed of delegates from all the Colonies.
2. **Describe Grandfather's feeling toward Washington.**
Grandfather revered General Washington.
3. **How and where were Washington's soldiers quartered?**
Washington's soldiers were quartered all around the peninsula of Boston living in "tents of sailcloth," "shanties rudely constructed of boards," and "huts of stone or turf."
4. **Describe Washington as he looked when seated in the great chair.**
Washington sat on the chair "with his hand resting on the hilt of his sheathed sword, which was placed between his knees, his whole aspect well befitted the chosen man on whom his country leaned for the defense of her dearest rights."
5. **Describe the lack of discipline in the American army before Washington took command.**
"The privates considered themselves as good as their officers and seldom thought it necessary to obey their commands unless they understood the why and wherefore."
6. **Do you know of any army in World War One that lost its power to fight because the privates "considered themselves as good as their officers and refused to obey their commands"?**
The French army was often considered to be disorganized and undisciplined.
7. **Compare Washington's army with the British army, as to numbers, training, and equipment.**
The American troops had approximately fourteen thousand men. They lacked discipline and had few weapons. The English army was more numerous, was well-equipped, and had veteran soldiers.
8. **What characteristic of Washington helped him most at this time?**
The characteristic that helped Washington most during this time was his ability to bring order out of chaos.
9. **Find the lines in which Hawthorne describes this power of Washington.**

The lines that describe this power of Washington's are on page 128, lines 27-33: "One of Washington's characteristics was the faculty of bringing order out of confusion. All business with which he had any concern seemed to regulate itself as if by magic."

10. **Describe the feeling Washington inspired in his men.**

Washington's soldiers felt as if "he had led them to a hundred victories."

11. **Give instances in which Washington submitted his plans to his generals and followed their judgment even though it differed from his own.**

Washington wanted to storm the English batteries, but his officers unanimously agreed against it. Another time his officer's disagreed with him was when he wanted to cross the Charles River on the ice.

12. **Why did he do this?**

He went with their opinion because he respected them.

13. **How did Washington's army spend the summer, autumn, and winter of 1775-1776?**

Washington's army spent the summer, autumn, and winter of 1775-1776 besieging Boston, preventing the enemy from obtaining food and supplies.

14. **What happened in Boston to the inhabitants and to the British army quartered there?**

Many of the inhabitants of Boston died due to "cold, hunger, and sickness."

15. **How did Washington finally take Boston?**

Washington finally took Boston by erecting a battery on Nook's Hill. When the British army were embarking on their ships, "Washington's troops marched over the Neck, through the fortification gates, and entered Boston in triumph."

16. **What do you know about the mansionhouse in Cambridge?**

Washington used the mansionhouse in Cambridge for his headquarters when he took command of the Continental Army. Later it became the home of poet Henry Wadsworth Longfellow.

17. **Laurence thought of Longfellow as the author of "Voices of the Night." Of what poems do you think of him as the author?**

Of the selections in *The Elson Readers, Book Six*, Longfellow wrote "Christmas Bells," "The Village Blacksmith," "The Old Clock on the Stairs," and "A Psalm of Life."

18. **Find in the glossary the meaning of: irreverent, auditors, conspicuous, befitted, deficiency, enterprise, faculty, hazardous, unanimous, tenanted, venerable, pilgrimages.**
19. **Pronounce: reconnoiter, hostile, decisive, eminent.**

SERVICE AND THRIFT

ABOU BEN ADHEM, P. 134

1. **Find the line that tells what Abou saw when he awoke the first time.**
   He saw "An angel writing in a book of gold."
2. **By what other names does the poet speak of the angel?**
   He speaks of the angel as a "vision" and a "presence."
3. **Read aloud the lines that answer Abou's questions.**
   The lines that answer Abou's questions are:
   "The names of those who love the Lord." and "Nay, not so."
4. **Find the line that tells how he wished to have himself recorded.**
   The line that tells how he wished to have himself recorded reads: "Write me as one that loves his fellow men."
5. **Why was it that "Ben Adhem's name led all the rest"?**
   Abou's name was above all the rest because he loved his fellow man so much that God blessed him.
6. **This kind of story is called a parable; what is its theme, or subject?**
   The theme is to love our fellow men.
7. **Read aloud, with the help of a classmate, the conversation between Abou and the angel.**
8. **Name some acts by which you think Abou might have shown his love for his fellow men.**
   Answers will vary.
9. **Find in the glossary the meaning of: thrift, rich, exceeding, accord, cheerly, wakening.**
10. **Pronounce: Abou Ben Adhem.**

The House by the Side of the Road, p. 135

1. **How does the thought of this poem compare with that of "Abou Ben Adhem"?**
   The theme of this poem is the same as "Abou Ben Adhem." They are both poems about helping others.
2. **Do you know persons of the kinds described in the first stanza? How does the poet describe himself in this stanza?**
   Answers will vary. The poet describes himself as a friend to man.
3. **What do you learn of the poet in the second stanza?**
   In the second stanza, we learn the poet is both good and bad.
4. **Tell in your own words the meaning of the third stanza.**
   Students' answers will vary but should include the idea that the third stanza describes the kinds of people who will pass by the poet's house, and that all these passersby are part of an infinite plan.
5. **In the fourth stanza the poet tells you that he has sympathy with his fellow men in their joys and sorrows; what does the first line of the stanza tell you? The second line?**
   The first line of the stanza tells you that there is hope ahead, and the second line tells you there will be bad times along with the good.
6. **Note in the poem that the road is compared to life; read the lines that describe the road and those that describe fellow travelers.**
   The lines that describe the road are stanza 4, lines 13-16:
   "I know there are brook-gladdened meadows ahead,
   And mountains of wearisome height;
   That the road passes on through the long afternoon
   And stretches away to the night."

   The lines that describe the travelers are in stanza 5, lines 23-24:
   "They are good, they are bad, they are weak, they are strong,
   Wise, foolish—so am I."
7. **Read lines that give the poet's reason for his love for his fellow men.**

The lines that give the poet's reason for his love for his fellow men are in stanza 5, lines 23-26:

"They are good, they are bad, they are weak, they are strong,
Wise, foolish—so am I.
Then why should I sit in the scorner's seat
Or hurl the cynic's ban?"

8. **Name characters about whom you have read that you think lived "by the side of the road."**

Answers will vary.

9. **Why do you think the poet repeats the second stanza, with slight changes at the end of the poem?**

Repetition in poetry is called a refrain or a chorus. Poets use this for emphasis and effect.

10. **Find in the glossary the meaning of: hermit, self-content, firmament, pioneer, blaze, highways, scorner, cynic, press, ardor, infinite, brook-gladdened.**

A Bird House by the Side of the Road, p. 138

1. **Time your reading of this story and compare your reading speed with that of your classmates.**
2. **After reading it through once, see how much of the story these topics suggest to you: Duncan's birthday; Duncan's father; the bird house; the tree swallows; the bluebird; the martins; Duncan's success.**
3. **In what respect was Duncan's act like that of the aged couple which inspired "The House by the Side of the Road"?**

   Duncan was very much like the aged couple. He helped those less fortunate, and in this case, those were the birds.
4. **What are the names of birdlovers about whom you've read?**

   Authors in *The Elson Readers, Book Six* who are birdlovers are Arthur Guiterman, Maurice Thompson, John Logan, John James Audubon, and Ralph Waldo Emerson.
5. **Find words in this story that tell characteristic acts of birds.**

   The following are some characteristics of birds learned in this story:

   a. Birds are attracted to different kinds of bird houses.

   b. Birds eat insects, including flies.

   c. Martins migrate south for the winter.
6. **Find in the glossary the meaning of: indignant, biddy, scapnet.**
7. **Pronounce: martin, gaping.**

Conductor Bradley, p. 142

1. **What noble service did Conductor Bradley perform?**
   Conductor Bradley warned others of the train's wreck.
2. **Why was it a "grand supreme endeavor"?**
   His act was a "grand supreme endeavor" because he gave his life to save others. The poet says his words were noble.
3. **In what sense was "the lost life" saved?**
   The "lost life was saved" because without his warning other lives would have been lost.
4. **What is the Biblical reference to "Others he saved; himself he could not save"?**
   The Biblical reference is found in Matthew 27:42—"He saved others; Himself He cannot save. If He is the King of Israel, let Him now come down from the cross, and we will believe Him."
5. **Why did not the poet say "beside the noble deed," instead of "the noble deed beside"?**
   He said "the noble deed beside" because "beside" rhymes with the other two lines. It has a nicer sound.
6. **Can you explain why this noble deed dwarfs "all our pride of virtue"?**
   This deed dwarfs "all our pride of virtue" because his deed cost him his life which is a far greater sacrifice than helping people in other ways.
7. **What wish does the poet express in the last line?**
   The poet wishes that we be willing to help others with the passion of Bradley.
8. **Can you tell why this poem belongs in this group of selections?**
   This poem belongs to this group of poems because the theme is helping one's fellow men.
9. **Can you tell of an instance of a similar kind of self-sacrifice? Read aloud the stanza in which the poet compares Bradley, who thought only of others, not of himself, to those who think only of themselves.**
   Answers will vary.
   The stanza that compares Bradley to others is found in stanza 10:
   "We bow as in the dust, with all our pride

Of virtue dwarfed the noble deed beside.
God give us grace to live as Bradley died."

10. Find in the glossary the meaning of: smitten, wreck, signals, electric, sensual, failing.

11. Pronounce: martyr, dramas, aureole.

Extended Activities:

1. Have students spend a week searching through the newspaper. Have them locate articles reporting on good deeds done by people in their community or elsewhere in America. Have students cut out the articles and report on their findings at the end of the week.

2. Have students perform an act of kindness.

3. Read the book *The Giving Tree* by Shel Silverstein. Have students write a thank you letter to someone who has sacrificed for them.

NAME________________________________CLASS__________DATE______

CONDUCTOR BRADLEY, p. 142

1. Spend a week searching through the newspaper. Locate articles reporting on good deeds done by people in your community or elsewhere in America. Cut out the articles and report on your findings at the end of the week.
2. Perform an act of kindness.
3. Read the book *The Giving Tree* by Shel Silverstein. Write a thank you letter to someone who has sacrificed for you.

The King of the Golden River; or, The Black Brothers, p. 144

SUMMARY

Chapter One: Once there was a very fertile valley called Treasure Valley. It was owned by three brothers: Schwartz, Hans, and Gluck. The two elder brothers were very ugly and greedy. The neighbors called them the Black Brothers. They would charge high prices for their produce and would kill any animal that might damage or eat from their crops. The younger brother, Gluck, was tender hearted and was often made to do the cooking for the other two.

One year it rained so much that the crops outside Treasure Valley were ruined. As a result people went hungry and came to the Black Brothers for food. Schwartz and Hans charged such a high price that only the rich could afford to buy any of their produce. One evening while Gluck was cooking, an "extraordinary looking little gentleman" appeared at the door. He was cold and hungry, so Gluck let him in to warm, and he fed him his one piece of mutton. When the two brothers returned home, they were very angry and tried to throw out the gentleman. However, the man threw them across the room seemingly without any effort. The old man told the brothers he would return that evening for his last visit. At midnight a great crash awoke the brothers. The roof was gone and rain poured on top of them. The gentleman appeared in a foam globe. He told the brothers he left the roof on Gluck's room and his calling card on the table. The next morning, the brothers found their home and valley in ruins. The visitor's card read "Southwest Wind, Esquire."

Chapter Two: The two brothers, now needing some other form of income, decided to become goldsmiths. They were not successful because they mixed the gold with copper and then spent any profit on drinking. Finally, they only had Gluck's favorite mug left to melt down. As Gluck went to melt his mug the face on the mug began to talk to him. A dwarf appeared out of the furnace and introduced himself as the king of the Golden River. He proceeded to tell Gluck that he had been enchanted and turned into a dwarf and that Gluck had freed him. The king told Gluck to pour three drops of holy water into the river and the river would turn to gold. However, if unholy water was poured into the river the person would turn into a black stone. The king then disappeared.

Chapter Three: Schwartz and Hans returned home to find the mug destroyed. Gluck relayed the story of the king and the river. As they argued over who should travel to the river, the police were called because of all the noise. Schwartz was put in jail. Hans, seeing his opportunity to seize the gold, stole some holy water and headed toward the river. On his way he met a dog, a child, and an old man who were dying of thirst. Hans refused to help them. When he reached the river, he was turned into a black stone.

Chapter Four: Gluck was upset that Hans did not return. He had no money and no food, so he hired himself out to another goldsmith. Making enough money, he freed Schwartz from jail. Schwartz, surmising Hans obviously poured stolen holy water into the river, went to a bad priest and secured holy water for himself. While on his journey to the river he met with a child and an old man, both of whom were dying of thirst. Schwartz refused to help them. He then thought he saw Hans, who also was dying of thirst. Schwartz just laughed at him and went on his way. Tossing his water into the river, he, too, turned into a black stone.

Chapter Five: Gluck decided he would go to the river. A priest happily gave him the holy water he needed. On his journey he met the old man and child. Overcome with sympathy for them, Gluck shared his water. He then came upon the dog. Having only a few drops of the water left, Gluck decided to share the water rather than try to retrieve the gold. The dog then transformed itself into the king of the Golden River. The king told Gluck that his brothers' water had been defiled with hatred and greed. The king replenished Gluck's flask and was told to empty it into the river. Gluck did as he was told. The river did not turn to gold, but Treasure Valley was restored to its fruition. There Gluck went to live, and the poor were never driven from his door.

1. **From what did the Golden River get its name?**
   The Golden River got its name because it flowed down the mountainside and shone like a shower of gold.
2. **To what was the fertility of the valley due?**
   The valley was so fertile because of all the streams that kept the ground moist.
3. **By what name were Hans and Schwartz known? Why were they given this name?**
   Hans and Schwartz were commonly known as the Black Brothers because they were so ugly and mean.
4. **How did Gluck differ from his brothers?**
   Gluck was handsome and kind unlike his brothers.
5. **What things happened during the little old man's first visit that tell you he was an extraordinary person?**
   During the little old man's first visit, he kept dripping with water and without much effort was able to fling Schwartz and Hans across the room.
6. **In what manner did Southwest Wind make his last visit?**
   Southwest Wind came for his last visit by tearing off the roof of the house and destroying the crops.
7. **What change came over the valley when the West Winds ceased to visit it?**
   The fields dried up when the West Winds ceased to visit.
8. **What chances to show kindness did Hans have as he climbed the mountain?**

Hans could have shown kindness by giving the dog, child and old man something to drink.

9. **Read lines that show how the sky changed each time he refused to help the suffering.**

Each time Hans refused to help the suffering the sky changed. When he refused to help the dog, " a strange shadow" came "across the blue sky." When he refused to help the child, "a dark gray cloud came over the sun, and long, snake-like shadows crept along the mountainside." When he refused help to the old man, "a flash of blue lightning rose out of the east, shaped like a sword; it shook thrice over the whole heaven and left it dark with one heavy, impenetrable shade."

10. **What opportunities to help others did Schwartz have as he ascended the mountain?**

Schwartz could have helped the child and the old man.

11. **What happened each time that he refused to help?**

Each time he refused to help, "black clouds rose out of the west and a mist of red came over the sun."

12. **How did the face of the mountain change after Gluck gave the water to the old man? After he gave water to the child?**

The face of the mountain became lively and grass sprouted. After Gluck helped the child, flowers began to bloom.

13. **What happened after he gave the water to the dog? Why was it hard for Gluck to give away all his water? What chance did he think he was giving up when he gave away the last drop of water?**

After Gluck gave water to the dog, the dog transformed into the king of the Golden River. It was hard for Gluck to give away all his water because he was hoping to pour it into the river. He gave up his chance to get the gold when he gave away his last drops of water.

14. **What words show that he was willing to lose his chance in order to save the dog?**

Gluck said, "Confound the king and his gold too." This showed he was willing to help the dog and foresake the gold.

15. **Find lines that show that Gluck's boyhood had been spent in service to others. Find lines that show how he helped others when he became a man.**

Lines that show Gluck's boyhood was spent in service to others are:

He was "kind in temper to every living thing. He did not, of course, agree particularly well with his brothers, or rather, they did not agree with him." Lines that show his kindness as an adult read: "And Gluck went and dwelt in the valley, and the poor were never driven from his door, so that his barns bcame full of corn, and his house of treasure."

16. **Commit to memory the following lines:**
    A poor man served by thee shall make thee rich;
    A sick man helped by thee shall make thee strong.
    What is the meaning of these lines?
    These lines mean that giving is better than receiving. One can find happiness in helping others.
17. **How did the dwarf account for the failure of Hans and Schwartz and for Gluck's success?**
    The dwarf accounted for Schwartz and Hans' failure due to their greed and refusal to help others. Gluck's success was due to his mercy on others.
18. **What lines of page 172 contain the main thought of the whole story?**
    The main thought of the whole story reads: "...the inheritance which had been lost by cruelty was regained by love."
19. **Why was this story placed in this group of selections?**
    This story fits with this group of selections because of its theme of the value of helping others.
20. **Select passages to be read aloud in class.**
21. **Tell the story briefly in your own words, using for your outline the ten topic headings given in the book.**
22. **Find in the glossary the meaning of: (I) secluded, dear, tithes; (II) refractory, doublet, swallowtail, hob, accommodated, dryly, knuckle; (III) bolster, stead, gutted, Esquire; (IV) effectually, plate, precipice, crucible; (V) proprietor, malice; (VI) massy, angular; (VII) traverse, lurid, recruited; (X) inumerable, emerges.**
23. **Pronounce: (I) cicada; (II) inundation, maledictions, venture, conical, concerto, savory, humility, meditatively; (III) administering, deprecatingly, incommode, ironically, admonition; (IV) momentous, averred, malicious, effervescent; (V) deigning; (VI) combatants, constable, gnashed; (VII) glacier; (VIII) zenith; (IX) gentians.**

Extended Activities:

1. To further gauge silent reading comprehension, give the students this short true/false quiz.

F. a. Schwartz, Hans and Gluck were three handsome brothers.

T. b. Gluck was made to cook in the kitchen while the other two brothers attended to business.

T. c. The mysterious visitor who came was Southwest Wind.

T. d. The brothers became goldsmiths after they left Treasure Valley.

F. e. The man in Gluck's mug was Southwest Wind.

T. f. Schwartz and Hans got into a rowdy fight which resulted in Schwartz being put in prison.

F. g. A priest agreed to give Hans holy water if he would share some of the gold.

T. h. A dog, a child, and an old man asked Hans for a drink.

F. i. Schwartz turned into a black stone because he threw drinking water into the river.

T. j. Gluck's gold at the end of the story was the fertility of the valley.

2. Pause between each of the chapters and predict what you think is going to happen in the next chapter. After reading chapter one, what was foreshadowed? Foreshadowing is when the author gives the reader clues as to what is going to happen later in the story. In chapter one we learn that Schwartz and Hans are called the Black Brothers and in the end of the story they are turned into black stones.

3. The story is told from the third person limited point of view. Third person limited is told by someone not in the story, but knows only the thoughts and feelings of one of the characters, in this case, Gluck. There are two other points of view: first person and omniscient. First person point of view is told by a character in the story and omniscient point of view is told by someone not in the story and reveals the thoughts and feelings of all the characters. Rewrite the story from first person point of view. Choose Schwartz, Hans or the king of the Golden River as the narrator. Share your story with the class and discuss how the story changed.

NAME______________________________ CLASS__________ DATE______

THE KING OF THE GOLDEN RIVER; OR, THE BLACK BROTHERS, P. 144

1. For a reading check, circle true or false to the following statements:

True False a. Schwartz, Hans and Gluck were three handsome brothers.

True False b. Gluck was made to cook in the kitchen while the other two brothers attended to business.

True False c. The mysterious visitor who came was Southwest Wind.

True False d. The brothers became goldsmiths after they left Treasure Valley.

True False e. The man in Gluck's mug was Southwest Wind.

True False f. Schwartz and Hans got into a rowdy fight which resulted in Schwartz being put in prison.

True False g. A priest agreed to give Hans holy water if he would share some of the gold.

True False h. A dog, a child, and an old man asked Hans for a drink.

True False i. Schwartz turned into a black stone because he threw drinking water into the river.

True False j. Gluck's gold at the end of the story was the fertility of the valley.

2. Pause between each of the chapters and predict what you think is going to happen in the next chapter. After reading chapter one, what was foreshadowed?

____

3. The story is told from the third person limited point of view. Third person limited is told by someone not in the story, but knows only the thoughts and feelings of one of the characters, in this case, Gluck. There are two other points of view: first person and omniscient. First person point of view is told by a character in the story and omniscient point of view is told by someone not in the story and reveals the thoughts and feelings of all the characters. Rewrite the story from first person point of view. Choose Schwartz, Hans or the king of the Golden River as the narrator. Share your story with the class and discuss how the story changed.

STANZAS ON FREEDOM, P. 175

1. **How does the poet define true freedom?**
   The poet defines true freedom in the lines "True Freedom is to share all the chains our brothers wear, And, with heart and hand, to be Earnest to make others free!"
2. **Mention cases to show that our country has been "earnest to make others free."**
   Answers will vary.
3. **What men and women do you know of in history who have helped "make others free"?**
   Answers will vary.
4. **How does this poem apply to America's going to the aid of Cuba and, more recently, to the aid of France and Belgium?**
   America helped Cuba in the Spanish-American War of 1898 to attain its independence from Spain. During World War One, Germany wanted to attack France by going through Belgium. Belgium was a neutral country. Germany did occupy Belgium, and it was at that time that America sent troops to France to help move Germany out of France and Belgium.
5. **Find in the glossary the meaning of: boast, fetters, fallen, scoffing.**

Our Noble Defenders, p. 176

1. **Read aloud Cardinal Mercier's words of gratitude to the wounded Belgian soldiers.**
2. **In what two instances does he say they were "saviors"?**

   The soldiers were our saviors at Liège and in Flanders.
3. **What does he point out as the foremost duty of every Belgium citizen?**

   The foremost duty of every Belgium citizen is gratitude to the army.
4. **Find words in this speech that we may apply to American soldiers who fought in World War One.**

   Words we could apply to American soldiers are "heroism," "valiant," and "respect."
5. **How has our country shown its gratitude to those who fought in World War One?**

   We have shown gratitude to those who fought in World War One by erecting monuments to them and honoring them on Memorial Day. Many communities hold special services for those who fought in the wars. Have students discuss how their community honors those who were in the armed forces.
6. **Find in the glossary the meaning of: vocation, onslaught, assuredly.**
7. **Pronounce: Mercier, Havre, Malines, Louvain, Liège, Calais.**

The Spires of Oxford, p. 178

1. **This poem describes Oxford University as seen from a train during World War One; what picture does the first stanza give you?**

   The picture presented of Oxford in the first stanza is an impressive building with spires set against a "pearl-gray sky."

2. **What tells you that Oxford is a college town?**

   When the poet says the Oxford men "went abroad to die" and that they "gave their merry youth away," the reader understands Oxford is a college town.

3. **Why does the poet say "hoary" colleges?**

   "Hoary" means white, like the hair on an elderly person. The colleges had been there many years.

4. **What does the poem say the Oxford men who went to war gave up?**

   The Oxford men gave up the "peaceful river," "the Cricket-field, the quad, and the shaven lawns."

5. **What did American college men who went to war overseas give up?**

   American college men who went to war gave up much of the same things the English college boys gave up: friends, family, education, peace.

6. **Find in the glossary the meaning of: colleges, cricket-field, quad, shaven.**

Extended Activity:

Have students write a poem describing a building they pass on their way to school. In the poem have students include answers to the following questions: Who do they imagine lives or works in that building? What kinds of sacrifices do they make for the good of the community?

NAME________________________________CLASS___________DATE_______

THE SPIRES OF OXFORD, P. 178

Write a poem describing a building you pass on your way to school. In the poem include answers to the following questions: Who do you imagine lives or works in that building? What kinds of sacrifices do they make for the good of the community?

The Birds of Killingworth, p. 179

1. **What season is described at the beginning of the poem?**
   The season described at the beginning of the poem is spring.
2. **When did the events described occur? What tells you this?**
   The events described in the poem take place within a year because the poem starts with spring then moves to autumn when the leaves have fallen and ends with Almira's wedding the following spring.
3. **Which of the signs of spring mentioned have you seen?**
   Answers will vary.
4. **What is meant by "the vanguard of the Spring"?**
   The "vanguard of the Spring" means those who come first in spring.
5. **What does the poet say are its "banners"?**
   The purple buds on the boughs are the "banners" of the spring.
6. **What are the "fluttering signals" of the rivulets?**
   The trickling of the melting snow in the rivulets are the "fluttering signals."
7. **Who does he say wrote "those lovely lyrics" the merle and mavis sing?**
   The poet says the lyrics were written "By His hand" which refers to God.
8. **What is said about the sparrows in Holy Writ? (See Matthew X:29-31).**
   "Are not two sparrows sold for a penny, yet not one of them will fall to the ground apart from the will of your father. And even the very hairs on your head are all numbered. So don't be afraid; you are worth more than the sparrows." New International Version.
9. **Who is it hears the ravens cry? (See Luke XII:24)**
   God hears the ravens cry.
10. **Read the prayer the crows utter incessantly.**
    The crows' prayer is on page 180, line 8: "Give us, O Lord, this day our daily bread."
11. **What tells you the direction from which "the birds of passage" came?**
    The "birds of passage" have come from the south. We know

this because they speak a language of "tropic isle remote."

12. What alarmed the farmers?

The cawing of the crow alarmed the farmers.

13. For what purpose was a town meeting called?

The town meeting was called to discuss what to do about the birds.

14. What kind of man was the squire? Read the lines that tell you this.

The squire was a man who thought well of himself for he said, "A town that boasts inhabitants like me Can have no lack of good society."

15. Read lines that describe the parson.

The parson did not respect life for his "favorite pastime was to slay the deer" and he "lopped the wayside lillies with his cane."

16. Tell about the preceptor; what do you think of his poetry?

The preceptor loved Almira. The poem says he would "gaze idly round, Now at the clouds, and now at the green grass and all absorbed in reveries profound of fair Almira."

Answers will vary.

17. Read lines that describe the Deacon.

Lines that describe the deacon read: "His form was ponderous, and his step was slow; There never was so wise a man before; He seemed the incarnate 'Well, I told you so.'"

18. Who championed the cause of the birds?

The preceptor championed the cause of the birds.

19. Where does his speech begin?

His speech begins on page 182, line 25.

20. Explain "as David did for Saul." (See I Samuel XVI:14-23)

David played the harp for Saul to sooth him. The birds' singing soothes passersby.

21. What services does the preceptor say the birds render to man?

The birds keep away the bugs and fill the air with music.

22. What was the effect of his speech?

The speech had no effect on the audience. It did not change their minds.

23. What action did the meeting take?

At the meeting it was decided to kill all the birds.

24. **What resulted from the destruction of the birds?**
The insects ate all the crops because the birds were not there to keep the bugs out.

25. **What comparison is made relating to Herod? (See Matthew II) To the schoolboys?**
Herod decided to kill all the baby boys in hopes of getting rid of the Christ child. However, this action did not accomplish what he had hoped. The towns people hoped to keep their crops by ridding themselves of the birds, but their actions were not successful. Thus, like schoolboys, they discovered their mistake too late.

26. **By whom were the birds restored?**
The birds were restored by Almira.

27. **How did the preceptor celebrate the restoration of the birds?**
He and Almira were married.

28. **Memorize lines 5-8, page 184.**

29. **Notice how Longfellow adds to the music of the poem by repeating certain sounds as "lovely lyrics," "winged wardens," and "melodious madrigals." The repetition of the same sound at the beginning of two or more words used closely together is called *alliteration*. Find other examples that please you.**

30. **One of the reasons why this poem is easy to read is that there is a pause somewhere near the middle of many of the lines; test a few of the lines for this.**

31. **Longfellow uses the following rhyming scheme in this poem: ABABABCC; that is, the first, third and fifth lines rhyme, the second, fourth, and sixth lines rhyme, and the seventh and eighth lines rhyme. Test the rhymes in several stanzas by this scheme.**

32. **Why has this poem a place in the service group?**
This poem is about helping something weaker than ourselves. It fits nicely into the selections about service.

33. **Find in the glossary the meaning of: merle, Saxon, vanguard, sound, jocund, tilled, convened, marauders, fervor, lopped, preceptor, sonnet, bombazine, incarnate, sundry, jargoning, weevil, dialect, windrows, man-at-arms, bounty, bard.**

34. **Pronounce: piteous, gibberish, prognosticating, august, austere, voluminous, perpetuate, madrigals, roundelay, omnipotence, vanquished, canticles.**

Industry and Thrift (A Letter to a Relative in Reply to His Request for a Loan), p. 189

1. **How did Lincoln regard the letter from Johnston (his half-brother), requesting eighty dollars?**
   Lincoln regarded the letter from Johnston as another of his many pleas for financial help.
2. **What reason did Lincoln suggest for Johnston's continued difficulty?**
   Lincoln felt his defect was his "idleness."
3. **What valuable advice did he give him?**
   Lincoln advised Johnston to find a job and allow his father and the boys to take care of things at home.
4. **What proposition was made if this advice was heeded?**
   Lincoln proposed that for every dollar Johnston earned Lincoln would match it.
5. **Do you think it was a good way to develop thrift in Johnston?**
   Answers will vary.
6. **What plan for developing thrift in its citizens did our government originate during the World War?**
   During World War One, our government instituted Savings Bonds and encouraged thrift through propaganda (advertising).
7. **Find in the glossary the meaning of: comply, idler, discharging, deed.**
8. **Pronounce: request, indebtedness, contrary.**

A THRIFT PROVERB, P. 192

1. **How did Frankin's wife help him to prosper?**
Franklin's wife assisted him by "folding and stitching pamphlets, tending shop, purchasing old linen rags for the paper-makers, etc."
2. **What habits of thrift can boys and girls establish for themselves?**
Answers will vary.
3. **Tell about thrift stamps and other ways of saving.**
There are many ways of saving today, such as savings accounts, Savings Bonds, etc. Use this question to prompt a discussion of possible ways to be thrifty.
4. **Compare Franklin's habits of thrift with Lincoln's advice to his brother.**
Both Lincoln and Franklin believe in hard work and not being extravagant.
5. **Find in the glossary the meaning of: frugality, pamphlets, earthen, pewter.**
6. **Pronounce: thrive, porringer.**

The Pied Piper of Hamelin, p. 193

1. **Find Hanover and the Weser River on your map.**

2. **Whom did the people blame for the condition of their city?**
   The people blamed the mayor for their condition.
3. **What threat did they make?**
   The people threatened to send the mayor "packing" if something was not done about the rats.
4. **What effect did this have upon the mayor?**
   The mayor "quaked with a mighty consternation."
5. **Describe the appearance of the mayor's strange visitor.**
   The strange visitor wore a robe half yellow and half red. He was "tall and thin."
6. **What did the Pied Piper offer to do?**
   He offered to rid the town of the rats.
7. **How did the mayor and corporation receive his proposal?**
   They were overjoyed at his proposal.
8. **How soon did the notes of the pipe take effect?**
   The notes of the pipe took effect immediately.
9. **Read aloud lines in the report to Rat-land telling how the music sounded to a rat.**
   The lines can be found on page 197, lines 4-21.
10. **What did the mayor order when the rats had been destroyed?**
    The mayor ordered the town to make sure all the rats were gone and to block up all their holes.
11. **Whom had he forgotten?**
    He had forgotten to pay the pied piper.
12. **Find the lines that show why the mayor dared dispute the piper's claim.**

The mayor dared to dispute the Piper's claim because the rats could not return. "Our business was done at the river's brink; We saw with our eyes the vermin sink, And what's dead can't come to life I think."

13. **How did the mayor reward the piper for his services?**
The mayor rewarded the piper by offering him food and drink.
14. **Compare the sound made by the gathering of the children with the noise made by the rats.**
The rats came "rumbling," "grumbling," and "tumbling" and the children came "bustling," "hustling," "clattering," and "chattering."
15. **Where did the piper lead the children?**
The piper led the children to a chasm in the side of a hill.
16. **Tell the story of the little lame child.**
The lame child was slow keeping up and so was left behind when the children entered the chasm and it closed.
17. **What comparison is made on page 201, lines 7-9?**
The lines are being compared to a Bible verse, Matthew 19:24. The Bible verse states that it is easier for a camel to go through the eye of a needle than a rich man to enter the kingdom of God.
18. **How do you account for the strange tribe in Transylvania?**
Answers will vary, but students should conclude that they are the lost children.
19. **What does the selection teach about service?**
This selection teaches that one should keep his or her promises.
20. **Give examples showing how the rhymes add to the fun of the story.**
21. **Find words that the author "coined" to add to the rhythm.**
22. **Find in the glossary the meaning of: pied, ditty, vermin, sprats, noddy, corporation, dolts, quaked, hap, swarthy, brawny, tawny, commentary, puncheon, pottage, scorpion, ribald, enraptured, pate, decree, tabor, alien, subterraneous, trepanned.**
23. **Pronounce: ermine, obese, guilder, newt, vesture, conserve, psaltery, replenish, caliph, bereft, burgher.**

True Citizens, p. 204

1. **For what does our flag stand?**
   Our flag stands for America and symbolizes the love the citizens have for their country.
2. **Mention some sacrifices that true citizens made for the good of all during the World Wars; what sacrifices did children make?**
   Citizens and children had to be thrifty. They rationed materials such as rubber to help with the war effort.
3. **Did "meatless" and "wheatless" days mean sacrifice?**
   Yes. Many people gave up eating extravagantly to help in the war effort.
4. **Tell what sacrifice "Oxford men" made (page 178); what service the Belgian soldiers performed for the world.**
   The Oxford men sacrificed their youth and education to fight in the war. The Belgian soldiers did as well.
5. **What can an American boy or girl do for his school? For his home?**
   Answers will vary.
6. **What does our country ask us to do?**
   Answers will vary.
7. **How should a true citizen feel and act toward his country?**
   Answers will vary.

Extended Activity:

Questions 5, 6, and 7 lend themselves to a class discussion. Draw a map on the board, see example below, and record student responses. Have students copy the map when it is completed and write an essay.

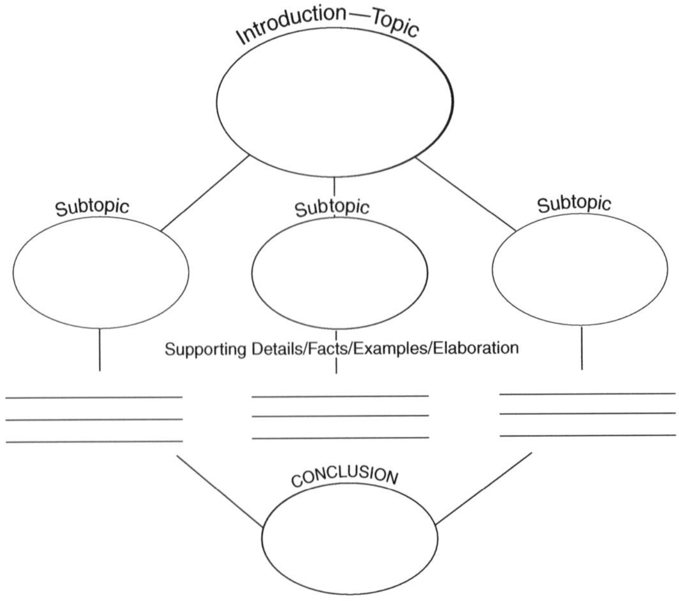

NAME______________________________CLASS__________DATE______

TRUE CITIZENS, P. 204

Following class discussion, copy the map you have created as a group and write an essay.

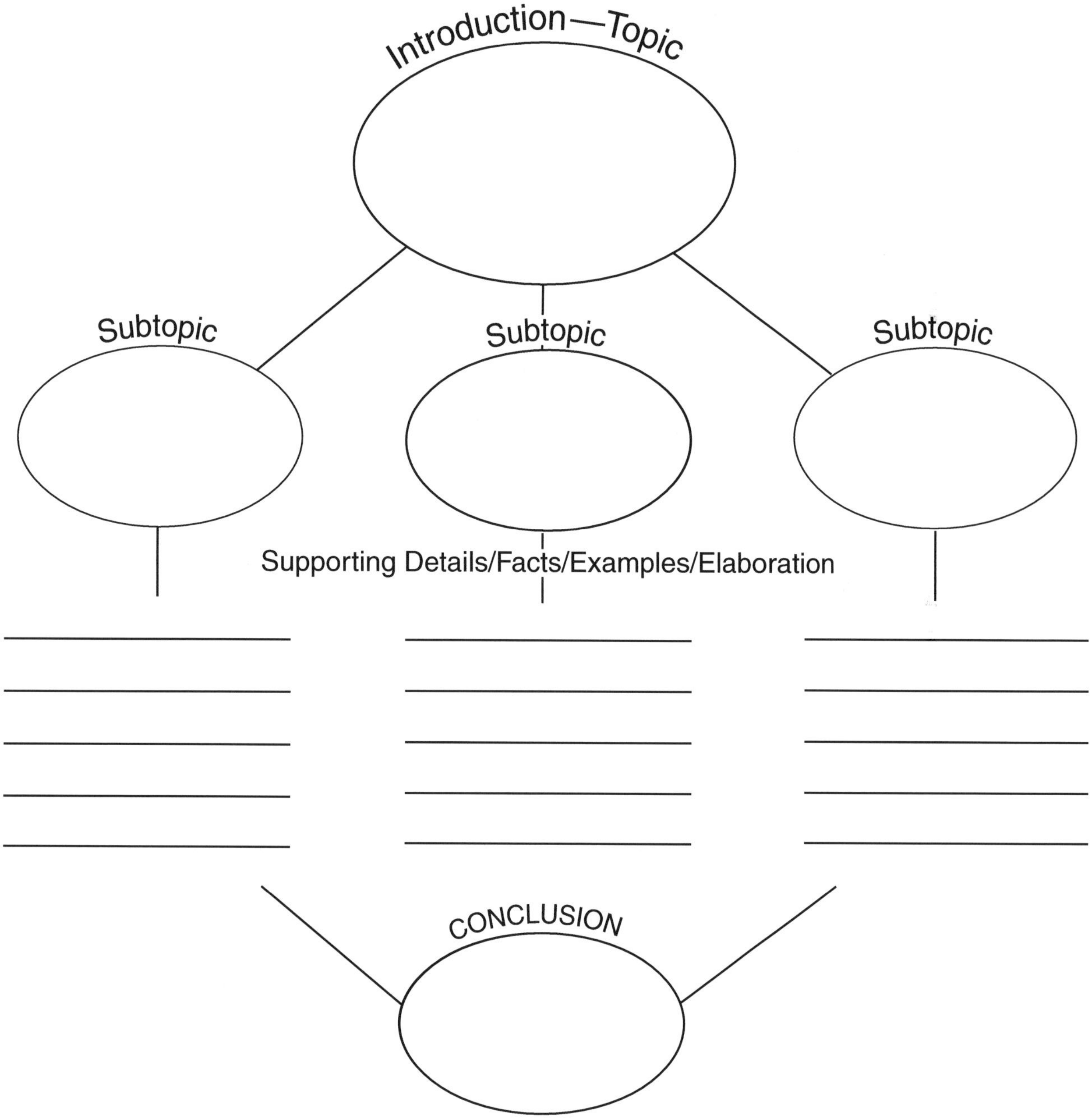

Go Forth To Serve, p. 205

1. **When was this letter written and to whom was it addressed?**
   The letter was written after World War One at the beginning of the school year to all children.
2. **What was the purpose of the letter and what reason does President Wilson give for writing it?**
   The purpose of the letter was to encourage children to volunteer for the Junior Red Cross.
3. **What kinds of peacetime work does the letter say the Junior Red Cross will teach you to do?**
   The Junior Red Cross will teach you "simple lessons of citizenship."
4. **President Wilson said World War One was the greatest of all wars: in what respects does he say this is true?**
   He says that this was a great war because "more men and nations were engaged in it than any other war of history." As a result, "people have seen a vision of a different kind of world from the world of the past."
5. **He says the Junior Red Cross will teach you to be a good citizen; in what ways?**
   The Junior Red Cross will teach you to be a good citizen by helping those less fortunate.
6. **How has your school helped the children of other countries?**
   Answers will vary.
7. **Mention other ways in which the pupils of your school have done the work of good citizens.**
   Answers will vary.
8. **Find in the glossary the meaning of: associated, systematic, invaded, formerly, generation.**
9. **Pronounce: duty, fortunate, foreign.**

Extended Activity:

Have students choose an organization or a cause they think is important for others to be a part of. Have them write and present a persuasive speech convincing their audience to become involved. Introduce students to the faulty methods of persuasion and have them avoid these in their speech.

Bandwagon—This method of persuasion says because everyone else is doing, saying, or buying it; you should too.

Testimonial—This method of persuasion says because a famous person is doing, saying, or buying it; you should too.

Red Herring—This method of persuasion brings in unrelated issues to distract the listener from the real issue.

Overgeneralization—This method of persuasion exaggerates the facts and uses words such as never, always, everyone, etc.

Rubric for Teacher Evaluation:

	Poor		Satisfactory		Excellent
Eye Contact	◇	◇	◇	◇	◇
Emphasis	◇	◇	◇	◇	◇
Volume	◇	◇	◇	◇	◇
Length	◇	◇	◇	◇	◇
Visual	◇	◇	◇	◇	◇
Organization	◇	◇	◇	◇	◇

Gradatim, p. 207

1. **Where does the poet imagine the foot of the ladder to be?**
   The foot of the ladder is on the "lowly earth."
2. **How is the ladder built?**
   The ladder is built as we climb it.
3. **By what kind of deeds do we ascend this ladder?**
   The deeds that help us ascend the ladder are things "we have mastered of good or gain, By the pride deposed or the passion slain."
4. **What foes does the third stanza tell us we must conquer if we wish to mount the ladder?**
   We must conquer pride and passion.
5. **Notice how Longfellow in the following lines from his poem, "The Ladder of St. Augustine," has expressed the same thought in a different way:**

   Saint Augustine! Well hast thou said,
   That of our vices we can frame
   A ladder, if we will but tread
   Beneath our feet each deed of shame!

   We have not wings, we cannot soar;
   But we have feet to scale and climb
   By slow degrees, by more and more,
   The cloudy summits of our time.
6. **Mention some noble deed of which you have read in this book.**
   Answers will vary.
7. **What opportunities have boys and girls to do noble deeds?**
   Answers will vary.
8. **Many opportunities are offered American boys and girls for *individual* service; what opportunities do the Boy Scouts, the Camp Fire Girls, and the Junior Red Cross offer for *organized* service?**
   These organizations allow American boys and girls to help others and to learn about those things that make them good citizens. They learn about household activities as well as career opportunities.

9. What part does your school take in these national organizations for service?

Answers will vary.

10. Find in the glossary the meaning of: gradatim, grandly, mastered, deposed.

11. Pronounce: vaulted, passion, vanquished.

NAME______________________________ **CLASS**__________ **DATE**______

Story	***Find in the glossary the meaning of:***
Reader p. 25	**roundup**__________
	cowpuncher__________
	corral__________
	bottom__________
	prongbuck__________
	sheer__________
	picketed__________
	loom__________
	quarry__________
Reader p. 34	**arrested**__________
	jungle__________
	reverberating__________
	interspersed__________
	margin__________
	crevices__________
	inspection__________
	respective__________
	compact__________
	velocity__________
	rendered__________
	whip-thong__________
	concealment__________
	momentarily__________
	acute__________
Reader p. 39	**indicated**__________
	towering__________
	majestic__________
	imposing__________
	doubling__________
	rejoined__________
	antlers__________
	swerved__________
	wolverine__________
	persecution__________
	visible__________
	mortal__________
	assailed__________
	defied__________
	accounted__________

Reader p. 45	**lyrics**	______
	prelate	______
	rubicund	______
	livery	______
	unconventional	______
	commending	______
Reader p. 46	**swarm**	______
	thrills	______
	gush	______
	greening	______
	splendor	______
	gladden	______
	vales	______
Reader p. 48	**cuckoo**	______
	decks	______
	hail	______
	bowers	______
	starts	______
	lay	______
Reader p. 50	**expand**	______
	pinions	______
	baffles	______
	competition	______
	precaution	______
Reader p. 52	**forbearance**	______
	wood-rose	______
	pulse	______
	high	______
	behavior	______
Reader p. 54	**slopes**	______
	paraded	______
	selfsame	______
Reader p. 56	**mavis**	______
	crumpled	______
	brawling	______
	bridal	______
	render	______
Reader p. 58	**ancient**	______
	fanes	______
	clime	______
	sparry	______
	lyre	______
Reader p. 60	**range**	______

gossipy________________________________
nook________________________________
gracious________________________________
token________________________________
rigor________________________________
foretells________________________________
Reader p. 62 **cranny**________________________________
emerald________________________________
Reader p. 63 **grazing**________________________________
prevailing________________________________
laureate________________________________
Reader p. 65 **nearing**________________________________
clearing________________________________
warbler________________________________
Reader p. 68 **element**________________________________
constant________________________________
upward________________________________
Reader p. 70 **mark**________________________________
bound________________________________
deep________________________________
bursting________________________________
aloft________________________________
tame________________________________
billowy________________________________
dolphins________________________________
outcry________________________________
range________________________________
Reader p. 79 **wanderlust**________________________________
vagabond________________________________
milestone________________________________
tollgate________________________________
Reader p. 81 **distressed**________________________________
baffled________________________________
Reader p. 82 **cataract**________________________________
cot________________________________
rude________________________________
iron-bound________________________________
yield________________________________
glowing________________________________
inclined________________________________
Reader p. 84 **luxuriance**________________________________
Castilian________________________________
veering________________________________

affright____________________
properties____________________
extremity____________________
Reader p. 87 **annuity**____________________
asylum____________________
infirmities____________________
committeeman____________________
inmate____________________
legacy____________________
overseer____________________
mused____________________
incubator____________________
juniper____________________
lurked____________________
tense____________________
commissions____________________
wake____________________
panorama____________________
flusterated____________________
Reader p. 98 **strand**____________________
realm____________________
sway____________________
bays____________________
reverence____________________
sires____________________
hallowed____________________
Reader p. 99 **tapers**____________________
devices____________________
fascination____________________
counselor____________________
mammoth____________________
sinister____________________
perpetually____________________
free-irons____________________
garnished____________________
nectar____________________
inadvertently____________________
dissolved____________________
versatility____________________
indifferent____________________
talismans____________________
Ali Baba____________________
cricket-bats____________________

stumps_____________________________________

Reader p. 107 **carols**_____________________________________

belfries_____________________________________

chime_____________________________________

Reader p. 108 **saps**_____________________________________

mankind_____________________________________

modes_____________________________________

spite_____________________________________

common_____________________________________

Reader p. 111 **immortality**_____________________________________

clarion_____________________________________

empire_____________________________________

coronal_____________________________________

clod_____________________________________

Reader p. 114 **chafes**_____________________________________

nurtured_____________________________________

ample_____________________________________

azure_____________________________________

fawn_____________________________________

Reader p. 115 **Tories**_____________________________________

customhouse_____________________________________

coffee house_____________________________________

incensed_____________________________________

ministry_____________________________________

Faneuil Hall_____________________________________

Liberty Tree_____________________________________

common_____________________________________

garrisoned_____________________________________

battery_____________________________________

provincial_____________________________________

exhorted_____________________________________

affirmed_____________________________________

provocation_____________________________________

ascertained_____________________________________

aspect_____________________________________

diorama_____________________________________

Reader p. 122 **shrine**_____________________________________

prevail_____________________________________

trump_____________________________________

Reader p. 124 **trail**_____________________________________

unsullied_____________________________________

crag_____________________________________

Reader p. 126 **irreverent**_____________________________________

auditors__________
conspicuous__________
befitted__________
deficiency__________
enterprise__________
faculty__________
hazardous__________
unanimous__________
tenanted__________
venerable__________
pilgrimages__________
Reader p. 134 **thrift**__________
rich__________
exceeding__________
accord__________
cheerly__________
wakening__________
Reader p. 135 **hermit**__________
self-content__________
firmament__________
pioneer__________
blaze__________
highways__________
scorner__________
cynic__________
press__________
ardor__________
infinite__________
brook-gladdened__________
Reader p. 138 **indignant**__________
biddy__________
scapnet__________
Reader p. 142 **smitten**__________
wreck__________
signals__________
electric__________
sensual__________
failing__________
Reader p. 144 **secluded**__________
dear__________
tithes__________
refractory__________
doublet__________

swallowtail__________
hob__________
accommodated__________
dryly__________
knuckle__________
bolster__________
stead__________
gutted__________
Esquire__________
effectually__________
plate__________
precipice__________
crucible__________
proprietor__________
malice__________
massy__________
angular__________
traverse__________
lurid__________
recruited__________
innumerable__________
emerges__________
Reader p. 175 **boast**__________
fetters__________
fallen__________
scoffing__________
Reader p. 176 **vocation**__________
onslaught__________
assuredly__________
Reader p. 178 **colleges**__________
cricket-field__________
quad__________
shaven__________
Reader p. 179 **merle**__________
Saxon__________
vanguard__________
sound__________
jocund__________
tilled__________
convened__________
marauders__________
fervor__________
lopped__________

preceptor___
sonnet
bombazine
incarnate
sundry
jargoning
weevil
dialect
windrows
man-at-arms
bounty
bard
Reader p. 189 **comply**
idler
discharging
deed
Reader p. 192 **frugality**
pamphlets
earthen
pewter
Reader p. 193 **pied**
ditty
vermin
sprats
noddy
corporation
dolts
quaked
hap
swarthy
brawny
tawny
commentary
puncheon
pottage
scorpion
ribald
enraptured
pate
decree
tabor
alien
subterraneous

Reader p. 205

trepanned____
associated____
systematic____
invaded____
formerly____
generation____

Reader p. 207

gradatim____
grandly____
mastered____
deposed____

Pronounce:

buttes, fortnight, haunting, route, plateau, cañon, leisure, gorge, supple, wary, clamber, often, ponderous, François, wapiti, toward, wounded, reappearance, creature, farther, shoal, pursuit, beauteous, visitant, genial, poised, recesses, resplendent, stalk, hoary, subtle, beneath, violet, Italian, loosed, Hesperian, verdure, unsheathes, elm, melodious, alders, partridge, blithesome, aspiring, regions, porpoise, calm, exquisite, ardent, situation, populous, gestures, raiment, ceremony, Miltiades, nary, Ishmael, whoppingest, writhed, bouquet, ghastly, panniers, Parliament, diminutive, profile, miniature, dissembling, scimitar, genie, redress, valiant, imperious, patriots, prospect, grandeur, bounteous, wharf, warriors, hoisted, metropolis, desolate, conducive, strewn, yeomanry, precincts, valor, impious, reconnoiter, hostile, decisive, eminent, Abou Ben Adhem, martin, gaping, martyr, dramas, aureole, cicada, inundation, maledictions, venture, conical, concerto, savory, humility, meditatively, administering, deprecatingly, incommode, ironically, admonition, momentous, averred, malicious, effervescent, deigning, combatants, constable, gnashed, glacier, zenith, gentians, Mercier, Havre, Malines, Louvain, Liège, Calais, piteous, gibberish, prognosticating, august, austere, voluminous, perpetuate, madrigals, roundelay, omnipotence, vanquished, canticles, request, indebtedness, contrary, thrive, porringer, ermine, obese, guilder, newt, vesture, conserve, psaltery, replenish, caliph, bereft, burgher, duty, fortunate, foreign, vaulted, passion, vanquished.

Part II: Stories of Greece and Rome

In This Section—

Objectives—

STORIES OF GREECE AND ROME

By completing "Part II," the following objectives will be met.

1. The student will use effective reading strategies to construct meaning and identify the purpose of a text including:
   a. defining unfamiliar words
   b. retelling and summarizing
2. The student will determine the main idea or essential message and identify relevant supporting details and facts of a text.
3. The student will read and organize facts from the text and other sources to make a report, outline and/or perform an authentic task.
4. The student will prepare for writing by focusing on the topic and organizing supporting details in a logical sequence.
5. The student will draft and revise writing.
6. The student will produce final documents that have been edited for correct spelling, punctuation, and grammar.
7. The student will write for a variety of audiences and purposes.
8. The student will write in a variety of genres including narrative and expository writing.
9. The student will use reference materials such as: dictionaries, encyclopedias, and maps.
10. The student will identify the development of plot and how conflicts are resolved in a story.
11. The student will identify and understand similarities and differences among the characters, settings, and events presented in various texts.
12. The student will respond critically to fiction.
13. The student will understand the elements of the epic and the epic hero.
14. The student will recognize cause-and-effect relationships in literary texts.
15. The student will respond to a text by explaining how the motives of the characters or events compare with those in his/her own life.
16. The student will use context clues to understand words and ideas.
17. The student will predict events that may occur in the text and explain the reasoning behind the prediction.
18. The student will understand the qualities necessary to develop good character and apply those qualities to his/her personal life.
19. The student will identify adjectives and the nouns they describe.
20. The student will identify appositives.

The Story of Achilles, p. 215

SUMMARY

I. WHY THE GREEKS SAILED TO TROY

King Tyndareus of Sparta was searching for a suitable husband for his daughter, Helen, the fairest of all the women. So many men wanted to be chosen that the king feared the men would turn against him. Therefore, he asked the men to swear that once a husband was chosen, they would support him and protect Helen. Helen then chose Menelaus for her spouse. In Troy, Thetis, the goddess of the sea, and Peleus, King of Thessaly, did not invite Discord to their wedding feast. Discord appeared anyway with an apple. The apple had a note attached that read, "To the fairest." Three goddesses, Hera, Athena, and Aphrodite fought over the apple. Zeus decided that Paris should be the judge of who received the apple. He chose Aphrodite who promised him to give him in marriage to the most beautiful woman. This woman happened to be Helen of Sparta. So, Aphrodite stole Helen from Menelaus and gave her to Paris. All the men of Sparta, remembering their promise to King Tyndareus, agreed to go to Troy to retrieve Helen.

II. WHY THERE WAS STRIFE BETWEEN AGAMEMNON AND ACHILLES

While Greece was battling with Troy over the abduction of Helen, Agamemnon took the daughter of Apollo's priest as part of his spoils. This angered Achilles who thought Agamemnon was taking more than his fair share of the treasures. Agamemnon agreed to send the daughter of Apollo's priest back, causing strife between Agamemnon and Achilles. Achilles plotted to kill Agamemnon, but Athena convinced him not to. Achilles then spoke to his mother, Thetis, and asked her to petition Zeus to allow Troy to win thus getting revenge on Agamemnon. Zeus then sent a Dream to Agamemnon which told him to go fight the men of Troy.

III. HOW THE GREEKS BATTLED WHILE ACHILLES SULKED IN HIS TENT

Paris decided to fight Menelaus, and the two agreed the victor would win Helen. During the battle between the two, Aphrodite came and swooped Paris back to his chamber in Troy. The battle raged again. Hector was urged to return to Troy to ask the mothers to pray. While there he visited his wife and child.

IV. HOW PATROCLUS WENT INTO BATTLE WEARING THE ARMOR OF ACHILLES

Because Achilles was angry with Agamemnon, he refused to participate in the battle against Troy. His good friend Patroclus convinced Achilles to allow him to wear his armor, thus scaring the men of Troy. Achilles agreed as long as Patroclus agreed to stay away from the city of Troy. Patroclus went into battle against Hector and did not do as he promised Achilles. With the help of Apollo, Hector slew Patroclus.

V. HOW THE DEATH OF PATROCLUS AROUSED ACHILLES

Hector took the armor off Patroclus and put it on himself. The Trojans wanted to keep Patroclus's body. When Achilles heard the news of his good friend, he wanted to avenge his death. He did not have any armor, thus he could not fight. Distressed, his mother, Thetis, came to him and promised to fetch him some armor. The next morning she had kept her word and Achilles went into battle.

VI. HOW ACHILLES AVENGED THE DEATH OF PATROCLUS

Achilles and Hector began to fight. Achilles chased Hector three times around the city of Troy before Hector turned to face Achilles in battle. The gods were with Achilles, and Achilles, knowing of a weak link in the armor Hector was wearing (it was Achilles's armor to begin with), he slew Hector.

VII. HOW KING PRIAM RANSOMED THE BODY OF HECTOR

King Priam, Hector's father, was visited by a messenger of Zeus. The messenger told the king to offer Achilles ransom for the return of Hector's body. King Priam made the offer, and Achilles accepted and agreed to stop fighting for twelve days so the people of Troy could give Hector a proper burial. When the twelve days passed, the Greeks and Trojans went to war again. Achilles, whose one weak spot was his heel, was slain by Paris. Now led by Ulysses, the Spartans overtook Troy, and Menelaus was able to take Helen back, thus ending the war.

I. Why the Greeks Sailed to Troy, p. 215

Questions for testing silent reading:

1. **Who was Helen?**
Helen was the daughter of the king of Sparta. She was the fairest of all the women.
2. **What promise did the king force the suitors to make?**
The king forced the suitors to promise to protect Helen and whomever she chose as a husband.
3. **Why did Ulysses suggest this promise to the king?**
This was suggested because the king was afraid the suitors would be angry if one of them was not chosen for Helen.
4. **Whom did Helen choose?**
Helen chose Menelaus.
5. **Who was Paris?**
Paris was the son of Priam, the king of Troy.
6. **Tell about the apple of Discord.**
The apple was brought to the wedding feast of Paris's parents. A note was attached reading, "To the fairest." Three goddesses, Hera, Athena, and Aphrodite, argued over who should receive the apple.
7. **Why did Zeus decide to have Paris, a mortal, make the choice?**
Zeus decided to allow Paris to make the decision since he was mortal and would someday die. If Zeus chose then he would have to live with the goddesses' wrath for eternity.
8. **What were the promises given to Paris by Hera, Athena, and Aphrodite?**
Hera promised Paris lordship over all of Asia. Athena promised to make Paris "wise in counsel and skillful in war above all others." Aphrodite promised to give Paris the fairest woman as his wife.
9. **To whom did Paris award the apple?**
Paris awarded the apple to Aphrodite.
10. **How did Aphrodite reward Paris?**
She awarded Paris by presenting Helen to him as his wife.
11. **What did Menelaus do then?**
Menelaus called upon the men of Greece who swore to protect Helen and asked them to retrieve Helen from Paris, a Trojan.

12. **How did Ulysses try to avoid keeping his promise?**
    He tried to avoid keeping the promise by working in the fields and pretending to be out of his mind.
13. **How large an army went from Greece to Troy?**
    The Greek army was made of 100,000 men and 1,200 ships.
14. **What was the family relationship between Helen and each of the following?**

    Tyndareus
    Father of Helen

    Menelaus
    Helen's husband

    Agamemnon
    Menelaus's brother

    Penelope
    Helen's cousin and married to Ulysses

    Ulysses
    Advisor to the king and a great warrior

    Paris
    Son of Priam, took Helen from Menelaus

    Priam
    King of Troy

II. Why There Was Strife between Agamemnon and Achilles, p. 219

1. **How long did the Greeks besiege Troy?**
   The Greeks besieged Troy for nine years.
2. **Why did the seige last so long?**
   The seige lasted so long because Agamemnon and Achilles were fighting.
3. **What started the quarrel between Agamemnon and Achilles?**
   The quarrel started when Agamemnon took the daughter of Apollo's priest as a prize.
4. **In the end, who gave up his prize?**
   Agamemnon gave up his prize.
5. **How was Achilles prevented from slaying Agamemnon?**
   Achilles was prevented from slaying Agamemnon when Athena was sent by Hera to stop him.
6. **What was the wish Achilles told his mother, Thetis?**
   Achilles told his mother, Thetis, he wished Troy would win in the battle to disgrace Agamemnon.
7. **How was the wish carried out?**
   The wish was carried out when Zeus sent a Dream to Agamemnon telling him to go to battle.
8. **What did Agamemnon do?**
   Agamemnon prepared to attack Troy.

III. How the Greeks Battled While Achilles Sulked in His Tent, p. 223

1. **Name the Greek leaders.**
   The Greek leaders were: Menelaus, Ajax the Greater, Ajax the Lesser, Nestor, Achilles, and Ulysses.
2. **Who were the Trojan leaders?**
   The Trojan leaders were: Hector and Aeneas.
3. **What additional reason does this chapter give you for Aphrodite's favoring Aeneas and the other Trojans?**
   Aphrodite was Aeneas's mother.
4. **By what act did Paris show his nature?**
   After Hector rebuked Paris for being a coward, he took on the challenge and agreed to fight.
5. **What was the result of the hand-to-hand conflict between Paris and Menelaus?**
   Paris was taken away by Athena, and so neither man won the battle.
6. **Why did Hector return to the city?**
   Hector returned to the city to ask the mothers to pray to Athena for the Trojans to win the war.
7. **Which was Andromache most anxious about—her husband or her country?**
   She was most anxious about her husband.
8. **Tell the incidents that make you think Hector was a good husband and father.**
   Answers will vary.
9. **What was the family relationship between Hector and each of the following?:**
   Priam
   King of the Trojans, Hector's father
   Hecuba
   Hector's mother
   Paris
   Hector's brother
   Helenus
   Hector's brother, a wise seer
   Andromache
   Hector's wife

IV. How Patroclus Went into Battle Wearing the Armor of Achilles, p. 228

1. **Why did Patroclus come to Nestor?**
   He came to see who Nestor was carrying wounded.
2. **What was Nestor's advice, and how was it carried out?**
   Patroclus was to go dressed as Achilles. The Trojans would be scared to see a man they thought was Achilles.
3. **How large a host were the Myrmidons?**
   They were made of fifty ships with fifty men on each ship.
4. **What did Achilles do before he made his prayer? What was the meaning of these acts?**
   Before Achilles made his prayer he cleaned the cup with sulfur and water then poured wine into it for Zeus. This showed Achilles's thoughtfulness and respect for the gods.
5. **What did the Trojans think when they saw Patroclus?**
   The Trojans thought Achilles had forgotten his wrath when they saw Patroclus dressed as Achilles.
6. **In what ways did Apollo help the Trojans?**
   Apollo kept Patroclus back from the city. Apollo stirred the spirit of Hector so that he would go after Patroclus. Hector hit Patroclus so hard that his eyes grew dim and his armor fell off.
7. **What happened to Hector's brother, the driver of his chariot?**
   Patroclus hit him in the head with a stone.
8. **How was Patroclus killed?**
   He was slain by Hector's spear.
9. **What is said about the helmet of Achilles?**
   The helmet never touched the ground.

V. How the Death of Patroclus Aroused Achilles, p. 232

1. **What became of the arms of Achilles which Patroclus wore?**
   Hector took the armor and wore it himself.
2. **How did the Greeks try to protect the body of Patroclus?**
   Ajax the Greater stood by it, protecting it.
3. **Who was sent to Achilles with the news of Patroclus's death?**
   Antilochus came to Achilles with the news of Patroclus's death.
4. **What did Achilles do when he heard of the death of his friend?**
   Achilles poured dust on his head, then laid on the ground and tore his hair.
5. **What did Achilles feel about what had happened?**
   He was extremely distraught and wanted to seek revenge for Patroclus's death.
6. **Who came to comfort him and what did she promise to do for him?**
   Thetis, Achilles's mother, came to comfort him.
7. **Who called Achilles to the battle, and who helped him?**
   Zeus called Athena to help Achilles in battle. Athena gave Achilles her shield and a golden halo around his head.
8. **What was the result of his appearance?**
   The Trojans were scared and fell back.
9. **Why was Achilles able to fight the next day?**
   Achilles was able to fight because his mother brought him new armor to wear into battle.
10. **What did the gods do to prevent the fighting between Hector and Achilles?**
    Athena and Apollo made the men's spears miss their target each time they were thrown.
11. **How was Troy saved at this time?**
    Apollo took the form of a Trojan chief whom Achilles chased away from the city.

VI. How Achilles Avenged the Death of Patroclus, p. 237

1. **How did Achilles happen to be far from the walls of Troy?**
   He was far from the city walls because he was chasing Apollo, who took the form of a Trojan chief.
2. **What did Achilles do when Apollo made himself known?**
   He said, "Thou hast done me wrong...Had it not been for this, many more Trojans would have been killed...O that I had the power to take vengeance on thee!" Then he ran swiftly back to the city.
3. **What did Priam and Hecuba urge Hector to do?**
   Priam and Hecuba urged Hector to go inside the city gates and avoid fighting.
4. **Describe Achilles's pursuit of Hector around the city walls.**
   Achilles chased Hector three times around the city walls "as a hawk pursues a dove around a mountain."
5. **Who helped Hector?**
   Apollo helped Hector.
6. **Why did Apollo leave Hector?**
   Apollo left Hector because Hector was losing.
7. **How did the fact that Hector wore the armor taken from Patroclus help Achilles?**
   Achilles knew the weak spots in the armor. There was a problem with the armor where the neck joins the shoulder. Achilles knew he could attack Hector on this spot.
8. **Why did Hector want the Trojans to have his body?**
   They wanted to give Hector proper burial.

VII. How King Priam Ransomed the Body of Hector, p. 242

1. **Who saw Achilles taking away the body of Hector?**
Andromache, Hector's wife, saw Achilles taking away the body.
2. **Who persuaded Achilles to give up the body?**
Thetis, who was sent by Zeus, persuaded Achilles to give up the body.
3. **Who went after it and how?**
King Priam went after the body alone. He took with him a ransom for the body.
4. **What sign did Zeus send to Priam?**
Zeus sent an eagle as a sign to Priam.
5. **How did Priam touch the heart of Achilles?**
Priam reminded Achilles of his father and his friend Patroclus.
6. **After Hector's body was returned to Priam, what favor did Priam beg of Achilles?**
Priam begged Achilles to allow the fighting to stop for twelve days so the city could mourn properly for Hector.
7. **How was the body of Hector met?**
All of the town people came to meet Hector's body when King Priam returned to the city with it.
8. **Describe the funeral rites.**
They first burned the body then put the bones in a chest of gold. The chest was covered with a purple cloth and put inside the tomb. It was then buried under rocks.
9. **What was the fate of Achilles?**
Achilles was killed when Paris pierced him in the heel with his arrow. As a child, Achilles was dipped in a magic river by Thetis. She held him by the heel, the only spot left untouched by the magic water.
10. **What happened when Troy fell?**
After Troy fell, Menelaus took Helen back to Greece to be his wife.

The Story of Achilles—Discussion, pp. 215-252

1. **The *Iliad* is full of beautiful comparisons such as the two at the beginning of III; find another one.**

   The two comparisons are:

   "The face of Achilles grew black as a thunderstorm." p. 219, line 27

   "But when the spoil is divided, yours is always the lion's share." p. 220, lines 4-5

   Other comparisons are:

   "As is the flare of a great fire when a wood is burning on a hilltop, so was the flash of their arms." p. 223, lines 17-18

   "As thick as the bees swarm in the spring, when the milk pails are full, the Greeks thronged to the battle." p. 223, lines 20-21

   "But the Trojans were like a flock of bleating sheep." p. 226, line 1

   "Achilles pursued him, as a hawk pursues a dove upon the mountains." p. 238, lines 31-32

2. **Another characteristic of the *Iliad* is the double adjective: yellow-haired; shrill-voiced. Can you find others that are striking?**

   Some other double adjectives are:

Double Adjective	*Noun described*	
Long-yellow	hair	p. 220
Long-shafted	spear	p. 225
White-armed	Andromache	p. 242
Four-wheeled	wagon	p. 244

3. **Which of the gods are favorable to the Greeks and which to the Trojans?**

   Greeks: Hera, Athena, and Thetis

   Trojans: Zeus, Aphrodite, Ares, and Apollo

4. **Notice how the gods themselves are not free to act as they wish; give an example.**

   Zeus will consult with the other gods before he makes a decision.

5. **Compare the trenches, armor, and implements of war in the *Iliad* with those of the World Wars.**

   The tools used in war in the *Iliad* are bows and arrows and spears. The Greeks and Trojans wore heavy armor because the combat was hand-to-hand. In the World Wars, people used airplanes, bombs and guns to fight. Most fighting in the World Wars was not hand-to-hand. Men stood great distances apart when they fought.

6. **What was the first cause of the Trojan War?**
The first cause of the Trojan War was Paris's theft of Helen from Menelaus.
7. **Read aloud in class: the story of the golden apple, page 217, line 7, to page 219, line 8; Patroclus goes into battle, page 230, line 10, to page 232, line 28; Achilles arouses himself, page 235, line 23, to page 236, line 8, and page 240, line 18, to page 242, line 21; burial of Hector, page 246, line 15, to page 247, line 20; the death of Achilles, page 247, line 21, to page 248, line 17.**
8. **Tell in your own words the story of Achilles, using for your outline the topic headings for the various chapters (7 pupils).**
9. **You will enjoy the illustrations as well as the stories in Colum's *The Children's Homer*. In *Stories of Greece and Rome, Retold from St. Nicholas* you will find interesting information about Greek and Roman life.**
10. **Find in the glossary the meaning of: (I) assembled, resolve, avenge, overlord, reared, immortal, counsel; (II) pressed, ill, spoil, scabbard, scepter; awful, array, doom, beside; (III) herald, apart, pierced, shrank, seer, fared, loathes, shuttle; (IV) warning, entreating, nigh, archer, corselet, waxed; (V) halo, ointment, drawing; (VI) dread, sacrifice, heart, dismayed, ransom; (VII) mantle, kinsfolk, litter, minstrels, shun.**
11. **Pronounce: (I) suitors, grievous; (II) besieged, naught, due; (III) thronged, allies, rebuked, bleating, wroth, nymphs; (IV) chariot, smote, forehead, bade, tunic, prophesy; (V) bier, mourning, locusts; (VI) whirl, pounce, vengeance, stature; (VII) truce, decreed.**

Extended Activities:

1. While students are reading, have them keep track of the characters by using the following chart:
2. Discuss with students how the story might have been different

GREEK CHARACTERS	IDENTIFICATION
Tyndareus	king of Sparta, father of Helen
Ulysses	chief, advisor to the king
Penelope	Ulysses's wife
Menelaus	Helen's husband
Agamemnon	chief, Menelaus's brother
Achilles	chief, mother is Thetis, a goddess
Ajax, the Greater	chief
Ajax, the Lesser	chief
Nestor	old man who counseled peace

TROJAN CHARACTERS	IDENTIFICATION
Paris	son of King Priam
King Priam	king of Troy
Aeneas	great warrior
Peleus	king of Thessaly
Anchises	Aeneas's father
Hector	brother of Paris

GODS AND GODDESSES	IDENTIFICATION
Zeus	king of the gods
Hera	queen of the gods
Athena	goddess of war
Aphrodite	goddess of love
Hermes	messenger
Ares	god of war
Apollo	god of music, poetry, and medicine
Thetis	goddess of the sea

had the gods not interfered with the actions of the humans. Have students write a story excluding the gods. Once stories are written, have students explain the reasoning for their plot. Have students share their stories with the class. This activity would also work well with students in groups of twos, threes or fours.

NAME________________________________ CLASS____________ DATE________

THE STORY OF ACHILLES, PP. 215-252

1. **While reading, keep track of the characters by using the following chart:**

GREEK CHARACTERS	IDENTIFICATION

TROJAN CHARACTERS	IDENTIFICATION

GODS AND GODDESSES	IDENTIFICATION

2. **Write a story excluding the gods. Once stories are written, explain the reasoning for your plot. Share your stories with the class.**

The Story of Ulysses, p. 253

SUMMARY

I. HOW ULYSSES OUTWITTED POLYPHEMUS

Because of the Greeks' haughtiness after the Trojan War, Ulysses and his men did not find a quick and safe passage home. They first traveled to the land of the Ciconians where they were attacked. Leaving there they landed on the shore of the Lotus-eaters. Eating of the lotus would make one forget his home and country and care not to return. Ulysses had to bind his men and drag them back to the ships. Next they landed where the Cyclops live. Having ventured into a cave they were captured by the Cyclops Polyphemus, who was Poseidon's son. The men eventually devised a plan of escape where they gave Polyphemus much wine to drink then poked out his eye. Being blind, he could not see the men exiting the cave hidden underneath the bellies of his rams and sheep.

II. HOW CIRCE TURNED THE MEN TO SWINE

Again the men landed on another foreign island. This time it was the home of Aeolus, the god of the winds. Aeolus gave Ulysses a bag made of ox skin which contained the contrary winds. This helped Ulysses and his men make their way home. When they came within sight of Ithaca, Ulysses's men decided to open the ox skin to see what was inside. They thought Ulysses was being greedy and keeping treasure for himself. When they opened the bag, the winds escaped and blew them back to the island of Aeolus. For a second time Ulysses asked for Aeolus's help. Aeolus refused because he said the gods did not favor Ulysses. Sailing away from Aeolus's island the men came near the Laestrygonians who threw rocks at the ships and sunk many of them. Ulysses then landed on the island where dwelt Circe, the daughter of the Sun. Eurylochus was sent with some men to investigate. Circe turned many of these men to swine. When Ulysses found out, he went to see her. Along the way he met Hermes who gave him a plant to eat that would protect him from Circe's charms. While at dinner with Circe, she asked Ulysses why he was so quiet. Telling her his lament for his men, she turned them back into men. Then, being on good terms, they stayed with Circe a whole year. At the end of the year, Circe told Ulysses he was to go on a journey to visit the spirit of Tiresias, the seer.

III. HOW ULYSSES SAILED BETWEEN SCYLLA AND CHARYBDIS

As they left Circe, she warned them not to harm the oxen of the Sun and they would return safely to Ithaca. Ulysses visited Tiresias who told him that Ulysses had angered Poseidon by hurting his son the cyclops and that he would have a difficult time returning home. Ulysses and his men next came to the island of the Sirens. Ulysses's men bound him to the mast, and the men put wax in their ears so as not to hear the beautiful sounds and then not want to return home. Having successfully passed this trial they came to Scylla and Charybdis. They chose the path near Scylla, a monster with six heads. The monster ate six of Ulysses's men, which was better than Charybdis destroying all of Ulysses's men. Finally they set joyfully for home. However, Poseidon spied Ulysses and was angry that he was almost home, so he sent all the winds of heaven down upon him. Ulysses was thrown from his ship and had to swim for two days and two nights, with Athena helping him. On the third day he made his way into the mouth of a river and landed on a shore of another island.

IV. HOW CALYPSO HELPED ULYSSES BUILD A RAFT

Zeus sent Hermes to tell Calypso to allow Ulysses to return home. She agreed and helped Ulysses build a raft on which he would sail.

V. HOW THE PHAEACIANS RECEIVED ULYSSES

He landed on the shore of the Phaeacians. Nausicaa, the king's daughter, was washing her clothes at the river when she found Ulysses and brought him back to her father. The Phaeacians clothed and fed Ulysses. They made a big ship for him, and the king gave him a crew to sail home. On the night before his departure, the minstrels sang of the Trojan War. This made Ulysses sad and he revealed his identity to the Phaeacians.

VI. HOW ULYSSES FOUND HIS OLD SWINEHERD STILL FAITHFUL TO HIM

When Ulysses and his crew landed on Ithaca, they set Ulysses down on the shore and left him. He met Athena and the two of them decided not to reveal Ulysses's identity. Many suitors were destroying Ulysses's house and wanting to marry Penelope. Athena, plotting to help Ulysses get rid of the suitors, turned Ulysses into an old beggar. He went to Eumaeus, the swineherd, who fed him and took care of him. Athena then went and helped Ulysses's son, Telemachus, return to Ithaca safely, avoiding the suitors who were waiting to kill him. Telemachus came to Eumaeus where he met Ulysses. Ulysses revealed himself to his son.

VII. HOW THE OLD NURSE RECOGNIZED ULYSSES

Telemachus and Eumaeus took Ulysses to the city where they went to see Penelope. Along the way they met Argus, Ulysses's old dog. Upon seeing Ulysses, the dog died. Penelope spoke with Ulysses, the beggar, then asked her nurse Eurycleia to wash him. When Eurycleia took Ulysses aside, she recognized him because of a scar on his thigh. That night Penelope had a dream. She saw an eagle killing geese.

VIII. HOW THE SUITORS TRIED THE BOW OF ULYSSES

Penelope had decided to marry the suitor who could accurately shoot Ulysses's bow. All the men lined up to demonstrate their skill. None of the men could even bend the bow.

IX. HOW ULYSSES WAS RESTORED IN HIS OLD HOME

Ulysses instructed Penelope's nurse to have the ladies depart and lock them in their chamber until the battle was over. He then shot the bow accurately and then fought the suitors. He sent word to Penelope that he had returned. She did not believe him at first as many men had tried to deceive her in the past. Finally, Athena restored Ulysses to his handsome self and Penelope and Ulysses were reunited.

I. How Ulysses Outwitted Polyphemus, p. 253

1. **How did the number of ships and men which Ulysses had when he came to Troy compare with those he had when he left?**
   He had twelve ships with fifty men on each ship, and he only had one when he left Troy.
2. **How many men did he lose in his adventure with the Ciconians?**
   He lost six men from each ship.
3. **What would have happened if a south wind instead of a north wind had blown after they sailed around the southern point of Greece?**
   They would have returned home to Ithaca.
4. **Tell about the adventure with the Lotus-eaters.**
   Eating the lotus would make one care not to see wife and country again. Ulysses had to bind and drag his men back to the ship after they ate the lotus.
5. **Where did Ulysses and his men go next?**
   They went to the country of the Cyclops.
6. **Who was Polyphemus?**
   Polyphemus was a Cyclops who was Poseidon's son.
7. **Tell the story of Ulysses's dealings with the Cyclops.**
   The Cyclops captured Ulysses and his men and locked them in his cave. He ate some of the men for his meals. One evening they gave the Cyclops wine then poked out his eye. The next morning the men hid themselves under the bellies of the Cyclops's sheep and rams. Because the Cyclops was blind, he could not see the men escaping.
8. **How many men were lost in this adventure?**
   Six men were lost in this adventure.
9. **What was the plan of escape Ulysses carried out?**
   See the answer to question number seven.
10. **What was the prayer of Polyphemus to Poseidon?**
    Polyphemus prayed that Ulysses never reach home, and if he did that he would find trouble in his house.

II. How Circe Turned the Men to Swine, p. 260

1. **What did the king of the winds do to help Ulysses?**
   Aeolus, the king of the winds, bound the contrary winds in the skin of an ox and gave it to Ulysses.
2. **How near to Ithaca did the west wind carry Ulysses?**
   Ulysses and his men were so close to Ithaca that they could see the lights on the shore.
3. **What happened while Ulysses slept?**
   While Ulysses slept, his men opened the bag of the contrary winds.
4. **Why was Aeolus not willing to help Ulysses a second time?**
   He was not willing to help Ulysses a second time because he said the gods were against Ulysses.
5. **How did it happen that Ulysses's ship was saved when all the others were destroyed by the Laestrygonians?**
   Ulysses's ship was saved because it was anchored by a cliff. The other ships went into the harbor.
6. **Where did they next sail?**
   Next they sailed to the island of Circe, daughter of the Sun.
7. **Who went exploring?**
   Eurylochus and twenty-two men went exploring.
8. **What did Eurylochus report when he fled back to the ship?**
   He reported that Circe had changed the men into swine.
9. **How did Hermes help Ulysses?**
   Hermes gave Ulysses a plant to eat that would protect him from Circe's charms.
10. **How long did the men stay with Circe?**
    The men stayed with Circe for one year.
11. **What new adventure did Circe declare to Ulysses?**
    She declared that Ulysses would journey to see the spirit of Tiresias, the seer.

III. How Ulysses Sailed between Scylla and Charybdis, p. 266

1. **What warning regarding the oxen of the Sun did Tiresias give Ulysses?**
   Tiresias warned Ulysses not to harm the oxen if he wanted to return to Ithaca safely.
2. **Why was it well for Ulysses that he returned to Circe?**
   He could return to Circe since they were now friends.
3. **How did Ulysses prepare to resist the attraction of the Sirens?**
   To resist the attraction of the Sirens, Ulysses's men would put wax in their ears and bind him to the mast of the ship.
4. **How did Ulysses and his men pass between Scylla and Charybdis?**
   Ulysses and his men passed between Scylla and Charybdis by allowing Scylla, a monster with six heads, to eat six of the men. While Scylla was busy eating, they could pass close to the monster and get through. If they went close to Charybdis, they would all have perished in the the rush of waters.
5. **Why did Ulysses land at the island where the oxen of the Sun fed, when both Tiresias and Circe had warned him?**
   He landed because his men were tired of the sea, and he could not go against his men.
6. **What wrong did the men do, and how were they punished?**
   The men ate some of the oxen. As punishment, Zeus brought a great storm, breaking the mast of the ship and lightning hit the men. All perished except Ulysses.
7. **How was Ulysses saved?**
   Ulysses was saved by attaching the keel to the mast and using it to float.
8. **Where did he land?**
   He landed on Ogygia where the goddess Calypso lived.
9. **How long did he stay with Calypso?**
   He stayed with Calypso seven years.
10. **What did Zeus promise Athena?**
    Zeus promised Athena that if all the gods were of one mind, he would have Poseidon put aside his anger to let Ulysses return to Ithaca.

11. What happened in Ithaca?

Suitors were after Queen Penelope and were ransacking Ulysses's home. Telemachus, Ulysses's son left to find word of Ulysses.

IV. How Calypso Helped Ulysses Build a Raft, p. 270

1. **Why do we not find Ulysses in the beautiful cave listening to the lovely song of Calypso?**
   Ulysses was at the shore weeping and groaning for his wife.
2. **What was the message of Hermes to Calypso?**
   Hermes told Calypso that Zeus wanted her to allow Ulysses to return home.
3. **How did Calypso help Ulysses?**
   Calypso helped Ulysses by building him a raft on which to sail.
4. **How long did he sail and how near was he to Phaeacia?**
   He sailed for seventeen days until he could see the hills of Phaeacia.
5. **What did Poseidon do?**
   Poseidon "sent all the winds of heaven down upon him."
6. **How did Ulysses finally reach the mouth of the river?**
   He reached the mouth of the river by swimming for two days with Athena's help.

V. How the Phaeacians Received Ulysses, p. 273

1. **Why did Nausicaa decide on this particular day to wash the clothes?**
   She decided to wash clothes because Athena appeared to her as a friend who convinced her she needed to wash her clothes for her suitors.
2. **What reason for washing the clothes did Nausicaa give her father?**
   She told her father he needed clean clothes for his council meetings and her brothers needed clean clothes for the dance.
3. **How did Nausicaa and her maidens go to the river?**
   They went to the river riding on a wagon.
4. **What did the girls do after the clothing was washed?**
   After the clothing was washed, they ate and played.
5. **Why was Nausicaa not afraid of the stranger?**
   She was not afraid of the stranger because she thought the gods would protect her.
6. **Describe the home of Alcinous.**
   The home of Alcinous had "walls of brass, and doors of gold hanging on posts of silver; and on either side of the door were dogs of gold and silver. Along the wall from the threshold to the inner chamber were seats, on which sat the chiefs of the Phaeacians, feasting; and youths wrought in gold stood holding torches in their hands to give light in the darkness." "And round about the house were beautiful gardens with orchards of fig, and apple, and pear, and pomegranate, and olive. There was also a vineyard, and beds of all kinds of flowers; and in the midst of all were two never-failing fountains."
7. **How was Ulysses received?**
   Ulysses was received kindly. They fed him and clothed him.
8. **How was he entertained on the following day?**
   They gave him a feast.
9. **When did Ulysses tell his name?**
   Ulysses told his name when the minstrel began to sing of the war between the Greeks and the Trojans.
10. **What did Ulysses tell the Phaeacians?**
    He told the Phaeacians of all his adventures since the war.

11. How did Ulysses express his appreciation of their kindness to him?

Ulysses expressed his appreciation by praying to the gods and asking them to bless the Phaeacians.

VI. How Ulysses Found His Old Swineherd Still Faithful to Him, p. 280

1. **Describe the arrival of Ulysses in Ithaca.**
   When they arrived on the shore of Ithaca, Ulysses was asleep, so the men left him there and departed.
2. **What did Ulysses do when he recognized his own country?**
   He kissed the ground when he recognized his own country.
3. **How and why did Athena change him?**
   Athena changed him into an old beggar so that no one would recognize him. They were plotting to get rid of Penelope's suitors.
4. **How did Ulysses test Eumaeus?**
   Ulysses told Eumaeus a strange tale and asked about the king.
5. **What acts of Eumaeus must have impressed Ulysses favorably?**
   Eumaeus spoke of his love for Ulysses and showed hospitality to the beggar.
6. **Who helped Telemachus to return safely?**
   Athena helped Telemachus return safely. She gave him an alternate path to take to avoid the suitors who were lying in wait for him.
7. **How did Ulysses caution Telemachus?**
   Ulysses revealed himself to Telemachus and warned him not to tell anyone who he was.

VII. How the Old Nurse Recognized Ulysses, p. 283

1. **How did Penelope greet the returning Telemachus?**
   She greeted him with a hug.
2. **What information did he give her?**
   He said he had learned that Ulysses was not dead.
3. **What was the goatherd's treatment of Ulysses?**
   The goatherd kicked Ulysses in the thigh.
4. **Tell about the dog, Argus.**
   Argus was Ulysses's dog. When he saw Ulysses, he recognized him, then died. Argus had been holding on to life to see his master one more time.
5. **How did Antinous treat Ulysses?**
   Antinous mocked him and told him to leave, then hit him with a stool.
6. **What did Ulysses and Telemachus do after the suitors had departed?**
   After the suitors departed, they took the armor from the hall.
7. **What was the story of the mantle and the tunic which Ulysses told Penelope?**
   Penelope asked the beggar what Ulysses was wearing, to see if he was telling the truth about having seen Ulysses alive. Ulysses told her correctly.
8. **How did Eurycleia recognize Ulysses?**
   She recognized Ulysses from the scar on his thigh.
9. **What was Penelope's dream?**
   Penelope dreamed an eagle was killing geese in her home.
10. **What did Ulysses say concerning the trial of the bow?**
    Ulysses said that Penelope ought to continue with her trial of the bow. She had agreed to marry the man who could accurately shoot Ulysses's bow. The plan was for Ulysses to return and shoot the bow himself.

VIII. How the Suitors Tried the Bow of Ulysses, p. 288

1. **How did the suitors regard the kindness of Telemachus toward the beggar?**
   The suitors did not like that Telemachus was being kind to the beggar.
2. **What did Penelope invite the suitors to do?**
   She invited the suitors to try and shoot an arrow through the holes of twelve axes.
3. **Who was the first to try the bow, and who were the last?**
   The first to try the bow was the priest, and Antinous and Eurymachus were the last to try the bow.
4. **How did Ulysses make himself known to Eumaeus and the herdsman?**
   He showed them his scar made by a wild boar.
5. **How did Eurymachus feel when he found that he could not bend the bow?**
   He was sad not that he lost Penelope, but that he was so much weaker than Ulysses.
6. **What explanation did Antinous give?**
   Antinous said he could shoot the bow because it was the holy day of the archer god.
7. **Why did Telemachus speak as he did to his mother?**
   Telemachus was defiant to his mother because he had to protect the identity and plan of Ulysses.
8. **What help did the faithful servants give?**
   The faithful servants helped keep the women locked up so they would not come out and see the men fighting.
9. **How did Ulysses handle the bow and with what success?**
   He handled the bow without toil and sent an arrow through every hole of the axes.

IX. How Ulysses was Restored in His Own Home, p. 291

1. **At what mark did Ulysses take aim?**
Ulysses aimed at Antinous.
2. **What surprised the suitors when they tried to defend themselves?**
There was no armor on the walls with which to protect themselves.
3. **How did Ulysses make himself known to the suitors?**
Ulysses shouted that he had returned and said, "destruction is come upon you all."
4. **How did Eurymachus try to excuse himself?**
Eurymachus blamed the situation on Antinous and told Ulysses that they would pay him back twentyfold for all they had devoured.
5. **Whom did Ulysses spare?**
Ulysses spared the minstrel and the herald.
6. **How did Penelope receive Eurycleia's news of the return of Ulysses?**
Penelope thought Eurycleia had lost her reason, and Penelope mocked her.
7. **Why was Penelope so slow in being convinced that the beggar was Ulysses?**
She was slow in believing the beggar was Ulysses because she had been deceived so many times before.
8. **Where did Ulysses find his father, Laertes?**
Laertes was in his garden digging a plant.
9. **What signs did Ulysses show him to prove that he was his son?**
Ulysses showed Laertes his scar on his thigh, then told about all the trees that had been given to him as a boy.
10. **What was the prayer of Laertes?**
The prayer of Laertes was, "Father Zeus, truly ye gods yet bear sway on high Olympus, for now my son has returned and the suitors have paid for their insolent pride."

The Story of Ulysses—Discussion, pp. 253-295

1. **Which one of the gods befriended Ulysses, and which one was hostile to him?**
   Athena befriended Ulysses, and Poseidon was hostile to him.
2. **Notice that the Cyclops lacked three qualities which were valued by ancient Greeks, just as they are valued by good citizens today: caring for the welfare of others; reverence; kindness to strangers.**
3. **How did Poseidon answer the prayer of Polyphemus?**
   He answered the prayer of Polyphemus by not allowing Ulysses a quick and safe trip home. When Ulysses did return home, he found trouble in his house.
4. **Give illustrations of Ulysses's cunning and craftiness.**
   a. Ulysses told the Cyclops that his name was No Man. When Ulysses attacked the Cyclops and others came to find out what the screaming was about, the Cyclops answered that No Man was attacking him.
   b. Ulysses often did not give into temptation and took steps to avoid it. For example, he did not eat the lotus and had his men bind him to the mast when the passed the Sirens.
   c. In the end, Ulysses plotted to kill the suitors and carried out his plan in disguise.
5. **Notice Ulysses's determination to return to his country in spite of all the dangers and the charms of Circe, the Sirens, Calypso, and Nausicaa.**
6. **Find a passage showing Ulysses's love for Ithaca, and another showing why Nausicaa thought no enemy could harm the Phaeacians.**
   As the minstrels sang of the Trojan war, "Ulysses wept to hear the tale."
   Nausicaa thought no enemy could harm the Phaeacians because they were favored by the gods.
7. **Tell about the treatment of strangers in the time of Homer, noting the order which was followed: (1) refreshing the stranger with bath and food; (2) questioning him as to name, country, and purpose of coming; (3) exchanging gifts.**
   Zeus, the king of the gods, insisted that strangers be treated graciously. It was not only a social custom to be

hospitable but also a religious duty. Even so, treatment of strangers varied from country to country. Polyphemus only questioned who they were; he offered no bath or food, and his gift offer was to eat Ulysses last of all his men. The Laestrygonians tried to crush them with stones, and Circe gave Ulysses's men wine, barleymeal, cheese, honey and drugs before she turned them into swine. However, Calypso met Hermes with meat and drink and asked about his errand. She supplied the men with bread, water, wine, clothes, and fair winds for their journey. The Phaeacians also treated Ulysses and his men with special regard. They offered Ulysses a seat, poured an offering to "Zeus, who is the friend of strangers," and "the keeper of the house gave him meat and drink." When Ulysses was left alone with the queen she inquired of his name and country. At the end of his visit, he was given "rich gifts" so that "he might go forth as befitted so illustrious a guest."

8. **Compare the sports in Phaeacia with our modern sports.**

The Phaeacians valued dance and running around. They did not participate in competitive sports like we do today.

9. **How are Laertes, Penelope, Telemachus, Eurycleia, Eumaeus, and Argus connected with Ulysses?**

Laertes is Ulysses's father, and Penelope is Ulysses's wife. Telemachus is his son; Eurycleia is his nurse; Eumaeus is his servant, the swineherd; and Argus is Ulysses's dog.

10. **Make a list of ten or more interesting double adjectives with the nouns they describe.**

Double Adjective	*Noun described*	
Honey-sweet	fruit	p. 254
Sweet-smelling	skin	p. 255
Silver-studded	sword	p. 264
Rosy-fingered	dawn	p. 272
Far-off	Troy	p. 272
Well-wooded	land	p. 294
Well-ordered	farm	p. 294

11. **Make a list of ten or more nouns used to describe other nouns, as: Eurycleia, the nurse; Athena, daughter of Zeus.**

Noun as Adjectives	*Noun described*	
a mighty giant	Cyclops	p. 255

king of the winds	Aeolus	p. 260
their country	Ithaca	p. 261
daughter of the king of the land	Maiden	p. 262
giants	Laestrygonians	p. 262
daughter of the sun	Circe	p. 262
the seer	Tiresias	p. 265
his son	Polyphemus	p. 266
a horrible monster	Scylla	p. 267
thy messenger	Hermes	p. 269
the aged father of Ulysses	Laertes	p. 270
one daughter	Nausicaa	p. 273
daughter of Zeus	Athena	p. 280

Nouns that are used to describe other nouns are called *appositives*. Appositives rename or give further information about the prior noun.

12. Locate on a map: Sparta, Troy, Home of the Cyclops (Sicily), Scylla and Charybdis (Straits of Messina), Phaeacia (Corcyra), Ithaca.

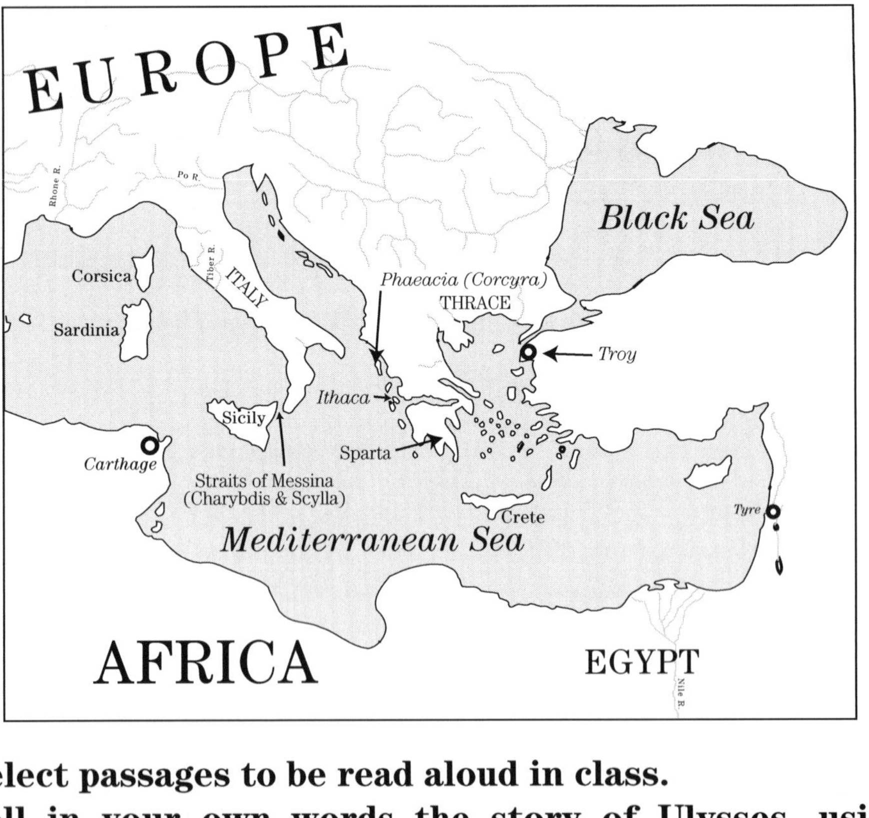

13. Select passages to be read aloud in class.

14. Tell in your own words the story of Ulysses, using for your outline the topic headings for the various chapters (9 pupils).

15. Find in the glossary the meaning of: (I) laurels, fold,

curdled, pirates, hospitality, craft; (II) launched, lofty, fawning; (III) violence, monster, spits; (IV) donned, cypress, adz, augers, yard, moored; (V) council, quoit, illustrious; (VI) substance, wayfarers, loyalty; (VII) marvelous, seapurple, brooch; (VIII) scoffed, quiver, authority, flaw; (IX) manifest, terraced, insolent.

16. Pronounce: (I) forbade; (II) threshold, acorns, herb; (III) bellowed, guise; (V) pomegranate, escort; (VI) route; (VII) alms; (IX) mock.

Extended Activities:

1. Have students select one of Ulysses's adventures they liked the most. Using the outline below, have them write about one reason it was their favorite. Students should plan their writing then revise and edit before drafting a final copy.

Outline:

Topic—State the favorite adventure
Reason—state the reason for liking this adventure
Elaboration—write a further explanation of the reason
Example—give an example from the text to support the reason
Example—give another example from the text to support the reason
Summary sentence

2. Have students create a cartoon with five sections, depicting their favorite adventure of Ulysses.

3. Discuss the following with the class: It took years for Ulysses to return home. Along the way he faced many extraordinary and dangerous adventures. He had to possess many different kinds of survival skills. If you were to go on an adventure such as Ulysses, what kinds of survival skills do you think would be the most important to possess? Make a list of these skills on the board. What kind of survival skills are necessary in day to day life? (Examples: CPR, calling 911)

4. Ulysses met all kinds of strange creatures such as the Cyclops and the Scylla. Have students create another fanciful creature that Ulysses might have met. Give the creature a name and display student works in the classroom.

NAME______________________________CLASS__________DATE______

THE STORY OF ULYSSES, PP. 253-295

1. Select one of Ulysses's adventures you liked the most. Using the outline below, write about one reason it was your favorite. Plan your writing then revise and edit before drafting a final copy.

   Outline:

   Topic—State the favorite adventure
   Reason—state the reason for liking this adventure
   Elaboration—write a further explanation of the reason
   Example—give an example from the text to support the reason
   Example—give another example from the text to support the reason
   Summary sentence

2. Create a cartoon with five sections, depicting your favorite adventure of Ulysses.

4. **Ulysses met all kinds of strange creatures such as the Cyclops and the Scylla. Create another fanticiful creature that Ulysses might have met. Give the creature a name and display your work in the classroom.**

THE STORY OF AENEAS, P. 299

SUMMARY

I. THE FALL OF TROY; THE WOODEN HORSE

The Greeks laid siege to Troy for ten years. Minerva, favoring the Greeks, helped Ulysses devise a plan to take Troy. The Greeks built a large wooden horse. The Greek chiefs hid inside as the other Greeks pretended to depart Troy. The Trojans were deceived into thinking the horse was a gift to Minerva for a safe trip home. After much discussion, the Trojans brought the horse inside the city gates. That evening a Trojan traitor, Sinon, opened a secret door in the horse letting the chiefs out. They, in turn, opened the city gates allowing the Greek armies into the city to attack. Pyrrus, son of Achilles, killed Polites and his father, King Priam.

II. HOW AENEAS FLED FROM TROY

Aeneas left the battle and returned to his home to check on his family. There he saw a vision of Hector, who told him to flee. Then his mother, Venus, appeared and showed him that the fate of Troy was in the hands of the gods, and there was nothing more he could do to save the city. Aeneas took his family and they began to flee the city. Along the way, Aeneas's wife, Creusa, became separated from Aeneas. Other Trojans followed Aeneas. They went to Mount Ida where they hid and began to build ships to leave Troy.

III. HOW AENEAS CAME TO ITALY

After the ships were completed the people set sail for a new land. They first went to Thrace, then to Crete. At Crete, many of the people became ill, and Aeneas learned from his household gods that they were to travel to Italy to set up permanent residence. So, they set sail again. On their way to Italy they passed Ithaca, and on the island of Sicily, Anchises died. They then landed on Carthage where they stayed for some time. Leaving Carthage, they finally landed in Italy and began to build a city that would later become Rome. Aeneas mysteriously disappeared in a battle for the land. In the end, Juno begged Jupiter to change the Trojans' name to Romans.

Note: This story of Aeneas's visit to Carthage has also been retold musically in a short Baroque opera titled Dido and Aeneas, *by Henry Purcell.*

I. The Fall of Troy; the Wooden Horse, p. 299

1. **Why did the siege of Troy last so long?**
The siege lasted so long because the gods; Apollo, Mars, and Jupiter; loved Troy.
2. **What were the Trojans made to believe regarding the horse of wood?**
They were led to believe the horse was a gift to Minerva for a safe trip home.
3. **What did the Greeks pretend to do?**
The Greeks pretended to leave Troy.
4. **Who was the first to advise that the horse should be brought inside the walls?**
One of the elders of the city was the first to advise bringing the horse inside the walls.
5. **What was Laocoon's opinion?**
Laocoon's opinion was that the horse was a trap.
6. **How did Sinon deceive the Trojans?**
Sinon deceived the Trojans by leading them to believe the Greeks had departed.
7. **What happened that made the Trojans think Laocoon was punished for his treatment of the horse?**
A serpent came out of the sea and devoured Sinon and his two sons.
8. **How was the horse brought into the city?**
The horse was brought into the city by opening the gates, tearing down one adjoining wall and putting the horse on wheels.
9. **What did Cassandra say, and how was her prophecy received?**
She prophesied that the horse was evil, but no one believed her.
10. **What did Helen do when she saw the horse?**
When Helen saw the horse she walked around it and called out the names of the Greek chiefs.
11. **How did the Greek army enter the city?**
The Greek army was able to enter the city because the chiefs came out of the horse and opened the city gates.
12. **What vision did Aeneas see and what did the spirit tell him to do?**

He saw the slain Hector who told him the Greeks were inside the city and he needed to flee.

13. In what part of the city was there the most fighting?

The most fighting took place at the palace of King Priam.

14. What was Hecuba's advice to Priam?

Hecuba's advice to Priam was for him to not fight, but rather worship the household gods.

15. What happened to Polites?

Polites was killed by Pyrrhus, Achilles's son.

16. What other cruel thing did the son of Achilles do?

He killed King Priam.

II. How Aeneas Fled from Troy, p. 305

1. **Where was Aeneas going?**
   Aeneas was going home to his wife and child.
2. **What effect did the sight of Helen have upon Aeneas?**
   When he saw Helen, his fury was enraged. He blamed her for the fall of Troy.
3. **What truth did Venus reveal to Aeneas?**
   Venus revealed that it was the gods who were destroying Troy.
4. **What gods especially were hostile to Troy?**
   Neptune, Juno, and Minerva were hostile to Troy.
5. **Why did Anchises at first refuse to flee with Aeneas?**
   He did not want to leave to live in a strange land.
6. **What happened that made Anchises change his mind about going with Aeneas?**
   Jupiter appeared as a light on Ascanius's head, and Anchises thought this was a sign for him to leave Troy.
7. **Describe the picture you see of Aeneas and his family leaving their home.**
   Answers will vary. Refer to page 308, lines 19-29.
8. **What happened to Creusa?**
   She was separated from Aeneas.
9. **What did the spirit of Creusa reveal to Aeneas?**
   She revealed that she was to stay in Troy and that Aeneas would eventually prosper and marry a woman of royal blood.
10. **What had happened while Aeneas was returning to the city?**
    While Aeneas was returning to the city, the city was being destroyed and other Trojans decided to flee as well.
11. **Where and how was the winter spent?**
    The winter was spent under Mount Ida building ships.
12. **What was the family relationship between Aeneas and each of the following:**
    Venus
    Aeneas's mother
    Anchises
    Aeneas's father
    Creusa
    Aeneas's wife
    Ascanius
    Aeneas's child

III. How Aeneas Came to Italy, p. 310

1. **Where did they go first, and where did they settle later, on Anchises's advice?**
The first went to Thrace then to Crete, the island of the ancestors of the Trojan people.
2. **What did the household gods tell Aeneas as he slept?**
They told him that they were to settle in Italy, not Crete.
3. **What did the Trojans do as they passed Ithaca?**
They cursed Ithaca because it was the home of the hated Ulysses.
4. **Where did they meet Andromache and Helenus?**
They met Andromache and Helenus on an island in a grove by a river.
5. **Tell about the Greek, the companion left behind by Ulysses.**
The man was left in the Cyclops's cave. The Trojans had pity on him and took him aboard.
6. **What happened on the island of Sicily?**
On the island of Sicily, Anchises died.
7. **What did Juno do when she saw the Trojans nearing their destination?**
She went to Aeolus, king of the winds, and asked him to let a storm rage against the Trojans.
8. **Why did the action of Aeolus anger Neptune?**
Aeolus's action angered Neptune because Neptune had dominion over the sea. He told Aeolus to keep to his rocks.
9. **What comforting facts did Jupiter tell Venus?**
"Aeneas shall make war with nations of Italy and shall subdue them, and build a city, and rule therein for three years. After thirty years the boy Ascanius shall change the place of his throne to Alba, where for three hundred years there shall be kings of the kindred of Hector. Then shall a priestess bear twin sons, whom a wolf shall nurse; and one of these, Romulus, shall build a city, dedicating it to his father, Mars, and shall call it Rome, after his own name. To this city have I given power without bound or end. Even Juno shall repent of her wrath and join with me in cherishing the men of Rome, so that they shall rule even over the land of the Greeks."

10. **To what country had Aeneas and his companions come?**
 They came to Italy.
11. **Who told Aeneas about Carthage?**
 Venus, in the form of a maiden, told Aeneas about Carthage.
12. **Why was Aeneas well received by Dido?**
 "Jupiter sent Mercury, his messenger, to turn the hearts of Dido and her people so that they would deal kindly with people."
13. **What did Dido offer the Trojans?**
 She offered them homes.
14. **Why was she unwilling to let Aeneas go?**
 She was unwilling to let him go because he moved her heart.
15. **How did Aeneas know of Dido's fate?**
 He saw the fire and knew in his heart what had happened.
16. **How long did Aeneas wander?**
 Aeneas wandered for seven years.
17. **What did Aeneas learn from Anchises in the regions of the dead?**
 He learned of the glorious future of Rome.
18. **How did Aeneas and his men escape the enchantment of Circe?**
 They were "aided by favorable winds" and were able to escape Circe.
19. **Who was Latinus?**
 Latinus was the king of the country where Rome would be built.
20. **How did Aeneas become king?**
 Aeneas married Latinus's daughter and became king when Latinus died.
21. **How did the life of Aeneas end?**
 During a conflict, he mysteriously disappeared.
22. **What last favor did Juno beg of Jupiter?**
 Juno begged Jupiter that the name of Troy perish and the people be called Romans.

The Story of Aeneas—Discussion, pp. 299-319

1. **Notice points of resemblance in the stories related in Homer's poems and those related in the Aeneid by Vergil, who lived at least seven centuries after Homer.**
2. **Which gods were favorable to the Trojans, and what were the reasons for Venus's partiality?**

   Apollo, Mars, and Jupiter were favorable to the Trojans. Venus was partial because Aeneas was her son.
3. **In this conflict between the gods, which side seems to you to have won?**

   Answers will vary.
4. **Did Aeneas show his bravery in the same way Hector showed his? Who was braver, Creusa or Andromache?**

   Answers will vary.
5. **How did Hector and Venus make Aeneas willing to flee from Troy?**

   Aeneas learned from them that the fate of Troy was in the hands of the gods, not the actions of the people.
6. **Do you know of any World War heroes who served their country in a way similar to Sinon's service? What are such people called?**

   Such people are called spies who carry out espionage. In World War One, the Germans used many spies. The most famous was a woman named Mata Hari who posed as an Indian dancer in Paris. Most nations had poor intelligence agents during World War One. Because of improved technology, espionage was helpful to all nations during World War Two. Today, the Central Intelligence Agency (CIA) is the American organization that controls the actions of our spies and identifies spies of other countries.
7. **Relate an instance of kindness to an enemy in World War One of which you are reminded by the Trojan's treatment of the Greek companion to Ulysses.**

   Answers may vary. One example can be found in Article 218, Paragraph 1, of the Versaille Treaty which makes provisions for repatriating prisoners of war regardless of their offences.

8. Trace on a map the wanderings of Aeneas, locating: Troy; Thrace; Crete; Sicily; Carthage; Italy.

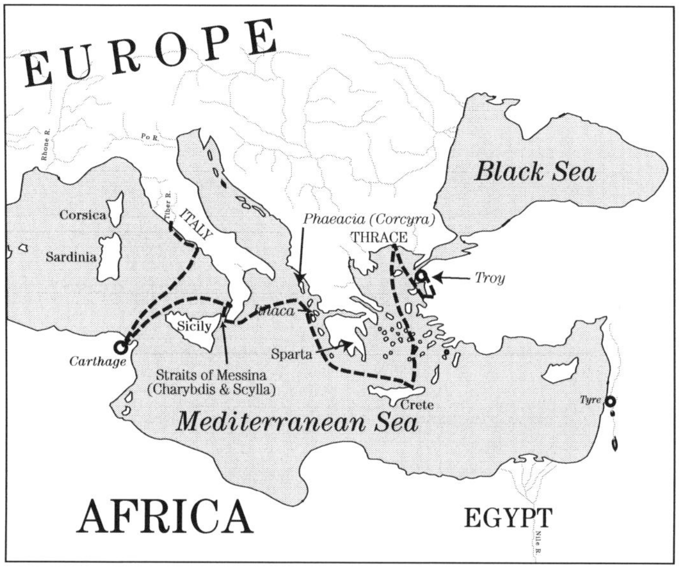

9. Read aloud in class: the story of the death of King Priam, page 304, line 16 to page 305, line 29; Aeneas flees with his family, page 307, line 19, to page 310, line 20; Dido entertains the Trojans, page 313, line 27, to page 315, line 25; Aeneas reaches the promised land, page 316, line 10, to page 317, line 7.

10. Tell in your own words the story of Aeneas, using for your outline the topic headings for the various chapters (3 pupils).

11. Find in the glossary the meaning of: (I) delayed, devised, scheme, citadel, appease, marvel, treacherously, bewitched, reverenced, knob, unworthy; (II) handmaidens, consumed, trident, javelins, well-nigh, fleeting; (III) oracle, blight, tumult.

Extended Activities:

1. Have students research and prepare a report on one of the following topics to give them further knowledge of common Roman and Greek history:

   Augustus Caesar
   Julius Caesar
   Pompeii
   Pantheon
   Olympics

2. Have students construct a model of the Pantheon, the temple of the gods. They may use toothpicks, clay, or other building material.

NAME______________________________CLASS__________DATE______

THE STORY OF AENEAS, PP. 299-319

8. Trace on a map the wanderings of Aeneas, locating: Troy, Thrace, Crete, Sicily, Carthage, Italy.

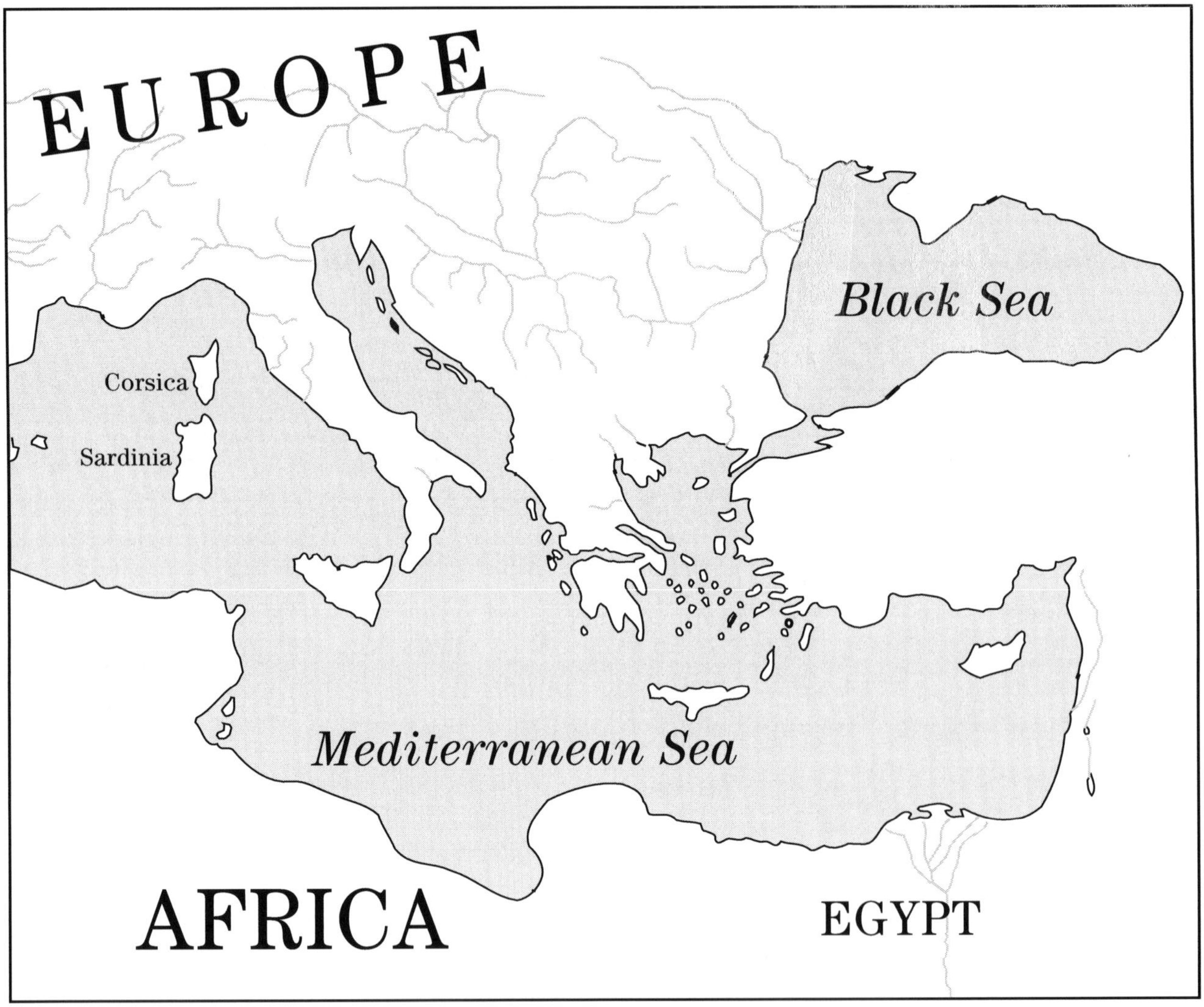

NAME______________________________ **CLASS**__________ **DATE**______

Story	***Find in the glossary the meaning of:***
Reader p. 215	**assembled**____________________
	resolve____________________
	avenge____________________
	overlord____________________
	reared____________________
	immortal____________________
	counsel____________________
Reader p. 219	**pressed**____________________
	ill____________________
	spoil____________________
	scabbard____________________
	scepter____________________
	awful____________________
	array____________________
	doom____________________
	beside____________________
Reader p. 223	**herald**____________________
	apart____________________
	pierced____________________
	shrank____________________
	seer____________________
	fared____________________
	loathes____________________
	shuttle____________________
Reader p. 228	**warning**____________________
	entreating____________________
	nigh____________________
	archer____________________
	corselet____________________
	waxed____________________
Reader p. 232	**halo**____________________
	ointment____________________
	drawing____________________
Reader p. 237	**dread**____________________
	sacrifice____________________
	heart____________________
	dismayed____________________
	ransom____________________
Reader p. 242	**mantle**____________________

kinsfolk____
litter____
minstrels____
shun____
Reader p. 253 **laurels**____
fold____
curdled____
pirates____
hospitality____
craft____
Reader p. 260 **launched**____
lofty____
fawning____
Reader p. 266 **violence**____
monster____
spits____
Reader p. 270 **donned**____
cypress____
adz____
augers____
yard____
moored____
Reader p. 273 **council**____
quoit____
illustrious____
Reader p. 280 **substance**____
wayfarers____
loyalty____
Reader p. 283 **marvelous**____
seapurple____
brooch____
Reader p. 288 **scoffed**____
quiver____
authority____
flaw____
Reader p. 291 **manifest**____
terraced____
insolent____
Reader p. 299 **delayed**____
devised____
scheme____
citadel____
appease____

marvel____________________________________
treacherously______________________________
bewitched_________________________________
reverenced________________________________
knob_____________________________________
unworthy__________________________________
Reader p. 305 **handmaidens**_______________________________
consumed__________________________________
trident___________________________________
javelins___________________________________
well-nigh__________________________________
fleeting___________________________________
Reader p. 310 **oracle**___________________________________
blight____________________________________
tumult____________________________________

Pronounce:
suitors, grievous, besieged, naught, due, thronged, allies, rebuked, bleating, wroth, nymphs, chariot, smote, forehead, bade, tunic, prophesy, bier, mourning, locusts, whirl, pounce, vengeance, stature, truce, decreed, forbade, threshold, acorns, herb, bellowed, guise, pomegranate, escort, route, alms, mock.

Part III: Great American Authors

In This Section—

Objectives—

GREAT AMERICAN AUTHORS

By completing "Part III," the following objectives will be met.

1. The student will use effective reading strategies to construct meaning and identify the purpose of a text including:
   a. using illustrations
   b. defining unfamiliar words
   c. retelling and summarizing
2. The student will determine the main idea or essential message and identify relevant supporting details and facts of a text.
3. The student will read and organize facts from the text and other sources to make a report, outline, and perform an authentic task.
4. The student will prepare for writing by focusing on the topic and organizing supporting details in a logical sequence.
5. The student will draft and revise writing.
6. The student will produce final documents that have been edited for correct spelling, punctuation, and grammar.
7. The student will write for a variety of audiences and purposes.
8. The student will use reference materials (dictionaries, encyclopedias, maps, charts, photos, and electronic reference) to gather information.
9. The student will identify the development of plot and how conflicts are resolved in a story.
10. The student will identify and understand similarities and differences among the characters, settings, and events presented in various texts.
11. The student will identify author's purpose and point of view.
12. The student will identify and use literary terminology such as rhyme scheme, personification, simile, end rhyme, and alliteration.
13. The student will respond critically to fiction, nonfiction, poetry, and drama.
14. The student will recognize cause-and-effect relationships in literary texts.
15. The student will respond to a text by explaining how the motives of the characters or events compare with those in his or her own life.
16. The student will understand the qualities necessary for people to become good citizens and apply those qualities to his/her personal life.
17. The student will understand the qualities necessary to develop good character and apply those to his/her own life.

BENJAMIN FRANKLIN—

MY ARRIVAL IN PHILADELPHIA, P. 329

1. **What tells you that the events related in this story happened many years ago?**
   Franklin's mode of travel, type of money, communication, and the printing machinery he describes all indicate that this story happened long ago.
2. **Why do you think Franklin remembered so well all the details of his ridiculous appearance when he arrived in Philadelphia?**
   He probably remembered them so well because he wanted to make a good impression on the people he met, but he was painfully aware of not measuring up to their standards of appropriate dress and overall appearance.
3. **How did he fall in with the Quakers in Philadelphia?**
   He was walking up the street and met "many clean-dressed people in it, who were all walking the same way," so he joined them and ended up in the Quaker meetinghouse.
4. **What trade did Franklin learn, and to whom did he apply for work?**
   Franklin learned the printing trade. He applied first to Andrew Bradford, a local printer, who had no work for him. Bradford referred him to a new printer in town by the name of Keimer, who eventually hired him.
5. **What interest did Sir William Keith show in him?**
   Sir William Keith saw that Franklin "appeared a young man of promising parts, and therefore should be encouraged." He visited Franklin at work where he "made me many compliments, desired to be acquainted with me, blamed me kindly for not having made myself known to him when I first came to the place, and would have me away with him to the tavern, where he was going with Colonel French to taste, as he said, some excellent Madeira."
6. **Why did he return to Boston?**
   He returned to Boston at Sir William Keith's request who recommended that Franklin prevail upon his father to set him up in his own printer's business in Philadelphia where

the existing printers were "wretched." He promised that he would procure for Franklin the "public business."

7. **What tells you that Franklin was fond of reading?**

He became acquainted with the young people of the town who loved to read, and together they spent their evenings reading.

8. **What traits in Franklin's character are indicated in this selection?**

Students are encouraged to identify as many traits as they can support with details from the story. Among them would be the traits of courage in facing a new town, job, and faces with little money, and leadership in putting Keimer's press "into fit order to be worked with." Thrift and hard work are also evident in this story.

9. **Which of them may account for his later greatness?**

Responses will vary based on answers to the previous question. Clearly, courage, leadership, thrift, and hard work contributed to his greatness.

10. **What habit of Franklin's does the picture on page 327 suggest?**

The picture on page 327 (p. 195 of this *Guide*) suggests that Franklin enjoyed reading.

11. **Make a list of expressions peculiar to Franklin's time and give modern substitutes for them.**

Possible peculiar expressions could include: "one of them was a crafty old sophister, and the other a mere novice"; "there I lodged and dieted"; "a good deal of the knave in his composition"; "stared like a pig poisoned"; "we had a blustering time at sea." Encourage students to "translate" the terms into popular teen expressions.

12. **How do you connect Franklin's name with *The Saturday Evening Post?***

The Saturday Evening Post is published by the nonprofit Benjamin Franklin Literary and Medical Society. For more information visit http://www.magazinesofamerica.com/1520.html.

13. **Find in the glossary the meaning of: passage, thereby, sly, hand, discovering, artful, font, dieted, illiterate, condescension.**

14. **Pronounce: fatigued, accosting, reputable, sophister, novice, compositor, apprehended, affable.**

FRANKLIN'S "ONLY AMUSEMENT," P. 336

1. **What habit of using the library did Franklin make?**
   Franklin "set apart an hour or two each day" to read at the library.
   Have you a fixed habit of reading outside the school?
   Answers will vary.
2. **What kind of books do you think Franklin read?**
   It is likely that among Franklin's books were the classic works of great authors, biographies of great leaders, and works of Greek and Roman authors. Student responses may vary.
3. **What amusement did he allow himself?**
   "Reading was the only amusement I allowed myself."
4. **What two habits combined to make Franklin's income increase?**
   His habits of frugality and industry helped his income to increase.
5. **What proverb did his habit of industry prove true?**
   "Seest thou a man diligent in his calling, he shall stand before kings; he shall not stand before mean men." Franklin stood before five kings and dined with the King of Denmark.
6. **What habits of saving have you?**
   Answers will vary.
7. **Find in the glossary the meaning of: repaired, degree, learned, education, frolics, contend, mean.**
8. **Pronounce: indefatigable, distinction.**

Great American Authors—*Benjamin Franklin*, pp. 327-336

Extended Exercises

1. Both of these stories describe brief glimpses into Franklin's life at two very different times. The first was written before he was married, and the second piece was written when he had a family to support. Throughout his life, Franklin was an editor, printer, inventor and statesman, as well as a soap maker and a cabbage farmer. Have students research his life using the brief biography in this reader, as well as encyclopedias and the Internet. Have them develop a timeline from his birth to his death (1706-1790) and highlight the major events they find. Have them locate where on the timeline these two stories might fit best.

2. Benjamin Franklin is famous for his book, *Poor Richard's Almanac,* which included brief sayings still used today. Have students locate some of his sayings and translate them into twenty-first century language. Possible Internet resources include:

http://www.sfheart.com/almanac.html

http://www.brittanica.com/seo/p/poor-richard/

Have students dress up as Franklin may have looked and present their twenty-first century adaptations of his adages to the class. See if fellow students can guess the original adage.

3. After students have read these stories about Franklin's experiences, have them choose one of the following topics and write a short descriptive essay on their experience.

They say clothes describe the man. One time when my clothes described me was…

My favorite place to be alone and read is…

I'm saving my money for…

Someday I would like to invent…

One thing I am really good at is…

NAME______________________________CLASS__________DATE______

GREAT AMERICAN AUTHORS—*BENJAMIN FRANKLIN*, P. 327-336

1. Both of these stories describe brief glimpses into Franklin's life at two very different times. The first was written before he was married, and the second piece was written when he had a family to support. Throughout his life, Franklin was an editor, printer, inventor and statesman, as well as a soap maker and a cabbage farmer. Research his life using the brief biography in this reader, as well as encyclopedias and the Internet. Develop a timeline from his birth to his death (1706-1790) and highlight the major events you find. Locate where on the timeline these two stories might fit best.

2. Benjamin Franklin is famous for his book, *Poor Richard's Almanac,* which included brief sayings still used today. Locate some of his sayings and translate them into twenty-first century language. Dress up as Franklin may have looked and present your twenty-first century adaptations of his adages to the class. See if fellow students can guess the original adage.

3. Choose one of the following topics and write a short descriptive essay on your experience.

   They say clothes describe the man. One time when my clothes described me was...
   My favorite place to be alone and read is...
   I'm saving my money for...
   Someday I would like to invent...
   One thing I am really good at is...

WILLIAM CULLEN BRYANT—

MARCH, P. 339

1. **What peculiarities of March weather have you observed?**
   Responses will vary depending on what part of the country the students reside.
2. **How does the poet regard March? Why?**
   The poet calls March stormy because it comes "With wind, and cloud, and changing skies."
3. **What reasons does the poet give for calling March "a welcome month"?**
   The poet regards March as "a welcome month" because it brings back "The glad and glorious sun" and wears "the gentle name of Spring." It brings in the reign of "a long, bright, sunny day."
   Another poet, Helen Hunt Jackson, says: "Oh, March! we know thou art Kind-hearted, spite of ugly looks and threats, And, out of sight, art nursing April's violets!" Do you agree with her?
   Responses will vary.
4. **Why does the poet say "the full springs are just set out to meet the sea"?**
   The "full springs" are the melted ice "from frost set free, That, brightly leaping down the hills, Are just set out to meet the sea."
5. **What season is indicated in lines 21 and 22, page 339?**
   "The year's departing beauty hides Of wintry storms the sullen threat;" speaks of the season of winter.
6. **How does "the year's departing beauty" hide the threat of winter storms?**
   The "departing beauty" may refer to the snowfalls that blanket the earth and hide the threat of the cold winter storms.
7. **What "kindly promise" is meant?**
   The promise is "the hope of those calm skies And that soft time of sunny showers when the wide bloom, on earth that lies, Seems of a brighter world than ours."
8. **In whose "sternest frown" does it abide?**
   It abides in the stern frown of March.

9. **To what month does the last stanza refer?**
   The last stanza refers to April with its "sunny showers."
10. **Memorize the last stanza.**
11. **How does the March of Bryant's poem compare with that described by Wordsworth (page 63)?**
    Bryant's poem describes a "stormy March" that comes "With wind, and cloud, and changing skies" and brings "blast and storm." Wordsworth's poem describes only the positive images of March—crowing cocks, flowing streams, twittering birds, glittering lakes, sleepy fields, etc.
12. **Find in the glossary the meaning of: train, sullen.**

Extended Activity:

Bryant uses vivid words and phrases to help the reader experience the contrasting images of March. Have students identify all the adjective/noun pairs in this poem that reflect those contrasts and write them in the accompanying chart based on their positive, negative, or neutral connotations. Which image is reflected most often? Possible noun/adjective pairs: stormy March; changing skies; snowy valley; passing few; wild, stormy month; loud and bleak winds; welcome month; northern lands; glad and glorious sun; gentle train; gentle name; long, bright, sunny day; soft and warm changed winds; gushing rills; full springs; departing beauty; wintry storms; sullen threat; sternest frowns; kindly promise; calm skies; soft time; sunny showers; wide bloom; brighter world.

Positive Images	Negative Images	Neutral Images

See "Extended Activities" at the end of Bryant's poetry for further study.

NAME______________________________**CLASS**__________**DATE**______

MARCH, p. 339

Bryant uses vivid words and phrases to help the reader experience the contrasting images of March. Identify all the adjective/noun pairs in this poem that reflect those contrasts and write them in the accompanying chart based on their positive, negative, or neutral connotations. Which image is reflected most often?

Positive Images	Negative Images	Neutral Images

The Planting of the Apple Tree, p. 340

1. **Read the stanza that tells how we plant the apple tree.**
   "Come, let us plant the apple tree! Cleave the tough greensward with the spade; Wide let its hollow bed be made; There gently lay the roots, and there Sift the dark mold with kindly care, And press it o'er them tenderly, As round the sleeping infant's feet We softly fold the cradle sheet; So plant we the apple tree."
2. **What comparison is there in the first stanza?**
   The poet compares the planting of an apple tree with putting a baby to bed.
   The soft soil, like the cradle sheet covering the child, covers the roots in their shallow bed.
3. **In the second stanza what does the poet say we plant in the apple tree?**
   We plant buds that will "lengthen into leafy sprays," boughs in which the thrush will "haunt and sing and hide her nest," and shade that will provide "shelter from the summer shower."
   In the third stanza?
   We plant sweets so that May's winds can pour "Its fragrance through our open door," blossoms for bees, flowers for a sick girl's room, and "For the glad infant sprigs of bloom."
   In the fourth?
   We plant fruits that grow in June, ripen in August, and drop in September where "children come, with cries of glee, and seek them."
4. **Why did the poet follow this order?**
   The poet followed this order because it is the process through which the tree must pass to become full-grown: buds become leafy branches that produce sweet aromas and develop fruit that ripens and is finally gathered.
5. **Why is the grass called fragrant?**
   The grass is fragrant with the aroma of apples hiding in it.
6. **In the fifth stanza, what is said of the apple tree in the winter season?**
   "Girls whose young eyes o'erflow with mirth Shall peel its fruit by cottage hearth."
7. **With what is "cottage hearth" compared?**

The "cottage hearth" is compared to "prouder homes" where guests will find apples heaped together with grapes and oranges.

8. **What is the meaning of lines 7-9, page 342?**

The image of the apple tree, like our flag, an image of freedom, will travel to countries far away and remind people around the world of the freedom of their "long, long hours of summer play In the shade of the apple tree."

9. **How would you answer the poet's questions in the seventh stanza?**

The poet asks these questions: "Oh! when its aged branches throw Thin shadows on the ground below, Shall fraud and force and iron will Oppress the weak and helpless still?" "What shall the tasks of mercy be Amid the toils, the strifes, the tears Of those who live when length of years Is wasting this apple tree?" Encourage a class discussion of these questions from the students' perspectives.

10. **What do you think Bryant would say about the work of the American Forestry Association as a "task of mercy"? This association sent 35,000,000 tree seeds overseas to plant new trees on the battlefields of France and Belgium.**

Answers will vary.

11. **To whom does "a poet of the land" refer?**

"A poet of the land" refers to the man who planted the apple tree.

12. **Why do you like this poem?**

Answers will vary.

13. **How does the picture on page 337 compare with the picture you imagined when reading the first stanza?**

The picture shows children and a man planting a young tree very much as the poet describes planting the apple tree in the first stanza of this poem.

Student responses may vary.

14. **What thoughts about the apple tree were uppermost in Bryant's mind?**

Bryant thinks about the wonder of the apple from its beginning as a tiny sapling to its end as an old tree.

In the mind of the poet who wrote "Apple Blossoms," on page 56?

This poet describes only the beauty and magic of the apple blossom.

15. The last paragraph on page 338 mentions the kind of "adventures" that made Bryant's life full of interest. Was the poet's experience in planting an apple tree one of these adventures?

As indicated in the paragraph, Bryant's poetry describes the magic and adventures he has experienced in nature. Undoubtedly, Bryant considered the planting of an apple tree an adventure.

How does this kind of adventure differ from the adventures that made the life of Roosevelt thrilling?

Students will find a brief biography of Roosevelt on page 32 of the reader. Roosevelt found adventure in nature, as did Bryant. However, Roosevelt's adventures focused on Western life and the magic of the animal world, including his ranch experiences and hunts for wild game, while Bryant found adventure in the changing seasons.

16. Find in the glossary the meaning of: mold, betrays, fraud, wasting, quaint.

17. Pronounce: hearth, sojourners.

Extended Activity:

Have students create a strip consisting of eight panels—one panel for each stanza. Beginning with panel one, illustrate each stanza in order, ending with panel eight and stanza eight. Their artwork should reflect the visual image that Bryant describes.

Students should use the plan below to construct their panels. Using the front and the back will provide eight panels.

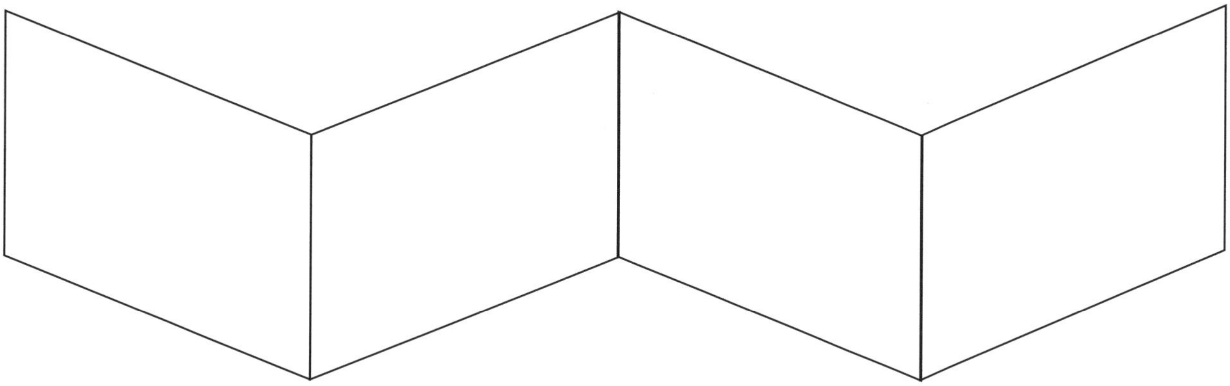

See "More Extended Activities" at the end of Bryant's poetry for further study.

NAME______________________________ CLASS__________ DATE______

THE PLANTING OF THE APPLE TREE, P. 340

Create a strip consisting of eight panels—one panel for each stanza. Beginning with panel one, illustrate each stanza in order, ending with panel eight and stanza eight. Your artwork should reflect the visual image that Bryant describes.

Use the plan below to construct your panels. Using the front and the back will provide eight panels.

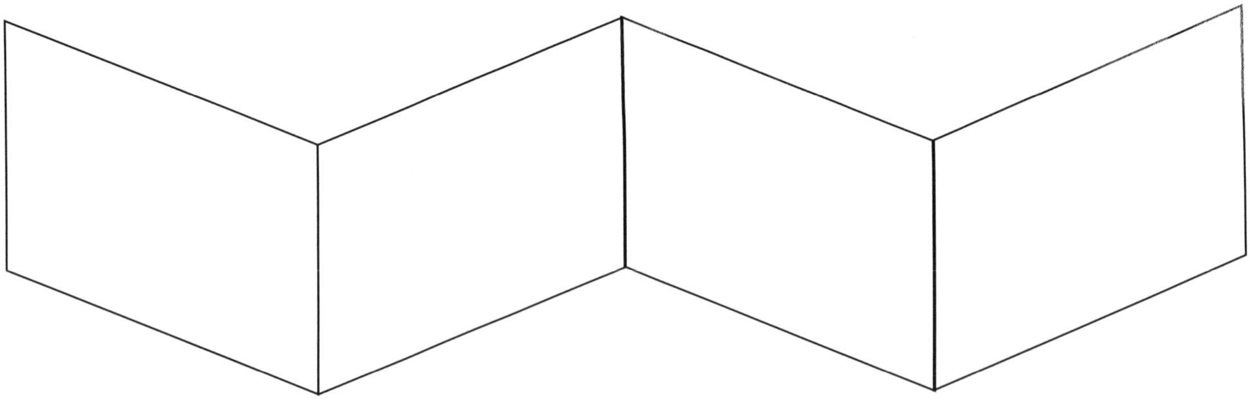

The Death of the Flowers, p. 344

1. **To what season does the poet refer in the opening stanza?**
   The poet refers to the season of autumn.
2. **Why does he call it "the saddest of the year"?**
   The winds wail, the woods are bare, the meadows are brown and dry, the leaves are dead, and the birds have flown south.
3. **What does Bryant say makes the leaves "rustle" at this time of year?**
   "The eddying gust" and "the rabbit's tread" make the leaves rustle.
4. **What is an "eddying gust"?**
   The glossary defines an eddying gust as a "sudden wind that blows back and forth."
5. **What is meant by "a beauteous sisterhood"?**
   The "beauteous sisterhood" refers to "the flowers, the fair young flowers, that, lately sprang and stood In brighter light and softer airs."
6. **What spring flowers does the poet name?**
   The spring flowers are the windflower, the violet, the brier rose and the orchis that died in summer's heat.
   What fall flowers?
   The fall flowers are the goldenrod, the aster, and the yellow sunflower.
7. **What comparison is made in the third stanza?**
   The poet compares the "frost from the clear cold heaven" to a plague that falls on men, destroying "the brightness of their smile."
8. **Which line contains the best description of autumn?**
   The poem makes many references to autumn from its "melancholy days" to the flowers "in autumn beauty." Students will have varying answers.
9. **How does your feeling of autumn compare with Bryant's?**
   Responses will vary.
10. **Are the brooks and the wind and the rain really sad in autumn, or is it the poet's fancy that makes them seem so?**

A fancy is an image or representation of something formed in the reader's mind. The poet forms an image of sadness using the figurative language of personification, giving human actions or feelings to nonhuman objects, to help the reader fancy or imagine that the these things are sad.

Do these same things seem sad in "March," page 339?

No, the poet in "March" describes these things with positive terms. He refers to them as "gushing rills," "changed winds" which he describes as "soft and warm," and "sunny showers."

11. Find in the glossary the meaning of: sear, sprang, glade, glen.

12. Pronounce: orchis, upland.

Extended Activity:

In question ten, students should recognize that the poet uses personification to describe the brooks, wind and rain. Have them find other examples of personification in this poem. Possible answers include: melancholy days, wailing winds, naked trees, flowers are lying in their beds, November rain does not call them back out of the earth, bright smiles of flowers, the day calls to the squirrels and bees, the south wind searches for flowers and sighs to find them gone.

NAME________________________________CLASS__________DATE______

THE DEATH OF THE FLOWERS, p. 344

In question ten, you should recognize that the poet uses personification to describe the brooks, wind, and rain. Find other examples of personification in this poem.

GREAT AMERICAN AUTHORS—*WILLIAM CULLEN BRYANT,* PP. 337-345

More Extended Exercises

1. Have students choose one of Bryant's poems and identify its rhyme scheme.

"March"

ABAB CDCD, EFEF GHGH IJIJ KLKL MNMN.

"The Planting of the Apple Tree"

ABBCCADDA AEEFFAGGA AHHIIAJJA AKKLLAMMA ANNOOAPPA AQQRRASSA ATTUUAVVA AWWXXAYYA.

"The Death of the Flowers"

AABBCC DDEEFF GGHHII JJKKLL.

2. Have students read the biographies of Franklin (page 327) and Bryant (page 337). From the information they find, have them complete the Venn Diagram comparing and contrasting the lives of these two very famous men.

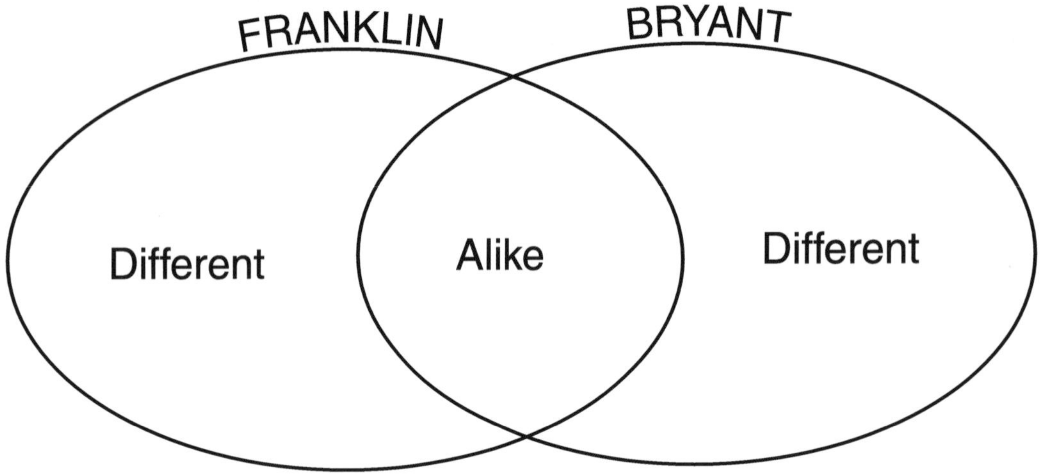

NAME________________________________CLASS__________DATE______

GREAT AMERICAN AUTHORS—*WILLIAM CULLEN BRYANT,* PP. 337-345

1. Choose one of Bryant's poems and identify its rhyme scheme.

"March"

____

____

"The Planting of the Apple Tree"

____

____

"The Death of the Flowers"

____

____

2. Read the biographies of Franklin (page 327) and Bryant (page 337). From the information you find, complete the Venn Diagram comparing and contrasting the lives of these two very famous men.

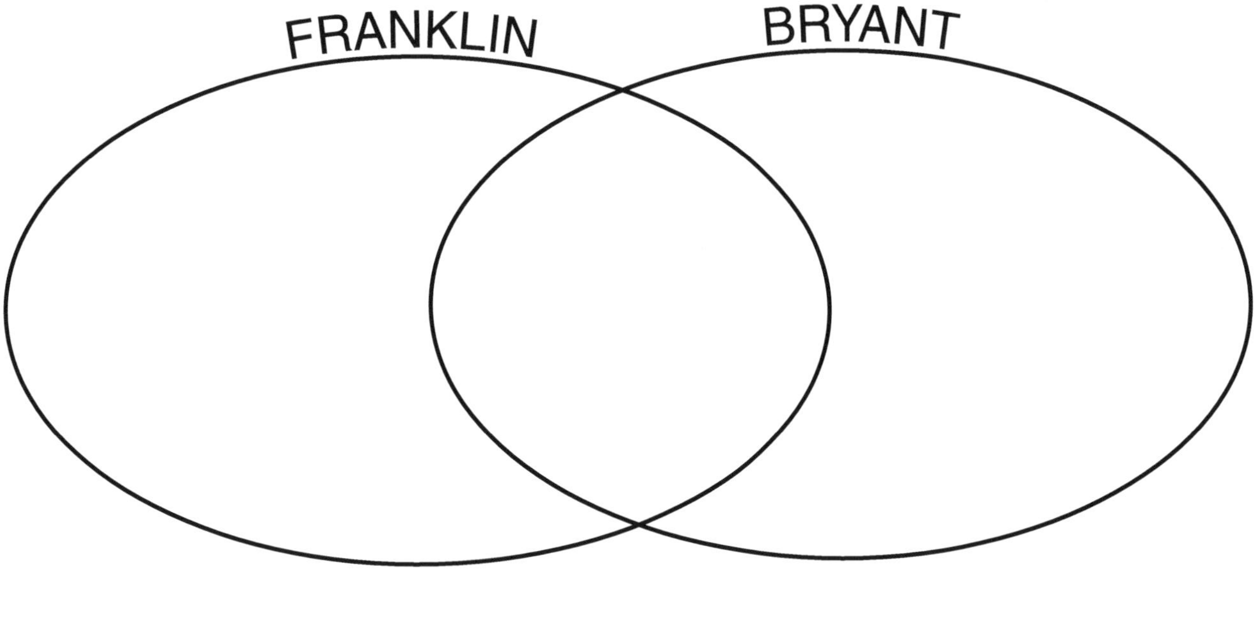

HENRY WADSWORTH LONGFELLOW—

The Village Blacksmith, p. 348

1. **What picture does the poet give you of the smith?**
The poet describes the smith as "a mighty man" who has "large and sinewy hands; and the muscles of his brawny arms Are strong as iron bands. His hair is crisp, and black, and long; His face is like the tan; His brow is wet with honest sweat; He earns whate'er he can."
2. **What is the result of the smith's owing nobody?**
Because he owes no man anything, he "looks the whole world in the face."
3. **What habits of the blacksmith does this stanza tell about you about?**
The blacksmith is a hard worker; "Week in, week out, from morn till night" he is always on the job. Then on Sunday he goes to church "and sits among his boys; He hears the parson pray and preach; He hears his daughter's voice Singing in the village choir, And it makes his heart rejoice."
4. **What "lesson" has the blacksmith taught?**
The blacksmith has taught the lesson of tenacity in the face of difficulty. "Toiling-rejoicing-sorrowing, Onward through life he goes." He begins a task in the morning and sees it through to completion, earning a good night of rest.
5. **What is compared with "the flaming forge"?**
"The flaming forge" is a metaphor of life—at the forge and in life we work out our "fortunes."
With "the sounding anvil"?
"The sounding anvil" is another metaphor of life—on the anvil and in life "each burning deed and thought" shapes and forms us.
6. **Which lines make an appropriate motto for all workers.**
Stanza seven is an appropriate model.

    Toiling-rejoicing-sorrowing,
    Onward through life he goes;
    Each morning sees some task begun;
    Each evening sees it close;

Something attempted, something done,
Has earned a night's repose.

7. **Find in the glossary the meaning of: smithy, brawny, crisp, tan, bellows, sledge, sexton, chaff, threshing.**
8. **Pronounce: sinewy, wrought.**

Extended Activity:

In the "Historical Note" students read about the fate of the "spreading chestnut tree" which resulted in the poem "From My Armchair." Have students locate the poem and compare it with "The Village Blacksmith," particularly noting his descriptions of the tree and the blacksmith in these two works.

("From My Armchair" can be located on the Internet at www.everypoet.com/archive/poetry/Henry_Wadsworth_Longfellow It is listed with Longfellow's complete poetical works under the title "Ultima Thule.")

Name______________________________**Class**__________**Date**______

The Village Blacksmith, p. 348

In the "Historical Note" you read about the fate of the "spreading chestnut tree" which resulted in the poem "From My Armchair." Locate the poem and compare it with "The Village Blacksmith," particularly noting his descriptions of the tree and the blacksmith in these two works.

The Old Clock on the Stairs, p. 350

1. **What picture do you have after reading the first stanza?**
   The poet describes a large tree-shaded country house in which a clock hangs and ticks away the hours.
2. **What do "old-fashioned" and "antique" add to your picture?**
   The "old-fashioned countryseat," the "antique portico," and the "ancient timepiece" give the reader the image of a house which has been on the "village street" a very long time.
3. **What picture of the clock do the first two stanzas give you?**
   The clock, which stands "halfway up the stairs," is referred to as "an ancient timepiece" in a "case of massive oak" that continually whispers to all who pass "Forever-never! Never-forever."
4. **Read the lines illustrated by the picture on page 346 (page 212 in *Teacher's Guide*).**
   "There groups of merry children played; There youths and maidens dreaming strayed."
5. **Why does Longfellow call this an "ancient" timepiece?**
   It is "ancient" because it has been there so long. "Through days of sorrow and of mirth, Through days of death and days of birth, Through every swift vicissitude Of changeful time, unchanged it has stood."
6. **What name is applied to this kind of clock?**
   It is frequently referred to as a grandfather clock.
7. **In what way does he say this clock is like a monk?**
   The poet says the clock in its oak case is like "a monk, who, under his cloak, Crosses himself, and sighs, alas! With sorrowful voice to all who pass: 'Forever-never! Never-forever!'"
8. **Why does the clock's voice seem low by day and loud at night?**
   During the day other noises drown out the clock's voice, but "in the silent dead of night" the clock "echoes along the vacant hall."
9. **With what does the poet compare the clock's voice at night?**
   It's voice is as "Distinct as a passing footstep's fall."

10. What habit of the clock does Longfellow mention in the fourth stanza?

Though time brings sorrow, mirth, death, birth, and change, the clock never changes. "And as if like God, it all things saw, It calmly repeats those words of awe: "Forever-never! Never-forever!"

11. Whose fire does he say once roared up the chimney?

The fire of "Free-hearted Hospitality" once roared up the chimney.

12. To what "precious hours" does he refer in the sixth stanza?

He refers to the "precious hours" when "There groups of merry children played; There youths and maidens dreaming strayed"

13. Find in the glossary the meaning of: portico, countryseat, station, massive, board, prime, shroud, incessantly.

14. Pronounce: vicissitude, affluence, horologe.

Extended Activity:

Just as in the "Historical Notes" under "The Village Blacksmith," so this poem's "Historical Notes" identifies another of Longfellow's poems titled "The Children's Hour." Have students locate the poem and find the names of Longfellow's three daughters mentioned in the notes. Their names are Alice, Allegra, and Edith.

This poem can be found in *The Elson Readers, Book 5*, page 323. (It can also be located at the Internet site: www.everypoet.com/archive/poetry/Henry_Wadsworth_Longfellow. The poem is listed under the heading titled "Birds of Passage.")

NAME____________________________**CLASS**__________**DATE**______

THE OLD CLOCK ON THE STAIRS, P. 350

Just as in the "Historical Notes" under "The Village Blacksmith," so this poem's "Historical Notes" identifies another of Longfellow's poems titled "The Children's Hour." Locate the poem and find the names of Longfellow's three daughters mentioned in the notes.

1. ____

2. ____

3. ____

A Psalm of Life, p. 354

1. **The poet says that life is not a dream, but a reality; quote the words that tell what the aim of life is.**
   "Not enjoyment and not sorrow Is our destined end or way; But to act that each tomorrow Find us farther than today."
2. **What do the lives of great men suggest to us?**
   "Lives of great men all remind us We can make our lives sublime, and departing, leave behind us Footprints in the sands of time." Just as we follow in the steps of great men that have lived before us, we can leave noble deeds behind us for those that follow our footsteps.
3. **What lines tell how our right living may be a help to others?**
   "Footprints, that perhaps another, Sailing o'er life's solemn main, A forlorn and shipwrecked brother Seeing, shall take heart again."
4. **What added meaning does *then* give to the last stanza?**
   It encourages the reader not to give up or quit but to "Let us, then, be up and doing, With a heart for any fate." Just as lives of great men before us challenged us, we should then pass it on to those behind us.
   What other word might be used instead of *then?*
   Encourage a variety of student responses. Some alternatives may include: therefore, so, consequently.
5. **Can you suggest another title to express the theme or thought of the poem?**
   Encourage the students to suggest another title based on the theme they perceive the poet is expressing.
6. **Compare the theme of this poem with that of the poem "Gradatim" (page 207).**
   Students are encouraged to read both poems and list the comparisons found in them. The theme in both poems reflects the concept that noble character and deeds are of great value, not only in this life but as examples for those who come after us.
7. **Commit to memory the seventh stanza.**
   "Lives of great men all remind us
   We can make our lives sublime,

And, departing, leave behind us
Footprints in the sands of time."

8. **Find in the glossary the meaning of: goal, destined, bivouac, sublime, main, achieving.**

Extended Activity

Have students identify someone whom they admire and respect. How has that person left footprints for others to follow? Have them complete the following web and write an essay on their hero's impact.

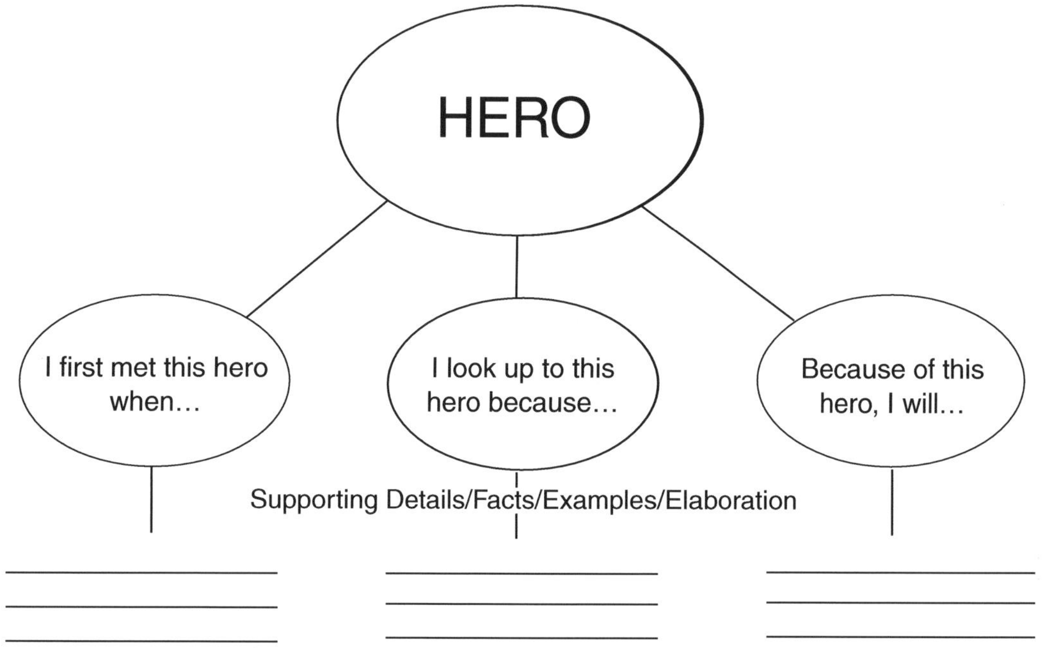

Have them edit their essay for correct spelling, punctuation, and grammar.

NAME________________________________ CLASS__________ DATE______

A PSALM OF LIFE, p. 354

Identify someone whom you admire and respect. How has that person left footprints for others to follow? Complete the following web and write an essay on your hero's impact. Edit your essay for correct spelling, punctuation, and grammar.

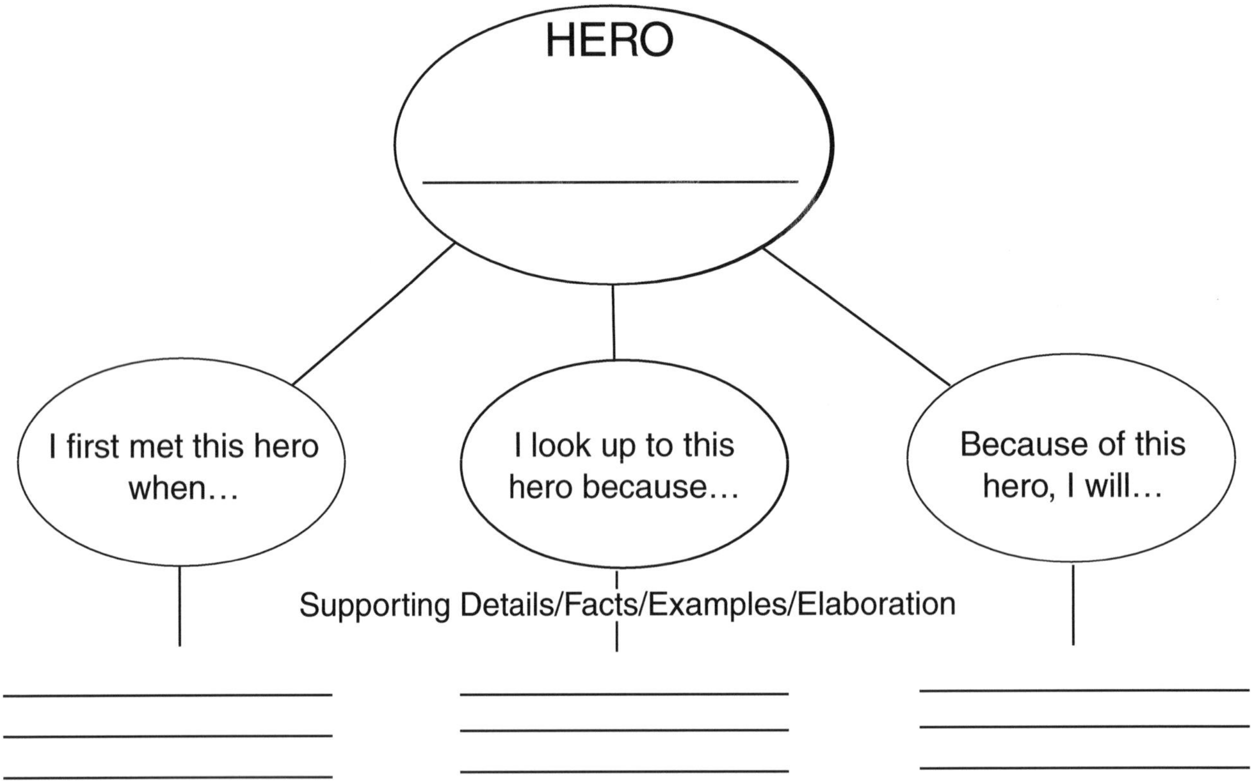

GREAT AMERICAN AUTHORS—*HENRY WADSWORTH LONGFELLOW*, PP. 346-355

More Extended Activities

1. Longfellow's poetry is rich in visual images and sensory details that capture the mind of the reader. One can hear, see, and feel the images he describes.

To reinforce these sensory details, have students choose one of Longfellow's works in this section. Have them prepare a presentation for the rest of the class that includes reading, sound effects, music, and a visual aid that portrays the main idea of the poem. To help them organize their presentation, have them complete the following organizer, writing down the specific lines, music titles, sound effects and aids they will use.

READING	Read lines that specifically describe the main idea.
SOUND EFFECTS	What sound effects would descibe the main idea, such as a ticking clock in "The Old Clock on the Stairs"?
MUSIC	Choose background music, with or without words, that best descibes the main idea.
VISUAL AID	How would you present the main idea in picture form?

2. Longfellow's poems are delightful to read because of their rhythm. In one of the extended activities under the section titled "Flowers," students learned that meter in poetry refers to the pattern of stressed and unstressed syllables that create the rhythm in the poem. Stressed or accented syllables are indicated with a '; unstressed or unaccented syllables are indicated with a ˘. To reinforce that concept, have students choose a poem from these selections, recopy the first stanza, then above each syllable mark a ' or a ˘ to indicate the meter of the poem.

NAME______________________________CLASS__________DATE______

GREAT AMERICAN AUTHORS—*HENRY WADSWORTH LONGFELLOW*, PP. 346-355

1. Longfellow's poetry is rich in visual images and sensory details that capture the mind of the reader. One can hear, see, and feel the images he describes.

   Choose one of Longfellow's works in this section. Prepare a presentation for the rest of the class that includes reading, sound effects, music, and a visual aid that portrays the main idea of the poem. To help organize your presentation, complete the following organizer, writing down the specific lines, music titles, sound effects and aids you will use.

READING	Read lines that specifically describe the main idea.
SOUND EFFECTS	What sound effects would descibe the main idea, such as a ticking clock in "The Old Clock on the Stairs"?
MUSIC	Choose background music, with or without words, that best descibes the main idea.
VISUAL AID	How would you present the main idea in picture form?

2. Longfellow's poems are delightful to read because of their rhythm. In one of the extended activities under the section titled "Flowers," you learned that meter in poetry refers to the pattern of stressed and unstressed syllables that create the rhythm in the poem. Stressed or accented syllables are indicated with a '; unstressed or unaccented syllables are indicated with a ˘.

To reinforce that concept, choose a poem from these selections, recopy the first stanza, then above each syllable mark a ' or a ˘ to indicate the meter of the poem.

NATHANIEL HAWTHORNE—

LITTLE DAFFYDOWNDILLY, P. 358

SUMMARY

Little Daffydowndilly was a young boy who had been sent away to school by his mother. Daffydowndilly thought the schoolmaster, Mr. Toil, was a cruel taskmaster and decided to run away where he would never see Mr. Toil again. No sooner had he begun his journey than he met a stranger who also confessed that he had a dislike for Mr. Toil, and together they continued on their way. In the course of their ramblings they met a variety of people with whom Daffydowndilly wanted to stay. However, every group had a leader who looked and acted exactly like Mr. Toil, and upon hearing from his companion that the leaders were Mr. Toil's brothers, Daffydowndilly kept walking, determined to stay away from anyone that had any connection to Mr. Toil. At last, in desperation, Daffydowndilly discovered that Mr. Toil was all over the world, in fact, was his traveling companion. He learned the lesson that diligence was a noble trait and decided to return to school and practice it.

1. **Why was Daffydowndilly so named?**
   He was named Daffydowndilly "because in his nature he resembled a flower, and loved to do only what was beautiful and agreeable and took no delight in labor of any kind."
2. **Do you think he disliked school because of the work or because of Mr. Toil?**
   Since he "took no delight in labor of any kind," he probably disliked school because of the work. But he also disliked Mr. Toil because of his stern demeanor and harsh demands.
3. **Which sentences tell you this?**
   "Nevertheless, Mr. Toil had a severe and ugly countenance, especially for such little boys or big men as were inclined to be idle; his voice, too, was harsh; and all his ways and customs seemed very disagreeable to our friend Daffydowndilly."
   "No wonder, therefore, that poor Daffydowndilly found it a woeful change, to be sent away from the good lady's side and put under the care of this ugly-visaged schoolmaster, who never gave him any apples or cakes, and seemed to think that little boys were created only to get lessons."
4. **What was his purpose in running away from school?**
   He ran away from school to find his mother and to "never find anybody half so disagreeable as this old Mr. Toil!"

5. **Who joined him?**
   He was joined by "a man of grave and sedate appearance, who was trudging at a moderate pace along the road."
6. **On their way they met several groups of workers; what happened in each case?**
   First they passed a field where haymakers were at work. Daffydowndilly thought it would be wonderful to work all day in the sunshine and blue sky surrounded by singing birds. Then he noticed the owner of the field who looked and acted exactly like Mr. Toil, and he grabbed his companion's hand and ran from the field in fright. The companion told him the owner was Mr. Toil's brother who was "more disagreeable" than Mr. Toil. Next Daffydowndilly and his companion came upon some carpenters building a house, and Daffydowndilly thought how wonderful it would be to build his own little house where Mr. Toil could never bother him. Then he noticed the man in charge of the carpenters who, again, looked exactly like Mr. Toil. Daffydowndilly grabbed his companion's hand and ran in fear. He was told again that this was another of Mr. Toil's brothers. Soon they ran into a company of soldiers and Daffydowndilly thought he would gladly follow them to war in their bright clothes with feathered caps and shining muskets. Then he heard the voice of the captain of the company and ran in fear once more, for the captain looked exactly like Mr. Toil. Again his companion assured him that the captain was a brother to Mr. Toil. The two continued on their journey and met a group of smiling people dancing to a fiddle. Daffydowndilly was sure this would be the place to stay, until he noticed the fiddler who looked just like Mr. Toil. To him it seemed "as if there was nobody but Mr. Toil in the world!" His companion informed him that the fiddler was another brother, "more disagreeable than his brothers." So they walked on along highways and through villages, and Mr. Toil seemed to be everywhere—standing like a scarecrow in a cornfield and sitting in parlors and kitchens from cottages to mansions. The companion told Daffydowndilly that these were all Mr. Toil's brothers. They came at last to a shady place where Daffydowndilly begged to sit down and rest. There he saw yet one more person, "the laziest and heaviest, and most torpid" of all the people at rest under the shade. Alas!

Another brother of Mr. Toil's! At seeing this, Daffydowndilly burst into tears and begged to be taken back to school, so his companion agreed to take him back. It was then that he recognized his companion's voice—the voice of Mr. Toil who had traveled with him all day.

7. **What conclusion did Daffydowndilly finally draw?**
He concluded that if Toil was everywhere, he may as well return to school.

8. **Find the lines that tell you.**
"If there is nothing but Toil all the world over, I may just as well go back to the schoolhouse!"

9. **Why should everyone do his part of the world's work?**
The world can only work when everyone does their part. Encourage students to explore reasons why we should all do our part.

10. **Why should we learn to enjoy work?**
Student responses will vary. Encourage a class discussion of the value of enjoyable work.

11. **What was Hawthorne's purpose in writing this story?**
Hawthorne wanted to entertain his readers with a humorous story about work, but more importantly, he wanted to impress upon his readers the importance of work. As Daffydowndilly learned, "diligence is not a whit more toilsome than sport or idleness."

12. **Which of all the experiences that Daffydowndilly had in his walk with the stranger surprised him most?**
Student responses may vary, but likely the biggest surprise was when Daffydowndilly discovered that he had been walking with Mr. Toil all day, even as he was trying to run away from him.

13. **Who are more easily tired, persons like Monsieur le Plaisir who constantly seek pleasure, or persons who enjoy their everyday life and tasks?**
Encourage students to discuss these contrasts and support their conclusions based on Hawthorne's moral that "diligence is not a whit more toilsome than sport or idleness."

14. **Whom do you know that finds pleasure in doing work that seems to you uninteresting and tedious?**
Answers will vary.

15. **Find the lines illustrated by the picture to the left of Hawthorne's portrait on page 356 (p. 224 in this *Guide*).**

The lines illustrated by the picture are on page 360, beginning at line 12. "They had not gone far, when the road passed by a field where some haymakers were at work, mowing down the tall grass and spreading it out in the sun to dry."

16. Read aloud in class the best descriptions of Mr. Toil.

The best descriptions of Mr. Toil can be found on page 358, lines 14-26, beginning with: "Nevertheless, Mr. Toil had a severe and ugly countenance, especially for such little boys or big men as were inclined to be idle; his voice, too, was harsh; and all his ways and customs seemed very disagreeable to our friend Daffydowndilly…" An additional description can be found on page 359, line 3-8: "No wonder, therefore, that poor Daffydowndilly found it a woeful change, to be sent away from the good lady's side and put under the care of this ugly-visaged schoolmaster, who never gave him any apples or cakes, and seemed to think that little boys were created only to get lessons." Students should be encouraged to draw from other passages that describe Mr. Toil's brothers who looked and acted like him.

17. Tell the story of Daffydowndilly's various encounters.

See the summary in response to question number six.

18. Find in the glossary the meaning of: resembled, affirmed, hitherto, indulgent, ugly-visaged, trudging, sociable, precisely, erecting, clapboards, molest, compasses, exhorting, diligent, besought, composedly, flourishing, innumerable, entreated, torpid, whit.

19. Pronounce: countenance, quoth, epaulets, Monsieur le Plaisir, Signor Far Niente, approbation.

Extended Activity:

It is suggested that this story be read silently. Check student comprehension of silent reading with these true/false questions.

F. 1. When Daffydowndilly's mother took him to school, he was a diligent, hard working student.

T. 2. Daffydowndilly was known for telling the truth.

F. 3. Daffydowndilly ran away from school with plenty of supplies in his pocket for the journey.

F. 4. Daffydowndilly's journey took him far from the school.

F. 5. When Daffydowndilly ran away from school, he left Mr. Toil behind in the classroom.

T. 6. The family of Toils had been around since the beginning of time.

F. 7. Mr. Toil's only brothers included a farmer, a carpenter, a captain, a fiddler, and an idler.

F. 8. Monsieur le Plaisir was proud to belong to the family of Toils.

T. 9. Signor Far Niente was the laziest of the Toil brothers.

T. 10. After his journey, Daffydowndilly developed good study habits.

NAME______________________________CLASS__________DATE______

LITTLE DAFFYDOWNDILLY, P. 358

For a reading check, circle true or false to the following statements:

True False 1. When Daffydowndilly's mother took him to school, he was a diligent, hard working student.

True False 2. Daffydowndilly was known for telling the truth.

True False 3. Daffydowndilly ran away from school with plenty of supplies in his pocket for the journey.

True False 4. Daffydowndilly's journey took him far from the school.

True False 5. When Daffydowndilly ran away from school, he left Mr. Toil behind in the classroom.

True False 6. The family of Toils had been around since the beginning of time.

True False 7. Mr. Toil's only brothers included a farmer, a carpenter, a captain, a fiddler, and an idler.

True False 8. Monsieur le Plaisir was proud to belong to the family of Toils.

True False 9. Signor Far Niente was the laziest of the Toil brothers.

True False 10. After his journey, Daffydowndilly developed good study habits.

Mr. Higginbotham's Catastrophe, p. 367

SUMMARY

Mr. Higginbotham's Catastrophe is a tale of gossip run amok. A peddler met a stranger on the road who told him that Mr. Higginbotham had been murdered. The peddler repeated the story, adding details as he went, at every stop he made. Along the way he met fellow travelers who either denied the story or contributed to it, so that the catastrophe became a confusion of times, dates, location, and details. The peddler finally solved the mystery when he accosted the murderer in the act of murdering Mr. Higginbotham. The peddler, responsible for the rumors, became the hero in the end.

1. Tell in your own words the story of Mr. Higginbotham's catastrophe, using the following topics:

a. the peddler meets the traveler;

The peddler, Dominicus Pike, traveled from village to village trading tobacco. He was known for his good character and inquisitive nature. One morning he met a traveler from whom the peddler asked the latest news. Sullen and shifty, the traveler whispered that Mr. Higginbotham had been hanged last night at eight o'clock in his orchard by an Irishman and a Negro. No one would find him till morning. With that, the traveler scurried off, and the peddler was left to imagine the details of the story.

b. the peddler retells the sensational news;

At the peddler's evening stop, he retold the story to his fellow travelers, adding details of his own so that the telling took him half an hour. However, a farmer in the group contradicted the peddler's story by saying that he had personally drunk bitters with Mr. Higginbotham that very morning, and Mr. Higginbotham knew nothing of his own murder. In disgrace, the peddler retired for the night, dreaming of being hanged. However, on his journey the next morning, the peddler encountered another traveler, a Negro, who at the peddler's questioning, told him that Mr. Higginbotham had been hanged the night before, and his death would not yet be discovered. Leaving the peddler in great confusion, the traveler hurried on.

c. the excitement at Parker's Falls;

When the peddler arrived in Parker's Falls, he set the town in an uproar with his story of Mr. Higginbotham's murder.

While they were milling in the street with the news, the mail stage drove into town. They mobbed the coach asking for news of the murder, only to learn from the lawyer who had arrived in the stage that he had personally spoken with Mr. Higginbotham the evening before, and had the murder occurred, the lawyer would certainly have heard it when he passed through Mr. Higginbotham's town that morning. In addition, the lady on the stage, Mr. Higginbotham's niece, confirmed that she had spoken to Mr. Higginbotham that very morning before leaving on the stage, so the story could not possibly be true. The peddler was driven from the town in disgrace, meditating on Mr. Higginbotham's niece who seemed to him an angel.

d. the peddler solves the mystery.

The peddler determined to visit Kimballton, Mr. Higginbotham's town, to see for himself whether Mr. Higginbotham was still alive. Passing through the toll booth, he inquired of the toll man if he had seen Mr. Higginbotham recently. The toll man assured him that he had seen Mr. Higginbotham, that he was, in fact, riding right ahead of the peddler in the dusk. The peddler shook the reins of his horse and headed for Kimballton. When he arrived, he drove to Mr. Higginbotham's gate to see for sure that he was not hanging in his orchard. The peddler noticed movement in the orchard, rushed forward, whipped an Irishman he found there, and discovered Mr. Higginbotham under the tree with a noose around his neck. The mystery was solved when the peddler realized three men had plotted the death of Mr. Higginbotham, the two travelers he'd met on the road who had chickened out but told it as fact, and this one whom he'd caught in the act. The peddler became a hero, was given Mr. Higginbotham's niece in marriage and received his wealth when he died.

2. **Read again the first chapter of the story and list all the suggestions made by the author to increase the reader's suspicion that the traveler is one of the three men who plotted the murder.**

"Dominicus noticed that he carried a bundle over his shoulder on the end of a stick and traveled with a weary, yet determined, pace. He did not look as if he had started in the morning, but as if he had footed it all night and meant to do the same all day." "The man pulled the broad brim of a gray hat over his eyes and answered, rather sullenly, that he did not come from Parker's Falls." "The traveler—an ill-looking fellow—appeared to hesitate a little." "As soon as this horrible intelligence was communicated, the stranger betook himself to his journey again, with more speed than ever, not even turning his head when Dominicus invited him to smoke a cigar and relate all the particulars." "The stranger on foot must have worn seven-league boots to travel at such a rate."

3. **Point out suggestions that make you think the Negro whom the peddler met was also one of the three plotters.**

"On hearing this sudden question, the Ethiopian appeared to change his skin, its yellow hue becoming a ghastly white, while, shaking and stammering, he thus replied..." "Scarcely had the yellow man spoken, when he interrupted himself, and though he seemed weary enough before, continued his journey at a pace which would have kept the peddler's mare on a smart trot...If Mr. Higginbotham's corpse were not yet discovered by his own family, how came the mulatto, at about thirty miles distance, to know that he was hanging in the orchard, especially as he had left Kimballton before the unfortunate man was hanged at all?"

4. **At what point in your reading of this story did you connect the traveler or the Negro with the plot to hang Mr. Higginbotham?**

Answers will vary.

5. **What reason can you give for the travelers telling the sensational news?**

They wanted to throw suspicion off of themselves by suggesting others had murdered Mr. Higginbotham.

6. **At what point in the story was your interest the greatest?**

Answers will vary.

7. **Select passages to read aloud in class.**

8. **Find in the glossary the meaning of: (I) depicted, communicated, pondering, perpetrated, manifested; (II) gospel; (III) population, narrative, shifted, rumbled, excessive; (IV) hoax, equivalent, instinct, solitary.**

9. Pronounce: (I) catastrophe, narrator, occurrence; (II) mentioned, perplexity, meditations, hostler, originated, pathos; (III) edition, apprehended, signature, supplicate, ablution; (IV) autograph, discern, emergency, champion.

Extended Activity:

It is suggested that this story be read silently. Check student comprehension of silent reading with these true/false questions.

T. 1. The peddler is described as young, curious, talkative, and having good character.

F. 2. The two travelers with bundles over their shoulders were eager to share their stories of Mr. Higginbotham's murder with the peddler.

F. 3. Mr. Higginbotham lived in Parker's Falls.

T. 4. The first news of Mr. Higginbotham's murder traveled faster than railroads.

T. 5. A neighbor, a lawyer, and a lady had all spoken with Mr. Higginbotham after his supposed murder.

T. 6. The first thing the peddler did when he arrived at Parker's Falls was to feed his horse.

T. 7. The people of Parker's Falls were angry when they heard that Mr. Higginbotham was not murdered.

F. 8. The lawyer read from his notebook that Mr. Higginbotham had been robbed of $1000.

F. 9. Mr. Higginbotham's niece worked in his cotton factory for a living.

F. 10. When the peddler arrived in the orchard he found Mr. Higginbotham hanging from St. Michael's pear tree just as he had been told.

Name______________________________Class__________Date______

Mr. Higginbotham's Catastrophe, p. 367

For a reading check, circle true or false to the following statements:

True False 1. The peddler is described as young, curious, talkative, and having good character.

True False 2. The two travelers with bundles over their shoulders were eager to share their stories of Mr. Higginbotham's murder with the peddler.

True False 3. Mr. Higginbotham lived in Parker's Falls.

True False 4. The first news of Mr. Higginbotham's murder traveled faster than railroads.

True False 5. A neighbor, a lawyer, and a lady had all spoken with Mr. Higginbotham after his supposed murder.

True False 6. The first thing the peddler did when he arrived at Parker's Falls was to feed his horse.

True False 7. The people of Parker's Falls were angry when they heard that Mr. Higginbotham was not murdered.

True False 8. The lawyer read from his notebook that Mr. Higginbotham had been robbed of $1000.

True False 9. Mr. Higginbotham's niece worked in his cotton factory for a living.

True False 10. When the peddler arrived in the orchard he found Mr. Higginbotham hanging from St. Michael's pear tree just as he had been told.

THE THREE GOLDEN APPLES, P. 379

SUMMARY

The story of The Three Golden Apples tells of the exploits of Hercules, a mythical Greek hero, who conquered impossible odds to retrieve three golden apples for the king. He encountered numerous dangers, killing terrible beasts, and holding up the sky in his efforts to get the apples as he was directed. But he, alone of all the young men who attempted the feat, returned at last with his apples.

1. **Tell the story of Hercules and the Golden Apples, following this outline:**

a. Hercules seeks the garden of the Hesperides;

The garden of the Hesperides was renowned for growing golden apples. Countless adventurous young men had gone in search of the apples but returned empty-handed, if they came back at all, because it was rumored that the garden was guarded by a dragon with one hundred heads: fifty heads stood guard while the other fifty slept. Hercules, a kind, generous, noble but fierce young man, set out to reach the garden and claim the apples, clothed in the skins of a fierce lion that he had killed and carrying an enormous club.

b. the flower maidens;

On his way to the garden, Hercules came to a river bank where he encountered the beautiful young flower maidens twining flowers into wreaths. When he asked them for directions to the garden of Hesperides, the maidens were shocked that anyone would want to go there. Recalling the dragon that guarded the garden, they begged him to return to his home, but he refused their pleas. Instead he told them stories of his conquests—the death of two huge serpents, an enormous lion, a hydra, a stag, and people that were half-human and half-horse. In addition, he related his exploits of cleaning a stable with rivers, shooting enormous birds, catching a wild bull, taming wild horses, conquering Hippolyta, queen of the Amazons, and giving her girdle to the king's daughter. Last he told them of his fight with Geryon, the six-legged man. After hearing of his victories, the flower maidens crowned him with flower wreaths and sent him on his way with directions to the Old Man of the

Sea who could show him the way to Hesperides.

c. the Old Man of the Sea;

As Hercules left the flower maidens, they cautioned him to hold fast to the Old Man of the Sea when he found him. Hercules left, swinging his huge club, knocking down a giant oak in his path. At last he came to the sea where he found the Old Man of the Sea asleep. His arms were covered with scales, and he had webbed feet and fingers and a long beard. Hercules crept up and grabbed the Old Man by an arm and a leg. Awaking in fright, the Old Man fought desperately to escape Hercules' grasp to no avail. He changed his appearance to become in turn a stag, a seabird, a three-headed dog, the six-legged Geryon, and a huge snake, hoping to force Hercules to let him go. But the Old Man gave up at last and returned to his original form, begging Hercules to release him. Upon hearing that it was Hercules he was facing, the Old Man gave him directions to the garden of Hesperides and sent him on his way.

d. the giant Antaeus;

As he traveled toward his final destination, Hercules met the giant Antaeus, a powerful giant who became ten times stronger every time he touched the earth. Hercules attempted to conquer Antaeus with his club, but every time he knocked him down, Antaeus rose ten times stronger, so the only way Hercules finally ended the battle was to pick up the giant and squeeze the strength out of him. As he continued his journey, Hercules walked through Egypt where he was taken prisoner and had to kill the king of the country in order to escape. Traveling on through Africa he came at last to the shore of the ocean where it seemed his journey must end.

e. the golden cup and the mighty Atlas;

As he stood on the shore of the ocean, Hercules saw in the distance a large, golden object that seemed to be heading toward him. As it approached he saw it was an enormous cup of gold, sent to carry him across the ocean. He climbed inside, spread out his lion's skin and settled down for a nap while the giant cup carried him softly across the sea to an island. When he landed, he saw an enormous giant with eyes the size of lakes and a nose and mouth a mile long. It was the mighty Atlas, the giant who held up the sky. When Hercules explained to Atlas that he wanted to know how to get to Hesperides, Atlas invited him to take his place holding up the sky and he would go and retrieve the apples for Hercules. Hercules agreed and shifted the sky to his own shoulders, settling in to wait for Atlas's return with the golden apples.

f. the ending.

Elated with his freedom, Atlas shook off the forest trees that had grown around his feet, dancing and laughing as he stepped into the water on his way to Hesperides. Hercules, trying hard to hold the sky steady, tried not to worry about what calamities might occur if he shook the sky even a little bit. At long last, he saw Atlas on the horizon returning from Hesperides with three golden apples the size of pumpkins. Eager to be on his way with the apples, Hesperides asked Atlas to take back the sky, to which Atlas replied that he could carry the apples to the king much faster than Hercules could. But Hercules grew impatient with him and shrugged his shoulders which caused some stars to fall from the sky. Atlas laughed and declared that he had not lost so many stars in five centuries of holding up the sky. He accused Hercules of being impatient and needing more practice at holding up the sky. Hercules agreed if only Atlas would take the sky for just a moment while Hercules shifted his lion's skin for more comfort. When Atlas took back the sky, Hercules grabbed the apples and ran with Atlas bellowing after him to come back. And to this day, the giant Atlas, or a mountain named after him, holds up the sky with forests growing around his feet.

2. **Which incident of the story interested you most?**

Answers will vary.

3. **What incidents of his life did Hercules narrate to the flower maidens?**

See question number one, letter b.

4. **Find all the different names the author uses in speaking of the flower maidens.**

The author used the following names: beautiful young women, damsels, maidens, young maidens, fair auditors, sisters, fair young girls.

5. **Which of the exploits of Hercules seems to you most wonderful?**

Answers will vary.

6. **What made Antaeus so strong?**
   He was "so wondrously contrived by nature that every time he touched the earth he became ten times as strong as he had ever been before."
7. **How did Hercules overcome the giant?**
   He lifted "Antaeus off his feet into the air, and squeezing and squeezing and squeezing him until finally the strength was quite squeezed out of his enormous body."
8. **What do you learn of the beauty of the garden of Hesperides?**
   When Atlas returned from his visit to the garden, he told Hercules, "Very fair apples they are. I took the finest that grew on the tree, I assure you. Ah, it is a beautiful spot, that garden of Hesperides! Yes, and the dragon with a hundred heads is a sight worth any man's seeing. After all, you had better gone for the apples yourself."
9. **Read aloud in class: the story of Hercules's adventures, page 382, line 17, to page 384, line 33; the encounter with the Old One, page 388, line 15, to page 390, line 29; the description of Atlas, page 393, line 21, to page 394, line 20.**
10. **Find in the glossary the meaning of: (I) graft; (II) pastime, heroic, remonstrances, intervals, auditors, valiant, ponderous, illustrious; (III) impressive, riven, verdant, figurehead, uncivil; (IV) prodigious, contrived, lustrous, immeasurably, circumference, reverberated; (V) intolerably, disconsolate, sustain, obscurity, intelligibly; (VI) immersed, wistfully, ajar.**
11. **Pronounce: (I) Hesperides; (II) destiny, stripling, hydra, exploit, gigantic, choral; (III) hospitable, minutely; (IV) Antaeus, horizon, tumultuous; (V) pother, incalculable; (VI) aerial, firmament, fissure, posterity, variety.**

Extended Activity:

It is suggested that this story be read silently. Check student comprehension of silent reading with these true/false questions.

F. 1. Hercules wanted the golden apples in the garden of Hesperides because they were "sweet, mellow, and juicy."

F. 2. Hercules wanted the apples to give to his father, the king.

T. 3. The flower girls did not want the sword belt of Mars.

F. 4. The Old Man of the Sea told Hercules exactly where to find the garden of Hesperides.

F. 5. Hercules used his club to beat the strength out of Antaeus.

F. 6. A church bell woke Hercules when he arrived on the island of Atlas.

T. 7. The author compares the sky to cares of the earth.

T. 8. Atlas was the only person on earth who could get to the garden of Hesperides.

T. 9. Hercules would rather hold up the sky than to slay a dragon with one hundred heads.

T. 10. Holding up the sky gave mighty Atlas a backache.

NAME______________________________CLASS__________DATE______

THE THREE GOLDEN APPLES, P. 379

For a reading check, circle true or false to the following statements:

True False 1. Hercules wanted the golden apples in the garden of Hesperides because they were "sweet, mellow, and juicy."

True False 2. Hercules wanted the apples to give to his father, the king.

True False 3. The flower girls did not want the sword belt of Mars.

True False 4. The Old Man of the Sea told Hercules exactly where to find the garden of Hesperides.

True False 5. Hercules used his club to beat the strength out of Antaeus.

True False 6. A church bell woke Hercules when he arrived on the island of Atlas.

True False 7. The author compares the sky to cares of the earth.

True False 8. Atlas was the only person on earth who could get to the garden of Hesperides.

True False 9. Hercules would rather hold up the sky than to slay a dragon with one hundred heads.

True False 10. Holding up the sky gave mighty Atlas a backache.

GREAT AMERICAN AUTHORS—*NATHANIEL HAWTHORNE*, PP. 356-401

More Extended Activities

The following activities can be adapted to use with any of Hawthorne's stories.

1. Plot tells the events as they occur in the story. It follows the design of a pyramid and usually consists of four main parts: a. the exposition explains the background and setting of the story including any of the following: who, what, where, when; b. the rising action includes events that lead to the climax; c. the climax is the turning point, the height of the action, the highest part of the pyramid from which we can begin to predict accurately the end of the story; and d. the resolution is the satisfying end of the story when the problems are all solved. Apply any of the stories to the pyramid diagram.

"Little Daffydowndilly"

Exposition: Daffydowndilly, a lazy school boy; Mr. Toil, his harsh schoolmaster; the traveling companion with whom Daffydowndilly ran away from Mr. Toil.

Rising action: Daffydowndilly and his companion meet many groups of people all controlled by Mr. Toil's brothers; students should list several of the groups (See question number six, p. 225).

Climax: Daffydowndilly discovers his companion is Mr. Toil.

Resolution: Daffydowndilly returns to the classroom and becomes a diligent student.

"Mr. Higginbotham's Catastrophe"

Exposition: the peddler who travels from town to town trading goods and gossip; Mr. Higginbotham, the man who is known to be murdered.

Rising action: the peddler meets strangers who tell him of the murder, as well as people who deny the murder, and confusion reigns.

Climax: the peddler meets Mr. Higginbotham in the orchard.

Resolution: the peddler becomes a hero for saving Mr. Higginbotham from being murdered.

"The Three Golden Apples"

Exposition: Hercules, the hero who goes in search of the garden of Hesperides to find the golden apples.

Rising action: Hercules meets obstacles on his way to the garden of Hesperides.

Climax: Atlas's return from the garden.

Resolution: Hercules gets the apples at last and escapes to the king.

2. Asking questions as they read helps students to understand the characters and the problems they meet. Have students choose any of the stories and answer these questions as they read. Who had a problem? What was it? Why was it a problem for the character? How did he try to solve the problem? How was the problem finally solved?

3. All authors write for a purpose: to inform, to teach, to entertain, to persuade. Some stories may have more than one purpose. Have students complete the following chart to identify the purpose of each story, writing details from the story in the boxes that support their opinion.

	INFORM	ENTERTAIN	TEACH	PERSUADE
"Little Daffydowndilly"				
"Mr. Higginbotham's Catastrophe"				
"The Three Golden Apples"				

4. Hawthorne's writing is rich with details that help the reader visualize the scene. Have the students choose a descriptive scene from one of Hawthorne's stories and illustrate it including all of Hawthorne's details to bring the picture to life.

NAME______________________________CLASS__________DATE______

GREAT AMERICAN AUTHORS—*NATHANIEL HAWTHORNE*, PP. 356-401

1. Plot tells the events as they occur in the story. It follows the design of a pyramid and usually consists of four main parts: 1. the exposition explains the background and setting of the story including any of the following: who, what, where, when; 2. the rising action includes events that lead to the climax; 3. the climax is the turning point, the height of the action, the highest part of the pyramid from which we can begin to predict accurately the end of the story; and 4. the resolution is the satisfying end of the story when the problems are all solved. Apply the stories to the pyramid diagram.

"Little Daffydowndilly"

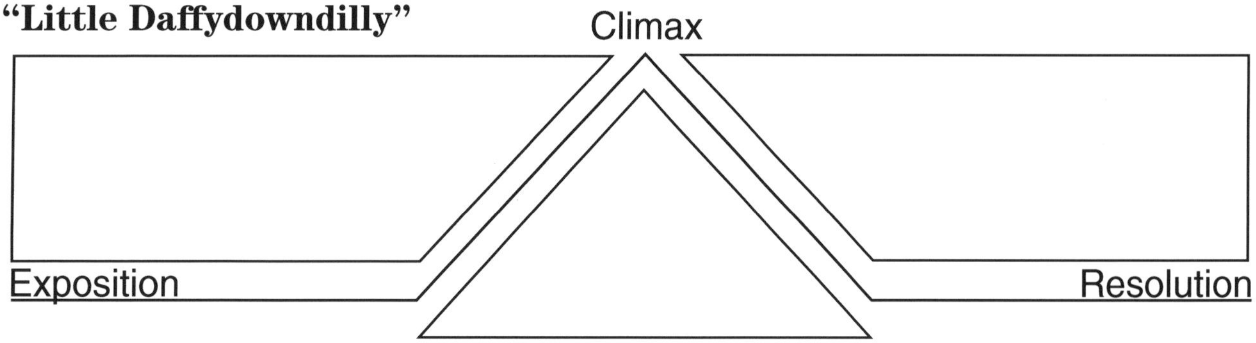

"Mr. Higginbotham's Catastrophe"

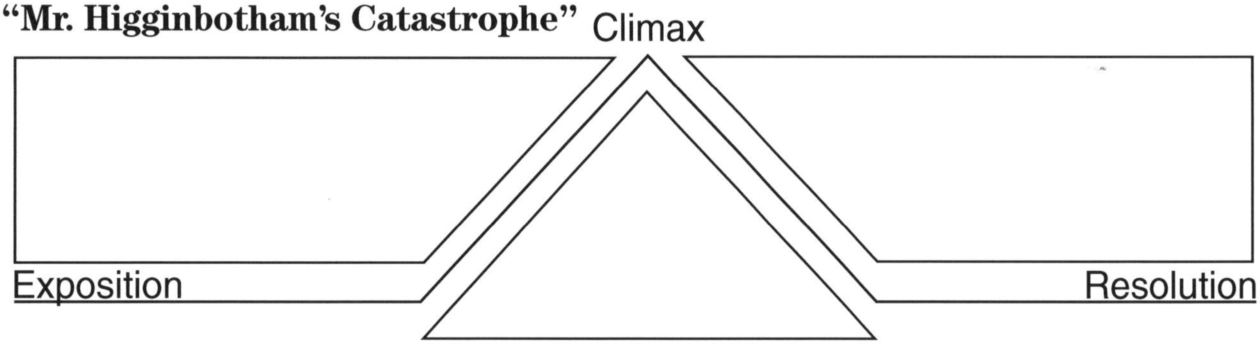

"The Three Golden Apples"

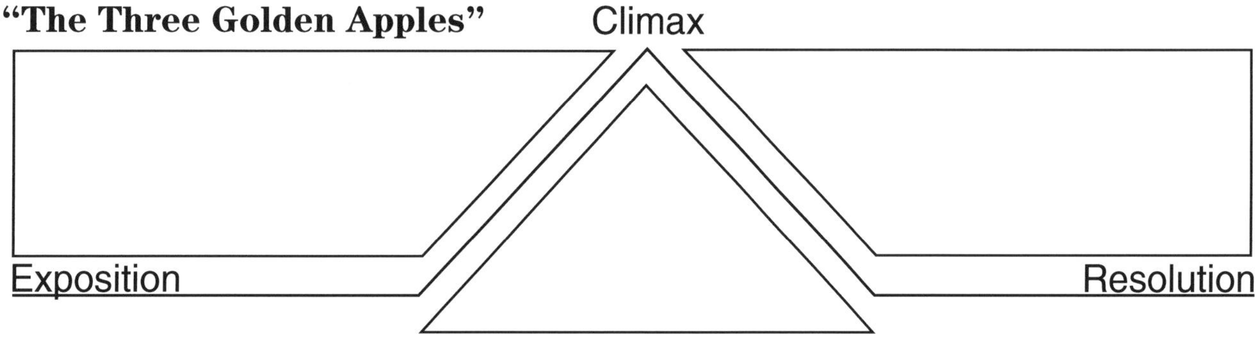

2. **Answer these questions as you read:**

"Little Daffydowndilly"—

Who had a problem?____

What was it?____

Why was it a problem for the character?__________________________

____

____

How did he try to solve the problem?___________________________

____

____

How was the problem finally solved?____________________________

____

____

"Mr. Higginbotham's Catastrophe"—

Who had a problem?____

What was it?____

Why was it a problem for the character?__________________________

____

____

How did he try to solve the problem?___________________________

____

____

How was the problem finally solved?____________________________

____

____

"The Three Golden Apples"—

Who had a problem?____

What was it?____

Why was it a problem for the character?__________________________

____

____

How did he try to solve the problem?___________________________

____

____

How was the problem finally solved?____________________________

____

____

3. All authors write for a purpose: to inform, to teach, to entertain, to persuade. Some stories may have more than one purpose. Complete the following chart to identify the purpose of each story, writing details from the story in the boxes that support your opinion.

	INFORM	ENTERTAIN	TEACH	PERSUADE
"Little Daffydowndilly"				
"Mr. Higginbotham's Catastrophe"				
"The Three Golden Apples"				

4. Hawthorne's writing is rich with details that help the reader visualize the scene. Choose a descriptive scene from one of Hawthorne's stories and illustrate it including all of Hawthorne's details to bring the picture to life.

JOHN GREENLEAF WHITTIER—

THE PUMPKIN, P. 404

1. **Which line tells where the gourd and melon vines are found?**
   Line one says the gourd and melon are found "Oh, greenly and fair in the lands of the sun."
2. **Explain the reference to Jonah, "Nineveh's prophet" (See Jonah IV:4-11).**
   This reference to Jonah describes his actions after warning the people of Nineveh that they were to obey God or perish. He left the city of Nineveh, built a shelter, and sat under it, waiting to see what God would do to the city. God caused a vine to grow up and shade Jonah from the heat, but the next day a worm ate up the vine. The hot sun caused Jonah so much discomfort that he wanted to die, or in the words of the poet, he "longed for the storm-cloud, and listened in vain For the rush of the whirlwind and red fire-rain."
3. **Which line tells that the Yankee delights in his pumpkin crop?**
   Line 13 says, "Yet with dearer delight from his home in the North, On the fields of his harvest the Yankee looks forth."
4. **What "calls back the past" on Thanksgiving day?**
   "The rich Pumpkin pie" "calls back the past."
5. **Why does boyhood love the pumpkin?**
   Boyhood loves the pumpkin because it brings back memories of purple wood-grapes, falling nuts, carved pumpkins, and corn heaps where children sat on pumpkins telling fairy tales with the moon for a lantern.
6. **Find lines that you think refer to "Cinderella."**
   Page 405, lines 7-8 refer to "Cinderella" as "the fairy who traveled like steam, In a pumpkin-shell coach, with two rats for her team!"
7. **To whom do you imagine the poet addresses the last stanza?**
   The poet addresses the pumpkin in the last stanza.
8. **Read the poet's prayer.**
   The last stanza is the prayer to the pumpkin.
9. **What is compared to the pumpkin pie in this prayer?**

The pumpkin pie is compared to the life of the pumpkin itself. "And thy life be as sweet, and its last sunset sky Golden-tinted and fair as thy own Pumpkin pie!"

10. **How did the artist illustrate this poem on page 402?**
    The artist illustrated this poem with a field of pumpkins growing between corn rows.
11. **Commit to memory the third stanza.**
12. **Find in the glossary the meaning of: greenly, gourd, Creole, crooknecks, matron.**
13. **Pronounce: purpling, pumpkin.**

The Barefoot Boy, p. 406

1. **Why was Whittier able to make so good a picture of the barefoot boy?**
   Whittier was himself "once a barefoot boy!"
2. **What picture of the barefoot boy does the first stanza give you?**
   The poet pictures a tanned, barefoot boy with a torn hat and "turned-up pantaloons" whistling merrily through red lips made redder from eating "strawberries on the hill."
3. **Why does the poet call him a "prince"?**
   He is not "republican"—equal to his peers; he stands taller than his peers, a prince.
4. **What does the boy have that "the million-dollared" cannot buy?**
   The boy has "Outward sunshine, inward joy."
5. **What does the barefoot boy know that he "never learned" from books?**
   The second stanza defines all that the boy knows: bees, flowers, birds, habits of animals, tortoises, woodchucks, moles, robins, orioles, lilies, berries, nuts, grapes, wasps and hornets.
6. **Who taught him these things?**
   "Nature answers all he asks."
7. **Read the lines which show that Nature and the boy are on intimate terms.**
   Page 407, lines 16-19 tell us "Hand in hand with her he walks; Face to face with her he talks, Part and parcel of her joy—Blessings on the barefoot boy."
8. **Why is June "boyhood's time"?**
   June crowds "years in one brief moon."
9. **What is meant by "all things" waiting for him, "their master"?**
   The barefoot boy was the master of all he heard or saw; Nature was there waiting for his enjoyment.
10. **Read the lines that tell the riches of the boy.**
    The riches of the boy are expressed in stanza three, lines 24 to the end of the stanza. They include hummingbirds, honeybees, the squirrel, the mole, the blackberry cone, the brook, the pond, and walnut and apple trees.

11. **What is the mole's spade?**
The mole's spade refers to his long nose that he uses to burrow through the ground.
12. **Where in this book have you read about "Apples of Hesperides"?**
Hawthorne writes about the "Apples of Hesperides" in his story titled "The Three Golden Apples" on page 379.
13. **Explain the comparison of the sunset rays to a tent, page 408, line 16.**
Like a tent the sunset rays bent over him, "Purple-curtained, fringed with gold, Looped in many a wind-swung fold."
14. **What fly lights "his lamp of fire"?**
The firefly, or lightning bug, lights "his lamp of fire."
15. **What does Whittier think are the boy's greatest troubles?**
The boy's greatest troubles are the "flinty slopes" and "stubble-speared" meadows.
16. **Why did the poet say "I was monarch"?**
He was the "monarch" of his barefoot world, the ruler of all that transpired around him.
17. **What does the poet call "prison cells of pride"?**
The "prison cells of pride" are the shoes the boy will eventually have to wear when he becomes a man.
18. **Why does he call them this?**
By wearing shoes the boy will "lose the freedom of the sod."
19. **What wish does the poet express for the barefoot boy in the last stanza?**
"Ah! that thou couldst know the joy Ere it passes, barefoot boy."
20. **Which stanza do you like best?**
Answers will vary.
21. **Do you think the artist, on page 402 (p. 246 in this *Guide*), has illustrated the poet's word-picture?**
The artist illustrates a barefoot boy with fishing rod and pail in hand wandering down the road. Student responses will vary. It could be argued that the artist does not accurately illustrate the poem since the poet makes only one brief reference to the pickerel pond.
22. **Find in the glossary the meaning of: republican, tenants, groundnut, mason, artisans, plied, snouted, complex, fashioned, monarch, flinty, moil.**

23. **Pronounce: habitude, architectural, eschewing, orchestra.**

All's Well, p. 410

1. **How do clouds "which rise with thunder" appear?**
   They appear as storm clouds, or thunderheads.
2. **What feeling do they inspire?**
   They may inspire anxiety and fear.
3. **What do these clouds bring?**
   They bring rain to "slake our thirsty souls."
4. **What is the "shadowy lens of even"?**
   The glossary defines the "shadowy lens of even" as the "gathering darkness of evening, as through a magnifying glass."
5. **When does the eye look "farthest into heaven"?**
   The eye looks "farthest into heaven" in the evening.
6. **In what three ways does Whittier illustrate the title, "All's Well"?**
   The poet uses the images of clouds that quench our thirst, blows that break our chains, and wrongs that enhance God's love to illustrate the title, "All's Well."
7. **To what is "the love of God" compared?**
   The wrongs of men, like the darkness of evening, enhance the "love of God" which appears as "gleams of star and depths of blue."

Great American Authors—*John Greenleaf Whittier*, pp. 402-410

Extended Activities

The following activities can be adapted to use with Whittier's poems.

1. At the beginning of Whittier's poems, the students noted Whittier's portrait along with illustrations of the poems in this section. In the discussion questions, students were asked to describe the artist's renditions of the poems. To represent "The Pumpkin," the artist chose a field of corn and pumpkins. "The Barefoot Boy" was illustrated carrying a fishing rod and pail. Have students read the poems and choose a descriptive scene that they would use to best represent the poem. Students should create the illustration using the details in the poem to bring the picture to life.

2. In a brief scanning of Whittier's poems in this section, students will see that the poet frequently uses hyphenated words to express his thoughts. Hyphenated words are two or more words joined together with hyphens to form a single thought. The hyphenated words may be nouns, describing a person, place, thing or idea; or they may be adjectives, describing a noun. Have students identify all of Whittier's hyphenated words and identify in the chart whether they are nouns or adjectives. If they are adjectives, students are to list the noun they describe.

"THE PUMPKIN"

NOUNS	ADJECTIVES
storm-cloud	gray-haired New Englander
fire-rain	care-wearied man
orange-leaves	pumpkin-shell coach
wood-grapes	golden-tinted life
corn-heap	
pumpkin-vine	

"THE BAREFOOT BOY"

NOUNS	ADJECTIVES
million-dollared	turned-up pantaloons
ground-mole	grown-up man
wood-grape	sand-rimmed pond
	cloudy-ribbed sunset
	purple-curtained sunset
	wind-swung fold
	stubble-speared sward
	new-mown sward

3. Have the students choose hyphenated words from the noun or adjective list they have identified in the poems and write a brief definition of the word. What image does the hyphenated word imply that the two separate words do not? Students should look at the words in context to help determine meaning.

NAME______________________________**CLASS**__________**DATE**______

GREAT AMERICAN AUTHORS—*JOHN GREENLEAF WHITTIER,* PP. 402-410

1. At the beginning of Whittier's poems, you can find Whittier's portrait along with illustrations of the poems in this section. In the discussion questions, you were asked to describe the artist's renditions of the poems. To represent "The Pumpkin," the artist chose a field of corn and pumpkins. "The Barefoot Boy" was illustrated carrying a fishing rod and pail. Read the poems and choose a descriptive scene that you would use to best represent the poem. Create the illustration using the details in the poem to bring the picture to life.

2. **In a brief scanning of Whittier's poems in this section, you will see that the poet frequently uses hyphenated words to express his thoughts. Hyphenated words are two or more words joined together with hyphens to form a single thought. The hyphenated words may be nouns, describing a person, place, thing or idea; or they may be adjectives, describing a noun. Identify all of Whittier's hyphenated words and identify in the chart whether they are nouns or adjectives. If they are adjectives, list the noun they describe.**

"THE PUMPKIN"

NOUNS	ADJECTIVES

"THE BAREFOOT BOY"

NOUNS	ADJECTIVES

3. **Choose hyphenated words from the noun or adjective list you have identified in the poems and write a brief definition of the word. What image does the hyphenated word imply that the two separate words do not? You should look at the words in context to help determine meaning.**

Word	Definition

OLIVER WENDELL HOLMES—

CONTENTMENT, P. 413

1. **With what statement does the first stanza open?**
   "Little I ask; my wants are few."
2. **How is this statement contradicted in the same stanza?**
   "I only wish a hut of stone (A very plain brownstone will do) That I may call my own." "Brownstone" is defined in the glossary as "a kind of stone used for fine city houses."
3. **What do the words "cold victuals" usually mean?**
   The glossary defines "cold victuals" as "left over food."
   What seems to be the poet's idea of "cold victuals"?
   He seems to consider "cold victuals" as ice cream since his "choice would be vanilla-ice."
4. **Find a statement in each stanza which is contradicted by other statements in the same stanza.**
   Stanza one: "Little I ask" is contradicted by "a hut of (brown)stone."
   Stanza two: "Plain food" is contradicted by "vanilla-ice."
   Stanza three: "I care not much for gold or land" is contradicted by "Some good bank-stock, some note of hand, Or trifling railroad share."
   Stanza four: "Jewels are baubles: 'tis a sin" is contradicted by "One good-sized diamond in a pin."
   Stanza five: "I would not have the horse I drive So fast…" is contradicted by "Perhaps for just a single spurt."
   Stanza six: "Of books but few—some fifty score For daily use, and bound for wear" is contradicted by "Of red morocco's gilded gleam And vellum rich as country cream."
   Stanza seven: "Wealth's wasteful tricks" is contradicted by "carved tables" made "of buhl" or as found in the glossary, "wood with fancy metal inlays."
   Stanza eight: "Nor long for Midas' golden touch" is contradicted by "I shall not miss them much."
5. **What does the poet say of his wants in the first line of the poem?**
   He says his "wants are few." He asks for little in life.

What have you learned of his wants from the succeeding lines of the poem?

He really wants rich food, gold and land, jewels, a fast horse, many richly adorned rare books, fancy furniture and fame.

6. **For what does he say that he is grateful?**

He is "Too grateful for the blessing lent Of simple tastes and minds content."

7. **What furnishes the fun in the poem?**

The fun comes in his contrasts; pretending to be a man of "simple tastes and minds content," he really longs for all life's riches.

8. **What do you think was the poet's purpose in writing this poem?**

Answers will vary. Encourage students to explore the author's purpose from their perspective. Include the concept that perhaps the author was poking fun at the outward humility we profess versus our inner thirst for power, wealth, and fame.

9. **Find in the glossary the meaning of: brownstone, subsist, baubles, unfruitful, vellum, recumbent.**

10. **Pronounce: victuals, mortgage, buhl.**

To An Insect, p. 415

1. **Who is addressed in the poem?**
   The poet addresses the insect.
2. **Why does the poet say the insect reminds him of certain old folks?**
   The poet says the insect is like certain old folks because "thou say'st an undisputed thing In such a solemn way."
3. **Can you account for the question asked in the last line of the second stanza?**
   "Do Katydids drink tea?" The poet uses a metaphor to compare a "knot" of Katydids under a tree with a "knot of spinsters" at a tea party. The glossary defines a spinster as "an unmarried woman, no longer young."
4. **What wish and prophecy are expressed in the last stanza?**
   The poet's wish is for "Peace to the ever-murmuring race!" He prophesies that "the child of future years Shall hear what Katy did."
5. **Point out instances of the poet's quiet humor in this poem.**
   The poet believes the Katydid is female because of her "petulant and shrill" voice. He also compares the Katydid to the naughty girls in his childhood who took their secrets to the grave. Students may identify additional instances of humor.
6. **Find in the glossary the meaning of: testy, trill, spinster, warrant, rend.**
7. **Pronounce: dogmatist, petulant, mystic.**

LEXINGTON, P. 417

1. **Where is Lexington?**
   Lexington is located in Massachusetts, west of Boston.
2. **When did the Battle of Lexington occur?**
   Students will read in the "Historical Note" that the Battle of Lexington occurred on April 19, 1775.
3. **What made this a famous battle?**
   It was the opening battle for independence from the British government. The British were defeated, losing about three hundred men to about eighty-five Americans. Further information on the Battle of Lexington can be found in *A History of the United States and Its People*, by Edward Eggleston, Lost Classics Book Company, Lake Wales, Florida.
4. **Who is meant by the "bold rebel"?**
   The "bold rebel" refers to the American soldiers who rebelled against the British government.
5. **To what is the beat of the drum compared in the third stanza?**
   The beat of the drum is compared to "the thunder-burst rolling" through storm clouds
6. **What word in the third stanza refers to the American volunteers?**
   The "yeomanry," or farmers, were the volunteers that fought the British
7. **To whom does the word "soldier" in the same stanza refer?**
   The "soldier" refers to the British; "Long have they gathered and loud shall they fall."
8. **Find something in the fourth stanza which tells you that "the horseman" was a British soldier.**
   The poet refers to the horseman's "belted breast," the British military dress.
9. **Why is the English flag called "silken-fringed red cross"?**
   The red cross is the emblem on the British flag. Have students research the British flag to discover its design.
10. **What is meant by the word "her" in the last stanza?**
    "Her" refers to the colonies for which the Americans fought.

Who are "her martyrs"?

"Her martyrs" are the American soldiers who fought and died for the colonies.

11. What is the "starry fold"?

The "starry fold" is the American flag. Have students research the flag design at the time of the Battle of Lexington. The Continental Colors flag flew from 1775-77, the time period of the Battle of Lexington. It had thirteen red and white stripes for the thirteen colonies and included the crosses of the British flag in the upper left corner, symbolizing the loyalty of the colonists to Great Britain. The first flag that had stars and stripes, to which the "starry folds" refers, was adopted in 1777, two years after the Battle of Lexington.

12. What is meant by "eagle" in the last stanza?

The "eagle" refers to the proud bald eagle, adopted as our national bird in 1782. Just as we protect our national bird, the author infers that we work to protect our nation. "Heaven keep her ever free."

13. What is the "fair emblem her heroes have won"?

The "fair emblem," or sign refers to the flag that symbolizes our national pride and freedom.

14. How does the last stanza apply to our heroes of the World Wars?

They also rest in green graves, "Shroudless and tombless," where they died while fighting for freedom and democracy in the war.

15. Notice the interesting rhyming scheme in this poem. As you read the poem aloud, notice the pleasing effect produced by the two-syllabled rhyme in the first and third lines of every stanza.

The rhyme scheme in this poem is as follows: ABABCCDEED FGFGHHIJJI KLKLMMNOON PQPQRRSTTS UVUVWWXYYX.

16. Read the stanza that you think the picture on page 411 (p. 257 in this *Guide*) illustrates.

The illustration refers to stanza three which describes the "red glares (of) the Musket's flash" and the "Sharp rings (of) the rifle's crash."

What other lines might the artist have chosen for illustrations?

Answers will vary.

17. Find a copy of Holmes's poems in the library and read "Grandmother's Story of Bunker-Hill Battle."

18. Find in the glossary the meaning of: spire, death-volley, knell, yeomanry, mustering, reeking, herd, ashes.

19. Pronounce: plume, prancing, shroudless, tombless.

Extended Activity:

To enhance Holmes's poem "Lexington" have students find and read a copy of "Paul Revere's Ride," by Henry Wadsworth Longfellow. It was his ride that roused the farmers to fight in the Battle of Lexington. (Longfellow's poem can be found in *The Elson Readers, Book Eight.*)

Great American Authors—*Oliver Wendell Holmes*, pp. 411-420

More Extended Activities

The following activities can be adapted to use with Holmes's poems.

1. Oliver Wendell Holmes uses a variety of rhyme schemes in his poems. In order to achieve the proper rhyming effect, the poet rearranges words, thus making the meaning unclear at times. Have students find several pairs of rhymed lines whose arrangement is restructured to achieve the correct rhyme. Have them copy the lines then put them in their own words to achieve the meaning the poet intended. Example: "To An Insect," Old gentlefolks are they…In such a solemn way." They are old, solemn people.

2. Stopping to review what they have read as they progress through the poem helps students to clarify meaning and make sense of the poem. To help students clarify meaning in Holmes's poems, have them choose a poem, read each stanza and stop to clarify those lines. Students should paraphrase the meaning, putting it in terms that they understand. At the end of the poem, students should have a clear meaning of the poem's intent.

NAME________________________________CLASS__________DATE______

GREAT AMERICAN AUTHORS—*OLIVER WENDELL HOLMES*, PP. 411-420

1. Oliver Wendell Holmes uses a variety of rhyme schemes in his poems. In order to achieve the proper rhyming effect, the poet rearranges words, thus making the meaning unclear at times. Find several pairs of rhymed lines whose arrangement is restructured to achieve the correct rhyme. Copy the lines then put them in your own words to achieve the meaning the poet intended.

Poem: "To an Insect"
Old gentlefolks are they
In such a solemn way.
Meaning:
They are old, solemn people.

Poem: ________________________________

____

____

Meaning:

____

Poem: ________________________________

____

____

Meaning:

____

Poem: ________________________________

____

____

Meaning:

____

Poem: ________________________________

____

____

Meaning:

____

2. Stopping to review what you have read as you progress through the

poem helps to clarify meaning and make sense of the poem. To help clarify meaning in Holmes's poems, choose a poem, read each stanza and stop to clarify those lines. You should paraphrase the meaning, putting it in terms that you understand. At the end of the poem, you should have a clear meaning of the poem's intent.

Poem: "Contentment"

Stanza 1: ______________________________

Meaning: ______________________________

Stanza 2: ______________________________

Meaning: ______________________________

Stanza 3: ______________________________

Meaning: ______________________________

Stanza 4: ______________________________

Meaning: ______________________________

Stanza 5: ______________________________

Meaning: ______________________________

Stanza 6: ______________________________

Meaning: ______________________________

Stanza 7: ______________________________

Meaning: ______________________________

Stanza 8: ______________________________

Meaning: ______________________________

Poem: "To an Insect"

Stanza 1: ______________________________

Meaning: ______________________________

Stanza 2: ______________________________

Meaning: ______________________________

Stanza 3: ______________________________

Meaning: ______________________________

Stanza 4: ______________________________

Meaning: ______________________________

Stanza 5: ______________________________

Meaning: ______________________________

Stanza 6: ______________________________

Meaning: ______________________________

Poem: "Lexington"

Stanza 1: ____

Meaning: ____

Stanza 2: ____

Meaning: ____

Stanza 3: ____

Meaning: ____

Stanza 4: ____

Meaning: ____

Stanza 5: ____

Meaning: ____

GREAT AMERICAN AUTHORS, PP. 323-423

More Extended Activities:

The following activities can be adapted to further enhance students' exposure to these important authors.

1. With the exception of Benjamin Franklin (1706-1790), all the authors in this section were born and lived in the same general span of American history. They share many similarities, as well as differences. Have students read each biography and complete the following chart:

	Birth/Death	Place of Birth and Boyhood	Education	Profession & Interests	Best Known For
FRANKLIN					
BRYANT					
LONGFELLOW					
HAWTHORNE					
WHITTIER					
HOLMES					

When the chart is complete, have the students list the similarities and differences they have noted in the chart.

2. After they have researched the authors, have the students choose an author and one of his works in this section, or if they choose, another piece they have read by that author. Have students plan an authors' reunion in which these authors meet and share their work. Students should dress in character and present their work as they think the author would want it told.

3. Have students choose an author from this section and research him further using the Internet and/or encyclopedias. Students are to write an essay titled, "If I could step back in time, I would like to meet...." They must develop a thesis statement that identifies their reasons for choosing that author. Using relevant data from their research, students must explain in their essay why that author would be a good choice with whom to meet. They are not to copy directly from their research; paraphrasing and summarizing must be used throughout the essay except for short quotes taken directly from the author, indicated with quotation marks. At the end of the essay the student should prepare a Works Cited page that acknowledges his/her sources. The MLA (Modern Language Association) style is commonly used when citing works of literature. The list of resources are alphabetized by the author's last name or, if there is no author, by the first main word in the title. A sample Works Cited outline follows:

Elson, William H. and Christine M. Keck. "Henry Wadsworth Longfellow." *The Elson Readers, Book 6*. Lake Wales, FL: Lost Classics Book Co., 2001. 346-347

Hoffman, Kathryn. " A Family That Digs Together..." *Time for Kids* 1 May 2001: 4-5.

Lukes, Bonnie L. *Henry Wadsworth Longfellow: America's Beloved Poet* (*World Writers*). Greensboro, NC: Morgan Reynolds, Inc., 1998.

Rabe, Roberto. "Henry Wadsworth Longfellow." 28 June 2001 http://eclecticesoterica.com/longfellow_bio.html

Robbins, J. Albert. "Henry Wadsworth Longfellow." *The World Book Encyclopedia*. 1985 ed.

(Note: Titles of works are italicized; underlining indicates italics when not possible to italicize, such as when using a typewriter.)

NAME____________________________ CLASS__________ DATE______

GREAT AMERICAN AUTHORS, PP. 323-423

1. **With the exception of Benjamin Franklin (1706-1790), all the authors in this section were born and lived in the same general span of American history. They share many similarities, as well as differences. Read each biography and complete the following chart:**

	Birth/Death	Place of Birth and Boyhood	Education	Profession & Interests	Best Known For
FRANKLIN					
BRYANT					
LONGFELLOW					
HAWTHORNE					
WHITTIER					
HOLMES					

When the chart is complete, list the similarities and differences you have noted in the chart.

____

____

____

____

____

____

NAME______________________________ **CLASS**__________ **DATE**______

Story	***Find in the glossary the meaning of:***
Reader p. 329	**passage**__________
	thereby__________
	sly__________
	hand__________
	discovering__________
	artful__________
	font__________
	dieted__________
	illiterate__________
	condescension__________
Reader p. 336	**repaired**__________
	degree__________
	learned__________
	education__________
	frolics__________
	contend__________
	mean__________
Reader p. 339	**train**__________
	sullen__________
Reader p. 340	**mold**__________
	betrays__________
	fraud__________
	wasting__________
	quaint__________
Reader p. 344	**sear**__________
	sprang__________
	glade__________
	glen__________
Reader p. 348	**smithy**__________
	brawny__________
	crisp__________
	tan__________
	bellows__________
	sledge__________
	sexton__________
	chaff__________
	threshing__________
Reader p. 350	**portico**__________
	countryseat__________

station____
massive____
board____
prime____
shroud____
incessantly____

Reader p. 354 **goal**____
destined____
bivouac____
sublime____
main____
achieving____

Reader p. 358 **resembled**____
affirmed____
hitherto____
indulgent____
ugly-visaged____
trudging____
sociable____
precisely____
erecting____
clapboards____
molest____
compasses____
exhorting____
diligent____
besought____
composedly____
flourishing____
innumerable____
entreated____
torpid____
whit____

Reader p. 367 **depicted**____
communicated____
pondering____
perpetrated____
manifested____

Reader p. 369 **gospel**____

Reader p. 372 **population**____
narrative____
shifted____
rumbled____

	excessive__________
Reader p. 375	**hoax**__________
	equivalent__________
	instinct__________
	solitary__________
Reader p. 379	**graft**__________
Reader p. 380	**pastime**__________
	heroic__________
	remonstrances__________
	intervals__________
	auditors__________
	valiant__________
	ponderous__________
	illustrious__________
Reader p. 385	**impressive**__________
	riven__________
	verdant__________
	figurehead__________
	uncivil__________
Reader p. 390	**prodigious**__________
	contrived__________
	lustrous__________
	immeasurably__________
	circumference__________
	reverberated__________
Reader p. 393	**intolerably**__________
	disconsolate__________
	sustain__________
	obscurity__________
	intelligibly__________
Reader p. 397	**immersed**__________
	wistfully__________
	ajar__________
Reader p. 404	**greenly**__________
	gourd__________
	Creole__________
	crooknecks__________
	matron__________
Reader p. 406	**republican**__________
	tenants__________
	groundnut__________
	mason__________
	artisans__________

plied ______

snouted ______

complex ______

fashioned ______

monarch ______

flinty ______

moil ______

Reader p. 413 **brownstone** ______

subsist ______

baubles ______

unfruitful ______

vellum ______

recumbent ______

Reader p. 415 **testy** ______

trill ______

spinster ______

warrant ______

rend ______

Reader p. 417 **spire** ______

death-volley ______

knell ______

yeomanry ______

mustering ______

reeking ______

herd ______

ashes ______

Pronounce:

fatigued, accosting, reputable, sophister, novice, compositor, apprehended, affable, indefatigable, distinction, hearth, sojourners, orchis, upland, sinewy, wrought, vicissitude, affluence, horologe, countenance, quoth, epaulets, Monsieur le Plaisir, Signor Far Niente, approbation, catastrophe, narrator, occurrence, mentioned, perplexity, meditations, hostler, originated, pathos, edition, signature, supplicate, ablution, autograph, discern, emergency, champion, Hesperides, destiny, stripling, hydra, exploit, gigantic, choral, hospitable, minutely, Antaeus, horizon, tumultuous, pother, incalculable, aerial, firmament, fissure, posterity, variety, purpling, pumpkin, habitude, architectural, eschewing, orchestra, victuals, mortgage, buhl, dogmatist, petulant, mystic, plume, prancing, shroudless, tombless.

Appendix I
Instructional Aids

The first section of this appendix, "Silent and Oral Reading," appears in the original *Elson Readers, Book Seven* and offers the teacher and parent a useful method of assisting the student(s) in attaining the objectives in this guide. The remaining aids have been written specially for this guide by the authors as additional resources for the teacher and parent.

Silent and Oral Reading

Silent Reading. This book includes abundant material for both silent and oral reading. Some stories and poems must be read thoughtfully in order to gain the author's full meaning; such reading cannot be done rapidly. In other selections the meaning can be grasped easily, and the reading can be rapid; in such cases we read mainly for the central thought, for the story element.

You read silently more often than you read aloud to others; you should, therefore, train yourself in rapid silent reading, concentrating your mind on the thought of the selection. You will soon discover that as you give closer attention to a story you will not only understand it better, but you will also remember more of it. In previous grades your training in silent reading has enabled you to gather facts from individual paragraphs and to hold in mind the thread of the narrative in shorter selections. But you are to extend this power steadily until you can gather facts and follow the unfolding plot in selections of considerable length. A number of stories in this book are long enough to train you to read with intelligence a newspaper, a magazine article, or a book. And this is precisely the ability you most need, not only in preparing lessons in history and other school subjects, but in all your reading throughout life. As you train yourself to grasp swiftly and accurately the meaning of a page, you increase your capacity to enjoy books—one of the most pleasurable things in life. Theodore Roosevelt trained himself to be such a rapid reader that he was able to grasp the central thought of a page almost as quickly as he could turn the leaves of the book.

In preparing lessons in geography and history and in the use of geographical and historical stories, you have a splendid opportunity to increase your ability to gather facts quickly from the printed page. These informational studies, however, do not take the place of the reading lesson in literature. They merely offer additional opportunity for you to increase your ability in rapid silent reading.

Notice that the rapid silent readers in your class generally gain and retain from their reading more facts than the slow readers do. Notice, too, that you read more rapidly when you are looking for the answer to some particular question or looking for a certain passage than you do when you read merely to follow the thread of the story. Moving your lips or pointing to the words with your finger retards your speed. In the selections in this book suggested for silent reading you may test your ability at thought-getting in any of the following ways:

1. By using a list of questions covering the most important ideas of the selection
2. By telling the story from a given outline
3. By making a list of questions yourself, allowing some classmate to use them to test his or her ability at thought-getting, while you make similar use of his or her questions.
4. By telling the story from an outline that you have made. Telling the substance of the story from your own outline is an excellent kind of test because you test not only your understanding of the story, but also your memory and your power to express the thought of what you have read.

In all your reading, both at home and at school, you should read as rapidly as you can, but not so fast that you fail to get the thought. In preparing your lessons on selections in this book, test yourself by seeing how many of the questions, under "Discussion," that develop the most important thoughts of the story, you can answer after one reading. You may have to read parts of the story more than once in order to gain the full meaning. If, from time to time, you record your reading speed and your thought-getting ability, comparing your standing with that of your classmates and with the standard for seventh grade pupils, you will be able to see whether or not you are making satisfactory progress. The standard for seventh grade boys and girls is 250 words per minute, with the ability to reproduce after one reading 50% of the ideas in a 400-word passage.

The following form will suggest a way to record the results of your test:

INDIVIDUAL RECORD

Date	Titles	Speed		Comprehension
		No. of minutes required to read story	No. words per minute	Ten points for each of ten test questions*
	Hunting the Grizzly Bear Total No. Words, 1957			
	The Great Stone Face... Total No. Words, 7475			

*Questions to be selected by the teacher.

CLASS RECORD

Date	Speed			Comprehension			
	No. words per minute			Ten points for each of ten test questions			
	Lowest	Highest	Median	Lowest	Highest	Median	

Oral Reading. In the prose selections suggested for silent reading, you will wish to read aloud certain passages because of their beauty, their dramatic quality, or the forceful way in which the author has expressed his thoughts. In these selections, "Class Readings" are listed for this purpose. Sometimes these readings are intended for individual pupils; sometimes, particularly in dialogue, they are intended for groups. "Class Readings" include also supplementary poems and stories suggested for oral presentation.

In general, all poetry should be read aloud, for much of the beauty of poetry lies in its rhythm. The voice, with its infinite possibilities of change, is an important factor in interpreting a poem. As you listen to your teacher or some other good reader, you will appreciate how much pleasure one who has learned the art of reading is able to give others. Oral reading trains the ear of the listener to become sensitive to a pleasing voice, to correct pronunciation, and to distinct articulation. The sympathetic reading of many of the poems in this book will reveal to you the beauty of the language that we speak and by which we express our thoughts. Longfellow says, "Of equal honor with him who writes a grand poem is he who reads it grandly."

Outline for Oral Presentations

The following rubric is a general guideline to consider when critiquing student oral presentations. As the teacher, you may want to assign a point value to each of the items which you consider to be pertinent to the assignment.

General Guidelines

	Points Possible	Points Earned
Completed on time		
Fulfilled the guidelines of the assignment		
Message: **Clear and pertinent**		
Appealing and detailed		
Research: **Current and varied**		
Properly cited		
Technology: **Used technical materials, i.e., computer, puppets, tools appropriately**		
Used art materials i.e. wood, paint, paper creatively		
Presentation: **Good posture**		
Eye contact with the audience		
Voice control, volume, rate and expression		
Body language shows enthusiasm		

Presentation Checklist:

The following checklist is designed to assist the student in gathering materials and information for an oral presentation. The student should be encouraged to complete the proposal and review it with the teacher to ensure a well-organized presentation.

Proposal

Topic on which I'll speak

Supporting facts I plan to use

Supporting anecdotes or stories to interest my listeners

Visual aids to enhance my speech

Musical background to accompany my speech

Technological equipment I will need

What do I want my listeners to learn from this presentation

My concluding punch line

The Stages of the Writing Process

Throughout the reader, students are encouraged to write essays on a variety of topics for a variety of audiences and purposes. The following general guideline for the stages of the writing process will assist the student in producing a meaningful, well-organized, well-crafted essay. The writing process includes four stages: prewrite, draft, edit/revise, final copy.

Prewrite Planning Guide:

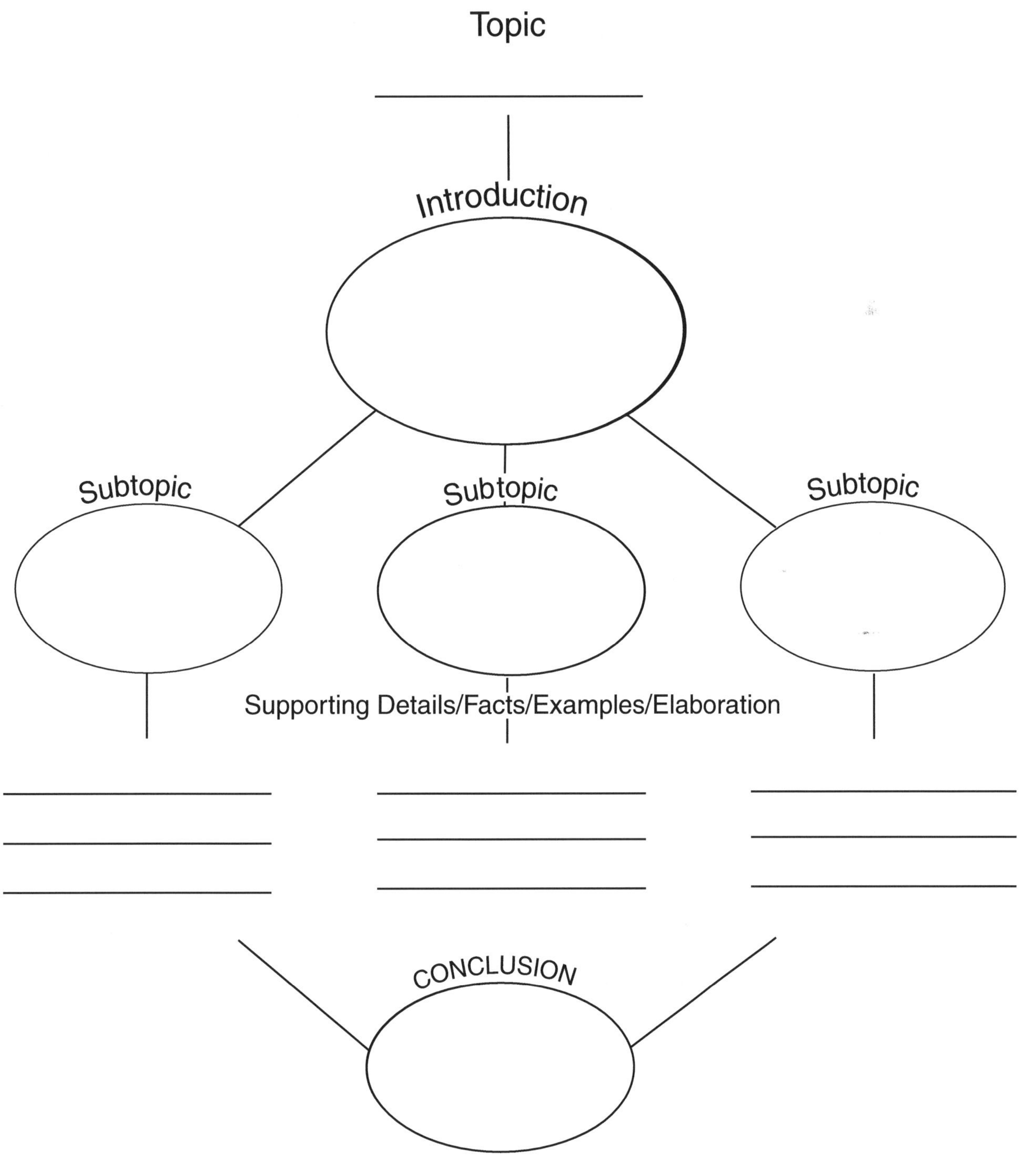

1. Introduction:

I. Students should develop their paper with the following elements:

A. Introduction:

a. Hook sentence—This sentence "hooks" the interest of the reader. A hook sentence can be a quote, a question, an interesting fact, or anecdote.

b. Thesis sentence—This sentence must include the subject about which the paper is written and an opinion. For example: Those living near the Mississippi River need to be prepared for floods. NOT: I'm going to write about floods along the Mississippi River.

c. Map sentence—This sentence lists the three main points of the body of the paper.

2. Body:

Develop the main reasons, one paragraph for each reason, using vivid sensory details. As appropriate use statistics, quotations, stories, and examples to support the reason. Use transitions appropriately at the beginning and within each body paragraph.

TREEES paragraphs

Topic
Reason
  Elaboration
Example
  Elaboration
Summary

3. Conclusion:

Restate the thesis and summarize your main reasons. Challenge the reader with a closing thought, action, or recommendation. In the conclusion, do not use exact words or phrases from the introduction.

Edit/Revise:

Review the essay to make sure it is organized with vivid details and examples that support the thesis, the tone is appropriate for the audience, and word choice is precise and lively. Sentences should be complete and varied in length and structure. Grammar should be appropriate, and spelling and punctuation are generally correct.

Final Draft:

Rewrite the essay to include the revisions made in the editing stage.

Evaluation Rubric (Checklist):

At right.

	Points Possible	Points Earned
Planning:		
Draft:		
Revision/ Editing:		
Final Copy: **Conventions** spelling, punctuation, grammar		
Supporting Details		
Neatness		
Introduction		
Conclusion		
Organization		

Appendix II

> World War One had ended just a few years before the original *Elson Readers* appeared. This event was fresh in the mind of Americans and profoundly changed the way they looked at themelves and their role in the world. This changed outlook is reflected in *The Elson Readers*, in both the literature that was included and in the study questions. This brief description of that great event is provided as both a source of background information and a starting point for parents, teachers, and students to begin discussions on this turning point in American history.

A Brief Description of World War One

by Andy Jameson

World War One (also known as the Great War) lasted for four years—from 1914 to the end of 1918. The war was fought between Germany and its allies (Austria-Hungary of the Hapsburg Empire and Turkey of the Ottoman Empire) known as the Central Powers (or the Triple Alliance), and Great Britain, France, Russia, Italy, Japan, and, from 1917, the United States called the Allies. Germany was forced to fight the war on two fronts: the Western Front against the Allies and the Eastern Front against Russia. It was the first international conflict in which the United States participated.

The leading causes of the war were the alliance system of the late nineteenth century, which divided European states into two contending camps; the German victory over France in the Franco-German War (1870-71); the unification of Germany under Chancellor Otto von Bismarck and its rapid industrialization; the nationalist and ethnic agitation in the Balkans; and the fact that by 1900, European states were engaged in an escalating arms race and building vast military and naval forces in peacetime. The alliance system was symptomatic of the tension in European society between the growth of an international economy—the competition for goods and markets—and the political outlook of European states based on their own narrow national interests.

Bismarck set out to build a German empire based on the nationalistic premise that Germany also deserved a "place in the sun"—which meant an international political, economic, and military position like that of the British Empire. In Europe, the Germans claimed that they were being encircled by France and Russia. The entrance of Germany into the world scene exacerbated the intense rivalry for power and colonial markets in Africa, the Near East, and the Far East, as well as control of the seas. When the Germans decided to build a navy in 1891, they began the Anglo-German naval race.

The "race for empire" led to crises in Morocco, where Germany sent a gunboat to protect German interests, and in the Balkans, where Germany supported its Austrian ally against the national liberation movements which threatened the integrity of the Austro-Hungarian Empire. The three Balkan Wars (1912-1913), which were a prelude to World War One, also involved the Turks, whose Ottoman Empire had been disintegrating under the liberation movements of the Greeks and the southern Slavic peoples (Serbs, Croats, Bulgarians), and the Russians, who intervened in the Balkans as the "big Slavic" protectors of the Orthodox Christians—thus posing a threat to the Central Powers.

It was the nationalist movements in the Balkans which provided the "spark" that began World War One. On June 29, 1914, the heir to the Hapsburg Empire, Archduke Franz Ferdinand, was assassinated in Sarajevo (the capital of Bosnia). The Germans supported their Austrian ally, while the French supported the Russians. Protected by their navy, the British tried to maintain their policy of "splendid isolation," but the threat to the British naval forces in the North Sea from the German fleet, and with the French coast of the Channel open to German naval attack, the British were forced to protect their sea lanes and defend their French ally. When the Russians refused a German demand to stop their mobilization on the eastern border, Germany declared war (August 1, 1914), and France followed with its declaration (August 3). And when the Germans launched their Schlieffen Plan—a military strategy which involved a rapid thrust through Belgium to crush the French forces (in violation of the treaty which guaranteed the neutrality of Belgium)—Great Britain also declared war on Germany (August 4).

To supply their Russian ally, the British and French launched a disastrous naval attack on Turkey via the Dardanelles (1915), but the campaign was called off when the Allies lost 143,000 killed or wounded in the Gallipoli campaign.

On the Eastern Front, the early Russian offensive of 1914, which had driven into German territories in Prussia, Poland, and Galicia, was stopped and driven back by the Austro-German offensive of 1915.

By 1916, the war of maneuver on the Western Front ground to a halt, and it became a war of position and attrition—the massive armies were deadlocked in trench warfare. The machine gun—a new weapon—immobilized the troops which could advance only with staggering losses, while the tank, which was to become the antidote to the machine gun, and the airplane, the future antidote to the tank, were still in the experimental stages of development as weapons of war. The stalemate on the Western Front, however, ended when the Russians withdrew from, and the Americans entered, the war. The imperial Russian armies, plagued by poor military leadership and inadequate supplies, collapsed, and Czar Nicholas II was forced to abdicate from the internal pressure of the socialists (Marxists), especially from the leader of the Bolsheviks, the extreme faction of the Russian Marxists, V. I. Lenin (who formed the Communist party). When the czar abdicated, Lenin seized power in November, 1917, and the Bolsheviks signed the treaty of Brest-Litovsk with the Germans (December 3, 1917). At this point the war shifted to the Western Front, where the German High Command, under its Generals Hindenburg and Ludendorff, planned an offensive against the Allies. The Germans moved their army from the Russian front to the west via the railroad.

The German policy of unrestricted submarine warfare led United States President Woodrow Wilson to break off diplomatic relations with Germany, and when the British ship Lusitania was sunk with American passengers on board, and American ships were lost to U-boat action, he asked Congress for a declaration of war "to make the world safe for democracy,"(April 2, 1917). But it would be one year before the American military force and industrial production were prepared for war, and American soldiers arrived on the Western Front. With conscription administered by a Selective Service system, the armed services built a force of over four million. The government undertook the massive task of converting producers in the lumber, steel, automobile, and other industries to war production. Shipping tonnage increased from one million to ten million tons. The war effort encouraged citizens to conserve food (sugar was rationed and meatless Tuesdays were introduced) and fuel (daylight-saving time was adopted to save coal), and to purchase government Liberty bonds—the Treasury Department staged rallies at which Hollywood stars appeared to promote bond sales. At the same time, farmers were induced to grow more crops, and the production of civilian goods was cut (75,000 tons of tin were diverted to military production from children's toys and 8,000 tons of steel from the manufacture of women's corsets to munitions). The United States also provided loans to the Allies, which they used to purchase food and supplies.

While American military and economic power were geared up, the French and British suffered great losses in holding the line on the Western Front. When asked about an allied offensive, French General Pétain said, "I am waiting for the Americans and the tanks." In June, 1918, American troops under the command of General John J. Pershing, engaged the Germans at the Battles of Château-Thierry, Belleau Wood, and the Argonne, as 250,000 Americans were landing in France each month. Faced with this allied buildup, the German command realized that Germany could not win the war, and the government of Kaiser Wilhelm II began peace negotiations. By the time the armistice was signed (November 11, 1918), there were two million American soldiers in France and another million were heading for Europe. The Allies suffered ten million killed and twenty million casualties in the war, and the United States lost 115,000 dead and 315,000 casualties. While the allied losses far surpassed those of the Americans, it was the specter and the reality of American military and economic power that were decisive in ending the war.

In military history, World War One is notable for the brutal conditions under which the war was fought and for the incompetent leadership of the commanders—and the effect on the morale and discipline of the troops. The idea that soldiers were "manipulated from above" subject to the traditional military concept of obedience based on punishment resulted in revision of the military code of conduct.

Among the legacies of the war, which affected the course of the twentieth century, were the creation of the League of Nations (an international consortium), the rise of totalitarianism, and the imperial partition of the Near East (which resulted in the future states of Iraq, Syria, and Jordan).

Glossary

a as in m<u>a</u>t	ə as in b<u>a</u>nana	ä as in f<u>a</u>ther	∅ as in s<u>i</u>de
e as in b<u>e</u>d	ər as in f<u>ur</u>th<u>er</u>	aů as in l<u>ou</u>d	ŋ as in si<u>ng</u>
i as in t<u>i</u>p	ā as in d<u>a</u>y	ē as in n<u>ee</u>d	ō as in sn<u>o</u>w
ȯ as in s<u>a</u>w	ȯi as in c<u>oi</u>n	ü as in r<u>u</u>le	ů as in p<u>u</u>ll
	ᵊ as in eat<u>e</u>n	<u>th</u> as in hea<u>th</u>er	

A

a ban doned (ə-'ban-dənd) gave up
a beau te ous sisterhood ('byü-tē-es) a beautiful collection of flowers of different kinds
ab lu tion (ə-'blü-shən) wetting
A bou ben Ad hem ('a-bü ben 'a-dem)
ac com mo dat ed (ə-'käm-ə-dā-təd) conveniently put
ac com mo dat ed to my mind (ə-'käm-ə-dā-təd) arranged as I wished
ac cord (ə-'kȯrd) harmony
ac cost ing (ə-'kȯs-tiŋ) stopping to speak to
ac count ed (ə-'kaůn-təd) explained
a chieve this feat (ə-'chēv; 'fēt) do this great act
a chiev ing (ə-'chē-viŋ) accomplishing something
A chil les (ə-'kil-ēz)
a corns ('ā-kȯrnz) nuts of oak trees
ac quaint ed (ə-'kwān-təd) known; understood
across the Neck from one side to the other of the narrow strip of land
a cute (ə-'kyüt) sharp
ad hered (ad-'hird) stuck
ad min is ter ing (əd-'min-ə-striŋ) giving
ad mo ni tion (ad-mə-'ni-shən) warning
a dopt ed (ə-'däp-təd) chose to take
ad van ces of the sea son (əd-'vans-əz; 'sē-sən) oncoming of summer
adz ('adz) a tool for smoothing wood
Aen e as (i-'nē-əs)
Ae o lus ('ē-ə-ləs)
ae ri al ('ar-ē-əl) light and airy
af fa ble ('a fə bəl) kind
af fairs of the pe ri od (ə-'farz; 'pir-ē-əd) happenings of that time

af fect ed to laugh (ə-ˈfek-təd; ˈlaf) pretended I was amused
af firm (ə-ˈfərm) declare
af flu ence (ˈa-flü-əns) rich gifts
af fright (ə-ˈfrit) fear
aft (ˈaft) back
Ag a mem non (a-gə-ˈmem-nän)
a jar (ə-ˈjär) out of place
A jax (ˈā-jaks)
a kim bo (ə-ˈkim-bō) with hands on hips, and elbows turned out
Al ba (ˈal-bə)
Al bert Nyan za (ˈal-bərt ˈnyän-zə)
Al cin ous (al-ˈsin-ō-es)
al ders (ˈȯl-dərz) a kind of small trees that grow in moist ground
A li Ba ba (ˈa-li ˈba-ba) hero of a story in *The Arabian Nights*
al ien (ˈā-lē-ən) foreign
Al lah (ˈä-lə) the Mohammedan name for God
all Chris ten dom (ˈkri-sən-dəm) the whole Christian world
al lies (ˈa-lØz) men who fought on the same side
all ser vice ranks the same different kinds of unselfish deeds are of the same value
all the deer kind all the kinds of deer
alms (ˈälmz) charity
a loft (ə-ˈlȯft) on high
al pine staff (ˈal-pØn; ˈstaf) long stick used in climbing
al ter nate ly (ˈöl-tər-nət-lē) in turn
al ti tude (ˈal-tə-tüd) height
a maze ment (ə-ˈmāz-mənt) surprise; wonder
am mu ni tion (am-yə-ˈni-shən) what is shot; here, mud to throw
am ple (ˈam-pəl) large; generous
am ple se cur i ty (ˈam-pəl; si-ˈkyu̇r-ə-tē) complete safety
an ag o ny of ter ror (ˈa-gə-nē; ˈter-ər) the greatest fright
An chi ses (an-ˈkØ-sēz)
an cient (ˈān(t)-shənt) very old; olden
an cient forms (ˈānt-shənt) old kinds
ancient mother land from which your forefathers came
An dro ma che (an-ˈdrä-mə-kē)
An dros, Sir Edmund (ˈan-dräs) an earlier governor of the colony
an endless ca pac i ty (kə-ˈpa-sə-tē) unlimited power
an gu lar (ˈaŋ-gyə-lər) sharp and stiff without curves
an i ma tion (a-nə-ˈmā-shən) life and enthusiasm
an nual guest in other lands (ˈan-yə-wəl) visitor in other countries every year

an nu i ty (ə-'nü-ə-tē) sum of money paid each year
a non-a non (ə-'nän) continually
An tae us (an-'tē-əs)
an tic i pate (an-'ti-sə-pāt) get ahead of; see beforehand
An til o chus (an-'til-ō-kəs)
an tique (an-'tēk) old
An tin ous (an-'tin-ō-əs)
ant ler ('ant-lər) the entire horn, or any branch of it
a part (ə-'pärt) away from others
ape ('āp) imitate
Aph ro di te (a-frə-'dØ-tē)
A pol lo (ə-'pä-lō)
ap par ent (ə-'per-ənt) that can be seen or known
ap pease (ə-'pēz) make quiet
ap pre hend ed (a-pri-'hend-əd) understood; captured
ap pren tice (ə-'pren-təs) one who learns a trade by helping a skilled worker
ap pro ba tion (a-prə-'bā-shən) being pleased
A qui la Rose ('a-kwə-lə)
arch er ('är-chər) one who uses bow and arrow
arch er y ('är-chər-ē) shooting with bow and arrow
arch i tec tur al (är-kə-'tek-chə-rəl) house building
ar dent ('är-dənt) eager
ar dor ('är-dər) enthusiasm
Ar es ('ar-ēz)
armed in virtue fighting better because he is sure he is right
Arm i stice Day ('är-mə-stəs) November 11, because on Nov. 11, 1918, fighting in World War One ceased
ar ray (ə-'rā) the order for fighting
ar rest ed (ə-'rest-əd) caught; stopped
art ful ('ärt-fəl) meaning more than they seemed to
ar ti fi cial ly daz zling (är-tə-'fi-shəl-ē; 'daz-liŋ) unnaturally bright
ar ti sans ('är-tə-zənz) workers
Art is long beautiful objects long outlast their makers
art shall love true love real feeling be the cause of your music, painting, literature, etc.
As can i as (as-'kā-nē-əs)
as cer tain (a-sər-'tān) find out
ash es ('ash-əz) remains
as pect ('as-pekt) look
as pir ing (ə-'spØr-iŋ) struggling upward
as sail (ə-'sāl) attack

as sas si nate (ə-'sa-sən-āt) kill by unexpected attack
as sault (ə-'sölt) attack
as sem bled (ə-'sem-bəld) met
as so ci at ed (ə-'sō-shē-āt-əd) joined
as sort ment (ə-'sört-mənt) collection of different kinds
as sur ed ly (ə-shür-əd-lē) surely
a sy lum (ə-'sØ-ləm) a home for those who have none of their own
at all e vents (i-'vents) no matter what might happen
Athena (ə-'thē-nə)
at in ter vals ('in-tər-vəlz) with quiet periods of time between
at ran dom ('ran-dəm) as it happens
at tend (ə-'tend) listen carefully
at tend ant (ə-'ten-dənt) goes with it
at ten tive (ə-'ten-tiv) heedful
at the read y ('re-dē) held in position to shoot
au di tors ('ö-də-tərz) listeners; hearers
au gers ('ö-gərz) tools for boring holes
au gust ('ö-gəst) grand
au re ole ('ör-ē-ōl) circle of light, such as saints have
aus tere (ö-'stir) stern
au thor i ty (ə-'thär-ə-tē) one who has power; the right; proof
au to graph ('ö-tə-graf) name in his own handwriting
a venge (ə-'venj) punish
a verred (ə-'vərd) declared
a vert ed (ə-'vərt-əd) turned
aw ful ('ö-fəl) that filled others with awe or dread
az ure ('a-zhər) bright blue

B

baby-white pure white, like a baby's clothes
bade ('bād) ordered
baffled ('ba-fəld) kept from doing what they wish
baffles ('ba-fəlz) is wholly beyond
balance of doom ('ba-lənts) old-fashioned scales, in which the gods weighed the fortunes of men
bard ('bärd) poet
Baron Munchausen's messenger ('bar-ən; 'mən-chaü-zənz; 'me-sən-jər) the fastest person you can think of; Munchausen is famous for the exaggerations in his stories
bate a stiver ('stØ-vər) take off a cent

battery ('ba-tə-rē) fort with mounted guns
baubles ('bȯ-bəlz) trifles
bays ('bāz) honors. Famous men were crowned with a wreath of bay leaves in ancient Greece
be as one act in the same way at the same time
beauteous ('byü-tē-əs) beautiful
befitted (bi-'fit-əd) suited
be given hon or a ble bur i al ('ä-nər-ə-bəl; 'ber-ē-əl) be buried in the grand way suitable for a hero
be hav ior (bi-'ha-vyər) conduct
be in the hu mor ('hyü-mər) feel like it
bel fries ('bel-frēz) towers for bells
bel lowed ('be-lōd) made a loud hollow noise
bel lows ('be-lōz) tool for blowing fires
belted breast man wearing a wide belt over his shoulders and crossed on his breast
be my own man again be free from fears and fancies
be neath (bi-'nēth) under
ben e fit by the her o ism ('be-nə-fit; 'her-ə-wi-zəm) be better off because of the bravery
Be o wulf ('bā-ə-wu̇lf)
be reft (bi-'reft) robbed
be side (bi-'sØd) others
be siege (bi-'sēj) encamp about, fighting when they have a chance
be sought (bi-'sät) begged
be spat tered (bi-'spa-tərd) spattered all over
be trays (bi-'trāz) shows
be witched (bi-'wicht) led your thoughts away
beyond the just measure of their abilities more than they are able to do
bid dy ('bi-dē) hen
bier ('bir) framework for holding a dead body
bil low y breast ('bi-lə-wē; 'brest) bosom made of waves, sought as a child seeks refuge with its mother
birds of pas sage ('pa-sij) birds that go south in winter
bis cuits ('bis-kəts) crackers
bit ters ('bi-tərz) a tonic drink with a bitter flavor
biv ouac ('bi-və-wak) encampment
blaze ('blāz) mark, by cutting a piece of bark off a tree every little distance
bleat ing ('blēt-iŋ) complaining
blight ('blØt) killing
Blithe-Heart King ('blØth) king of happiness; God

blithe some ('blith-səm) merry
blow most dreaded, happening we have been most afraid of
blushed crim son with their shame ('bləsht; 'krim-zən) turned deep red, as a person does when ashamed
board ('bōrd) table
boast ('bōst) something to be proud of
bol ster ('bōl-stər) long pillow for a bed
bom ba zine (bäm-bə-'zēn) thin wool goods used for mourning
bore such a sin gu lar re sem blance to ('sin-gyə-lər; ri-'zem-blənts) looked so curiously like
borne on her northern pine carried on a mast made from a pine which grew in the north
bos oms beat ('bu̇-zəmz) hearts beat with fear
Bos ton Mas sa cre ('bȯs-tən; 'ma-si-kər) a small fight in 1770, when the British fired on Americans who were using them roughly
bottom valley
bound limit
boun te ous ('bau̇n-tē-əs) overflowing with riches
boun ty ('bau̇n-tē) small sum of money
bou quet (bō-'kā) a bunch of flowers
bow as in the dust feel very humble
bowed with years ('bau̇d) feeble because of old age
bow ers ('bau̇-ərz) homes
bran dish ing ('bran-dish-iŋ) shaking threateningly
brawl ing ('brȯl-iŋ) making a noise as they ripple over the stones
brawn y ('brȯ-nē) fat; strong
break ing the peace ('brāk-iŋ) being so rough and noisy he was dangerous
break neck gal lop ing ('brāk-nek; 'ga-ləp-iŋ) hard, fast riding
breast ing for ward ('brest-iŋ; 'fȯr-wərd) directly facing and coming toward them
breathed on the South ('brēthd) blown over the warm countries
breath ing space ('brē-thiŋ) little time to rest from fighting
breath of the night ('breth) odor carried by the breeze
bred to ('bred) trained in
brid al ('bri-dəl) wedding
brief moon ('brēf) four short weeks
broken links of affection restored the meeting again of relatives or friends who have been separated for some time
brooch ('brōch) large pin
brook ('bru̇k) bear; little stream
brook glad dened ('bru̇k; 'gla-dənd) refreshed and beautified by little streams

brown stone ('braůn-stōn) a kind of stone used for fine city houses
buhl ('bül) wood with fancy metal inlays
burgh er ('bər-gər) citizen
burn ished ('bər-nisht) polished
burst ing ('bərst-iŋ) about to break
bursting at the light opening when the sun shines on them
bursting tide full flood when the ocean is highest
but little to their liking not at all what they wished
buttes ('byüts) steep hills
buy your way with tears pay your dues by suffering
by vir tue there of ('vər-chü; t͟ha-rəv) because of which

C

Caed mon ('kad-mən)
Cal ais (ka-'lā) a French port
ca liph ('kā-ləf) a Mohammedan ruler
calm ('kälm) quietness
Ca lyp so (kə-'lip-sō)
canyon ('kan-yən) a narrow valley with high, steep sides
can ti cles ('kan-ti-kəlz) songs
canvas overhead ('kan-vəs; ə-vər-'hed) only the cloth cover between him and the sky
ca pac i ty (kə-'pa-sə-tə) ability
cap and gown costume of a student in college
capped the cli max ('klØ-maks) did the greatest
car ols ('kar-əlz) Christmas songs
Car ron ('kar-ən)
Car thage ('kär-thij)
Ca sa bi an ca (kä-sə-bē-'änk-ə)
cas cades were falling (kas-'kādz) petals were coming down continually, as water flows over a rock and falls in spray
case ('kās) tray for type
Cas san dra (kə-'san-drə) a Trojan prophetess who was never believed
cas tel lat ed ('kas-tə-lā-təd) shaped like a castle with towers
Cas til ian (ka-'stil-yən) Spanish
cat a ract ('ka-tə-rakt) a waterfall
ca tas tro phe (kə-'tas-trə-fē) sad accident
cau tion ('kȯ-shən) advice to be careful; warning
cease ('sēs) stop
cen ten ni al (sen-'ten-nē-əl) one hundred years

cer e mo ny ('ser-ə-mō-nē) formal act
Cey lon (si-'län)
chafes ('chāfs) washes back and forth against; rubs the skin until it is sore
chaff ('chaf) husks of grain
chain ('chān) something that binds; here, ice
Cham ('kam)
cham pi on ('cham-pē-ən) rescuer
chan nel ('cha-nəl) course
chant sub lime ('chant; sə-'blØm) grand, noble religious song
char ac ter is tics (kar-ik-tə-'ris-tiks) peculiar abilities
char i ot ('char-ē-ət) two-wheeled car used in racing and in war
charms them into tas sel ing (chärmz; 'ta-sə-liŋ) sings to them until the blossoms come out
Cha ryb dis (kə-'rib-dəs)
chased a gov ern ment po si tion ('gə-vərn-mənt; pə-'zi-shən) tried to get a place in the civil service without being fitted for it
chasms ('ka-zᵊmz) very large, deep cracks
checked their madness ('chekt) kept them from doing such a rash thing
cheer ly ('chir-lē) cheerfully
cher ished ('cher-isht) loved and cared for
child of future years someone in the far distant time to come
chime ('chØm) music made by bells
cho ral ('kōr-əl) sung in chorus
ci ca da (sə-'kā-də) insect which looks like a grasshopper, but makes a humming noise
Ci co ni ans (si-'kō-nē-ənz)
Cin tra's vine ('sin-trəz) a famous variety of grapes. Cintra is a town in Portugal.
Cir ce ('sər-sē)
cir cum fer ence (sər-'kəm-fərnts) the outer edge
cit a del ('si-tə-dᵊl) fortress in the midst of the city
civ ic slan der ('si-vik; 'slan-dər) lies told about the government
clam ber ('klam-bər) to climb with difficulty
clap boards ('kla-bərdz) boards which form the outer covering of a house
clar i on ('klar-ē-ən) trumpet-like
clear ing ('klir-iŋ) a small stretch of open land
cleave ('klēv) cut
clime ('klØm) climate; country
clod ('kläd) piece of earth; ground
close as a vise ('klōs; 'vØs) very stingy
clown ('klaůn) stupid fellow
coat of mail hard shell which protects him

cof fee house ('kȯ-fē) house of refreshment which served as a public meeting place
cold vict uals ('vi-təlz) left over food
col leg es ('kä-lij-əz) buildings of the different departments of the university
com bat ants (kəm-'ba-tᵊnts) fighters
come to thine own again get back your home and wife
com mand its whole circumference (kə-'mand) look clear around it
com mem o rat ed (kə-'me-mə-rāt-əd) honored
com mence ment (kəm-'ments-mənt) graduation
com mend ing (kə-'mend-iŋ) praising
com ment ('kä-ment) remark
com men ta ry ('kä-mən-ter-ē) story
com mis sions (kə-'mi-shən) errands
com mit tee man (kə-'mi-tē-man) one of the school directors
com mon ('kä-mən) belonging to everyone; ordinary; public square
com mon ly seen at New mar ket ('kä-mən-lē; 'nü-mar-kət) the usual kind shown for sale Newmarket is the name of a famous English fair.
common property known to everyone
com mu ni cat ed (kə-'myü-nə-kāt-əd) told
com pact ('käm-pakt) solid
com pass es ('kəm-pəs-əz) tool for measuring
com pe ti tion (käm-pə-'ti-shən) attempt to equal or surpass
com plex (käm-'pleks) made of many parts; not simple
com ply with (kəm-'plØ) grant
com pos ed ly (kəm-'pō-zəd-lē) calmly
com pos ing new lyr ics (kəm-'pōz-iŋ; 'lir -iks) making up new songs
com pos ing stick (kəm-'pōz-iŋ) a tray in which the typesetter arranges the letters of type
com pos i tor (kəm-'pä-zə-tər) typesetter
con cealed (kən-'sēld) hidden
con ceal ment (kən-'sēl-mənt) hiding
con cer to (kən-'cher-tō) piece of music which is first loud, then soft
con de scen sion (kän-di-'sen-shən) kind manner
con du cive (kən-'dü-siv) helpful
con duct himself (kən-'dəkt) act
con firmed the state ment (kən-'fərmd; 'stāt-mənt) agreed with what had been said
con i cal ('kä-ni-kəl) round and high
con se quenc es ('känt-sə-kwents-əs) what would happen
con serve (kən-'sərv) jam
con spic u ous (kən-'spi-kyə-wəs) striking
con sta ble ('känt-stə-bəl) officer who makes arrests

con stant ('känt-stənt) unchanging; one after another
con ster na tion (kän-stər-'nā-shən) greatest surprise mixed with fright
con su lar service ('kän-sə-lər) work of those who look after the business of the U S. in foreign countries
con sumed (kən-'sümd) destroyed
con tem plat ing ('kän-təm-plāt-iŋ) looking at
con tend (kən-'tend) struggle
con tend with the ad verse skies (kən-'tend; 'ad-vərs) struggles against the lack of rain
con tin ue to trans act (kən-'tin-yü; tran-'zakt) go on working at
con tra ry ('kän-trer-ē) other hand; unfavorable
con tra ry to all rime and reason ('kän-trer-ē) not in the least expected
con trib ute to (kən-'tri-byət) pay a share of
con trib u tor (kən-'tri-byə-tōr) writer
con trived (kən-'trØvd) managed; formed
con vened (kən-'vēnd) called
cop pered gold ('kä-pərd) gold mixed with copper
corn ('kȯrn) grain; wheat
cor o nal ('kȯr-ə-nᵊl) crown
cor o ner's ver dict ('kȯr-ə-nərz; 'vər-dikt) opinion of officer who examined him to find cause of death
cor po ra tion (kȯr-pə-'rā-shən) body of city officers
cor ral (kə-'ral) field for cattle
cor rob o ra tive (kə-'rä-bə-rə-tiv) which proved the story
corse let ('kȯr-slət) armor for body
cot ('kät) cottage
coun cil ('kau̇nt-səl) assembly
coun sel ('kau̇nt-səl) giving advice
coun se lor ('kau̇nt-sə-lər) lawyer
coun te nance ('kau̇n-tᵊn-ənts) face
coun try seat ('kən-trē; 'sēt) large country home
cow punch er ('pənch-ər) cowboy
cracked in rapid suc ces sion (sək-'se-shən) shot, one right after another
craft ('kraft) deceit
craf ty in coun sel ('kraf-tē; 'kau̇nt-səl) clever in giving advice
crag ('krag) projecting mountain rock
cramped ('krampt) hindered
cran ny ('kra-nē) corner
crea ture ('krē-chər) animal
Cre ole ('krē-ōl) a person of Spanish or French descent brought up in a colonial possession; here, Spanish

Crete ('kret)
Creusa (krə-'ü-sə)
crev ic es ('kre-və-səz) cracks or openings in the rocks
crick et bats ('kri-kət; 'bats) bats used in cricket, an outdoor game played with balls, bats, and wickets
crick et field *see* cricket-bats
crisp ('krisp) curly
Crook ed Bil let ('krů-kəd; 'bi-lət) bent stick of wood, name of an inn
crook neck ('krůk-nek) squash
crowd of vet er ans ('ve-tə-rənz) large number of old soldiers; here, white seed-wings of dandelions
crowned his modest temples praised him, though he did not admit he deserved it
crowning mis ad ven ture (mi-səd-'ven-chər) worst thing that happened
cru ci ble ('krü-sə-bəl) dish in which metals can be melted
crum pled ('krəm-pəld) curled tightly
crying hav oc on ('ha-vək) destroying wholly
cuck oo ('kü-kü) bird noted for its whistle, from which it gets its name
cur dled ('kər-dᵊld) separated into curds and whey
cu ri ous flo rist ('kyür-ē-əs) careful gardener
cur rent ('kər-ənt) of the present time
curse of the hungry light on him he knows what it is to be hungry
cus tom house ('kəs-təm) building where taxes on foreign goods brought into this country are paid
cutting the cattle driving some of the herd apart from the others
Cy clops ('sØ-kläps)
cyn ic's ban ('sin-iks; 'ban) entire disapproval of people, felt by one who has no faith in mankind
cy press ('sØ-prəs) tree with dark evergreen leaves

D

dale ('dāl) valley
dan gling ('daŋ-gliŋ) hanging very loosely
darken the waves of wrath the patriot's anger grows stronger
dark hunters patriot soldiers
darkness of the land ignorance throughout the country
dawn of history beginning of the world as far back as we know
dead of night quiet hours of night
dead Past bur y its dead ('past; 'ber-ē) things that are done; be forgotten
dealt death and de struc tion among ('delt; di-'strək-shən) killed and wounded many of

dealt largely ('delt) done a good deal of business
dear high-priced
death and fate death which is decreed by the gods
death vol ley ('vä-lē) shot that kills
de ci sive (di-'sØ-siv) that would end the war
decks ('deks) makes beautiful
de cree (di-'krē) law
de creed (di-'krēd) planned by the gods; commanded
deed ('dēd) make out a paper, giving
deemed it ad vis a ble ('dēmd; əd-'vi-zə-bəl) thought it wise
deep sea
de feat ed (di-'fēt-əd) kept from doing what it wanted to do
de fect in your con duct ('dē-fekt; 'kän-dəkt) fault in your actions
de fi cien cy (di-'fi-shən-sē) lack; shortage
de fied (di-'fØd) been able to resist
de filed with corpses (di-'fØəld) made impure by dead bodies
de grad ed (di-'grād-əd) put down from his rightful place; disgraced
de gree (di-'grē) part
deign ing ('dān-iŋ) lowering himself to give
de layed (di-'lād) put off
del e gates ('de-li-gəts) men sent to represent the different colonies
del i ca cy ('de-li-kə-sē) dainty
de light ing himself with this i de a (di-'lØt-iŋ; Ø-'dē-ə) enjoying this thought
de li ver pos ses sion (di-'li-vər; pə-'ze-shən) give it over to me
deliver them from death save their lives
de moc ra cy (di-'mä-krə-sē) country governed by its people
de pict ed (di-'pikt-əd) pictured
de posed (di-'pōzd) put down
dep re cat ing ly ('de-pri-kā-tiŋ-lē) as if trying to excuse himself
des ert land ('de-zərt) land which produced no cultivated crops
des o late ('de-sə-lət) empty
des o la tion (de-sə-'lā-shən) state of being like a desert
des tined ('des-tənd) intended
des ti ny ('des-tə-nē) lot in life
de ter mined pace (di-'tər-mənd; 'pās) rate as if he were bound to reach a certain place
de vel op ing a dif fer ent pic ture (di-'vel-əp-iŋ; 'di-fərnt; 'pik-chər) showing a picture on each square as it moved
de vic es (di-'vØs-əz) designs
de vised (di-'vØzd) made up
de void of hope (di-'vȯid) without any chance to save my life

dex ter ous ('dek-stə-rəs) skillful
di a lect ('dØ-ə-lekt) form of speech used only in some particular part of the country
Dido ('dØ-dō)
di et ed ('dØ-ət-əd) boarded
dil i gent ('di-lə-jənt) quick with their work
di min u tive (də-'mi-nyə-tiv) very small
di o ra ma (dØ-ə-'ra-mə) representation, partly by painting, partly by real objects of the battle
dis cern (di-'sərn) make out
discharge of artillery train of shot, here mudballs
dis charge their car goes (dis-'chärj; 'kär-gōz) unload their freight
dis charg ing (dis-'chärj-iŋ) paying off
dis ci pline themselves ('di-sə-plən) train themselves to be soldiers
dis con so late (dis-'kän-sə-lət) sorrowful; sad
dis cov er ing (dis-'kə-vər-iŋ) letting it be known
dis guise (də-'skØz) dressed so no one would know them
dis mayed (dis-'mād) without courage because of his loss
dis sem bling (di-'sem-bəl-iŋ) falsely pretending
dis solved (di-'zälvd) melted
dis tinc tion (di-'stiŋk-shən) position
dis tressed (di-'strest) troubled
dit ty ('di-tē) song
diz zy sum mit ('di-zə; 'sə-mət) top so high it made your head swim
dog ma tist ('dȯg-mə-tist) one who asserts things positively
dol phins ('däl-fənz) porpoises with brilliant and changing color
dolts ('dōltz) stupid fellows
Domes day Book ('dümz-dā) book of records
do mes tic (də-'mes-tik) for the house
Do min i cus (də-'mi-ni-kəs)
do min ion (də-'mi-nyən) rule
donned ('dänd) put on
doom ('düm) destruction
Dorchester ('dȯr-ches-tər)
do the brothers justice be fair to the two older ones
do their hearts good make them happy and better
doth fare ill ('dəth) is about all melted
do thy will act as happy as you please
doub let ('dəb-lət) close-fitting body garment formerly worn by men
dou bling ('də-bə-liŋ) running back and forth
dra ma ('drä-mə) play; scene
draw ing ('drȯ-iŋ) getting him to go by a trick

dread ('dred) fearful
driving bargains selling his goods
drowns the moon goes so high that it shuts the moon from sight
drum ming a wel come ('drə-miŋ; 'wel-kəm) making a sound like a soft drum-beat to greet
dry blows slaps or hits which do not cause bleeding
dry ly ('drØ-lē) jokingly
due ('dü) fitting
due rites ('dü; 'rØts) all the honors he deserves
dusty par a dise ('par-ə-dØs) here 'par-e-dØz for rhyme, place of beauty made dusty by continual passing
du ty ('dü-tē) tax on foreign goods; what they ought to do

E

ear nest to make others free ('ər-nəst) ready to work and give up that others may have the same freedom as we
earth en ('ər-thən) made of baked clay
ease and dex ter i ty ('ēz; dek-'ster-ə-tē) enjoyment and skill
easy-gait two forty-five ('gāt) moderate rate of speed—a mile in two minutes and forty-five seconds
ed dies ('e-dēz) whirlpools
ed dy ing gust ('e-dē-iŋ; 'gəst) sudden wind that blows back and forth
e di tion (i-'di-shən) retelling with added details
ed u ca tion (e-jə-'kā-shən) training
Edwards, Jonathan a famous preacher of colonial days, who emphasized God's punishments more than his forgiveness
ef fec tu al ly (i-'fek-chə-wə-lē) with such good effect
ef fer ves cent (e-fər-'ves-sənt) bubbling
e lec tric (i-'lek-trik) like electricity; quietly; swiftly
el e ment ('e-lə-mənt) natural home
elm ('elm) tree of a graceful kind
em barked (im-'bärkt) went on board their boats
em blem ('em-bləm) sign
em er ald ('em-rəld) bright green
e mer gen cy (i-'mər-jent-sē) sudden turn of events
e merg es (i-'mər-jəz) comes out
em i nent ('e-mə-nənt) famous
em pire ('em-pØr) rule over great lands
enameled with her lovliest dyes (i-'na-meld) made bright and shining with the most beautiful colors

en cir cling (in-'sər-kəl-iŋ) around it
en coun tered (in-'kau̇n-tərd) met
en dured on any terms (in-'du̇rd) seen without making me fearful
en rap tured (in-'rap-chərd) charmed
en rolled (in-'rōld) named in lists
en ter prise ('en-tər-prØz) plan of attack
en thu si as tic ag i ta tions (in-thü-zē-'as-tik; a-jə-'tā-shənz) lively speech-making accompanied by many gestures
en tranc ing (in-'trant-siŋ) most charming
en treat (in-'trēt) beg
ep au lets (e-pə-'lets) ornaments on the shoulders of uniforms
equal priv i leg es ('priv-lij-əz) the same rights
e quiv a lent (i-'kwiv-lənt) enough to disprove it
e rect ing (i-'rekt-iŋ) building
ere it pas ses ('er; 'pas-əz) before it is gone
er mine ('ər-mən) white fur used for garments of men in high office
es chew ing (e-'shü-iŋ) getting away from
es cort ('es-kȯrt) companions
Es quire ('es-kwØr) a former title corresponding to Mister
e ter nal (i-'tər-nᵊl) everlasting; never melting
E thi o pi an (ē-thē-'ō-pē-an) Negro
Eu mae us (yü-'mē-əs)
Eur y cle ia (yü-rik-'lē-yä)
Eur y lo chus (yü-'ril-ō-kəs)
Eur y ma chus (yü-'rim-ä-kəs)
e vap o rate (i-'va-pə-rāt) pass off; disappear
even though they offer gifts this has become a proverb, meaning that gifts may conceal bad intentions
everlasting fires fire was sacred, and altar fires were never allowed to go out
ever the same always looking the same
ex ag ger a tion (ig-za-jə-'rā-shən) thing much larger than usual
ex ceed ing (ik-'sēd-iŋ) more than usual
ex ces sive (ik-'se-siv) very great
ex cit ed this up roar (ik-'sØt-əd; 'əp-rōr) started this excitement
ex hort ed (ig-'zȯrt-əd) urged
ex pand (ik-'spand) open up
ex pect anything from arms (ik-'spekt) hope to do any good by fighting
ex pe di tion (ek-spə-'di-shən) trip
ex pend ed (ik-'spen-dəd) used up
ex pe ri enced (ik-'spir-ē-ənst) gone through; had
ex pi ra tion of which pe ri od (ek-spə-'rā-shən; 'pir-ē-əd) end of this time

ex ploit ('ek-splȯit) heroic act
ex quis ite (ek-'skwi-zət) greatest possible
ex quis ite work man ship (ek-'skwi-zət; 'wərk-mən-ship) careful, delicate make
ex treme ly doubt ful of him (ik-'strēm-lē; 'dau̇t-fəl) half afraid of him
ex trem i ty (ik-'stre-mə-tē) point farthest south

F

fab u lous days ('fa-byə-ləs) times we know nothing of but stories
fac ul ty ('fa-kəl-tē) power
fail ing ('fā-liŋ) dying
faint ing voice ('fānt-iŋ) weak voice which is about to stop forever
fair ('fār) good; beautiful
fair and good of ours beautiful and gentle of our race, i.e., people
faith less coldness of the times ('fāth-ləs) lack of faith and eagerness we have now
fall en ('fȯ-lən) those who have not succeeded
fall-like par don ('pär-dən) come down gently and as welcome as release to a prisoner
falls the plague on men ('plāg) sudden disease kills people
fame shall glow glory be seen and known everywhere
fanes ('fānz) churches
Fan euil Hall ('fan-əl) a public hall in Boston used for meetings during the Revolutionary War
fangs ('faŋz) long, sharp teeth
fan tas tic (fan-'tas-tik) queer
far beyond the might of much harder than could be done by
fared ('fārd) gone
far ham lets ('ham-ləts) distant villages
far ther ('fär-thər) more distant
fas ci na tion (fa-sən-'ā-shən) charm; magic
fash ioned ('fa-shənd) made
fa tigued (fə-'tēgd) tired
fawn ('fȯn) a young deer
fawn ing ('fȯ-niŋ) showing delight
fearful hour terrible time
feath ered glean ers ('fe-thərd; 'glēn-ərz) birds
fel low less fir ma ment ('fe-lō-ləs; 'fər-mə-mənt) world of their own
fe ro cious (fə-'rō-shəs) very fierce
fer til i ty (fər-'ti-lə-tē) richness in producing crops

fer vor (ˈfər-vər) enthusiasm
fes tal dain ties (ˈfes-tᵊl; ˈdān-tēz) refreshments for a party
fet ters (ˈfe-tərz) chains
feud of rich and poor (ˈfyüd) constant warfare between the rich people and the poor people
fig ure head (ˈfi-gyər-hed) carved figure on the prow
filling up the outline adding the details himself
find honor in death die fighting for his country, so that he would be remembered as a hero
find no market for it get no one to buy it
fine-spun sen ti ment (ˈsen-tə-mənt) delicate feelings
fire i rons (ˈfØr; ˈØ-ərnz) tongs, poker, etc., for fireplace
fir ma ment (ˈfər-mə-mənt) sky
first-born of glory first heroes who died
fis sure (ˈfi-shər) opening
fix (ˈfiks) make firm
flaw (ˈflȯ) fault
fleet (ˈflēt) number of boats; here, birds in a flock
fleet ing (ˈflēt-iŋ) swiftly passing
flick ered (ˈfli-kərd) waved, brighter, then fainter
flint y (ˈflin-tē) rocky
flist thy vo cal vale (ˈflØst; ˈvō-kəl; ˈvāl) art flying away from the valley where thou hast sung
floods the trees (ˈflədz) flows through every branch and twig
floun der ing (ˈflau̇n-də-riŋ) falling heavily and awkwardly
flour ish ing (ˈflər-ish-iŋ) waving
flus ter a ted (ˈfləs-tər-ā-təd) confused
flut ed col umns (ˈflü-təd; ˈkä-ləmz) grooved pillars
foam ing brine (ˈfōm-iŋ; ˈbrØn) ocean
fold (ˈfōld) inclosure for sheep
font (ˈfänt) set of type
footprints on the sands of time some impression on the age we lived in
for a spell during some little time
for bade (fȯr-ˈbād) did not allow them to
for bear ance (fȯr-ˈbar-ənts) refraining, by the exercise of self-control, from doing a thing
fore head (ˈfȯr-əd)
for eign (ˈfȯr-ən) other than our own
fore most in the race (ˈfōr-mōst) first to reach it
fore saw (fōr-ˈsȯ) thought of beforehand
fore tells (fōr-ˈtelz) tells us beforehand

for mer ly ('fȯr-mər-lē) before this time
forth com ing (fōrth-'kə-miŋ) about to appear
fort night ('fōrt-nØt) two weeks
for tu nate ('fȯrch-nət) lucky
forty feeding like one whole flock of sheep, each cropping the new grass
fought in Freedom's cause served in the Revolutionary War, which made the United States free
foun tain ('faủn-tᵊn) water thrown up into the air to fall again; any spring, brook, or river
fount of har mo ny ('faủnt; 'här-mə-mē) source of music, i.e., nature
Fran cois (frän-'swä)
fraud ('frȯd) dishonesty
frayed ('frād) raveled out; worn
freight ed with life ('frāt-əd) loaded with living people
French proph ets ('prä-fəts) a sect which had fought in France for religious liberty
fresh leaf is springing new grass is beginning to grow
frisk ers ('fris-kərz) ones that went playfully
frol ics ('frä-liks) amusements
frost ed nightcap ('frȯ-stəd) dark covering which protected the bud from the cold
frost pow dered wing ('frȯst; 'paủ-dərd) wing with tiny white specks of snow on its feathers
fru gal i ty (frü-'ga-lə-tē) economy
fuller min strel ('min-strəl) better poet
funny rogue ('rōg) jolly fellow
fur row ('fər-ō) shallow ditch dug by a plow
fur ry civ ic robe ('fər-ē; 'siv-ik) long ermine gown, worn because he was mayor; hence, his office
fu sil lade of terror ('fyü-se-läd) shooting that frightened

G

gap ing ('gā-piŋ) wide open
gar nished ('gär-nisht) decorated
gar ris oned ('gar-ə-sənd) guarded by troops
gath ered ('ga-t͟hərd) drawn together
gave their merry youth away gave up, while young, their prospects of happy life
general court state legislature, which in those times decided cases as well as made laws

gen er a tion (je-nə-'rā-shən) people who were born about the same time you were
ge ni al ('jēn-yəl) warm
ge nie ('jē-nē) powerful spirit in *The Arabian Knights*
gen tians ('jen-shənz) plants with handsome blue flowers
Ger y on ('jē-ri-ən)
ges tures ('jes-chərz) movements of the body which express ideas
ghast ly ('gast-lē) horrible
gib ber ish ('ji-bə-rish) nonsense
gi gan tic (jØ-'gan-tik) great
gird ed ('gər-dəd) made ready
gir dle ('gər-dəl) loose sash; belt
gir dled ('gər-dəld) killed by cutting away a ring of bark, which makes them dry up
give him the butt turn the rod so that the big end is toward the fish, in order to take the strain when the fish is struggling to get away
give thee joy wish happiness for thee
give thee lordship over make thee ruler of
gla cier ('glā-shər) slowly moving body of ice
glad den ('gla-dən) put forth their leaves
glade ('glād) open space among trees
glean ers ('glēn-ərz) those who pick up grain left by the reapers
glen ('glen) little valley
glit ter ing up start fool ('gli-tər-iŋ; 'əp-stärt) man who brags of his new wealth
glory is departed from great days are over for
glow ing ('glō-iŋ) hot
gnashed ('nasht) was biting together
goal ('gōl) final purpose
go a pretty good jog walk right along steadily
gob let ('gäb-lət) tall drinking glass with a stem
go down to the grave die
Golden Town Heaven
good knave's trade ('nāvz) suitable business for a dishonest man
good ly marriage por tion ('güd-lē; 'pōr-shən) large amount of money and valuable things given by her father when she is married
good speed may you succeed
gorge ('gȯrj) a narrow passage between hills or mountains
gor geous ('gȯr-jəs) beautifully colored
gos pel ('gäs-pəl) truth
gos sip y breezes ('gä-səp-ē) gentle winds that seem to talk together

gourd ('gōrd) a hard-shelled fruit, not good to eat, but dried and used for drinking cups
gra cious ('grā-shəs) pleasing
gra da tim (gra-'dē-tim) gradually; step by step
graft ('graft) branch made to grow on a tree of another sort
gran deur ('gran-jər) magnificence
grand ly ('gran-dlē) to the highest degree
grand su preme en deav or (sə-'prēm; in-'de-vər) last noble effort
granted in the char ter ('char-tər) given in the original deed of land from the king
grasp ing pomp ('grasp-iŋ; 'pämp) those who want to take more than their rights in order to make a show
graz ing ('grāz-iŋ) eating the grass
greening becoming green
green ly ('grēn-lē) green
green sward ('grēn; 'swȯrd) grassy sod
griev ous ('grē-vəs) grief-bringing
grim ('grim) fierce; stern
gripe ('grØp) part that holds
ground nut a plant with roots that are good to eat
guil der ('gil-dər) old coin worth about forty-eight cents
guise ('gØz) appearance
Gui ter man ('gē-tər-mən)
gush ('gəsh) outpouring; sudden downpour; flow freely
gut ted ('gət-əd) removed the contents of

H

habits of life ways of living
hab i tude ('ha-bə-tüd) habits
had a good deal of the knave in his com po si tion ('nāv; käm-pə-'zi-shən) was something of a rogue; was tricky
hail ('hāl) greet with joy
hal lowed ('ha-lōd) holy
hallowed shade highly respected spirit
ha lo ('hā-lō) circle of light
Ham el in ('hä-məl-in)
hand workman
hand maid ens ('hand-mā-dənz) girls who serve her
Han o ver ('han-ō-vər)
hap ('hap) happen

hard by close to
hardly less sparing upon themselves; just about as stingy in their own case
hardtack large, thick, square crackers
hard vis age (ˈvi-zij) stern face
haunt ing (ˈhȯn-tiŋ) frequenting; going often to
hav en (ˈhā-vən) harbor
hav oc (ˈha-vək) destruction
Havre (ˈhävrᵊ) French port
hawks' bells tiny round bells fastened to the birds' legs when the hawks were used in hunting
haz ard ous (ˈha-zər-dəs) dangerous
healthy de moc ra cy (di-ˈmä-krə-sē) feeling that all were equal, which was good for them
heart (ˈhärt) courage
hearth (ˈhärth) here ˈhərth for rime, fireplace
heart of the Bad Lands prop er (ˈprä-pər) very center of the wild, barren country
heav ing surges (ˈhēv-iŋ; ˈsər-jəz) tossing waves
Hec tor (ˈhek-tər)
Hec u ba (ˈhe-kyə-bə)
Hel en us (ˈhe-lə-nəs)
He mans, Fe li cia (ˈhe-mənz; fə-ˈlē-shə)
He ra (ˈhir-ə)
her ald (ˈher-əld) one who made announcements
herb (ˈərb) medicinal plant
her brow is to the morning she is always looking toward the new and better day which is coming
Her cu les (ˈhər-kyə-lēz)
herd (ˈhərd) British soldiers
her i tage (ˈher-ə-tij) something handed down from the past
Her mes (ˈhər-mēz)
her mit (ˈhər-mət) living apart from others
Her od (ˈher-əd) *see* Matthew II:16
he ro ic (hi-ˈrō-ik) very large
Hes per i an (he-ˈspir-ē-ən) Italian
Hes per i des (he-ˈsper-ə-dēz)
he who killed the wolf General Putnam was noted for killing a fierce wolf, single-handed, when he was a young man
high (ˈhØ) noble
high fa vor (ˈfā-vər) great liking
high way (ˈhØ-wā) road

hilt ('hilt) handle
Hip pol y ta (hi-'pä-lə-tə)
hired a furnace rented the tools of a goldsmith
his hand was against all men he felt that people were his enemies
his heart melted within him he began to feel very sorry
his steps ad dressed (ə-'drest) went
hith er ('hi-thər) to this place
hitherto ('hi-thər-tü) up to this time
hitherward ('hi-thər-wərd) in this direction
hoar y ('hōr-ē) white
hoax ('hōks) joke
hob ('häb) projection on a fireplace where things may be kept warm
hoist ed ('hȯist-əd) raised
hold a morning gossip exchange the news with someone
hold rev el ('re-vəl) have feasting and games
holy im ag es ('i-mij-əz) small statues of the gods
Holy Writ ('rit) the Bible
home ly ('hōm-lē) everyday
ho ri zon (hə-'rØ-zᵊn) the line where the earth and sky seem to meet
hor o loge of E ter ni ty ('hȯr-ə-lōj; i-'tər-nə-tē) timepiece that measures endless time
hos pi ta ble (hä-'spi-tə-bəl) kind
hospitality (häs-pə-'ta-lə-tē) welcome into a home
host ('hōst) whole army
hos tile ('häs-tᵊl) fighting against him
hos tler ('häs-lər) one who takes care of horses
household gods gods of the home and family; here, the images of the gods
hov er ing in the sky ('hə-vər-iŋ) flying low, ready to swoop
hue and cry shouting that calls citizens to pursue and capture a criminal
hu mil i ty (hyü-'mil-ə-tē) meekness
Hunt, Leigh ('hənt; 'lē)
hus tling ('hə-sə-liŋ) crowding
hy dra ('hØ-drə) mythological creature

I

i dler ('Ød-lər) one who does not work
Il i ad ('i-lē-əd)
ill ('il) bad; poor
il lit er ate (il-'li-tə-rət) ignorant of books
il lu mi nat ing (i-'lü-mə-na-tiŋ) lighting up

il lum ined (i-ˈlü-mənd) having gilt or colored letters
il lus tri ous (i-ˈləs-trē-əs) famous
im meas ur a bly (i-ˈmezh-rə-blē) so large that it could hardly be measured
im me di ate con se quence (i-ˈmē-dē-ət; ˈkänts-sə-kwənts) result which followed at once
im mersed (i-ˈmərst) under water
im mor tal (i-ˈmȯr-tᵊl) that can never die
im mor tal i ty (i-mȯr-ˈta-lə-tē) everlasting life
im pen e tra ble (im-ˈpe-nə-trə-bəl) so dark one could not see through it
im pe ri al (im-ˈpir-ē-əl) having great power
im pe ri ous (im-ˈpir-ē-əs) which demands obedience
im per ti nent (im-ˈpər-tᵊn-ənt) rude
im pi ous (im-ˈpØ-əs) disrespectful
im port (im-ˈpōrt) bring in from another country
im por tuned (im-pər-ˈtünd) begged
im posed (im-ˈpōzd) laid
im pos ing (im-ˈpō-ziŋ) stately
im pres sive (im-ˈpre-siv) important
in ad vert ent ly (i-nəd-ˈvər-tᵊnt-lē) accidentally
in a highly mag ni fied state (ˈmag-nə-fØd) very much larger looking than he really was
in a trice (ˈtrØs) instantly
in cal cu la ble (in-ˈkal-kyə-lə-bəl) so large it cannot be measured
in car nate (in-ˈkär-nāt) in living form
in censed (ˈin-senst) angered
in ces sant ly (in-ˈse-sᵊnt-lē) without ever stopping
in clined (in-ˈklØnd) tipped
in com mode (in-kə-ˈmōd) to cause trouble
in cu ba tor (ˈiŋ-kyə-bā-tər) artificial apparatus for hatching eggs
in debt ed ness (in-ˈde-təd-nəs) sum of money that is owed
in de fat i ga ble (in-di-ˈfa-ti-gə-bəl) tireless
in di cat ed (ˈin-də-kā-təd) pointed out
in dic a tive of (in-ˈdi-kə-tiv) showing
in dif fer ent (in-ˈdi-fərnt) unsteady
in dig nant (in-ˈdig-nənt) angry
in dom i ta ble spirit of av a rice (in-ˈdä-ma-tə-bəl; ˈa-və-rəs) greedy determination
in dul gent (in-ˈdəl-jənt) much in the habit of letting him do as he liked
in fant (ˈin-fənt) child
in fi nite (ˈin-fə-nət) boundless and everlasting
in fi nite ly (ˈin-fə-nət-lē) very much

in fir mi ty (in-'fər-mə-tē) weakness
in flict ed on (in-'flik-təd) given
in his rec ord still ('re-kərd) continually for what he has done
in lieu of ('lü) instead of
in mate ('in-māt) person or thing in the asylum
in nu mer a ble (i-'nüm-rə-bəl) many; countless
in sid i ous (in-'si-dē-əs) sneaking
in so lent ('in-s(ə)-lənt) impudent
in some de gree (di-'grē) partly; to some extent
in spec tion (in-'spek-shən) looking
in state in an honorable manner
in stinct ('in-stiŋkt) her own wish
in teg ri ty (in-'te-grə-tē) honesty
in tel li gi bly (in-'te-lə-jə-blē) clearly
in tense (in-'tents) the greatest
in ter est he re lied on ('in-trəst; rē-'lØd) influence in getting business he expected to have
in ter mis sion (in-tər-'mi-shən) stopping
in ter posed (in-tər-'pōzd) put between the two
in ter pret ed (in-'tər-prə-təd) explained; shown
in ter pret ers (in-'tər-prə-tərz) those who make the meaning clear
in ter spersed (in-tər-'spərst) mixed
in ter vals ('in-tər-vəlz) spaces of time between
in the flower of your days still young and vigorous
in the sod she breathes even the dead answer her
in tol er a bly (in-'täl-rə-blē) terribly
in trench ment (in-'trench-mənt) a trench and a wall made of earth
in un da tion (i-nən-'dā-shən) overflow
in vad ed (in-'vā-dəd) entered by force
iron-bound ('Ø-(ə)rn) held with iron hoops
i ron i cal ly (Ø-'rä-nik-lē) mockingly
ir rev er ent (i-'rev-rənt) disrespectful
Ish ma el ('ish-mā-əl) the son of Abraham and Hagar. It was said of him, "His hand shall be against every man, and every man's hand against him." (Genesis XVI:12)
is sue ('i-shü) come out
is sued from the deep ('i-shüd) come up out of the sea
I tal ian (ə-'tal-yən)
Ithaca ('i-thi-kə)
it is not for me to I should not

J

jagged ('jagd) notched
jag ged ('ja-gəd) rough
jammed ('jamd) crowded
jar gon ing ('jär-gə-niŋ) talking nonsense
jaun ty grace ('jȯn-tē) gay becomingness
jav e lins ('jav-lənz) spears
joc und ('jä-kənd) merry
jun gle ('jeŋ-gəl) thick and tangled forest growth
ju ni per ('jü-nə-pər) a prickly evergreen bush
Ju no ('jü-nō)
Ju pi ter ('jü-pə-tər)

K

keep away the sky shut out the sight of the starry heavens
kins folk ('kinz-fȯk) relatives
kith or kin ('kith; 'kin) family or country
knell ('nel) death-bell
knew no bounds was so great she could not express it
knight ed ('nØ-təd) made a knight; given the title Sir
knob ('näb) part in the center which stands out
knock er ('nä-kər) something fastened to a door for knocking
knuck le ('nə-kəl) small end of leg of mutton; joint
Kop pel berg ('kō-pəl-bərg)

L

La er tes (lā-'ār-tēz)
Laestrygonians (ləs-tri-'gō-nē-ənz)
lag gards and i dlers ('la-gərdz; 'Ød-lərz) slow and unwilling workers
La nier, Sid ney (lə-'nir; 'sid-nē)
La oc ö on (lā-'ä-kə-wän)
La o da mas (lə-'äd-ə-məs)
larger heart wider sympathies
last re treat (ri-'trēt) place where they were last seen
late he bore he carried recently
Lat i nus ('la-tᵊn-əs)
laugh ter of the year ('laf-tər) gayest time of the whole year
launched ('lȯncht) set afloat

lau re ate ('lȯr-ē-ət) honored; in England the poet appointed by the king to compose poems for national occasions is called "poet laureate"

lau rels ('lȯr-əlz) bay trees

La vin ia (lə-'vi-nē-ə)

law by law shall grow laws be made in a just way

lay song

laying their hands to taking hold of

leaf lat ticed ('lēf; 'la-təst) partly shaded by leaves instead of by strips of wood in a crossed pattern

learned gained from books

leg a cy ('le-gə-sē) gift left in a will

lei sure ('lē-zhər) ease; spare time

length of years old age

let the piping drop stop playing his flute

lev ied blackmail ('le-vēd; 'blak-māl) took what they wanted, though it did not belong to them

Lib er ty Tree ('li-bər-tē; 'trē) an elm tree formerly standing in Boston

lief ('lēf) soon; gladly

Li ège (lē-'ezh) a Belgian province

liege men to God ('lēj-mən) those who owe their best service to the right

life is a high way ('hØ-wā) we go on living in the same way that we march along a main road

lift her drooping lid open her eyes which are closing in death

like a cra dled crea ture lies ('krā-d^{ə}ld; 'krē-chər) is as smooth and peaceful as a child in its cradle

lit ter ('li-tər) stretcher for carrying a helpless person

liv er y ('li-və-rē) garments

living oak shall crash tree shall grow old, die, and fall

loathes ('lōthz) shrinks from

loath to grant ('lōth; 'grant) unwilling to agree to

lo custs ('lō-kəsts) kind of grasshoppers

loft y ('lōf-tē) placed on high

loom ('lüm) shadowy form; weaving frame

loosed ('lüst) unlocked; unhitched; untied

lopped ('läpt) cut off

lord it over all act as if he were better than anyone else

Lord of the Garden God

lost en deav or (in-'de-vər) useless attempt

Lou vain (lü-'vā^{n}) Belgian city

loy al ty ('lȯi-əl-tē) faithfulness

Lu cien ('lü-shən)

lu rid ('lü-rəd) pale; ghostly
lurk ('lərk) hide
lust of gold ('ləst) strong desire for money
lus trous ('ləs-trəs) bright
lux u ri ance (ləg-'zhür-ē-əns) richness
luxuriant (ləg-'zhür-ē-ənt) very great
lyre ('lØr) stringed musical instrument, similar to the harp
lyr ics ('lir-iks) melodies; poems made to be sung

M

Ma dei ra (mə-'dir-ə) wine from the Madeira Islands, near Spain
made of all sweet ac cord (ə-'kȯrd) like beautiful, soft music
made the ex traor di na ry ex it (ik-strȯr-dᵊn-er-ē; eg-zət) gone out in the strange way
mad ri gals ('ma-dri-gəlz) songs
mag i cal trans for ma tions ('ma-ji-kəl; trans-fər-'mā-shənz) most wonderful changes
magic slept power to charm was hidden
main ('mān) sea
main tain (mān-'tān) uphold and defend
ma jes tic (mə-'jes-tik) noble
make af fi da vit (a-fə-'dā-vət) swear before a justice
make a mends (ə-'mendz) make up for their wrongdoing
make the crop take care of what you plant, until it is ripe
make this o men sure ('ō-mən) promise us that things shall happen in the way this sign shows
making merry having a gay time
mal e dic tions (ma-lə-'dik-shənz) curses
mal ice ('ma-ləs) hatred
ma li cious (mə-'li-shəs) evil
Ma lines (mȧ-'lēnz) a Belgian city
Mal loch, Doug las ('ma-lək; 'dəg-ləs)
mam moth ('ma-məth) very large
man age mat ters ('ma-nij; 'ma-tərz) act so as to succeed
man-at-arms soldier
man gled frame ('maŋ-gəld; 'frām) torn body
man i fest ('man-nə-fest) visible; show
man i fest symp toms ('man-nə-fest; 'simp-təmz) plain signs
man kind (man-'kØnd) all people
man sion ('mant-shən) large house

man tle (ˈman-tᵊl) long, loose garment
man tled in a vol ume (ˈman-tᵊld; ˈväl-yəm) wrapped in a mass
many a good ly pros pect (ˈgu̇d-lē; ˈprä-spekt) large number of fine views
ma raud ers (mə-ˈrȯd-ərz) thieves
mar gin (ˈmär-jən) edge
mark (ˈmärk) limit; sear
mark the rolling year keep track of the changing seasons
Mars (ˈmärz)
mar tin (ˈmär-tᵊn) a purple bird belonging to the swallow family
mar tyr (ˈmär-tər) one who dies for his faith
mar vel (ˈmär-vəl) a wonder; wonderful happening
mar vel ous (ˈmärv-ə-ləs) wonderful
ma son (ˈmā-sᵊn) builder
mas sa cre (ˈma-si-kər) killing of a large number without any reason
mas sive (ˈma-siv) large; heavy
mas sy (ˈma-sē) great
mas tered (ˈmas-tərd) made our own
ma tron (ˈmā-trən) the woman who manages a household; mother
ma tur er (mə-ˈtu̇r-ər) of older growth
ma vis (ˈmā-vəs) song thrush
may his tribe in crease (in-ˈkrēs) we wish for many more such people
may not stay am not allowed to stop
mean (ˈmēn) common
med i tat ing (ˈme-də-tā-tiŋ) thinking
med i ta tions (me-də-ˈtā-shənz) serious thoughts
med i ta tive ly (me-də-ˈtā-tiv-lē) very thoughtfully
meet ing house (ˈmē-tiŋ-hau̇s) church
mel an chol y (ˈme-lən-kä-lē) very sad
me lo di ous (mə-ˈlō-dē-əs) musical
mel o dy sin cere (ˈme-lə-dē; sin-ˈsir) song really expressing the feelings of the singer
Men e la us (me-nə-ˈlā-əs)
men of the same blood relatives
men tioned (ˈment-shənd) spoken of
Mer cier, Car dinal (mer-ˈsyā; ˈkärd-nəl)
Mercury (ˈmər-kyə-rē)
merle (ˈmərl) blackbird
me trop o lis (mə-ˈträ-pə-ləs) chief city
Mi das golden touch (ˈmØ-dəs) according to the Greek legend, King Midas was able for a few hours to turn to gold everything he touched
might and main (ˈmØt; ˈmān) whole strength

mile stone ('mØəl-stōn) stone which marks distance-boundary mark
mil i ta ry sci ence ('mi-lə-ter-ē; 'sØ-ənts) knowledge of war
military stores ('mi-lə-ter-ē; 'stōrz) guns and ammunition
mills of toil life of work
Mil ti a des (mil-'tØ-ə-dēz) Athenian general; here, the turkey
mind take care of
mind's dumb whisper silence of the mind
mingle in the conversation talk to the other people
min i a ture ('mi-ni-chůr) tiny
Min er va (mi-'nər-və)
Min is try ('mi-nə-strē) heads of departments of state in England
min strels ('min-strəlz) singers
mi nute ly (mØ-'nüt-lē) much in detail
min ute men ('mi-nət-mən) men ready to go and fight whenever called
mir y ('mØ-rē) muddy
mists of splen dor ('splen-dər) beautiful veil-like effect of the maple flowers
mock ('mäk) make fun of
mocks the doctor's rules needs to pay no attention to laws of health
mod er ate stat ure ('mä-də-rət; 'sta-chər) medium height
modes ('mōdz) customs
moil ('mȯiəl) hard work
mold ('mōld) earth; dirt
mo lest (mə-'lest) harm
mo ly ('mō-lē) magic plant
mo men ta ri ly (mō-mən-'ter-ə-lē) every moment
mo men tous (mō-'men-təs) very important
mon arch ('mä-nərk) ruler
Mon sieur le Plais ir (məs-'yər; 'lə; plə-'zēr) Mr. Pleasure
mon ster ('män-stər) huge animal
moored ('můrd) fastened
mo roc co's gilded gleam (mə-'rä-kōz) shine of fine leather binding with gilt letters
mor tal ('mȯr-tᵊl) deadly
mortal looms ('mȯr-tᵊl; 'lümz) weaving frames invented by men
mort gage ('mȯr-gij) promise to give up some property if a debt is not paid at a time promised
Mo selle (mō-'zel) a kind of wine
mother-of-pearl hard inside layer of a shell, which has beautiful colors
mo tion thy rest ('mō-shən) never stopping
moun tain born ('maůn-tᵊn) rising among mountains
mourn ful numbers ('mōrn-fəl) sad, gloomy verses

mournful rimes ('mōrn-fəl; 'rØmz) sad poetry
mourn ing ('mōr-niŋ) weeping
mult i plied ('məl-tə-plØd) made greater
mused ('myüzd) thought
mu si cal a dept ('myü-zi-kəl; ə-'dept) skilled musician
Mus ke gon (mə-'skē-gən)
mus ket ry ('məs-kə-trē) sound of guns firing
mus ter ing ('məs-tə-riŋ) that is calling the men together
mut tered ('mə-tərd) spoke in a low, indistinct tone
my heart leaps up I feel a sudden joy
my ho ri zon grew (hə-'rØ-zᵊn) I came to have a broader outlook
myr i ads ('mir-ē-ədz) a countless number
Myr mi dons ('mər-mə-dänz)
mys tic ('mis-tik) mysterious

N

naked woods leafless trees
name shall shine reputation be the best
nar ra tive ('nar-ə-tiv) story
nar ra tor ('nar-ā-tər) teller
nar row ing lust ('nār-ō-iŋ; 'ləst) strong desire which crowds out nobler wishes
nar y ('nar-ē) not one
na tive ('nā-tiv) where I was born; natural; one born in
naught ('nȯt) not at all
Nausicaa (nȯ-'si-kā-ə)
near ing ('nir-iŋ) almost here
nec tar ('nek-tər) drink of the gods; hence, most delicious drink
needle of my nature dips I turn, as the compass needle is drawn north
neg a tive ('ne-gə-tiv) denying it
Nep tune ('nep-tün)
nerve less the i ron hand ('nərv-ləs; 'i-ərn) the strong arm is helpless in death
Nes tor ('nes-tər)
newt ('nüt) lizard
new voice of Spring first song of the cuckoo heard that year
nigh ('nØ) near
night-bird nightingale
Ni zam (ni-'zäm) native ruler
nod dy ('nä-dē) fool
nook ('nu̇k) corner

noon ing ('nü-niŋ) noon recess
note less ('nōt-ləs) not worth talking about
note of hand promises to pay money when called for
nov ice ('nä-vəs) one with a simple, unsuspecting mind
nursed a faith believed more and more
nur tured ('nər-chərd) taken care of
nymphs ('nimpfs) beautiful maidens, related to the gods and having some divine power

O

oak en sub stance ('ō-kən; 'səb-stənts) oak wood of which it was made
oath ('ōth) solemn promise
o bese (ō-'bēs) extremely fat
ob ject of ab hor rence ('äb-jikt; əb-'hȯr-ənts) person hated and feared
ob scured (äb-'skyu̇rd) hidden; covered
obscured Co lum bi a's day (kə-'ləm-bē-əz) made it look dark for the nation
ob scu ri ty (äb-'skyu̇r-ə-tē) gloom; darkness
oc cur rence (ə-'kər-ənts) happening
Od ys sey ('ä-də-sē)
of after time in the future
of doubt ful char ac ter ('dau̇t-fəl; 'kar-ik-tər) whom nobody knew anything about
of many tongues speaking several different languages
of pe cul iar del i ca cy (pi-'kyül-yər; 'de-li-kə-sē) hard to ask because it might offend
of prom is ing parts ('prä-mə-siŋ) who seemed to be going to make his mark in life
of set pur pose ('pər-pəs) by a plan
of ten ('ȯ-fən)
of their own ac cord became (ə-'kȯrd) changed themselves into
of the line grown near the equator
of untamed nature just as they grew
of whom he re quires (ri-'kwØrz) to whom he insists
O gy gia (ō-'jij-ē-ə)
oint ment ('ȯint-mənt) thick, perfumed oil
Old French War war between the French and the English (1754-1763)
old-time fire enthusiasm he had felt when a young fisherman
Olym pus (ə-'lim-pəs)
om nip o tence (äm-'ni-pə-tənts) almighty power
on closer in spec tion (in-'spek-shən) when looked at more carefully

on slaught (ˈän-slȯt) attack
on soil and sea on land and water the same; everywhere
on the rack in torment
on the road at a place on my way
on the score of e con o my (ˈskōr; i-ˈkä-nə-mē) for the sake of making money
op pres sive (ə-ˈpre-siv) very heavy
or a cle (ˈȯr-ə-kəl) wish of the gods, as told by some priest
o ral tes ti mo ny (ˈōr-əl; ˈtes-tə-mō-nē) proof by saying so
or ches tra (ˈȯr-kəs-trə) company of various musical instruments
or chis (ˈȯr-kəs) orchid; a rare wildflower
or dered bounds (ˈȯr-dərd) limits set for us
o rig i nate (ə-ˈri-jə-nāt) start
our dreams in vad ed (in-ˈvā-dəd) disturbed our sleep
out cry (ˈaüt-krØ) loud cry
out land ish (ˈaüt-ˈlan-dish) strange; foreign
out of his el e ment (ˈe-lə-mənt) not in his natural surroundings
o ver arched with (ō-vər-ˈärcht) having a round-topped cover of
overgrown with bar na cles (ˈbär-ni-kəlz) covered with small shellfish
o ver lord (ˈō-vər-lȯrd) ruler
o ver se er (ˈō-və(r)-sir) man in charge of the poor
o ver whelm (ō-vər-ˈhwelm) bury in its waters
owe man kind a debt (man-ˈkØnd; ˈdet) ought to do everything possible to help others

P

painless play amusement that leaves no weariness afterward
pale is the lip of scorn those who talked in a proud and insulting way are now dead
pam phlets (ˈpamp-fləts) small, paper-covered books
pan niers (ˈpan-yərz) baskets carried on either side
pan o ra ma (pa-nə-ˈra-mə) rapidly changing display of expressions
par a ble (ˈpar-ə-bəl) little story which teaches a lesson
pa rad ed (pə-ˈrā-dəd) were assembled, as if ready for marching
par a lyzed (ˈpar-ə-lØzd) affected so that he could not move
Par lia ment (ˈpär-lə-mənt) the British legislative body
Par nas sus (pär-ˈna-səs)
part and par cel of (ˈpär-cəl) belonging to
par tridge (ˈpär-trij) the bobwhite
party strife struggles between political parties
pas sage (ˈpa-sij) fare

pas sing few ('pa-siŋ) a very small number indeed
pas sion ('pa-shən) temper
pas sion ate ly ('pa-shə-nət-lē) very angrily
pas time ('pas-tØm) amusement
pate ('pāt) head
pa thos ('pā-thäs) sad writing
pa tri ots ('pā-trē-əts) those who love and give service to their country
Pa tro clus (pə-'trō-kləs)
paying court showing attention
peep-show having an object or pictures inside, to be looked at through a hole which contains a magnifying glass
Pe leus ('pēl-yüs)
Pe nel o pe (pə-'ne-lə-pē)
per i lous en cum brance ('per-ə-ləs; in-'kəm-brəns) dangerous burden
per pe trat ed ('pər-pə-trā-təd) done
per pet u al (pər-'pe-chə-wəl) continual
per pet u ate (pər-'pe-chə-wāt) keep alive
per plex i ty (pər-'plek-sə-tē) failure to understand
per se cu tion (pər-si-'kyü-shən) pursuing with intent to kill
per sist ed in (pər-'sis-təd) kept on
per ti na cious and in trac ta ble dis po si tion (pər-tən-'ā-shəs; in-'trak-tə-bəl; dis-pə-'zi-shən) stubborn, headstrong nature
pes tered ('pes-tərd) bothered
pes ti lence ('pes-tə-lənts) a contagious disease causing many and sudden deaths
pet u lant ('pe-chə-lənt) cross; sullen
pew ter ('pyü-tər) a white metal formerly much used instead of silver
Phae cia (fə-'ā-shyə)
Phae cians (fə-'ā-shyənz)
pick er el ('pi-kə-rəl) a common fish
pick et ed ('pi-kə-təd) tied
pie bald ('pØ-bȯld) spotted
pied ('pØd) of different colors
Pied Piper flute-player dressed in many gay colors
pierced ('pirst) went through
pi e ty ('pØ-ə-tē) love for God and man
pil grim ag es ('pil-grə-mi-jəz) journeys
pin ions ('pin-yənz) wings
pin na cles ('pi-ni-kəlz) high, slender points
pi o neer (pØ-ə-'nir) going before and preparing the way for others
pipes his story sings what he has to tell, in flutelike notes
pi rates ('pØ-rəts) sea-robbers

pit e ous (ˈpi-tē-əs) sad
place of their self con tent (ˈself; kən-ˈtent) state of being satisfied with themselves as they are
place that en ter tains stran gers (en-tər-ˈtānz; ˈstrān-jərz) inn
plate dishes
plateau a broad, level, elevated stretch of land
Pla to (ˈplā-tō) a Greek who wrote *The Republic,* in which he described an ideal country. In it he permitted no poets; and the men who write book reviews seem also to want to drive away the poets.
play of his proud flanks movement of the muscles in his great sides
play the master rule
please your honors gentlemen, please listen
plied (ˈplØd) used busily
plodders (ˈplä-dərz) ones that moved slowly
plume (ˈplüm) feather
ply the loom (ˈplØ; ˈlüm) weave cloth—one of the duties of a servant
poised (ˈpȯizd) balanced
Po li tes (pə-ˈlØ-tēz)
Poly phe mus (pä-lə-ˈfē-məs)
pom e gran ate (ˈpä-mə-gra-nət) a fruit looking like an orange, but having red pulp with many seeds
pon der ing (ˈpän-də-riŋ) thinking deeply
pon der ous (ˈpän-də-rəs) very heavy
pop u la tion (pä-pyə-ˈlā-shən) people who lived there
pop u lous (ˈpä-pyə-ləs) inhabited; occupied by many people
por poise (ˈpȯr-pəs) a deep-water fish
por rin ger (ˈpȯr-ən-jər) bowl
por ti co (ˈpōr-ti-kō) porch made with large pillars
Po sei don (pə-ˈsØ-dən)
pos ter i ty (pä-ˈster-ə-tē) people who come after you
poth er (ˈpä-t͟hər) noise and confusion
pot tage (ˈpä-tij) good dishes; a soup
pounce (ˈpau̇nts) jump down suddenly
poured out wine made an offering before prayer
pranc ing (ˈprant-siŋ) gayly springing
pre cau tion (pri-ˈkȯ-shən) care; plan to be careful
Pre cep tor (pri-ˈsep-tər) master of the school
pre cincts (ˈprē-siŋkts) space of land
prec i pice (ˈpre-sə-pəs) cliff
pre cise ly (pri-ˈsØs-lē) just
pre late (ˈpre-lət) minister

prem is es ('pre-mə-səs) grounds
pre scribed (pri-'skrØbd) ordered
press go forward
pressed attacked
pre vail (pri-'vāl) get and keep the mastery; win the victory in battle
prevailing (pri-'vā-liŋ) nearly everywhere
Pri am ('prØ-əm)
pride in place and blood glorying in position and family
prime ('prØm) best; best time
pris mat ic colors (priz-'ma-tik) colors into which light can be separated: violet, indigo, blue, green, yellow, orange, and red
priv i leg es ('priv-li-jəz) things people were allowed to do
pro ceed ing (prō-'sēd-iŋ) way of doing
pro dig ious (prə-'di-jəs) huge
prodigious spec tac le ('spek-ti-kəl) huge thing to look at
pro file ('prō-fØl) side view
prog nos ti ca ting (präg-'näs-tə-kā-tiŋ) foretelling
pro ject ed (prə-'jek-təd) with points reaching forward
prom ised glory ('prä-məst) fruit that is to come
prong buck ('pröŋ-bək) one of the antelope family; the horns have a long, sharp end, or prong
pro nounced it to be (prə-'naùntst) said positively that it was
proof against all wounds so that it could not be wounded in any way
prop er ties ('prä-pər-tēz) qualities
prophecy act of telling what is going to happen
proph e sy ('prä-fə-sē) tell beforehand
pro phet ic veil (prä-'fe-tik; 'vāl) hanging blossoms which promise leaves later
pro posed such meas ures as (prə-'pōzd; 'me-zhərz) set forth the necessary things to be done
pro pri e tor (prə-'prØ-ə-tər) owner
pros pect ('prä-spekt) view; chance
pros pered ('präs-pərd) got along
pros trate ('prä-strāt) fallen
pros trat ed ('prä-strā-təd) knocked down
proved a cool er to ('prüvd; 'kü-lər) taken away the fierceness from
pro vin cial (prə-'vint-shəl) of the colony
prov o ca tion (prä-və-'kā-shən) cause; reason
psal ter y ('säl-tə-rē) an old kind of stringed musical instrument
pulse ('pəls) peas, beans, etc., that is, plain food
pump kin ('pəmp-kən)
punch eon ('pən-chən) large cask

pur er laws (ˈpyür-ər; ˈlȯz) better rules of conduct
pur ple (ˈpər-pəl) ripen
pur suit (pər-ˈsüt) chase
put it into the heart of gave the thought to
Pyr rhus (ˈpir-əs)

Q

quad (ˈkwäd) college buildings
quaint (ˈkwānt) old-fashioned; curious
quaint at tire (ə-ˈtØr) strange, old-fashioned clothes
quaked (ˈkwākt) shook in fright
quar ry (ˈkwȯr-ē) game
quar tered (ˈkwȯr-tərd) lodged; housed
quar ter ing (ˈkwȯr-tə-riŋ) moving sidewise
quick and treach er ous sands of sin (ˈkwik; ˈtre-chə-rəs) wrongdoing that is like quicksand, which drags you down
quite (ˈkwØt) entirely
quite a re spect a ble nar ra tive (ri-ˈspek-tə-bəl; ˈnar-ə-tiv) a complete story
quiv er (ˈkwi-vər) case; tremble
quoit (ˈkȯit) iron ring
quoth (ˈkwōth) said

R

rac y sweetness (ˈrā-sē) fresh sap
rai ment (ˈrā-mənt) clothing
ran dom (ˈran-dəm) *see* at random
range (ˈrānj) wild; slant; movement; go where I like
ran som (ˈran-səm) price paid to get something back
rapt in (ˈrapt) wholly taken up by
re al i ty (rē-ˈa-lə-tē) truth; fact
realm (ˈrelm) region
realms of death places where the dead remain—showing that he must die
re ap pear ance (rē-ə-ˈpir-ənts) coming into view again
reared (ˈrird) brought up
re buked (ri-ˈbyükt) spoke, blaming
re cess es (ˈrē-se-səs) hidden corners
rec on noi ter (rē-kə-ˈnȯi-tər) inspect
re cruit ed (ri-ˈkrü-təd) refreshed
re cruits (ri-ˈkrüts) soldiers who had just enlisted

re cum bent (ri-'kəm-bənt) easy; reclining
re dress (ri-'dres) chance for justice
reek ing ('rē-kiŋ) steaming
re frac to ry (ri-'frak-tə-rē) stubborn
re fus al of hos pi tal i ty (ri-'fyü-zəl; häs-pə-'ta-lə-tē) rude way you would not have me as a guest
re gal tent ('rē-gəl) tent fit for a king
re gions ('rē-jənz) spaces
regions now un trod (ən-'träd) countries not yet settled
reg u late itself ('re-gyə-lāt) go on in an orderly manner
Reid, Mayne ('rēd, 'mān)
rein ing in ('rā-niŋ) stopping
re joined (ri-'jȯind) responded
re late all the par tic u lars (ri-'lāt; pər-'ti-kyə-lərz) tell the whole story
re laxed his grasp (ri-'lakst) loosened his hold
re mon stran ces (ri-'män-strənt-səz) urgings against doing something
rend ('rend) tear apart
ren der ('ren-dər) give
rendered ('ren-dərd) made
re nown (ri-'naủn) fame
re paired (ri-'pard) made up for
re pairs thy ru ral seat (ri-'parz; 'thØ; 'rủr-əl; 'sēt) furnishes newly your home in the country
re past (ri-'past) meal
re plen ish (ri-'ple-nish) fill again
re pub lic an (ri-'pə-bli-kən) a believer in all men being equal
rep u ta ble ('re-pyə-tə-bəl) with a good name
re quest (ri-'kwest) asking
re sem bled (ri-'zem-bəld) was like
re solve (ri-'zälv) plan decided on
resolved on death or liberty was determined to be free or die fighting for freedom
resolve themselves into become
re spec tive (ri-'spek-tiv) own
re splend ent (ri-'splen-dənt) brilliant
re sumed (ri-'zümd) started again
res ur rec tion (re-zə-'rek-shən) coming to life again
re treat ed (ri-'trē-təd) gone back; given way; melted
re turn ing (ri-'tər-niŋ) rising
re ver ber ate (ri-'vər-bə-rāt) echo
rev er ence ('rev-rənts) respect

rev er enced ('rev-rənsd) respected
rev er ies pro found ('re-və-rēz; prə-'faùnd) deep thought
re vived his spi rits (rə-'vØvd; 'spir-əts) cheered him up
re volved from night to day (ri-'valvd) turned on its axis so darkness changed to light
revolve the cir cum stanc es ('ser-kᵊm-stant-səs) go over the story
Rhen ish ('re-nish) a kind of wine
rib ald ('ri-bəld) coarse fellow
rich gloriously bright
rich fulfillment dawn (ful-'fil-mənt) beginning of the luxuriant growth promised by the buds in spring
rig or ('ri-gər) coldness
riv en ('ri-vən) split
rod of op pres sion ('räd; ə-'pre-shən) unjust rule
rogue el e phant ('rōg; 'e-lə-fənt) vicious beast which roams about alone, doing harm
roll a far ('rōl; ə-'fär) stretch for long distances
rolled ('rōld) passed
Ro mu lus ('räm-yə-ləs)
Roo se velt, The o dore ('rō-zə-vəlt, 'thē-ə-dȯr))
rosy-fingered Dawn sunrise with its red beams, like a goddess's fingers
roun de lay ('raùn-də-lā) song with a repeated chorus
round up ('raùn-dəp) collecting cattle by riding around them and driving them
route ('rüt) path; way
royal standard flag of the king
ru bi cund ('rü-bi-kənd) red
rud dy ('rə-dē) red
rude ('rüd) home-made
rum bled ('rəm-bəld) rolled heavily
ruth less ly ('rüth-ləs-lē) most cruelly

S

sa ble ('sā-bəl) black
sac ri fice ('sa-krə-fØs) offerings
Saint Gau dens ('sānt; 'gō-dənz) American sculptor, (1848-1907)
salm on ('sa-mən)
sanc tioned his ad dress es ('saŋk-shənd; ə-'dre-səs) favored his attentions
sank to their rest died
saps ('saps) weakens
sat in coun cil ('kaùn-səl) talked things over

saun tered ('sȯn-tərd) walked idly
save my house preserve my descendants
sa vor y ('sā-və-rē) inviting; appetizing
Sax on ('sak-sən) belonging to the Anglo-Saxon race, which had settled in England before 700 A.D.
scab bard ('ska-bərd) sheath
scap net ('skap-net) catching large numbers of insects in the air for food, as a scoopnet dips up many minnows at one time
scep ter ('sep-tər) rod of a ruler
scheme ('skēm) plan
scheme of bond age ('bän-dij) plan to keep us from being free
sci ence ('sØ-ənts) learning
science truth shall know learning be kept true
scim i tar ('si-mə-tər) curved sword
Scit u ate ('sitch-ə-wāt)
scoffed ('skäft) laughed; made fun
scof fing ('skäf-iŋ) making fun
scorn er's seat ('skȯr-nərz) place where I would look down on others
scorn of long fa mil i ar i ty (fə-mi-lē-'yar-ə-tē) contempt because he had seen them so often
scor pi on ('skȯr-pē-ən) stinging bug
Scyl la ('si-lə)
sea far ing ('sē-far-iŋ) pertaining to those who spend much time on the sea; living in or on the sea
sea pur ple ('sē; 'pər-pəl) bright purple, so-called because the dye came from an ocean shell-fish
sear ('sir) dry
sea wor thy ('sē-wər-t͟hē) able to float
se clud ed (si-'klü-dəd) lonely
se date ap pear ance (si-'dāt; ə-'pir-ənts) serious look
se er ('sir) prophet
seize upon my feet ('sēz) make me go forth
self same ('self-sām) exact
sen iors ('sə-nyərz) the ones older than he
sen sa tion al (sen-'sā-shnəl) excitingly interesting
sen su al ('sen(t)-shə-wəl) bodily; selfish
se ren i ty (sə-'re-nə-tē) calmness
sets men to strive makes men fight
set their faces determined to stand
sex ton ('seks-tən) man who takes care of a church
shad ow y grass ('sha-dō-ē) tall grass casting shadows on tiny flowers

shadowy lens of even gathering darkness of evening, as through a magnifying glass
shapes of foul dis ease (di-'zēz) kinds of sickness caused by dirt
shap ing out ('shā-piŋ) cutting and fitting boards to make
sharps and flats keys
shav en ('shā-vən) closely mowed
sheathed ('shēthd) in its case, or sheath
sheer ('shir) straight up and down; perpendicular
shift ('shift) change
shift ing and furl ing ('shif-tiŋ; 'fər-liŋ) changing and rolling up
shil ling ('shi-liŋ) an English coin, worth about twenty-four cents
shiv ered ('shi-vərd) much broken
shoal ('shōl) place where the water is very shallow
shrank ('shraŋk) bent
shrine ('shrØn) holy place
shroud less ('shraủd-ləs) without being dressed for burial
shroud of snow ('shraủd) pure white garment in which a person is buried
shun ('shən) keep away from
shut tle ('shə-tᵊl) tool for weaving
Sib yl ('si-bəl)
sig nals ('sig-nᵊlz) warning signs or lights
sig na ture ('sig-nə-chủr) name signed at the bottom of
Si gnor Far Ni en te (sē-'nyōr; 'fär; nē-'en-tā) Mr. Do Nothing
sil ver y main ('sil-və-rē; 'mān) shining ocean
sim i lar line of con duct ('si-mə-lər; 'kän-dəkt) same way of acting
sim ply ('sim-plē) merely; just
Sin on ('sØ-nən)
sin ew y ('sin-yə-wē) strong; powerful
sin gu lar ap pear ance ('siŋ-gyə-lər; ə-'pir-ənts) strange look
singular prop er ty ('prä-pər-tē) unusual quality
sin is ter ('si-nəs-tər) evil
si rens ('sØ-rənz)
sires ('sØrz) forefathers
sit u a tion (si-chə-'wā-shən) place
skel e ton at their feast ('ske-lə-tᵊn) something sad in the midst of pleasure. The Egyptians used to set up a death's head at their feasts
slake our thirsty souls ('slāk) bring encouragement to our discouraged minds as rain brings refreshment to plants
slashed ('slasht) made with slits, to show cloth of a different color
sledge ('slej) heavy hammer
sloped ('slōpt) tipped

slopes ('slōps) hillsides
slowly dying cause movement which is needed no longer
sly ('slØ) meant to catch me
smith y ('smi-thē) place where horses are shod
smit ten ('smi-tᵊn) struck; wounded
smote ('smōt) slapped
snout ed ('snau̇-təd) long-nosed
snuff box es ('snəf-bäk-səs) boxes for holding snuff, or powdered tobacco, which people used to carry around for smelling
so a ban doned a char ac ter (ə-'ban-dənd; 'kar-ik-tər) such a wicked man so as you never saw, in such a way as you have never seen
so cia bly ('sō-shə-blē) pleasantly talking together
so cial con di tions ('sō-shəl; kən-'di-shənz) state in which they live
so cruel and grinding a temper ('crül; 'grØn-diŋ; 'tem-pər) such a cross and stingy disposition
soft ness in the air ('sȯft-nəs) moist warmth about me
so journ ers ('sō-jər-nərz) travelers who remain
sol i ta ry ('sä-lə-ter-ē) lonesome
some de gree of cre dence (di-'grē; 'kre-dᵊnts) belief in part of what he said
something of all on oc ca sions (ə-'kā-zhənz) agreed in belief with the man he happened to be talking with
son net ('sä-nət) fourteen-line poem
son of E rin ('e-rən) Irishman
soph ist er ('sä-fis-tər) man pretending to have reasons which he really knew were false
sore ('sōr) very sad; very much
Sound ('sau̇nd) Long Island Sound
spare guns guns shot by the servants
spar ry ('spär-ē) bright because of the shining minerals in the walls
speak for me tell about me
speak within bounds to make a thing, in the telling, smaller than it is
spell-bound wholly charmed
spheres of gold ('sfirz) the pumpkin
spice of life seasoning; what makes it interesting
spin ster ('spin-stər) an unmarried woman, no longer young
spire ('spØr) slender tower
spite ('spØt) hate; meanness
spits ('spitz) long, pointed rods to hold meat roasting over an open fire
splen dor ('splen-dər) beauty
spoil ('spȯil) booty; plunder
sprang ('spraŋ) grew up quickly

sprats ('sprats) small fish
spread her broad banner ('spred) may the flag fly unfurled
sprigs ('sprigz) tiny branches
stalk ('stȯk) stem
star ry time ('stär-ē) time when the stars shine; night
start ing little doubts ('stär-tiŋ; 'dau̇ts) beginning sentences with "perhaps" or "I suppose"
starts is surprised and delighted
sta tion ('stā-shən) place
stat ure ('sta-chər) height
St. Bar thol o mew (bär-'thä-lə-myü) a terrible killing of human beings in Paris (1572)
stead ('sted) place
steed ('stēd) racehorse
stepped into the breach did the thing which needed to be done
still seeming best liking whatever weather comes
stin gy ('stin-jē) scanty; small
stood for ages still has been growing in the same place for a long, long time
storm of the Revolution war that affected the country as a storm does the ocean
strand ('strand) shore
strewn ('strün) scattered
strip ling ('stri-pliŋ) youth
stumps ('stəmps) wooden rods which form the wickets used in cricket
Styr i a ('stir-ē-ə)
sub ject ed to an in tense gaze (səb-'jek-təd; 'in-tens; 'gāz) compelled to meet a searching look
sub lime (sə-'blØm) noble
sub sist (səb-'sist) live
sub stance ('səb-stents) wealth; possessions
sub ter ra ne ous (səb-tə-'rā-nē-əs) underground
sub tle ('sə-tᵊl) delicate
suc ces sive gen er a tions (sək-'se-siv; je-nə-'rā-shənz) classes that went through the school
sugarplums round candies
suit ors ('sü-tərz) men who are seeking to marry
sul len ('sə-lən) gloomy
sullen and gro tesque (grō-'tesk) hard, gloomy, and fantastic looking
sum mit ('sə-mət) top
sun dry ('sən-drē) several
sunlit oceans great stretches of water gleaming in the sunshine
sup ple ('sə-pəl) possessing the power to move easily; nimble

sup pli cate ('sə-plə-kāt) beg
Su preme Re pub lic (sə-'prēm; ri-'pə-blik) greatest government of the people, the United States
surf ('sərf) foam where the waves break on the shore
sur prised the hill (sər-'prØzd) took the hill by surprise, as in a battle
sus tain (sə-'stān) bear
swal low-tail ('swä-lō-tāl) an evening coat
swarm ('swȯrm) crowd thickly
swarth y ('swȯr-t͟hē) dark
sway ('swā) rule
sweeter manners kinder ways of acting
sweetmeats candied fruit; candy
swerved ('swərvd) turned
swift doom sudden death
sym bols ('sim-bəlz) signs
sys tem at ic (sis-tə-'ma-tik) thoroughly planned

T

ta bor ('tā-bər) small drum
take my glory from me gain the name of being as great a hero as I
take no account of pay no attention to
take thought for have the care of
taking the points of the com pass ('käm-pəs) looking about to see which way was north, etc.
talent of gold worth about $1,446 [1921]
tal is mans ('ta-ləs-mənz) magic objects worn to bring good luck
tam bou rine (tam-bə-'rēn) small drum with one head
tame shore land, which is not so exciting as the sea
tan ('tan) brown caused by sun
ta per ('tā-pər) candle; grow smaller
tasks of mercy ('tasks; 'mər-sē) kind deeds
taw ny ('tȯ-nē) yellowish-brown
Te lem a chus (tə-'le-mə-kəs)
tem pest tune ('tem-pəst; 'tün) loud, fierce song of the storm
ten ant ed ('te-nən-təd) lived in
ten ants ('te-nənts) dwellers
Ten e dos ('te-nə-däs)
tense ('tents) tightly stretched
ten to one but almost surely
ter raced ('ter-əst) having a series of raised level platforms of earth

tes ti fied ('tes-tə-fØd) told as a fact
tes ty ('tes-tē) quick-tempered
thanks giv ing had been pro claimed (thaŋks-'gi-viŋ; prō-'klāmd) everyone ordered to give thanks
the earth shall tread ('tred) be remembered as if he were still living
the ev er mur mur ing race ('e-vər; 'mər-mə-riŋ; 'rās) that family of insects which is always making low, indistinct sounds
their names are breathed they are spoken of with the low tone of respect and awe
there by (thar-'bØ) by doing so
there in (tha-'rin) in it
Thes sa ly ('the-sə-lē)
the thoughtful and the free the thinking men who loved liberty
The tis ('thē-təs)
the way may lead we may go
Thrace ('thrās)
thrash ing ('thra-shiŋ) tossing about violently; where grain is beaten to separate the kernel from the husk
Three Mar i ners ('mar-ə-nərz) three sailors, name of an inn
thresh old ('thresh-hōld) piece of wood or stone under a door
thrice ('thrØs) three times
thrift ('thrift) economy
thrills ('thrilz) makes joyous
thrive ('thrØv) succeed; get along well
thronged ('thrȯŋd) went in crowds
thrush with crim son breast ('thrəsh; 'krim-zən) robin
thy cer tain voice ('sər-tən) note we are sure of
thy God is God above you worship the true God
Ti ber ('tØ-bər)
tiles ('tØəlz) flat pieces, square or oblong, used for decoration
tilled ('tild) plowed; worked
Time is fleeting time seems always to be passing rapidly
Ti re si as (tØ-'rē-sē-əs)
tithes ('tØthz) taxes
to bac co stop per (tə-'ba-kō; 'stä-pər) a wooden peg with round top, to put in a pipe
to deal with fight
to his heart's con tent (kən-'tent) as much as he could want
toil and blood hard work of war, and even wounds
to ken ('tō-kən) sign
toll gate ('tōl-gāt) place where a tax is collected for using the road

tomb less ('tüm-ləs) without a prepared grave
took no delight in did not like
To ries ('tōr-ēz) colonists who sympathized with the English during the Revolutionary War
tor pid ('tȯr-pəd) slow; sluggish
tor rents ('tȯr-ənts) swift mountain streams
to the trump of Fame ('trəmp; 'fām) in the list of heroes
to ward ('tō-ərd)
tow ered ('tau̇-ərd) reached up
tow er ing ('tau̇-ər-iŋ) high
to your hurt and do you some harm
trail ('trāl) let touch the ground
train ('trān) crowd who wait upon
train-oil ('ȯil) whale oil
tran sact (tran-'zakt) do
trans formed (trans-'fȯrmd) completely changed
Tran syl va ni a (trant-səl-'vā-nyə)
trav erse (trə-'vərs) cover; cross
treach er ous ly ('tre-chə-rəs-lē) disloyally
tread to it march after it
tre panned (tri-'pand) trapped
tri dent ('trØ-dᵊnt) a three-pronged spear
trill ('tril) high, shaking note
trin kets ('triŋ-kəts) little ornaments, such as chains or rings
tripe ('trØp) part of a cow's stomach, used as food
trod ('träd) walked upon
troop er band ('trü-pər) company of soldiers
trop ic isle re mote ('trä-pik; 'Øl; ri-'mōt) distant island in the hot regions
trou ba dours ('trü-bə-dōrz) poets who composed songs in France in the 12th and 13th centuries
troubled sea state of confusion and uncertainty
truce ('trüs) time in which there is no fighting
trudg ing ('trə-jiŋ) walking
trump ('trəmp) trumpet; call
trump of doom's tone ('dümz; 'tōn) sound of a trumpet on the resurrection day
tuft ('təft) small bunch
tum bler ('təm-blər) acrobat
tu mult ('tü-məlt) noise and confusion
tu mul tu ous (tu̇-'məl-chə-wəs) stormy
tu nic ('tü-nik) short, loose undergarment

tur ban (ˈtər-bən) loose cap with a scarf wound around it, worn by men in Eastern countries
turn spit (ˈtərn-spit) one who turns an arrangement for holding meat while it is roasting before an open fire
turn the heart of persuade
Tyn dar e us (tin-ˈdar-ē-əs)
Tyre (ˈtØr)

U

ugly vis aged (ˈvi-zijd) homely
Ulys ses (yu̇-ˈli-sēz)
un am bi tious sim plic i ty (ən-am-ˈbi-shəs; sim-ˈpli-sə-tē) in a simple, way without any attempt to make it impressive
u nan i mous (yu̇-ˈna-nə-məs) agreed to by everyone
un bound ed sea (ən-ˈbau̇n-dəd) ocean that seems endless
un bro ken (ən-ˈbrō-kən) endless
un civ il (ən-ˈsi-vəl) rude
un con ven tion al (ən-kən-ˈvench-nəl) careless; natural
un du lat ing (ˈən-jə-lā-tiŋ) wavy
un fruit ful (ən-ˈfrüt-fəl) useless; only for show
un in ter rupt ed peal (ən-in-tə-ˈrəp-təd; ˈpēl) continuous roaring
un sheathes its blades (ən-ˈshēt͟hz) puts forth narrow leaves again
un speak a ble (ən-ˈspē-kə-bəl) great
un sub stan tial (ən-səb-ˈstan-shəl) formless
un sul lied (ən-ˈsə-lēd) spotless
un wor thy (ən-ˈwər-t͟hē) worthless
up land (ˈəp-lənd) high land
up ward like thee (ˈəp-wərd) looking up or aspiring as you are
up wind (əp-ˈwind) the direction from which the wind was blowing
ush ered (ˈə-shərd) taken in a polite way
ut most (ˈət-mōst) farthest; highest; greatest
ut ter most reaches (ˈə-tər-mōst) farthest parts

V

vag a bond (ˈva-gə-bänd) an idle wanderer; idle fellow
vales (ˈvālz) valleys
val iant (ˈval-yənt) brave and heroic
val ley and crag (ˈva-lē; ˈkrag) plain and mountain, i.e., the whole country
val or (ˈva-lər) courage

val ue less pat ri mo ny (ˈval-yü-ləs; ˈpat-rə-mō-nē) land now become worthless which they had received from their father
vam pire bats (ˈvam-pØr; ˈbatz) small flying animals that drink blood
van guard (ˈvan-gärd) first comers
van quished (ˈvaŋ-kwisht) conquered
van tage point (ˈvan-tij) high lookout
va ri e ty (və-ˈrØ-ə-tē) change
vault ed (ˈvȯl-təd) arched; rounding
veer ing (ˈvi-riŋ) turning
veiled with wreaths (ˈvāld) covered with flowers and vines
vel lum (ˈve-ləm) heavy, cream-colored paper
ve loc i ty (və-ˈlä-sə-tē) speed
ven er a ble (ˈve-nər-ə-bəl) old and worthy of deep respect
ven er a tion (ve-nə-ˈrā-shən) great respect
venge ance (ˈven-jənts) punishment
ven ture (ˈvent-shər) dare
venture on dare to do
Ve nus (ˈvē-nəs)
ver dant (ˈvər-dᵊnt) green
ver dure (ˈvər-jər) greenness
ver min (ˈvər-mən) small, disgusting insects or animals which usually thrive in dirt; here, rats
ver sa til i ty (vər-sə-ˈti-lə-tē) ability to do different things
very sum mit of the mor al scale (ˈsə-mət; ˈmȯr-əl; ˈskāl) highest point of goodness that can be reached
ves pers (ˈves-pərz) evening service
ves sel of fered for (ˈve-səl; ˈȯ-fərd) ship was ready to sail to
vessel of mercy dish put to kind uses
ves ture (ˈves-chər) clothing
vi cis si tude (və-ˈsi-sə-tüd) change
vict uals (ˈvi-tᵊlz) food
Vin de Grave (vin-də-ˈgräv) a kind of wine
vi o lence (ˈvØ-ə-lənts) fierce, determined natures
vi o lent (ˈvØ-ə-lənt) very great
vi o let (ˈvØ-lət) early spring flower
vis age (ˈvi-zij) face
vis i ble (ˈvi-zə-bəl) within sight
vis it ant (ˈvi-zə-tənt) guest; visitor
vo ca tion (vō-ˈkā-shən) occupation
vo lu mi nous (və-ˈlü-mə-nəs) large, flowing
voy a geurs (ˈvȯi-ə-zhərz) travelers

W

waited for just existed for my pleasure
wake ('wāk) track
wak en ing ('wāk-niŋ) which awoke him
wakening earth world coming out of winter as one comes out of a deep sleep
wan der ers from afar ('wän-dər-ərz) immigrants from distant countries
wan der ing breed ('wän-də-riŋ) kind that roams about
wan der lust ('wän-dər-ləst) longing to travel
wan ton ly ('wȯn-tən-lē) recklessly
wa pi ti ('wä-pə-tē) the American elk
war bler ('wȯr-blər) songster
war dens ('wȯr-dənz) guards
ward robe ('wȯr-drōb) a movable closet for clothes
warn ing ('wȯr-niŋ) sign of danger
war rant ('wȯr-ənt) am sure
war rant ed a sup po si tion ('wȯr-ən-təd; sə-pə-'zi-shən) made it seem true
war riors ('wȯr-yərz) fighters
wa ry ('wār-ē) very cautious
was given to me was granted me as a privilege
wast ed his sub stance ('wā-stəd; 'səb-stənts) spent his money foolishly
wast ing ('wa-stiŋ) making die
wa ter ing places ('wȯ-tə-riŋ) places one goes for boating, bathing, etc.
waxed ('wakst) grew; grown
way far ers ('wā-far-ərz) travelers
wealth of promised glory richness of fruit foretold by full blossoming
wee vil ('wē-vəl) beetle
weigh ing the ex pe di en cy ('wā-iŋ; ik-'spē-dən-sē) thinking over the fitness
well nigh ('nØ) almost
were divided had different opinions
We ser ('vä-zər)
wharf ('hwȯrf) landing place for boats
what justice have I done to how much I have enjoyed
what time when
whence ('hwents) from where
whip thong ('hwip; 'thȯŋ) whip made of a strip of leather
whirl ('hwərl) drag very swiftly
whit ('hwit) bit
whith er ('hwi-<u>th</u>ər) to where
whith er so ev er ('hwi-<u>th</u>ər-sō-'ev-ər) to whatever place
whop ping est ('hwä-piŋ-əst) very largest

wide bloom blossoming flowers everywhere
wil der ness of doubt ('wil-dər-nəs; 'daůt) uncertainty which seems to have no landmarks
wilds ('wØəldz) wildernesses
wind rows ('wind-rōz) rows of hay raked up to dry
wip ers of scores out ('wØ-pərz) people who act fairly and honestly
wist ful ly ('wist-fə-lē) longingly
with des per ȧte efforts at ex act i tude ('des-pə-rət; ig-'zak-tə-tüd) trying as hard as he could to place it just right, so the cut would not show
without bound or end so great that it cannot be measured
without the slightest re gard (ri-'gärd) while they did not care
with the na ked eye ('nā-kəd; 'Ø) without a spyglass
wit nessed ('wit-nəst) seen; lived through
wol ver ene (wůl-və-'rēn) an animal about two and one-half feet long, of heavy build and with long, shaggy hair; it is very cunning and difficult to trap
won der at the view ('wən-dər; 'vyü) be astonished at the sight
wood land crests ('wůd-lənd; krests) tree-covered hilltops
won drous por tal ('wən-drəs; 'pōr-tᵊl) magic gate
wood-rose wild rose
worked the herd ('wərkd; 'hərd) divided the cattle into groups and branded them
work "tooth and nail" work just as hard as you can
wor thy char ac ter ('wər-t͟hē; 'kar-ik-tər) good, able man
wound ed ('wün-dəd) injured
wrangl ing ('raŋ-liŋ) quarreling
wreath of ragged cloud ('rēth) long, uneven, straggling cloud
wreck ('rek) injured body
writhed ('rØt͟hd) turned and twisted
wroth ('ȯth) angry
wrought ('ȯt) carved; made; worked

X

Xan tip pe (zan-'ti-pē) a Greek woman of olden times, famous for her scolding
Xe nil ('zē-nəl) river in Spain
Xer xes ('zərk-sēz) king of Persia (486-465 B.C.)

Y

yard ('yärd) long pole to attach a sail to
yearn ing to meet her May ('yər-niŋ) eager for May to come

yeo man ry (ˈyō-mən-rē) farmers
yield (ˈyē(ə)ld) give
your brain be wil ders (bi-ˈwil-dərz) puzzles your mind; troubles you

Z

za ny (ˈzā-nē) foolish person
ze nith (ˈzē-nəth) point of sky directly overhead
zest (ˈzest) eagerness
Zeus (ˈzüs)